FEVER

A novel by Dan Churach

Cover design by Dan Churach.

Copyright © 2019 by Dan Churach

All rights reserved.

ISBN: 9781070458830

DEDICATION

For Aimée De Corte Kelly, a part of my *hānai* family... Aimée not only provides a wealth of her expertise to me as a resource for my writing but most of all, she is my friend.

CONTENTS

ACKNOWLEDGMENTS

I could never complete a creative work like this without a great deal of help. I offer my sincere thanks to Janice Wentworth, Aimée De Corte Kelly, Martin Houchin, Leon Hallacher, Paul Keenan, Graeme Thompson, Val De Corte, Angela Bollard, Roger Severn, Ken Seymour and Randall Hendriks. I'd be remiss if I didn't mention our pups, Bomber and Rocky. Every day they dutifully join me in the study during my somewhat hectic writing sessions. Finally, thanks once again to my wife and best friend, Karn.

PART ONE

"What is wanted is not the will to believe, but the will to find out, which is the exact opposite."

— Bertrand Russell

DAN CHURACH

1

Tuesday, 16 April; Lady Lyman Beach
near Townsville, Queensland

Lester lay on a beach towel under a clump of coconut palms. He had watched for half an hour, and now finally, the four figures seemed to be about finished loading their equipment onto the *Reef Explorer*. As he swept his gaze up and down the shoreline, the only other people he could see were a few beachcombers strolling away from the dock a half a kilometre to the north. The morning was picture perfect – deep blue sky spotted with a few fluffy cumulus clouds, almost no wind and the temperature somewhere in the mid-20s. The only sound he could hear was the gentle surf washing the shoreline and a flock of playful finches darting about the palms above his head.

He had been following the professor for a week now and knew he'd have his same small band of graduate students surrounding him. Pratt and his students drove up to this beach yesterday to do a series of dives on the reef using one of the university research vessels docked here. It was obvious why Pratt would work from this pier at Lady Lyman Beach. It offered an excellent jumping-off point to the Great Barrier Reef in that the coral outcrops were unusually close to the shore. Yes, it was a beautiful morning, and Lester was there to watch. He smiled confidently knowing that he had done his homework, and all would go as planned.

Lester adjusted his binoculars and confirmed Professor Sean Pratt sitting on the bench seat at the back of the boat while Becky Whitehall, one of his doctoral students, sat next to him pointing at a clipboard she held between them. Another PhD student, John Rivkin, was on the bridge checking the boat's gages. The last of Pratt's students, Nikki

Vasquez, stowed the last of the diving gear they would need and jumped back onto the dock. She walked to the bow, stooped down and started to unwrap the boat's lines from the cleats. Finally, Vasquez tossed the ropes onto the deck and stepped back aboard the boat. Within a minute or so, Rivkin nudged the throttle, and the *Reef Explorer* moved away from the dock.

The beeping of his mobile distracted Lester's attention. He glanced at the phone's screen and answered. "Yep."

"How'd you go with the arrangements?"

"No worries, mate. I stowed the gear right where we wanted it, all according to plan."

"All clear there?"

"Damned straight! There's no one around here this morning."

"Are our friends there now?"

"Sure are... just leaving the dock at this point."

"Pratt?"

He nodded his head absent-mindedly as if the person on the other side of the conversation could somehow see him. "Yeah, Pratt is here... and three of his students."

"Four all up then?"

"Yep, four."

"Make sure they're all clear... just like we planned..."

"Yeah, yeah... I'll make sure. Everyone will be just fine, but it'll be a good bang and will sure as hell send a good signal." He watched as the boat cleared the dock enough to open the throttle.

"Let me know when it's done."

"Will do, mate... and look, don't sweat – I have everything under control." Lester put his mobile away and raised his binoculars again. His eyes followed the *Reef Explorer* as she headed away from the small dock. He knew they wouldn't go more than a kilometre or so before dropping anchor out over the shoal. He put his binoculars in his beach bag and again looked around the area. Besides his academic targets, the only other people he could see were the two beach walkers now another couple of hundred metres farther down the beach.

Lester stood, grabbed his beach towel and shoved it into his bag. He walked back to his Toyota HiLux ute parked under trees about hundred metres away. When he had arrived, only Pratt's James Cook University Landcruiser was parked there under a shady tree, but now there was a newish red Nissan Micra parked a hundred-plus metres away at the far end of the unsealed car park. He reckoned that the two beachcombers he saw way up the shoreline had driven here in that which would make sense since they hadn't been around when he pulled in. He opened the door, dropped his duffle bag onto the passenger's seat and slid in. Lester grabbed the binoculars from the bag, set them on his lap and pulled the door closed behind him. He knew the wait wouldn't be too long now.

The *Reef Explorer* had quickly crossed an expanse of azure-blue water and slowed over a patch of dark blue that marked the shallow waters below the reef. As he focused his glasses on the boat, he watched Whitehall leaning over the bow and dropping the anchor while Rivkin pushed the throttle nudging the boat just enough to set the anchor. Within a minute or two, the grad student climbed down the ladder from the bridge to join his mates on the back deck. The professor was already there, looking down towards the water and chatting to an unseen person over the far side of the vessel. Lester spoke out loud to himself. "Damn, that was quick... maybe Vasquez had already gone into the water." Eyes glued to his binoculars, the big bloke watched patiently as the divers pulled on fins, checked regulators and adjusted straps.

His beeping phone interrupted his surveillance as he placed his glasses on the seat and grabbed his mobile. "Hi, honey."

"Are we still on for lunch, Lester?"

"Sure thing... at the Noodle Box, right?"

"Yeah... the Noodle Box."

"Is twelve-thirty still good for you?"

"Sure is."

"Okay, honey. Is everything okay there?"

"Yep... no worries at all, here."

"Good. Ah... Lester..." Her voice trailed off.

"Yes?"

"I love you."

"Love you, too, hon."

He traded his mobile for the binoculars and watched as Professor Pratt, Rivkin and Whitehall rolled off the stern dive platform and into the water. Just to make sure, he scanned the length of the *Reef Explorer,* and there was no sign of anyone left aboard.

Lester returned his binoculars to the seat next to him and picked up his phone. Pulling a piece of paper from his shirt pocket, he looked at the numbers written on it and punched them into his mobile as he started his ute. The big man turned on his stereo, selected his favourite AC/DC song, *"Highway to Hell"* and raised the volume as loud as he could make it. He looked over his shoulder at the unsealed road behind, reversed out from under the trees and started to roll forward. Just as his ute moved away from the trees, he pressed the send button. Lester couldn't hear the explosion offshore, but as he pulled away, he did see the big fireball in his rear-view mirror.

2

Tuesday, 16 April; Hospital of the University
of Pennsylvania, Philadelphia, Pennsylvania

"I'm Asha Sharma from GNN. I believe she is expecting me."

The receptionist made a few clicks on her screen and spoke into her headset. "I believe you are expecting Ms Asha Sharma. Yes, she is right here in the lobby... Of course." The receptionist looked back at Asha. "Yes, Doctor Stetzer is expecting you. Please go down this corridor to your left through those big doors under the 'University of Pennsylvania Medical Research' sign." She pointed towards some glass doors fifty metres away. "Once you go through there, you'll see another sign that says 'Epidemiology'. The receptionist there will direct you to Doctor Stetzer."

"Thanks so much."

Asha walked down the hallway and through the doors. It was noticeable that the 'research' wing was decidedly not patient-oriented since several of the doors she passed were either offices or laboratories. Another receptionist quickly directed her to a door with a plaque on it: "Dr Lawrence Stetzer, Director of Epidemiology".

Her hand no sooner began to knock when the wooden door opened. "Ms Sharma?"

"Yes... Asha Sharma. I'm so glad you were able to see me."

"Hello, Ms Sharma. I've been expecting you. Please come in." He took a few steps towards an oval-shaped wooden table and pulled a chair out for her. "Can I get you a coffee?"

"No, I'm... Look, I would actually love a glass of water."

"Certainly." He took two glasses from a tray on top of a small refrigerator behind his desk. He pulled out a pitcher of cold water and topped both glasses. "Of course, I read your notes and familiarised myself with some of the articles you published over the past year or two." He sat one of the glasses in front of her and took a seat on the other side of the table.

"Thank you." She had a sip.

"I read a few pieces you wrote about the Marburg viral outbreak in Uganda a few years back... that was a very nasty occurrence. You also followed that outbreak to some spillover into Frankfort, Germany and Belgrade, Serbia." He shook his head. "I think there were ten or twelve laboratory workers who lost their lives in that incident. Excellent writing, Ms Sharma."

"I appreciate that, Doctor. I've covered a wide array of topics in my career so far, but I admit to having a strong interest in medical stories." A big grin crossed her face. "I guess I always wanted to go to medical school, but just didn't have high enough tertiary entrance scores to get accepted into medicine when I was applying to university."

"Tertiary entrance scores... Do I detect a bit of down under in that accent?"

"You do."

"And where exactly did you grow up, Ms Sharma? That accent certainly doesn't sound like South Philly..." Now it was Stetzer's turn to smile.

"No, you're correct on that. I'm Australian – Western Australia – though I've lived in the States for the past several years."

"I've been to Sydney, but never out west there." He sipped his water. "For that matter, I've – we've – done some good collaborative work with researchers down under... Australian National University."

"ANU... in Canberra?"

"Yes, that's the one. That's your national capital, yes?"

"It is." Asha leaned forward. "Let me get to the point, Dr Stetzer. We're working on a series of in-depth pieces looking at the 'next-big-thing' as it were, and my GNN colleagues have been learning of a cluster of infectious diseases up in Alaska. Can you give me any insight to that?"

"On the record or off?"

"Well, how about 'off' for starters."

Stetzer gulped his water. "If you don't mind my asking, what have you heard?"

"Anthrax." Asha was to the point.

"Humm." He leaned back in his chair while looking directly at her. "I believe that a small outbreak of anthrax was reported in the news, yes? ...probably GNN reported that story."

"Sure, we did report that a few months back. The big news there – other than that this was in a U. S. state – was that it was anthrax from an animal that died... maybe died a long time ago, correct?"

The doctor nodded yes.

"I think they call it 'zombie anthrax', right?"

"I've heard the term." Stetzer was happy to listen until he could size up just how much she knew.

"Well, I believe that is pretty much what made it into the popular press. It isn't a new phenomenon, and I believe there have been a few reports of zombie anthrax in several places in Siberia. I imagine there are a lot of infected reindeer carcasses frozen there for hundreds... thousands of years. Thaw them out, and the little *Bacillus anthracis* bacteria wake up like Sleeping Beauty, yes?"

"For sure you have the right idea, but I don't know about Sleeping Beauty, Ms Sharma. *Bacillus anthracis* doesn't need a kiss... just extended temperatures above 32 degrees." He caught himself. "Ah... above zero degrees Celsius."

She smiled. "I've been in the States for a while now, and I understand Fahrenheit, though god knows why such a technologically advanced country would still use that scale."

"Fair enough, but don't hang hundreds of years of culture on my shoulders..." He laughed. "So, it sounds to me that you are very much on top of this story. I don't see how I could help you much here."

"My understanding is that you wear more than one hat and also do work for the CDC."

"You understand correctly. I think I've been affiliated with the Center for Disease Control for a decade or more now."

"Does this occurrence demonstrate the same manifestations of all anthrax outbreaks? Does the CDC have any information leading them – you – to believe this anthrax is of a different variety?"

"If you have researched this as much as I think you have, you must understand that *Bacillus anthracis* doesn't tend to mutate easily. I don't want to patronise you Ms Sharma, but you know that mutations occur when DNA is replicated. In the case of anthrax, it spends much of its lifecycle as a spore – in hibernation, if I can say it that way. These long periods of dormancy, whether in the permafrost or in more temperate soils, are not conducive to mutation since DNA replication does not happen at this time. What I'm saying is that anthrax preserved in permafrost may be thousands of years old, but when it 'awakens' as it were, it's just the same old DNA that it had when it became dormant."

"You are correct, Doc... we have researched this quite thoroughly. I fully understand what it is you are saying about the long periods of dormancy that result in slow or no mutations. But that doesn't rule out mutations that may have occurred 10,000, 20,000 or 30,000 years ago that have been frozen in place all that time, does it?"

Doctor Stetzer sat back in his chair and unconsciously rubbed at his chin. "Are we still off the record, Ms Sharma?"

"Please, Doctor Stetzer... I have a job to do. I am trying to write a story here."

He looked her right in the eye. "Please understand that on my end, I am unable to release data that has not been supported by laboratory work." Without breaking eye contact with her, his head rocked back and forth quite obviously in the affirmative. "As to whatever may have happened to our newly awakened *Bacillus anthracis* before they were cryogenically preserved 10,000, 20,000 or 30,000 years ago, we simply cannot say at this point."

3

Tuesday, 16 April; Suvarnabhumi Airport Hotel, Bangkok, Thailand

"Felly!" The middle-aged man spotted her from twenty metres away and increased his pace to where she and Geoff were sitting.

Felly stood and spread her arms wide and giving him a big hug when they met. "It's so nice to see you, Nigel. What a surprise it was when I heard you'd be passing through Bangkok the same time as us." She kissed him on one cheek and then the other before breaking their embrace.

"Good to see you, mate." Geoff was standing now and firmly gripped Nigel's hand and pumped it. "I think the last time I saw you was in London several years ago."

"Yes indeed, old chap. I think you were able to sneak away long enough to attend that IEA conference with Felly, right?"

"Yes, that was it." Geoff released his handshake and patted Nigel on the back. "I remember since it was a big deal when Felly was honoured at the award banquet that night... It's not every day a true blue Aussie gets such a prestigious award from the International Epidemiological Association."

"Stop it, Geoff." Felly almost blushed.

"Sorry, honey."

Felly smiled at her husband. "From what you mentioned in your email, I assume you have enough time for a drink, Nigel, yes?"

"Right-O. My flight isn't for..." He looked at his watch. "...over four hours yet, so we can have a bite to eat too if you are game." He spoke with a decidedly English accent.

"Let's do it." Felly grabbed his sleeve with one hand and her travel bag with the other.

* * *

"How's that?" Geoff pointed to a corner booth at an international restaurant away from the bustle of the boarding gates.

"That looks great to me, honey. Nigel?"

"Excellent."

Felly slid onto the upholstered bench seat behind the table. Geoff pulled out a chair and extended his hand to Nigel. "What would you like, mate?"

"I think I need a beer."

"Felly?"

"Yes... I'll go along with that."

Geoff caught a waiter's eye. "Three Singhas, please."

"So, I know Felly has been hard at work on her research up here in Thailand, but how did she manage to coerce you to come along on this adventure, Geoff?"

Geoff laughed. "Well frankly, she didn't need to coerce me, Nigel. I'm still working the same Emergency Department back in Melbourne that I've been at for donkey's years now, and the hospital owed me time for professional development. Once we knew Felly's grant had been extended and that she was coming up here for three months, I put some feelers out for an experience of my own."

"So, I take it you lined up a cushy job in a touristy hospital in Phuket, right?"

Felly nearly broke down into hysterical laughter. "Cushy job! Please..."

"I only wish, mate." Geoff picked up the story. "I know you are aware of the work my dear wife has been doing on *Zaire Ebolavirus* for the past several years now."

"Of course, I am."

"Well, though I hear about EVD all the time from Felly, we thankfully never see it present in Royal Yarra Hospital. That said, since I've spent a career so far in emergency medicine, I reckoned it was an ideal time to spend a few months totally out of my comfort zone, expand my medical knowledge and help out some less advantaged people."

"Was it difficult getting a short-term position like that, Geoff?"

The waiter returned with three bottles of Singha and three glasses on his tray. He placed a glass in front of each of them and filled the glasses about halfway.

"Not really. I made some contacts through the Thai government." Geoff lifted his glass to Nigel and Felly. "Cheers."

"Cheers."

"Making a few connections was easier than I thought it'd be because I had a few friends with whom I had gone through medical school... they had some Thai friends and... well, you get the picture. The fact that I was looking to practise in remote areas helped" Geoff sipped his beer.

"True. I travelled through a lot of the bush areas. My purpose was to collect as much data as I could, see as many people as I could and learn more about how local conditions were contributing to the spread of EVD – Ebola virus disease." She set her glass on the napkin. "When I knew where I was headed, it was easy enough to arrange for Geoff to spend a few days in some of the more remote clinics near where I'd be."

Nigel took another gulp of his Singha. "Fascinating. I mean, I haven't spent time in Thailand and was only here in Bangkok for a few days at my conference. What's the healthcare system like?"

"In some ways, better than you'd think... but in others, downright awful. They have had the UCS – that's Universal Coverage Scheme – in place for 25 years or so now, but though everyone has health coverage, the coverage is only as good as the local facilities. Once you get in some remote areas, you're lucky to have more than a nurse, and sometimes not even that. Bangkok Hospital Phuket is a great facility, but out in the bush, you'd have trouble finding a band-aid."

"The EVD seems to be taking hold, doesn't it?" Nigel lowered his eyes and shook his head.

"It is. And I fear there may be changes with the whole genus *Ebolavirus*, but we need to do a lot more work looking into that before I can be more definitive." She wished that she could be more positive with her old friend but could only relate what she knew to be true. "In my case, I had an extremely successful three months, and I'm heading back to Melbourne with more data than I could have ever wished to have."

"And Geoff?"

"I'd say the same, though from a very different perspective. I wasn't gathering data as such, just rolling up my sleeves and contributing to patient care..." Geoff caught himself at once.

"Naturally I don't mean that literally! ED work in the tropics caring for EVD patients is an incredibly taxing experience from every point of view. We NEVER roll up sleeves! The PPE includes fluid-resistant coveralls, fluid-impermeable gowns, surgical hoods, two pairs of single-use gloves, goggles or face shields, leg and shoe covers and respirators. That all works out better in an air-conditioned ward, but in a temporary tent-hospital in the bush, you tend to sweat profusely."

"My god... I never thought of wearing personal protective equipment without aircon. Damn... At least you'd go away at the end of the shift knowing you were appreciated." Nigel tried to put the best interpretation on Geoff's experience as he could.

"Yes, another please." Geoff held his nearly empty beer glass up when the waiter reappeared. He looked from Felly to Nigel and then back to the waiter. "Make that three, please."

"Overall, a good experience, mate?"

Felly was frowning as she shook her head from side to side. "I don't want to answer for my husband, but you can't believe what a mixed bag it's all been."

Finally, Geoff responded. "Look, describing it as a mixed bag is putting it mildly. I've had a fantastic experience up here. I've learned much about medicine and people. Additionally, I've met many good, very caring people. I've seen things that will never leave my mind's eye. And frankly, I've grown so much more appreciative of Australia and our healthcare system that I swear to kiss the ground when we disembark at Tullamarine Airport in Melbourne."

"Jeez... it sounds like you've run the gamut."

"I did, Nigel. I had some great experiences, rewarding experiences. In some ways, I think I learned more up here about both medicine and human nature than I have since medical school."

Nigel's face squinted as though he was searching his memory. "Sorry Geoff, but I don't recall where you did your medical school, though I am sure that you or Felly have told me at some point. Where did you study... Melbourne?"

"No, no... I was a Perth boy and did both my undergrad work and medical training at the University of Western Australia there."

"Right-O. Now then, sorry I interrupted you, mate... you were saying you had some rewarding experiences."

"Yes, I did and to answer your question of feeling appreciated... many times I certainly did. But I also had some not-so-nice experiences, too. Again, there is such a contrast between urban and bush people and customs and culture. Living in another country means that there is always a language barrier. Many of the professionals get by in English, but most locals can't speak a word of it. They see friends and relatives go into a tent-hospital and never come out. And I mean NEVER since when people die, their bodies cannot just be released to rellies wanting to bury them. Their bodies are isolated, wrapped and sealed, never to be seen again. To many, white doctors speaking a foreign language sealed in double layers of protective equipment might as well be extraterrestrial alien invaders. Whenever these aliens show up in a village, so many friends and rellies disappear. It's not difficult to see how we are associated with bringing death. Hell, in one little village we tried to get into we literally ran for our lives when a band of armed villagers chased us away with guns blazing. Too often, the best we could do was to drip electrolytes into an infected patient's arm trying to alleviate dehydration a bit until death mercifully claimed him or her." Geoff was rescued by another Singha being poured into his glass. He took a big gulp. "Please understand... most Thais have been very grateful, but some feared us health professionals more than they feared Ebola."

4

Tuesday, 16 April; Lyman Health Services
near Townsville, Queensland

"Professor Sean Pratt?"

"Yes, sir."

"I'm Senior Constable Alan Grocott, Queensland Police Service. You've had a heck of a morning, Professor. The nurses tell me you check out fine."

"Yeah, yeah... I'm fine, but I can't work out what happened. Becky, John, Nikki... are they okay?"

The constable tilted his head. "Ms Whitehall and Mr Rivkin are just fine, same as you. Ms Vasquez should be okay, too, but they took her down the coast to the hospital in Townsville as a precautionary measure."

Sean rubbed his head. "So, what happened?"

"I was hoping you could help us answer that same question, Professor."

"Man... we drove up in one of the university's Toyota Landcruisers last night and were heading out for a dive on the Reef, over Lady Lyman Shoal. We set anchor, suited up and slipped into the water. I mean, we couldn't have been in the sea for more than a minute or two when I heard a loud concussion."

"All four of you were away from the boat at this point, yes?"

"Yes, that's correct. I'm just guessing, but we couldn't have been more than a body-length or two beneath the surface... maybe two metres, three at most."

"I take it the engine was off?"

"Yeah, yeah... John shut her off and came down the ladder from the bridge. I imagine he left the keys in the ignition – we generally do when we dive. You'll have to confirm that with John though. Is he here?"

"He is. As soon as I finish asking you a few questions, you can see both Mr Rivkin and Ms Whitehall."

"Excellent."

"Was this a work-related trip, Professor Pratt?"

"Yes, collecting samples out on the Reef. We generally do two dives a day for a few days – three days planned this time. We collect coral, flora and fauna to take back into the labs. We also make photographic records of where we dive that allow us to make visual comparisons at a later time. The Reef keeps changing, Constable, and generally, it's not for the better." Pratt shook his head from side to side.

"I see. Tell me, Professor, was the boat – the *Reef Explorer* I believe – was that a university vessel?"

"Yeah, it was. The university has equipment we can use at several locations up the coast here. We've used the *Reef Explorer* before. I think she's about 12 or 13 metres."

"Did the vessel's engine use petrol of diesel fuel?"

"Diesel. The university tech people would have had a full tank when they set it up on the dock for us yesterday, but from past use, I know it's diesel. The university protocol is for the technical staff to deliver a boat to a prearranged spot ready to go, lock it up and let us have a key. It's a pretty simple system."

"Humm... Interesting." Grocott scratched his chin. "So, there was no petrol aboard?"

"Well no, I didn't say that. There was an inflatable aboard, a Zodiac. When we would go farther out onto the Reef, we used to use that but had no need this morning. The Zodiac had a five or six horsepower outboard, and there were a couple of tinnies of petrol stored aboard. I didn't check today since we weren't going to use it and were staying close to shore."

"I see."

"I'm curious; why do you ask?"

"Well Professor, as you know, diesel isn't so explosive, but petrol can be if you ignite the vapours. I mean, a well-maintained boat like that with the engine off and no one aboard doesn't simply explode. Frankly, it does make you wonder."

"I see what you mean."

"Look, I needed to ask you all those questions. You are free to join your students in the tearoom down the hall."

* * *

"Becky... John..."

The young woman almost jumped from her seat and quickly threw her arms around the Professor and hugged him. He reached one of his arms from her embrace and shook Rivkin's hand, too. "I'm so glad you two are okay. What have you heard about Nikki?"

Whitehall released him from her hug. "The staff here tell us that she's okay... just a few cuts and bruises. I think she must have been closest to the surface and the boat because a piece of debris fell on her and the impact cut her leg. Thank god she never lost consciousness."

"Yeah, good thing on that. Becky and I are no worse for wear, either. And you, Doc?"

"No... no problems, John. Damn, I'm trying to figure out what happened though. The constable asked me if the engine was off. It was, right?"

"Yeah, of course. He asked us that too. I shut it off before I came down the ladder."

"Did he ask you about having petrol, too?"

"Yes. You know, I did give both of them a shove with my foot, and they seemed very full by feel, but I confess that I never opened the tops to visually to check because we weren't using the zodiac. I know you always tell us to check before we leave, but I thought this time I didn't need to eyeball it since we weren't heading that far offshore." Rivkin's eyes turned towards the floor.

"It's okay, mate. You did check then, and two cans were full to the touch. I'm just so happy you and Becky are okay... Now let's hope Nikki comes out of this with just scratches, too."

5

Tuesday, 16 April; Suvarnabhumi Airport Hotel, Bangkok, Thailand

"That wasn't a bad feed for an airport restaurant if I say so myself." Geoff patted his mouth with his serviette and placed it on the table. "So, how's your work been, Nigel?"

He grinned. "How's it going to be? I mean, fifteen years in the Public Health's Centre of Infectious Disease Surveillance and Control doesn't generally offer the excitement and challenge that you face in the ED or Felly faces in maintaining research grants."

"That's not fair, Nigel. You're here eating dinner with us in Bangkok, so your Public Health England at least sees fit to send you to international conferences."

"Well, sure... look, I make no bones about my position, as far as that goes. For the most part, I oversee nationwide data collection, vaccine programs and our education and research divisions, but I feel as though I contribute. I mean, what the hell, it isn't all that sexy, but it is an essential service, and I have grown comfortable in my role there."

"Speaking of sexy, Nigel... Have you found another significant person in your life?"

"You had to ask... Look, I've dated a bit here and there, but after Jean and I split – damn, that's almost twelve years now – I've sort of given up on the need to get married for married sake. Besides that, I do put in a lot of hours, and frankly, I am generally flat out knackered when I come home and going out on the town is about the last thing I am thinking about. I mean, if a relationship ever happens, I'm open to that, but I do not feel the need to replace Jean, not that she is replaceable in the first place."

Felly almost felt sad for asking. She placed her hand on top of his. "I understand, my friend."

"How's your research going, Felly?" Nigel leaned back from the table and swallowed a gulp of water.

"All good, Nigel. I'm not a whole hell of a lot different from when we used to see each other every day back in grad school... give me an unanswered question and a lab and let me go dig into it. I guess the biggest challenge anymore is dealing with bureaucracy, dealing with a system way more concerned with bean-counting than research. Fortunately, Geoff has a different set of obstacles in providing healthcare services."

"True enough, at least most people are well aware of the relationship between funding and how long you have to wait in the emergency department. Most taxpayers tune into front line services." Geoff sat back as the waiter cleared the table. "Could we have some tea, please?" He surveyed his two dinner mates, and they nodded their agreement. "Anyway, as for you and Felly and research grants... I guess the tenuous nature of on-going funding offers the same plight for scientists the world over.

"It surely is the case for us in the UK."

"Geoff is right, of course." Felly nodded her head. "I guess I shouldn't complain too much, though. At least working in the area that I am has almost guaranteed our grants into the near future. I just complain because we still need to spend too much time assuring ourselves of that."

"How big is your group now, Felly?"

"Jeez... Besides me, there are two other PhD-level researchers, a couple of medical doctors and then maybe six or seven support staff. The family *Filoviridae* is pesky..."

"Pesky?" Geoff couldn't help but interrupt his wife.

"Well... I don't mean to minimise things. Between the *Ebolavirus* and the *Marburgvirus*, we're dealing with a terrifying set of diseases. Pardon my scepticism, but one of the biggest insulators of medical research and funding from the family *Filoviridae* is so obviously racial... Consider once that until the first cases of Ebola showed up in Washington, Los Angeles and Chicago, most of the world was fearful of such a horrid bug, but not fearful enough fund it to any great extent. So, thousands of dark-skinned people could die with little more reaction than GNN camera crews showing up, but infect a few white healthcare professionals and amazingly enough, parliaments and congresses find research funds."

"Bloody hell, Felly! Of course, I agree with you, but you are a bit hard on parliaments and congresses, no?"

"I don't think so for... not for one second! The only vaccine that even has limited effectiveness wouldn't have been developed without Canadian government help. Even then, no big pharma companies were willing to go it alone. Frankly, though there was some early encouragement with the vaccine, it's proving to be more of a disappointment than a miracle."

I have read some of the more recent papers concerning just that. It is disturbing..."

"Disturbing... I'll say!" Felly's eyebrows arched up. "But there is more troubling news than that, Nigel. We certainly aren't ready to make any public statements just yet, but things are happening with the whole family, particularly with *Zaire ebolavirus*. It's just starting to behave very strangely."

"A strange way?"

Felly turned her head as though she were unconsciously paranoid that someone might be listening in to their conversation. "Listen, Nigel... it's not at all that I don't want to tell you, but I just don't know as yet. Funny things are happening. For starters, consider the fact that we are sitting here in Thailand. What... a year-and-a-half or two years ago, there was no Ebola Virus Disease in Asia. Then it mysteriously shows up in Bangladesh. Now? It seems to be Ebola is appearing in many places here in Thailand, in Malaysia, in Cambodia and Vietnam... And while we are speaking of changes, who knew that other species of bats could carry these viruses?"

"Aw man Felly... Look, I work in the area of communicable disease. I'm no stranger to epidemics. Fortunately, we haven't had any outbreaks of Ebola in the UK save for a few cases of returning healthcare workers. But we have to remain optimistic. The work you're doing will go a long way to alleviating the pain and suffering of many. I guess the whole idea is that groups like yours learn enough to be ready as this scourge spreads. Let's be thankful that at least it's been sticking to the bat population and hasn't jumped to rats or mosquitos or what have you."

An expression of concern crossed Geoff's face as he peered over his glasses at Felly, and she looked towards the floor.

6

Tuesday, 16 April; GNN Home Office, Chicago, Illinois

"Asha, what are you doing here? Do you know what time it is?"

"Sure." She looked at the big clock on the wall. "It looks like it's about 10:30 PM."

"You smart ass, you!" His smile confirmed his affection for one of his best investigative reporters. "I thought you were on the East Coast somewhere."

"I was – in Philly for a meeting this morning. You know, I could ask why the Editor in Chief is hanging around the office at this hour of the night. Don't you know that all the big bosses are home with their families by now?"

Rothchild laughed. "Right... big boss... like that's going to get tomorrow's headlines out before every other news organisation this side of the moon."

Asha threw both hands over her head. "All right, all right... I give up, Oliver. I accept the fact that you're up to your ears if you agree that I'm underwater!"

"Sounds like we both need a cup of coffee." He turned towards the staff room, and Asha followed. "How'd you go in Philly... The zombie bacteria story, yes?"

"Yes." She followed him into the staff room.

He reached for a coffee pod. "What do you like?"

"Just a Dolce Gusto there, Oliver." She pointed to the drawer that had a store of the pods she liked to use. "It's easy – coffee and milk all in one capsule."

"Me too. I guess it's a reflection on both our lives – no need to be complicating a cup of coffee." He rested one hand on the closed cabinet door and put a mug beneath the machine's spout. "So, what did you learn in Pennsylvania today?"

"Good question... I'm still trying to work that out. I met with Dr Lawrence Stetzer. He's the Director of Epidemiology there at the U Penn Medical Research Center."

"Smart fellow – I've heard about him."

"I'll give him that, but he wasn't too free with information. I don't know what his exact constraints are, but I think my sources are onto something with that anthrax outbreak last year. Try as I might though, I couldn't get him to commit to any new version of *Bacillus anthracis* showing up in the melted permafrost."

"Commit? This was an interview, not a date!" Rothchild laughed as he pulled the second mug from the machine and carried both to a small table. They both sat.

"For god sakes, I mean I couldn't get him to verbally confirm what we've found even though I know it's true. The funniest thing, though... he nodded his head yes to me the whole time he said he could not confirm what we found."

"Aha... that's kind of committing! Why didn't you say that to begin with?"

"Oliver!"

"So, was the trip worth it or not?"

"Damned if I know. In my mind, I have confirmed our findings that the world now has a mutated version of *Bacillus anthracis* to deal with, but as to how big a problem that is, I don't know. Furthermore, from my journo's point of view, I received nothing from Stetzer that will allow me to go public with any of this."

"Journo, huh? You damned Aussies."

"Speaking of Aussie, that's one of the reasons I stopped by so late. I thought I'd give my dad a ring on my computer. If it's 10:30 PM here, it'd be 11:30 AM tomorrow morning in Western Australia, so I can probably get him in his office before lunch."

"His office? I thought your dad was retired."

"I reckon it'll be a cold day in hell when he REALLY retires. I mean technically, he's an Emeritus Professor, but to him, that means that instead of working six days a week like before, now he works six days a week without pay. At least before he retired, he used to earn a salary!"

"Oh boy. Well, let me know where you get to with this story. I think you're onto something big, though it scares the hell out of me as to just what it is. You know you'll get all the support in the world from me and GNN."

"Aw, thanks, Oliver. You can never know how much your support means."

* * *

"Hi, Dad."

"Hi, Asha. You caught me just before lunch."

"Good. I thought that'd be the case... though from the looks of your study there, you aren't in your office, are you?"

"I'm working from home this morning. I have several papers I need to review... to write up some feedback. There's a big environmental conference coming up, and I promised to finish these and get them out of here."

"Dad, you always need to get papers done." She smirked at the screen.

"I do have some a sad story to tell you though... did you see any Australian news today?"

"No, not really, Dad. I had a meeting in Philadelphia and then flew back here to Chicago. I've been pretty much out of it all day."

"Humm..." He scratched his beard, knowing full well how to raise her dander. "You probably don't remember Sean Pratt?"

"DAD!" She practically yelled into her computer's microphone. "Are you crazy? How would I EVER forget Sean?" Quite unconsciously, she gave him the most wistful smile imaginable.

Sacha lightly slapped his half-balding head with his open hand. "All right... all right... I remember that YOU had a crush on him when you were in high school."

26

"A crush... Dad, he was the most handsome doctoral student you ever had! Besides that, he was such a nice bloke. Of course, I was infatuated when I was 15, but... wait a minute... you asked if I had seen the news. Did something happen?"

"Well, for sure something happened, but I'll start by telling you Sean is okay. He and three of his grad students were starting a dive on the Great Barrier Reef yesterday – over near Townsville – and the university dive boat exploded."

"Oh my god!"

"No, no... as I said, Sean is fine as are two of his students. One young woman though – Nikki something – is in hospital. The last I heard on the ABC was that she is stable."

"Damn! Do they know what happened?"

"Not really. While I was brushing my teeth this morning, I heard a constable on the radio saying they are looking into whether or not it was an accident, but at this point, they still need to pull up the remains of the boat."

"Whether or not it was an accident! What are you talking about? Do you mean there's a question?"

"No, no, no, honey... don't jump to conclusions. Damn, you sound just like an ambo-chasing journo!"

"Dad! It's just the way you said it. Besides that, I don't chase ambos!"

"Well, I'll make sure to catch up on that news before I go to bed tonight. I hope he's okay." She tapped a finger on her desk. "I doubt Sean would even remember that you had a daughter..."

"Somehow I think he remembers." Sacha smiled. "Now then, you were meeting with someone in Philly today... er, yesterday?"

"Don't get going on the dateline, Dad. I know it's Wednesday down there. And yes, I was meeting with an epidemiologist at the University of Pennsylvania. Remember I asked you about the anthrax outbreak in Alaska. I think GNN reported on it in January or February, but the incident happened the end of last summer... last northern summer in August or maybe September."

"So, what did you find out?"

"Not enough. He wasn't willing to TELL me anything, but he did communicate that I might be onto something concerning a mutated form of *Bacillus anthracis.*"

"He didn't tell you, but he communicated that?"

"Oh, Dad. I do make a living trying to learn from people in more ways than just verbal communication, you know. In this case, his facial expression told me he agreed with me, but he wasn't willing to go on record verbally about it."

"I gotcha." Woof! Woof! There was a sudden canine commotion interrupting the Skype transmission from one side of the planet to the other.

"Is that Seymour?"

"Damn, I hope so. If it's not, a giant wild beagle is attacking me!" Sacha turned his computer camera towards the study window, and a large beagle sat erect barking out the floor to ceiling window. "I think Seymour sees another dog on 'his' street, obviously an unforgivable crime in Western Australia."

"I wish I could visit, Dad. I miss you... miss Seymour... I wish I had a good excuse to come over."

Sacha rolled his head as though he was trying to stretch his neck. "You just might be in luck."

"How do you mean that?"

"Well, I mentioned Sean... You may have seen something of the work being done on the Reef over the other side with green sea turtles. As is the case with a variety of reptiles, the gender of hatchlings is particularly sensitive to temperature. The data collected now suggests more than 99% of the new hatchlings are female. Numbers counted in one green sea turtle rookery last week had the girls outnumbering the boys by at least 116 to 1."

"Holy cow!"

"At least holy turtle, my dear!" His smug look accompanied his attempt at humour.

"Now THAT was bad even for a 'dad joke', Dad!" Asha still laughed.

"My point is that I believe in gender equality with the best of them, but I'm also a scientist... no baby boys mean no babies, full stop! The Pacific green sea turtles seem the worst, but loggerheads, leatherbacks, hawksbills... the other species are close behind."

"Is this work being done by one of your former students?"

"It is... one Sean Pratt... the same Sean Pratt I have already confirmed that you remember somewhere in the deep, dark recesses of your mind." He smirked through his computer to the other side of the planet.

Asha gave him her best 'disgusted' look. "Dad..."

"Anyway, he's been leading the pack with all this – turtles, decline of biodiversity, bleaching corals... Thank goodness he won't be sidelined for long. I will at least leave him a message now that I know he's not hurt and, if I can, will speak to him this afternoon. But there's more than Sean and his exploding dive boat."

"More?"

"Do you remember my old mate Clive Moseley?"

"Dr Clive? Sure, I remember him. He lectures at Notre Dame in Fremantle, yes? In the Notre Dame Medical School, right?"

"That's Clive."

"And?"

"Well, I'm having dinner with Clive tonight, but the brief chat we had yesterday piqued my interest. He has done a bit of work with a biochemist, microbiologist, epidemiologist from Melbourne. I'm sorry I'm so vague here, but I don't know her personally at all and am just relaying a heads up to you very family-like and unofficial."

"Cross my heart, Dad."

"Well in light of the mutated *Bacillus anthracis* you have taken a liking to, you might start following whatever the hell is going on with our not-so-friendly Ebola virus of late. I know you are aware of the spread of Ebola into Southeast Asia."

"Well, of course, but I was under the impression that only reflected rising temperatures."

He slowly shook his head. "Don't believe everything you hear. Your mutating virus story may just about be ready to grow exponentially."

"Damn, Dad, what' in god's name is going on?"

"I don't know exactly, but I'm trying to find out."

Asha paused and scratched her head. "Do I hear you saying that maybe Ebola might be mutating, too?"

Sacha raised both hands over his head as if to give up. "I know nothing."

"I'm not sure I believe you, Dad. Well, whatever... don't forget your daughter if you DO find something out."

"Look, give me a couple of days... It's Wednesday here now – Tuesday there... How about we Skype Friday, tomorrow – Thursday night time for you folks in Illinois. I don't know your schedule, but..."

"That would be great, Dad. Same time 48 hours from now?"

"Righty-oh, honey. Maybe I'm just an old academic who spent a career watching Mother Nature, but she always has a knack for surprising us when we least expected it. Maybe she's got another shocker or two in store for us again this time."

7

Wednesday, 17 April; Habitat Serviced Apartments, Townsville, Queensland

"G'day Professor Pratt. I'm Inspector Leon Rumford, and this is Inspector Katie Hasler of the Queensland Police Service. Do you mind if we speak with you for a minute?"

Sean opened the door. "Please, please... come on in and have a seat. We just settled in here ourselves. Thanks to the Queensland Police Service for putting us up here for the night." He wasn't sure if he had just spoken a serious 'thank you' or communicated a 'why are we here' message.

"Sorry for any inconvenience putting all three of you together here in the rental unit, Professor, but we thought it important to keep the three of you together long enough for us to hear the whole story."

"Fair enough." Pratt led them into the small living area in the serviced apartment unit they had rented. Becky was seated on one side of the sofa tucked up in a lotus position. She looked up at the two officers from her tablet computer just as Sean waved his arm in her direction. "This is one of my doctoral students, Becky Whitehall. I'll see if John is in his room."

"Yes, I'm sure he is. JOHN..." She shouted his name. "Sorry for yelling."

"No worries." The two police officers sat across from Becky as John walked into the room.

"G'day. John Rivkin here. I'm another one of Sean's graduate students." He shook their hands, grabbed a chair from the kitchenette, flipped it around backwards and sat down.

"I'm so sorry you three had such a harrowing day. I've spoken on the phone with Senior Constable Grocott who you spoke with at the Lyman Health Centre up north there, and he tells me the ED doc there cleared all three of you medically. Thank goodness for that."

"Yes, we were very fortunate." Sean took another kitchen chair and sat across from the sofa. "Now we just hope that Nikki... Nikki Vasquez, is just as lucky. Constable Grocott was a real help, got us back to our university Landcruiser and made sure we got back down here to Townsville this afternoon. Now we have to wait on Nikki."

"The latest update we had about an hour ago was that she was admitted to Townsville Hospital for observation."

"That's right... I just spoke with a staff member on her ward right before you got here, and the nurse let me speak directly with Nikki. She's feeling better than we feared, has a bit of a gash on her leg, but they haven't found any breaks. It looks like, save for a few stitches, she's going to be fine."

Inspector Rumford pulled out and small notepad from his chest pocket and flipped over a few pages. "Have you asked yourself why?"

"Why?" John started to respond, then looked at the professor who nodded his head approvingly. "That's pretty simple. We were there to collect samples, coral mostly, but also water quality samples, phytoplankton, zooplankton, microbes... All four of us were in the water and breathing through our regulators. Becky, Sean and I had already started our descent and were probably... what, two or three metres down..."

Becky confirmed his estimate. "Yes, about that."

"Anyway, I looked up and noticed that Nikki was below the surface but trying to hook her sample bag onto her waist belt. The next thing I knew, there was a loud bang. The fact that three of us were insulated by ten feet of water easily answers your question as to why we were okay, and she got hurt."

The inspector jotted a few notes and looked up. "Thanks for that, John. I guess I also was asking if any of you had thought about why... why the explosion happened in the first place?"

"Understood. Constable Grocott asked about that, too. He asked about whether we had any petrol aboard since the *Reef Explorer* was diesel-powered twin shaft. Look, we've used the boat before, and she's a nice piece of equipment. I'm sure the university can give you a sheet of specs on it. Happily, the last several times we dove up this way using her, John was the pilot."

"I see. Did you check fuel levels and whatnot before you departed, Mr Rivkin?"

"I sure did, and the diesel tanks were topped up. The university has a checklist we are meant to go through, and we always do so. It makes you tick all the obvious – fuel, water, electrics, safety gear, flares, radio gear... anyway, I went through it all." John nodded towards his professor. "Sean always insists we don't take shortcuts with OH & S matters."

Sean spoke up. "I've had a colleague get into a hell of a lot of trouble for not going through the whole checklist. Besides that, I take my responsibility to the students seriously."

"That's an affirmative." Becky smiled at her mentor.

"Anyway, Nikki helped me out with the tick list while the professor and Becky were checking our research equipment."

"We usually split it up that way." Pratt stretched a leg.

"Does your checklist ask you to check petrol cans? Did you happen to notice if there was any petrol aboard?" The inspector looked at his notepad. "Constable Grocott indicates that there were fuel cans for the Zodiac's outboard?"

John rocked his head back and forth. "Petrol? Look, the *Reef Explorer* had a cabinet just for petrol cans. There were two 20-litre jerry cans, and though I confess that I didn't open the tops to visualise them, I nudged them with my foot, and they seemed to be pretty full. Nikki confirmed that with me, and she ticked the box."

"Two full jerry cans, huh? Did you notice anything suspicious? Did you see anything maybe out of place there with petrol cans?"

"Suspicious? Out of place? Nah... there was a fuel line hose laying there. You know, one that has a primer bulb and fittings used to attach it from the jerry can to the outboard. I don't remember seeing anything else there."

"Humm..." Rumford kept writing. "We do have our QPS divers working in the water now. Once they pull out whatever is there, the forensics team will do what they do."

"Damn, the Queensland Police must think something nefarious has happened here, yeah?" Pratt's face looked dour. "Do you have information here that we don't? I mean, try as I might, I can't think of anyone who would have done this on purpose."

"No, no, professor. Whenever something like this happens, it's the responsibility of the Police Service to do a routine investigation." Rumford's voice was calm and reassuring. "It's just a matter of clearing the records. Naturally, insurance companies, banks and other involved parties need to be confident in the fact that an accident is an accident."

Pratt's nodded his head in understanding.

Inspector Hasler had been quiet until now but leaned forward and looked towards John. "Tell me, Mr Rivkin... Actually, let me direct this question at all of you. Did any of you see anyone else around the boat? Did you see any other people around the dock? Anything at all suspicious?"

"You know, now that you mention it, I remember thinking out loud to Nikki about what a perfect day it was and that there wasn't a soul anywhere to be seen enjoying it." Becky untucked herself and let one leg hang to the floor now.

"Yeah, I remember that." John's lifted his chin from the seat back on his turned-around chair. "Then Nikki jumped on the dock and went to take the line off the cleat, and we scanned up and down the beach. I think I saw two people walking away from us, but hell, they'd have been nearly a kilometre away."

"No one else?"

"Nah." Becky surveyed her mates, and both slowly shook their heads in the negative.

John ran his fingers through his hair. "You know, we parked the Landcruiser in the car park around... maybe just before 9 AM and loaded all our tanks and equipment on the little cart the university keeps in the back of the vehicle. There may have been a ute way up the other end of the car park, but I'm not certain. I never saw a person. If there was a ute, it was probably a fisherman."

Inspector Hasler scratched her nose with her index finger. "But you didn't see anyone but the beachcombers?"

"Nah..." All three answered almost in unison.

"Professor, please don't take this the wrong way, but are you aware of anyone who would want to see harm come to you or your students?"

"Harm?"

The inspector looked up from his notes towards Pratt. "Yes, harm. Would you being injured or worse be of benefit to anyone you know?"

"Well, no... like I said, I can't for the life of me think of anyone who would intentionally do this. John? Becky?"

Both students shook their heads no.

8

Thursday, 18 April; Yunupingu Institute of Medical Research, Melbourne, Victoria

"You're sure in early, Felly?"

"Hell, we flew overnight Tuesday and didn't get to Melbourne until midday yesterday. Until we got home, unpacked some and took a nap... I was awake way too early."

"Jet lag?" Deshi stood in her doorway with a mug of coffee in his hand.

She let out a deep breath. "Not really jet lag... I mean the four-hour time difference is a pain, but I'm more tired of both travelling home and being away for so long. Believe me, three months out of the office seems like forever, even considering our daily briefs and video conferencing."

"Well, I'm glad you're back in one piece. And what's this rush-rush surprise meeting that was scheduled at the last minute yesterday."

"You think you're surprised. I heard about it by text message just as I was getting off the plane yesterday and heading to immigration. That's just what I need, hosting some American bloke on an unknown mission pretty much just as I step off a plane. Oh well, the things we do to maintain research grants."

"Is he from the Los Angeles group?"

"Frankly, Deshi, I don't know, but the director told me he's with the Pentagon. Now what in god's name the Pentagon would want with us is beyond my imagination."

"Damn..."

"You said it. I guess I had my fun playing research scientist and now I have to pay my dues playing international diplomat…"

"I gotcha. Just another sad case of mean old Mr Reality rearing his ugly head." He chuckled at his half-hearted attempt at humour. "But I trust from what you've been telling us, your time up there in Thailand and Malaysia was worthwhile."

"For sure." She frowned. "I don't know, though, Deshi. Things are happening with our friends in the whole family *Filoviridae* and with *Zaire ebolavirus* in particular." She suddenly caught herself referring to one of the most lethal viruses on Earth as 'our friends'. "Hell, we study viruses as a career and can often explain mutations down to a specific segment of a particular gene. Some of the work you and Liz were doing last year literally came down to counting atoms! But I swear to god we are now seeing mutations occur in front of our eyes… metaphorically at least."

"Well, I don't want to brag, but the work Liz and I did last year by vitrifying cells containing family *Filoviridae* viruses and then examining them by cryo-fluorescent light microscopy, and cryo-electron tomography wasn't metaphorical in any way. We did visualise them!"

Felly had to laugh. "Now, don't be so touchy! You take me too literally. You and Liz will win an award for that work, and certainly, I haven't forgotten it. I mean that things are happening so fast now… the mutations seem accelerated."

"Do you think it's just family *Filoviridae*, Felly?"

"We should be so lucky… You know, being out of the way in the middle of Southeast Asia for three months allowed me to catch up on so much reading. I know that sounds funny, but the remoteness of where we were at least half the time caused us to have more 'quiet time' when we were away from the laboratory or away from the hospital in Geoff's case. I was able to follow up on other research more than I can here in Melbourne. That said, no, it's not just our little baby. For that matter, it's not just viruses... other microorganisms may be getting one step in front of us, too."

"What have you learned?"

"Well, are you familiar with ARGs?"

"Yeah, Antibiotic-Resistant Genes, yes?"

"Yes, yes... and of course from ARGs, it's just a hop-skip-and-jump to multidrug-resistant microorganisms. We're cranking out these ARGs by the bucketful through our abuse of antibiotics in medicine and – worse yet – in agriculture. One mutated enzyme traced back to surface water in New Delhi less than a decade ago, and now it has covered the globe and has been found in over 100 countries and even into the High Arctic. Of course, the real problem is that it can confer multidrug resistance into many microorganisms making them resistant to Carbapenems, that hugely important group of antibiotic agents are among the most powerful antibiotics we have to fight these multidrug-resistant microorganisms."

"Jesus! I'm so glad you've come home filled with wonderful tales of such erotic side trips in Southeast Asia. I was hoping for a slideshow." Deshi laughed.

"Be quiet, or I just might have Geoff come over here and show you slides of work he was doing in Ebola tent clinics." She was interrupted by her phone. "Excuse me, Deshi, I no sooner mention Geoff, and suddenly he's ringing me from the hospital."

Felly held one finger up as if to say 'wait a minute' as she answered the phone. "Hi, honey." Her gaze focused on the far wall of her office. "They WHAT?" She flashed an expression of dread towards Deshi. "Well, how in god's name are they going to do that? I mean, you can't just do a breathalyser to test for EVD. Besides that, if you'd be infected, I'd be infected, our entire Qantas planeload would be infected, and a long trail people from Thailand to Victoria would be infected. For that matter, you haven't even been on a Thailand ward for what... over two weeks at this point. Just tell them they're crazy."

Felly. Leaned back in her chair and listened. "Yep... aha... No way..." The longer she talked, the more her face flushed with anger. After a few minutes, she finally finished up the call. "Damn honey – what a pain that you have to go through this! Look... take a deep breath. I'll see you when I get home." A quick glimmer of a smile crossed her face. "...and I love you too, Geoff." She dropped her phone on the desk and flicked it with enough force that it teetered near the edge on the far side.

Deshi felt self-conscious just standing there from what was a bothersome conversation for her. "I'm sorry I was interrupting, Felly."

"No, Deshi no... you weren't interrupting at all. Actually, I'm glad you stayed since I have YOU to vent on! Besides that, you probably saved my phone from being smashed with me throwing it against the wall." This time her smile was brighter. "You know that Geoff works at Royal Yarra Hospital, right?"

"Of course, I know Geoff works at Royal Yarra... he has been there for a long time, yes?"

"Yep. Well, you won't believe it, but he started his duty this morning in the Emergency Department, and everything was what you'd expect. At some point, the hospital director shows up in ED and takes Geoff aside. It seems he had a phone call from a 'top pollie'... Geoff reckons the 'top pollie' was probably the Premier. Anyway, the government must demonstrate that they are doing everything possible to keep the citizens of Victoria safe from Ebola Disease."

"Damn... Has Geoff been experiencing symptoms?"

"No, none at all, and that's exactly the problem. Who knows better than us that EVD generally shows up in a week or two, twenty days max. Geoff left the tent hospital he was working at outside Phuket two weeks ago, and he's had zero symptoms since then? Hell, for that matter, he's had zero symptoms forever!"

* * *

The door on Felly's office opened, and she ushered their visitor into the tearoom where the staff were all seated around the table with steaming mugs in front of most. She had three flat boxes in her hands. "Good afternoon, all. It seems like forever since we all sat around this table last. I know it's only three months and we did continue with our video meetings, but I can't tell you how nice it is to be home.

"First things first." She opened one box and slid it along with the other two into the middle of the table. "I highly recommend these macadamia nut chocolate elephants that Geoff and I have grown quite fond of up there."

"Sorry, you were regulated to second on the agenda, Milt." There were polite laughs around the table. "I want to introduce all of you to Mr Milt Warner visiting us from Washington, DC. Welcome first of all to Australia and welcome to Yunupingu Institute of Medical Research, Milt."

Milt held one hand up. "Thanks so much, Felly, even being bumped off the top of the agenda by chocolate elephants. Some of my colleagues warned me about you Aussies and something you call 'the tall poppy syndrome'. Somehow, I think I've just had a personal introduction to that piece of Australian culture." He smiled. "I will happily be the first to take one of those chocolate elephants, though." The young woman next to him quickly reached for the open box and pushed it in front of him.

"I do apologise for such late arrangements leading up to this visit. I realise Felly just returned to Melbourne herself. I had a few meetings in Sydney and Canberra, have followed your work for quite a while now and was only able to organise this side trip to Melbourne on Tuesday. I am so happy that you worked me into your busy schedules."

"We're only too happy to have you, Milt." Felly politely told her little white lie to Warner while sipping her tea. "Let me do a quick once around here, so you know who everyone is. You've already met Dr Liz O'Rourke and Dr Deshi Tang. The three of us are the lead researchers on the project. I'll continue around the table. That's Wendy Ingman, one of the best lab technicians anyone could have on their team. Of course, I get myself into trouble here, because Damien Falk seated right next to her would also be on anyone's 'best-ever' list for hands-on laboratory work. Pete Baghurst is our all-around problem solver – electronics, software, fix-anything-handyman – you name it, and Pete can do it." She continued her introductions by extending her hand to the far side of the table. "This is Jai Yang, another fellow with top-notch laboratory skills as well as a doctoral student at one of the local universities studying..."

Jai spoke up. "Microbiology with a lot of emphasis on virology."

"Thanks, Jai. Pam Shearing sitting right next to him is another outstanding doctoral student – also microbiology. Is that right, Pam?"

"Yes, Felly."

"And finally, that's Fiona Grantham who is an all-around researcher here, and you'd just as likely find her in the library doing background work or helping pull papers together. I've known Fiona for quite a while now."

"Seven years, Felly."

"Thanks all for letting me do a quick once-around. Regrettably, we don't have the time to delve too deeply into all of your work but suffice it to say that you couldn't beat this team in the States, in the EU, or anywhere else people research the sort of things we are looking into."

Milt Warner leaned forward in his chair and meticulously folded the candy wrapper left from his chocolate elephant. "I can't tell you how happy I am to be here and how fantastic it is meeting all of you." His accent had a touch of a southern drawl and screamed 'American' with every word out of his mouth. "I've been following much of your research for several years now and so much appreciate the update that Felly, Liz and Deshi have given me over the past hour or so. I'm here to tell you that the excellent work you do and the papers you are writing have caught the eye of Uncle Sam."

Felly tilted her head to the side. "You know Milt, we just spent the last hour together, and I realise how rude I have been in going on at length about the Yunupingu Institute. I assume you are with the Center for Disease Control, but we never got that far. Exactly what part of the US government do you represent?"

"Please don't apologise, Felly... I've been so interested in the overview you three have presented that I didn't see the need to spend a lot of time on my work. As for me, I work with the Pentagon in the Biological Defense Program, now officially called the National Biodefense Strategy."

9

Friday, 19 April; Murdoch University, Perth, Western Australia

Sacha looked out his office window and watched the morning sunlight wash down onto the lawn. He clicked on Asha's icon, and the Skype app started to ring. His gaze again turned to the lawn, and he smiled as a frisky quenda scurried behind a grevillea shrub near his office block. His mind drifted off to the quendas, one of several varieties of brown bandicoot sharing the same plight as so many other marsupials, namely losing their habitat to the urban sprawl of Metro Perth.

"Hi, Dad..." At first, there was no response. "Hey, Dad... I'm over here."

Sacha snapped back to the here and now and turned towards his computer screen. "Hi, honey."

"Jeez, where were you? I answer my Skype and see you off with the fairies."

He laughed. "Well, obviously, I am in my office today, and it's a beautiful morning here in Perth. I was just watching a little quenda darting about outside my window."

"Okay, you're forgiven. At least I'm glad to hear that we haven't wiped out all the marsupials down there... at least not yet."

"True, but for how long?"

"I've got some good news for you, Dad."

"After some of what I've been learning in the past 48 hours, I could do with some good news."

"Oh boy, you too? Well, we'll get to that in a minute, but I've also had a productive 48 hours. After my meeting with that Dr Stetzer, the epidemiology bloke in Philly that I told you about the other night, I thought I was hot on the trail of a story that was leading me to Alaska. But it seems that Alaska is just one tip of the same biological iceberg we are attempting to unravel. It turns out that I'm looking to book flights down there."

Sacha's eyes lit up. "You're coming home, honey?" His voice projected his excitement.

"Well, I will for sure get to Perth, but it seems that Australia may have several things happening that fit right into the mutant microbe project we're working on."

"Talk about a mixed bag... I'm thrilled to hear you may be coming home, but afraid to ask you what you're chasing."

"For starters, it's not 'may be coming', I AM coming down, Dad. I just had a chat with Oliver, my Editor of Chief, and he's already approved the trip."

"I knew I liked your boss! That's fantastic news! When are you coming?"

"If I can book a flight for tomorrow – that's Friday Chicago time – I'll be in Australia Sunday, though I can't guarantee I'll be in Perth that fast."

"So where are you heading?"

"For sure I'm going to Townsville – James Cook University. I did follow up on the Sean Pratt story you mentioned, and there's just too much happening there. You can help me organise meeting up with Sean, yes Dad?"

"Of course, honey."

"I know I'm going to Canberra, too. Some of the research happening with Commonwealth-funded projects is starting to pay off. I need to dig deeper with some of my Canberra spies. For that matter, I learned that Sean is the lead researcher for the ARC-funded Centre of Excellence for Coral Reef Studies headquartered at James Cook Uni. They certainly sound as though they're onto so much right now."

"Well, well... this is all well and good, Asha, but don't forget your Perth spies. I guess to be spot-on correct, don't forget your Perth SPY... that's singular! You can't believe what I have learned on my end since we talked two days ago."

"So, let's hear it, Dad... spill the beans."

"We must have both come across similar info on the Sean Pratt event. Police haven't found anything yet, but they are suspicious."

"Of whom?"

"I don't think there is a target as yet, but the Queensland Police have recovered pieces of the boat and are trying to sort through it. On the positive side, everyone is okay including the one grad student of Sean's who had her leg lacerated. She was in the hospital, but I followed up with Sean this morning, and they discharged her now. At the request of the police, the other three spent a night in a serviced apartment there in Townsville, but they are all in good shape and home now."

"So, you spoke personally with Sean?"

"I did. We had a long chat yesterday, actually. For that matter, I'm planning to ring him as soon as you and I finish up here."

"I guess his missus... his mate... is happy to have him home, thank god."

"If I didn't know you better, my dear, I'd think you were fishing! No, Sean doesn't have a family at this point, honey... The professor is a single, eligible bloke, Asha."

"Oh, Dad... now stop that!"

He smiled into the camera. "Okay, okay... Look, the work he and his group are doing is more than just adding to the data heap supporting the demise of the Reef. They are actually getting into some innovative ideas over there."

"Like?"

"Like things I've been telling you about since you were a little girl. Like all life is interrelated, not just clusters of organisms interrelated in localised ecosystems... ALL LIFE!"

"Yes, I always think of that, Dad. That's the whole *Gaia* thing. For that matter, I am sure you have several hundred PhD-types – let's call them 'Sharma Disciples' – running around all over the planet thinking about that too."

He ignored her 'disciple' reference. "And I hope – though I FEAR it, too – that we are getting to the point that this idea will finally become so self-evident that nobody will be able to ignore it."

"Damn... Look, I followed a couple of leads and have gotten a tip that something funny is going on with the Ebola spread into Southeast Asia. Frankly, I don't have detail at this point, but I've gotten a lead on some Aussie researchers up to the ears in this. That's why I want to talk to some contacts in the government in Canberra. They are funding a lot of this research. I think it's..."

"Asha, Asha, Asha..." The older man interrupted his daughter. "Apologies for butting in, but I might be able even to open that door wider. I told you I had dinner with my old mate Clive Moseley."

"You did... Dr Mosely who lectures at Notre Dame Medical School."

"That's the one. Anyway, I guess you know he's spent a great deal of his life in public health and lectures across that spectrum into areas like epidemiology, biostatistics, environmental health and public policy. Because of that, he has contacts and stays on top of research in exactly the area you just mentioned... the Ebola deal up in Southeast Asia. Anyway – you've gotta stay with me here – he went to medical school here in Perth with an ED doc now over east in Melbourne." Sacha looked down to read something on his desktop. "Ah... Dr Geoff Kovac at Royal Yarra Hospital..."

"Dear lord... please don't tell me they have Ebola in Melbourne!"

"No, no, honey... nothing like that. It's just that Dr Kovac's wife is Dr Felicia Kovac at the Yunupingu Institute of Medical Research there in Melbourne. She's either the director, the lead researcher or both. Anyway, their research is pretty specific and includes a range of viruses that broadly cause haemorrhagic fevers. Clive tells me that better than 90% of their funding and work is in family *Filoviridae* if that rings a bell to my journo daughter."

"It does, Dad... That's the Ebola one, yes?"

"Yes. There are half a dozen of them, but the one causing most of the problems is more specifically the *Zaire ebolavirus*. Anyway, the Kovacs just returned from three months up in Thailand and maybe Malaysia collecting samples, doing fieldwork, making contacts... You might start with the Australian Research Centre – the anal-retentive ARC bean counters there in Canberra – but I'll bet you a twenty-cent piece you'll wind up at Yunupingu Institute before you are done."

Wow, Dad, I think you might have just opened a door for me. Does Dr Mosely remember me? I wonder if I could chat with him – with both of you together – while I am in WA?"

"Trust me, dear, he remembers you. His ears burn hearing me go on and on about my Asha. I think he'd be honoured to have dinner with us some night while you are here."

"I love you so much, Dad. I'll send you a message once I know what my travel arrangements will be." She yawned into the camera as she looked at the clock. "Excuse me. Damn, it's nearly eleven PM. I'm going to check with Qantas or Air NZ and see when I can book a seat."

10

Friday, 19 April; Yunupingu Institute of Medical Research, Melbourne, Victoria

"So how is Geoff taking all of this?" Liz sat across the desk from Felly.

"Pretty much as you'd expect. He's resigned himself to it even though the whole thing is stupid. We all agree to err on the side of protecting the public, but there's a fine line between common sense and pollie sense if you know what I mean."

"Trust me, I know... damned politicians! I used to date a bloke who eventually became one several years back... that was the end..." Liz wiped her hands together a few times. "...just like that."

Fair enough."

"So, what's Geoff up to?"

"Catching up on his reading... taking longer runs the past few mornings..."

Liz interrupted. "Runs... I thought they didn't let him out."

Felly's mouth mockingly dropped open. "They simply ordered no personal contact, and he just runs." She arched her eyes. "He is also catching up on his sleep and has been napping in the afternoon. Look, at the end of the day, I think the big deal to the Department of Health people was that he was not working in the hospital."

"I gotcha. So how long must he stay away from the hospital?'

"They're still debating that, but his last day in one of the Thai tent clinics was Wednesday 3 April. The Victorian government has adopted the World Health Organisation's guideline of a 21-day quarantine for *Zaire ebolavirus*, so nominally he should be allowed to return to work on 24 April or next Wednesday. Some of the Victorian Public Health folks are still debating if the 21 days count from 3 April or from 17 April, the day we got back to Melbourne."

"Bugger all... to count from this past Wednesday is silly."

"Damned right it is. First of all, Geoff had no failure of his PPE, no breaks, leaks or failed seals. Second of all, Geoff has displayed zero symptoms, no fever, no muscle pain, no flu-like symptoms... It's not that big a deal... report any symptoms immediately and be home-monitored by a visiting nurse twice a day. I know Geoff is my husband, and I obviously have some personal skin in the game, but I do hope that sound judgement prevails, and he can go back to work next week."

"Agreed, Fell-O."

Felly laughed at her friend. "Damn, it's good to be back in Australia. I haven't been called 'Fell-O' for three months!"

"Speaking of you being back... what did you think of our new best friend Milt Warner yesterday?"

Felly let out a gush of air. "I don't... I don't know. I felt embarrassed that I – we – spoke with him for nearly an hour before the staff intros and were so happy to tell him what we were doing here with our research without ever learning why he was interested in us."

"Don't take that on yourself, Felly. Deshi and I were in the same boat. I mean I glanced at his card in your office here, but it has his name, NBS Program and a fancy Washington, DC address. The USA official seal made it all look legit enough. I just assumed he was CDC and never had the foggiest what NBS meant... I mean working out of the Pentagon. So, what, they want us to be helping them develop biological warfare?"

"Let's not be jumping to conclusions yet. I agree that it's troublesome, though, and I fear I told him more than I should have."

Liz gently tugged on her ear. "Nah... Everything you said – or that Deshi or I said, for that matter – he could have found in published papers. Seriously, it's not like Yunupingu Institute is hiding any military secrets."

"Spot on, Liz. I'm still trying to work out exactly what the Americans are interested in. After he left, I did look into the NBS – American's National Biodefense Strategy – and it all pretty much makes sense. I know that our Commonwealth government has a similar strategy for us, too. Basically, the idea is the surveillance of, preparation for and risk reduction against any biological threats either natural or manmade. The obvious follow up to that is to counter any threats, respond to them and finally to recover from any impact to the nation. I'll bet you that our Commonwealth policy would echo all this, though we encounter it much more up close and personal when coming through airport immigration and customs as well as in Commonwealth control over animal and food imports and exports."

"I'm sure you're right. It just freaks me out that Mr Warner may represent a part of the U. S. government that might wonder if *Zaire ebolavirus* might make a nifty little weapon."

"I sure hope you are wrong there, Lizzy!" Felly focused her gaze through the window in her wall looking out into the staff common area.

"Me too..." Liz noticed her mate's attention was distracted, and she turned to look out the window herself. "What's up out there, Fell-O?"

"Oh, nothing. I just wondered... Is that Mallory Fowler out there in the staff common area?"

"Yes, that's her. She's been around the past month or two."

"The past month or two... Any idea why?"

"Come on, Felly. Our group isn't the only team housed here at the Medical Science Building. I mean, there must be 500 people working somewhere in and on this campus with all sorts of different medical projects. Mallory has been working in our Microscopy Centre for several years now... probably right after she gave up on her doctoral work and left our group."

"Yes, I know that – she's a laboratory techie with them, I think. But I don't believe I have seen her in our offices since then."

"I'm sure you're right. She always stopped by to pick up samples when we needed to have work done, but she seems to show up more frequently since you and Geoff went off to Thailand. I think that she and Jai are mates... maybe more than mates. Bugger if I know, but I have noticed them in the café downstairs at tea and at lunch... I don't mean every day, but occasionally. Hey, maybe they're an item for all I know. For that matter, I'm pretty sure some of Jai's doctoral research has made use of transmission electron microscopy, and she does a lot of the prep for that. You know... plunge freezing, staining, prepping cross-sections, mounting samples..." Liz swiped a strand of hair from her eye. "I know you two had a falling out, but she's just doing what twenty-something-women do as far as I can tell. It's not a biggy, Fell-O!"

Felly's look of concern was quickly replaced with a broad smile. "No... no biggy, Liz. I was just curious."

11

Friday, 19 April; Professor Pratt's residence,
Bushland Beach, Queensland

Sean opened the door and saw two Queensland Police officers standing there. "G'day Inspector Rumford, Inspector Hasler... I hope you had no trouble finding the place."

"No, no... I know Townsville pretty well, and I love the Bushland Beach area. Jeez, what a lovely spot you have here." Katie Hasler almost wondered out loud why an eligible bachelor lived in such a large house.

"Thanks, Inspector Hasler. Yeah, I really like Bushland Beach too. Hell, I'm the first to admit that the place is way too big for me, but it's been in the family for donkey's years. My grand mum... Look, you don't want to hear all of that. I love the place, but frankly, it's bigger by far than I need, but it's been easy since I inherited it with no mortgage and it's damned convenient getting back and forth to campus."

"I'm glad you had time to see us, Professor. When I called, I wasn't sure if you'd be here or at the university. I just wanted to check in with you, ask another question or two and update you about the investigation. First things first – how is Ms Vasquez?"

"Thanks for asking. Nikki is going to be just fine. I assume you knew she was discharged from hospital and is back at her place now. She shares a unit with Becky Whitehall over near campus. The docs don't think she'll have any lasting effects save for a bit of a scar on one of her legs."

"That's excellent. I'm glad to hear she's doing well. We did know that she and Whitehall were roommates."

Inspector Hasler noticed the professor's expression of surprise when the inspector mentioned knowing the two women were roommates. "Please Professor, we don't want you to think we're nosing about your business, but in cases like this, it's Police Service policy to do background checks. It's just all routine."

"Of course, my partner here is correct, Professor. No doubt you'd have expected that we'd do thorough background checks on everyone involved here. You won't be surprised to hear that all four of you check out squeaky clean. It's a funny thing in police work – eliminate people one at a time until the only ones left are the perps... the perpetrators."

Sean nodded his head. "Of course, Inspector, of course." He realised they were all standing inside his front door. "Look, why don't we have a seat here." He extended his hand towards a comfortable looking living room just off to the side of the entrance. All three of them entered and took a seat. "You say you had a question or two, Inspector?"

"Yes, Professor. I know that John Rivkin was filling in as far as the boat's pilot responsibilities the other morning, but did you happen to check out the engine compartment to see if there were full petrol jerry cans there?" Rumford had his notebook in one hand and a pen in the other.

"No, sir... actually, no sir on two counts. First of all, the university follows strict OH & S guidelines and we are not permitted to carry extra fuel of any kind in the engine compartment. We have for-purpose fuel lockers on university vessels, and that has to be separated from the engine compartment. In the *Reef Explorer's* case, I think the locker was on the deck pretty much right over the diesel tanks in the aft there. Secondly, no sir, I didn't check the fuel cans. I've gone out with John many times over the past year or two, and he's a competent skipper. I trust him fully."

"That's all fine – I just needed to check. You were there when we spoke with him the other day, and Rivkin said there were two jerry cans in there, and they both seemed full when he nudged them."

"Two? Funny, I was there when he answered you, and I didn't hear him say two."

The inspector looked at his notepad. "No, I have it written here... two, 20-litre jerry cans. Is there something wrong there, Professor?"

"Well, I don't mean to contradict John, but I reckon there should have been three jerry cans there. Whenever we used the *Reef Explorer's* Zodiac in the past, there were always three, 20-litre cans. As far as I know, that's pretty much what the university's policy is. They reckon a day's fuel the way we use it consumes 40 or 50 litres, so the two jerry cans would not provide any reserve."

"Humm... That's funny."

"Why do you ask?"

"Well, our forensic people have lifted what's left of the *Reef Explorer* out of the water now. Let me start by saying we haven't released all of this to the press as yet and I'd hope you'd not shout all of this from the rooftops. That said, we've also spoken with your colleague, Dr Wentworth."

"Robbo Wentworth? Yeah, he's in physics."

"Yes, physics and chemistry... at least enough chemistry to make him an explosives expert."

"Explosives expert? I never knew that, and I've worked with him for years."

The inspector tilted his head. "Well, you no doubt didn't realise that he also moonlights for ASIO, though that isn't public knowledge either."

"ASIO! Now, wait a minute. That's the Australian Security Intelligence Organisation... How the hell is spy-stuff coming into this?"

"How the hell do you think we cleared your background checks so quickly?" Rumford brushed his chin with his hand. "But let's not get too far ahead of the game, Professor. I told you the other day that it's our responsibility to check in any case like this. I'm not at liberty to go into great detail as to why, but I can tell you that at this point, that we are fairly certain that the *Reef Explorer* explosion was not accidental. Besides that, ASIO isn't all about spies, you know. They have a responsibility to protect all Australians from a broad range of threats, both domestic and international, and that includes terrorism."

"WHAT! Terrorism! For Christ's sakes... I'm a university environmental science professor, not a terrorist!"

"Now calm down, Professor. No one suspects any of you of being anything but a university professor and three doctoral students. But that's exactly why I mention Dr Wentworth. I was aware that you two knew each other, so in all likelihood, you would have heard some of this from him already."

"Frankly, I haven't seen Robbo for a week or two and I sure as hell didn't know he was with ASIO, but please don't take me this far into your investigation and then just stop... I want to know what you have found."

Inspector Rumford nodded his head in the affirmative. "No, I won't just let you hang, Professor. I can certainly give you a bit of information here, at least. Let me start by acknowledging that I am far from being an explosive expert. Hell, I had trouble with chemistry when I was in high school. That said, I do know that diesel fuel isn't nearly as volatile as petrol. Of course, that also means it's not so explosive all by itself... that is to say, not so explosive without getting a little help. We kind of started with that idea the other day. Why does a boat explode with no one aboard, no engine running and on a perfectly beautiful autumn morning? One reason could be a malfunction, but a quick call to the mechanics in the Facilities Management Department at your university solved that problem. I chatted to a Mr Fernandez there, and he filled me in on the work report he filed just last Monday. The *Reef Explorer* passed all the mechanical checks your OH & S policy calls for within the past ten days. Seems she was in perfect running order. I even asked him about the jerry cans."

"And?"

"And he told me they made sure all three cans were filled to within thirty millimetres of the cap. Again, OH & S rules call for that gap, so expansion doesn't leak volatile petrol from the cans I guess."

"Now wait a minute. I can't believe John Rivkin would mislead you."

"Professor, I don't think John Rivkin would mislead us either. Let me continue. I give our Forensic Services blokes all the credit in the world for the work they do. They use something they call a TERK or Trace Explosives Recovery Kit. Now I've already confessed to being awful at doing chemistry, but I know enough to be able to use the results of a good chemist. Using these methods, they can actually collect samples as small as one-billionth of a gram."

"Sweet Jesus! That's a nanogram."

"Billionth, nanogram, whatever... Dr Wentworth tried explaining it all to me, but when that explosion went off, bits and pieces were ejected by a shockwave..." Rumford looked to his notes again. "...at velocities of 1000 metres a second or more. Think about that, Professor. Bits and pieces flew out of there at a kilometre A SECOND! Thank god Ms Vasquez didn't catch anything sizable."

Inspector Hasler had been quiet through her boss's whole explanation until now. "Yes, thank god for sure. She could have been a goner."

"Anyway, through it all, a few tiny bits of plastic from the jerry can – or cans – were found in our sweep." Rumford held two fingers millimetres apart to emphasise how small the bits of plastic were.

"Are you telling me that the forensic guys could sweep the ocean? Damn! If you don't mind my asking, how in the hell did they do that?"

"You made it easy for them. Let me ask you, Professor, where did you drop anchor?"

"Well..." His hand unconsciously reached up and scratched his head. "I remember Becky went up on the bow and waited until we were clear of coral and in the middle of a nice, sandy area. We always avoid damaging any coral."

The inspector smiled as he looked towards Hasler. She had a quiet chuckle as she looked back at Rumford. "You were spot on, boss."

Rumford's face flushed with an expression somewhere between satisfaction and swagger. "I love detective work, Professor. I told Katie – ah, Inspector Hasler – that a team of environmental scientists would never drop anchor right over the reef, not in a million years. And 'good on you' I say... anchors chipping up coral is a bad thing, sir. I've spent my entire life in and around Capricornia here, and we love our Great Barrier Reef, emotionally, recreationally and financially. All of that said, when the *Reef Explorer* blew, it blew 15 metres above a fairly pristine patch of sand. The bits flew out in a spherical pattern, and ones that went down were immediately cushioned somewhat by the water. What drifted to the bottom was pretty easy for our divers to rake up and sieve across the sandy area below. We found several interesting pieces."

"And let me guess... one of them was a piece of a bomb?" Pratt was both fascinated by the police work and terrified at the thought of someone trying to blow them up.

"Well, not exactly a bomb. Among other things, we did find shredded bits from the plastic jerry cans. Dr Wentworth did his magic and found traces of A. S. A., which is the priming charge along with PETN..." He looked up from his notes. "I doubt you want to hear me mispronounce these chemical names Professor, but what this means is that the explosion wasn't an accident. These chemicals have the precise markings of a standard blasting cap, the kind used in half or more of the all the mines in Australia."

"A blasting cap wouldn't sink a boat the size of the *Reef Explorer*, Inspector."

"You're spot on there. But a blasting cap definitely would ignite a 20-litre jerry can of petrol which in turn would easily detonate a tank of diesel fuel."

"Damn. And you know all of this or are hypothesising it?"

"Just consider that both you and Mr Fernandez – the mechanic at your university – assure me that the *Reef Explorer* should have had three jerry cans. Tuesday morning John Rivkin was sure he only saw two cans in the petrol locker. Well, sir, we found several dozen pieces of jerry cans and your mate Wentworth found residue on about a third of them. You're the scientist, not me, but I know how to use statistics. If a third of a sample has traces of explosive, that must mean one of three cans had a blasting cap fixed to it. At this point, I can't give you a photo of the third jerry can, but it sounds very likely that someone probably used some gaffer tape to fix a blasting cap to one of those cans and moved it down into the engine compartment very near to the fuel tanks."

"But how would it have been detonated?"

"I'm sorry, Professor... we just haven't found all the answers as yet, but we will keep looking."

12

Friday, 19 April; O'Hare Airport, Chicago, Illinois

Asha looked at the time on her phone – 6:38 AM in Chicago, so 8:38 PM Friday evening in Western Australia. She had been thinking about texting her dad, but since she had to catch an early flight to connect in Los Angeles, she could still catch him awake if he was at home. She pressed the call button.

"G'day."

"Dad... it's me... it's Asha."

"Hi, honey. Where are you?"

"I'm still in Chicago, but at O'Hare Airport. Did you get my text?"

"I did. That's so fantastic that you will come here first and organise your Aussie schedule from home."

"As soon as I finished Skyping with you last night, I noticed that Oliver's light was still burning. We had a chat, and he agreed I should head off ASAP. I booked some flights and basically just had to agree to give up my weekend by sitting in cattle class seats on Qantas for a skillion hours."

"Well, I doubt it's a skillion hours, but I know it's a long flight. I'm just so happy you'll be here so quickly."

"Well, the alternative was hanging around here over the weekend and maybe not being able to connect with people down there next week. I can organise my schedule as easily from WA as I can from Chicago and get to spend time with my flesh and blood as a bonus."

"So, remind me again of your cross-planet dash."

"Easy. I depart O'Hare in about an hour and fly to Los Angeles on a domestic airline. I think I only have a few hours layover there and then fly one of Qantas's new long-range 787s direct to Perth."

"Directly to Perth. Oh boy, that's some serious flight time."

"Yeah, eighteen-something hours I think, but at least I can avoid having to transfer in Sydney or Melbourne. I get into Perth sometime around Saturday midnight."

"I'll be there, honey."

"No, Dad... That's silly to lose sleep just to pick me up. I can hop a taxi."

"Miss sleep... fat chance of that! You don't think for one lousy minute I could be soundly sleeping when my little girl is coming home for the first time in... in what? A year?"

"Okay, Dad. But you had better be careful driving. There are crazy hoons out drink driving at that hour on a Saturday night."

"I'll be careful, honey."

"I'm so excited to see you."

"It won't be long. If you get through immigration and customs with no hitches, I should have you back here petting Seymour by 2:00 or 2:30... You may even get enough sleep so that I can take you out for fish and chips Sunday night."

"Now that's a deal, Dad."

"Aw, man... I'll be stuffed!"

"What's wrong, Dad?"

"No, no... it's not wrong, honey, but this Monday is Earth Day. I've committed to being on campus for a good part of the day because I'm giving the Earth Day talk at Murdoch Uni. They have one every year, and it's an honour to be asked to present it."

"Well, that's no problem – that's fantastic! I'll be there in the front row listening to your words of wisdom, Dad."

"Thanks, honey. I think there's a brunch or lunch or some event afterwards and we can go to that together. I'll be proud as a peacock with my Asha here."

"Oh, Dad... I can't wait to see you."

"Do you have a minute yet, honey?"

"Sure. I'm at the gate, and they don't board for half an hour yet."

"I won't keep you, but I did want you to know that Sean rang me a little while ago."

"And?"

"You won't like the sound of this... The boat explosion on Tuesday is now more than suspicious. The Queensland Police have all but confirmed that there was foul play. They seem to have some evidence of an explosive device being involved, but Sean didn't get into that kind of detail with me. Damn... how about that?"

"Who would want to hurt a university professor?"

"Excellent question... Who? The obvious source of threat would be someone working with or for Wynwood Coal."

"Wynwood... why Wynwood?"

"Honey, you don't need me to go on here... you're the journo. Australia may only be the fourth largest producer of coal in the world, but we are the biggest exporter by far. Like it or not for an environmentalist like me – or like Sean – coal mining pays one hell of a lot of the bills in Australia."

"But Dad, again... why Wynwood?"

"Sorry... why Wynwood... I don't have the numbers in front of me, but if the government approves Wynwood, they have BILLIONS of tonnes of coal reserves, and it would be the largest coal mine on earth. We're talking a HUGE amount of money and the political fights going on down here right now are enough to make you cry. I guess I wouldn't put anything past those people."

"What people?" Asha's journalist curiosity had kicked in now. "Who's building this mine?"

"No one as of yet. If it all gets approved, there is a consortium of investors, mostly foreign sources of money."

"Dad, I've been so wrapped up in following the mutating microorganisms that I just haven't put any time into this issue. It sounds as though we maybe need to shine a little daylight here, too. Does Sean think it's them... think it's Wynwood?"

"He didn't really say that, but when foul play pops up like this, don't you journos always use that old adage 'follow the money'? In this case, the money is spot on coal."

13

Saturday, 20 April; Professor Pratt's residence, Bushland Beach, Queensland

Sean Pratt got in front of his computer just to see the Skype software wink off. He clicked on the icon and could see that it was Sacha who had just called. He walked back to the kitchen counter where he had just fixed a cup of coffee and brought it back to his desk. He clicked on Sacha's image, and Skype started ringing.

"Sean. Thanks for ringing me back. How are you? I hope I didn't wake you."

"Wake me, Sacha... it's ten in the morning over here. I should ask why YOU are awake at 8 AM out there in the sunny west."

"It certainly is sunny this morning, mate. And it's even sunnier for me since Asha gets in around midnight. I haven't seen that girl for nearly a year!"

"Yes, you mentioned she was coming sometime soon. Wow, tonight already."

"She's tracking a story or two and has every intention of getting over there to chat with you."

"Any time, any time... I'm surprised she even remembers me."

Sacha smiled into the camera. "Believe me, she sure does remember you, Sean. You were always one of my best students."

"Thanks, Sacha."

"More on her work in a minute, but have you heard anything new over there?"

"Well, I told you yesterday what the police were thinking. I just keep going over it in my head time and again. Naturally, I believe what the police have found... hell, that's cold, hard evidence. But as to who could possibly have wanted to harm us. All four of us sat around here with a beer last night and went over it and over it."

"You mentioned Wynwood Coal yesterday."

Sean tipped his head and squinted. "I don't know, Sacha. I'm sure they don't like the work we're doing because the information we are collecting may threaten their licensing, but bombs? For bloody hell... this isn't the movies! I have my problems with many of the business backers here, but they are at least legitimate, not organised crime like the Yakuza or the Mafia for god's sake... Not only that, but we're such small potatoes compared to some of the bankers having second thoughts at going ahead with loans, the state pollies having second thoughts about approving the needed legislation, the Commonwealth pollies giving their go-ahead, about the Aboriginal Land Council... I mean a professor and three graduate students draw a potentially lethal signal from a business interest? It just doesn't make sense."

"Jeez Sean, I agree with you." Sacha's eyes drifted down, and a dower expression crossed his face. "I hate to suggest this, but could something sort of way out there be going on with one of your students? Possibly someone has an angry ex-lover or something like that trying to get even."

"Sacha, Sacha, Sacha... you have been at this game for a generation longer than I have. You're talking about three young people I have come to know for several years, back into undergrad days for Becky and John. We've laughed together, cried together, travelled together, worked together... I mean I feel that I know these people like you know Asha. There's just nothing like that there."

"I don't want to pry here, Sean, but are you... are you okay?"

"Of course, I'm okay. I inherited a nice house from my grand mum, I don't drive a fancy car, I have no outstanding bills to speak of, I don't have a serious love life... Hell, I've become the classic nutty professor, and I'm only in my forties. People around campus bust my chops for spending more time with Pacific green sea turtles than with colleagues on campus. If anyone is chasing me, they are damned well invisible... or have fins!"

"I gotcha Sean."

"It can't be personal with any of us. Besides, all that I just told you has passed the cops' research, too." Sean unconsciously looked around as though he was making sure no one was there. "...Inspector Rumford hinted that somehow ASIO is even involved with this, and they have looked into all our backgrounds and found nothing suspicious."

"ASIO?"

"Yeah, ASIO... tell me about it. This is all just bat-shit crazy!"

There was a 15 or 20-second pause on both sides of the country. "You know that Asha is employed by GNN and is working on a project looking at unusual mutations on microorganisms. I think she's been chasing some zombie microbes thawing out in the Arctic permafrost and maybe some Ebola viruses and other nasty bugs."

"Yes, I did know that both from our chats and from the few times I've seen her on GNN lately. I must admit I don't see much TV anymore, but when I do, it's generally news or docos."

"Fair enough. I just really have been thinking a lot about that. You mentioned some of your work with turtles to me... suggesting greater than 99% of the new hatchlings in some spots are female. Crazy... I wonder if you're seeing any other changes happening on the Reef that seem accelerated? Are you observing any particular mutations or adaptions that seem a bit... maybe a bit unusual?"

"Yeah, we are. I mean, I'm not going to bend your ear on Skype all morning for the simple reason that I have to be on campus for a meeting in another hour or so, but we do see changes. Some are expected, some aren't. Some expected ones are interesting. A few colleagues at James Cook Uni are using the term 'ecological memory' referring to changes we see in the actual coral. I don't need to explain the intricacies of coral polyps to you, Sacha, but basically, we have had a series of bleaching events over here back to back. As you would expect, the parts of the reef farther north had more coral bleaching. Now – I feel silly telling you this – bleaching just causes the corals to expel the zooxanthellae that live there and, without these algae, the corals lose something like 80 or 90 per cent of their food source. Because we have had back-to-back bleaching events and even three or four straight years in the past decade, we've observed more hardy corals that are less susceptible to bleaching. Why? The obvious reason is that the weakest corals have died, and dead corals can't die a second time. The only unusual thing here is the speed... we see these massive changes every year rather than over hundreds of years."

"So that would be a good thing, yes?"

"Well... yes and no. I guess if we keep getting these events closer and closer together, the remaining coral will be stronger and better adapted to heat, but there sure as hell won't be much left. Also – and this is right up your ally with your 'living planet' ideas – what happens to the thousands of species that rely on a 2,300-kilometre long ecosystem?"

"I know I sound like the doting dad here, but I appreciate in advance your helping Asha out."

"For god's sakes, Sacha, this is me you're talking to. First of all, I'd help because that's who I am. Second of all, I'd help because I'm a research scientist and want to help anyone else doing things to allow us to better understand what we are doing to old Mother Earth. Third of all is the most important reason... Asha is so important to you, mate, my greatest mentor. You know I'd help you in any way could."

"Thanks for that, Sean. You know the feeling is mutual. I don't know how much your work specifically will help Asha, but I know she's smart enough to take what fits."

"Don't forget, I'm not alone over here at James Cook Uni. We have the Australian Institute of Tropical Health and Medicine, and I have a good mate working over there. I don't pretend to know all of what they do, but I know they deal with a hell of a lot of vector-borne diseases like malaria, Zika, dengue, and what have you."

"Damn... That's some nasty stuff and sounds like it's right up my Asha's alley!" Sacha laughed.

14

Saturday, 20 April; Yunupingu Institute of Medical Research, Melbourne, Victoria

"Working Saturday?" Liz noticed Felly's door wide open.

"After three months away from my desk, I'd better be working Saturday. I'm just catching up on these reports. Obviously, I didn't ignore it all while up in Thailand, but I need to review all the work you people were doing. This synthetic virology research that you and Deshi have been working on fascinates me, but obviously makes me nervous."

"I understand that, Fell-O. We talked about this, and both Deshi and I have tried to keep you in the loop while you were away."

"No, no... Lizzy... I'm not at all bitching to you about it. I WANTED us to go down this path. The work our Canadian friends did by using synthesised horsepox virus DNA to develop a horsepox virus-based vaccine seems to have proved effective as well as showing fewer side effects than vaccinia virus-based vaccines. Obviously, the vaccinia virus-based vaccines work since we eliminated smallpox that way, but the side effects were severe. If we can somehow manage a similar path with *Zaire ebolavirus,* we could help the entire world in ways we can't even imagine."

"For sure. If we can do that, what other viruses can we conquer using the same, synthetic virology techniques."

"But bloody hell, there is a flip side to all of this, and I guess that's one of the reasons I'm in the office so early on a Saturday morning."

"You mean the so-called Ebola Outbreak Syndrome."

"Yes. And that's not mythical… it's a fair dinkum response to a terrifying disease. I know we get used to dealing with *Zaire ebolavirus* on a daily basis – sometimes too comfortable. That's exactly when accidents happen. I like to think our team always keeps that in mind. But all accidents are a result of failure to follow proper laboratory procedures. It crossed my mind about 4 AM that sometimes biological accidents can result from a failure to follow proper administrative procedures, and that's what got me out of bed so early."

"Help me out here, Fell-O."

"Administrative procedures! How could I have been so lax with Milt Warner Thursday? I guess I've been replaying that in my mind over and over. I let him flatter me – flatter our team – to the point that I didn't consider he might have other motives. I just can't get the word 'Pentagon' out of my head. Here we are practising synthetic virology and engineering manmade viruses, and I'm having tea with an unknown American bloke who might be thinking of ways to use this as a weapon."

"Don't be too hard on yourself, Felly. At some level, we have to trust that the Americans are at least allies and that they were one of the original signers back in the early 1970s Biological Weapons Convention. Hell, if that's gone out the window, we are all in bigger trouble than work being done here at Yunupingu Institute."

"I hope you are correct, but I still wonder... why do both the Americans and the Russians still keep samples of the smallpox virus if we truly meant to eradicate it?"

Liz scratched her neck. "I can't answer that Fell-O. I just think you tend to beat yourself up too much over things you can't control. At least take solace in the fact that we follow all the Commonwealth guidelines concerning the High Security Laboratory Quarantine rules governing the work we do. I needn't tell you that designing and maintaining a physical containment level 4 facility isn't cheap."

"Since I am usually the one who gets hit over the head with the budget, I am fully aware of that!" Felly at least cracked a smile.

"So, how's Geoff, anyway? I assume he's symptom-free this morning and nearly ready for the all-clear signal."

"You are spot on with him being ready for the all-clear, but he did say he felt more tired than he should this morning. Considering he's been off for several days, he should be about at the top of his game."

"Oh well, it is April. He might be getting an early-season touch of a cold."

"Damn! That would be about the worst thing right now... Tired, headache, runny nose... the Victorian government Gestapo would lock him away for another three weeks if he gets a cold!"

15

Saturday, 20 April; Townsville District
Police Headquarters, Queensland

Inspector Rumford was sitting at his desk when Hasler and Wentworth knocked on the half-open door. "Come in, come in... Sorry to get you two out so late on a Saturday evening, but we've worked this together all week, and I wanted you to hear from Agent Navarro firsthand." Rumford stood. "Let's go to the meeting room across the hall – we'll have more room there."

The four walked across the empty hallway, and Leon flicked the light on as they entered. "Bloody hell... there aren't many folks around Headquarters after dinnertime on a Saturday night."

The four of them sat on both sides of the steel table. Rumford dropped his pad and tilted his head to the side. "Again, sorry to get you out here now, but Clint has some results here, and I reckon it couldn't wait. For starters, let me introduce you to our ASIO contact, Intelligence Analyst Clint Navarro." Clint nodded his head. "And Clint, this is Inspector Katie Hasler, my partner, and Dr Robert Wentworth who lectures physics at James Cook University here in town."

Navarro smiled at them. "Glad to meet you, Inspector and good to see you Robbo. Robbo and I have worked together a few times."

"True enough."

"Okay, formalities are done here... over to you, Clint."

"Well, first of all, thanks to your forensic team for finding so many bits and pieces and thanks to you, Robbo, for the analysis you did on the jerry can shreds. By finding traces of lead azide, lead styphnate, aluminium and pentaerythritol-tetranitrate, you have basically confirmed there was a blasting cap used here. For that matter – and we still need to confirm all of this – every indication seems to say it is one of a few rather common blasting caps used in dozens of mine sites around Australia."

"That's all well and good, Clint. This is kind of where we were this morning, though. You told me there's more here."

"Oh, there is more. We sifted through so much of what came out of the sieve. Your people did a great job at picking up the fine stuff. Anyway, we found traces of several things, but the one that is of most interest to us is this." Navarro held up his mobile showing a photo of what seemed to be a small pile of indistinguishable junk sitting on a white plastic sample tray. "I think this will lead us to whoever did this."

Katie leaned in over the table and squinted at the mobile's screen. "Pardon me, Agent Navarro. What in god's name are we looking at here?"

"Well, Inspector Hasler, you're looking at leftover shreds from two things here. One – the bit pushed to the left in the photo – is a small pile of very tiny pieces of polyurethane, probably black in colour, though the explosion could have changed that. Two, that little pile on the right side here is what remains of some printed circuit board made from paper reinforced phenolic resin. Generally, this has some copper foil bonded to it and makes up a circuit board on some of the electrical devices you have around your home."

"Now you have me, Clint. Exactly how do you put these pieces together?"

"Well for starters, we'd anticipate finding bits of a cheap mobile – you probably would refer to these as burner phones. They are inexpensive, easy to dispose of and – best of all to the perpetrator – not easily traced. The polyurethane supports this hypothesis since it may be weaker but is a hell of a lot cheaper material to use than polycarbonate, a much more durable and tougher plastic to use as a mobile phone casing. Likewise, the printed circuit board made from paper reinforced phenolic also indicates a cheaper manufacturing product. Consider my phone that I'm showing you the photo from. This has a polycarbonate casing..." He tapped it with his finger. "...and has a fibreglass reinforced epoxy resin board with a copper foil bonded to it on the inside."

"So, could you put it all together for us, Clint." Robbo reached for the phone so he could get a closer look.

Clint's head twitched to the side, and a smile crossed his face. "Piece of piss, Robbo. Putting this all together, I'd bet my house that it happened something like this: the perpetrator used a burner phone rigged to a blasting cap, and probably gaffer taped it to the side of a jerry can with 20 litres of petrol in it. Then he or she placed the rig below the *Reef Explorer's* deck right near the diesel tanks. When the culprit dialled the number, the cap ignited the petrol which then blew the whole rig and triggered the diesel to go, too. I'm only speculating now, but it's likely the person who did this was nearby and waited until everyone was in the water. If that's the case – and I emphasise that I'm speaking out my ass here – that would mean there was no intention to hurt the professor or his students."

"Good on ya, Clint. Sounds to me as though your guys and Robbo all did a great job here, but we still have a way to go. Now I can't help but think that if whoever did this just wanted to send a message, who in the hell were they sending the message to?" Rumford turned both hands up as if to say, 'give me an answer'.

Katie responded. "They may have avoided killing anyone but setting a bomb off like that would still qualify as attempted murder as far as the Crown goes."

Navarro had to carry the conjecture one step farther. "As far as the Crown sees it, Inspector Hasler, this wasn't only attempted murder... this was terrorism."

16

Saturday, 20 April; The Kovac's residence, Melbourne, Victoria

Felly didn't mind the twenty-minute walk. For that matter, she looked forward to it as a way to clear her head between the office and home. She was a little surprised to not have heard from Geoff all day, but if he was sleeping, she didn't want to call and bother him.

She was only a block from home as she gazed at her watch… 9:45 PM. Probably Geoff would be asleep in his easy chair with the television on. No doubt he'd have microwaved the leftover Chinese they had from Friday night's dinner. She took in a deep breath of the autumn air, cool and fresh. She was set on taking Sunday off, and maybe she and Geoff could take a long walk in the park or else along the water in Port Melbourne.

She turned the last corner before home and noticed several police cars with their lights flashing. She could also see a fire truck blocking the middle of the street. Suddenly her brain seemed to kick in – that was their house that attracted all the attention. All these police and rescue vehicles were crowded around their home. She started to jog down the last hundred metres or so until she reached a stretch of police tape roping off the house and yard.

"Wait a minute, ma'am. You can't go through here." Two constables stood, both with walkie-talkies in their hands. One started to talk into his unit, and the other held his hand up to her. "Ma'am, this area is quarantined."

"No, you don't understand. I'm Dr Felicia Kovac. I live here. My husband is Dr Geoffrey Kovac, and he lives here too."

"Please wait a minute, Dr Kovac." He turned sideways, spoke softly into his walkie talkie and looked back at Felly.

"Ma'am, please wait just a minute, and we'll have this all straightened out for you."

Felly felt a tear trying to get out of the corner of her eye, but she willed it to stay where it was. After what seem to be hours, though Felly knew it was only a minute, a young woman walked over to her and put a reassuring hand on her shoulder.

"Dr Kovac. I'm Helen Trainor from the Victorian Department of Health and Human Services. Dr Kovac, I'm sorry to tell you that your husband Geoffrey has been taken to the hospital... More specifically, he's been taken to The Royal Melbourne Hospital."

"Ms Trainor, there must be some mistake. Your department has kept an eye on Geoff since we returned from Thailand last Wednesday and he has been fine. There is no need to quarantine him."

"I'm so very sorry Dr Kovac, but he evidently took a turn for the worse this afternoon. When the attending nurse came by today, she immediately called Ambulance Victoria, and they went through all proper procedures to protect your husband and the community. Surely you realise he is in the best place he could possibly be tonight, and the best place being isolated from your entire neighbourhood, ma'am."

"Ms Trainor, I want to see my husband... I have to see my husband..."

Helen Trainor looked visibly disturbed. "I don't think that would be possible tonight, Dr Kovac. I can give you a lift to the hospital, and we can inquire, but I believe he has been admitted to their maximum quarantine facility. From what I've been told about your research position, you probably know more about that than me, but I don't have high hopes on a visit this evening."

"Please take me to the hospital."

"I can do that, Dr Kovac."

"Let me just run in the house for a minute and..."

Trainor interrupted her. "Dr Kovac, I'm certain you understand that you aren't allowed to do that. Your house is now under quarantine, that is under biosecurity level 4 quarantine."

Felly looked at her front door as people moved in and out of the house fully outfitted in encapsulating protective chemical suits, boots, full-face masks, air-purifying respirators and the works. She thought she was looking at a scene from some science fiction movie. Again, she felt tears welling up in her eyes, but she was no longer able to contain them.

* * *

She sat in the hallway for fifteen minutes. Considering how awful the whole experience had been, she at least gave Helen Trainor credit for trying to reassure her, trying to somehow help in a helpless situation. Trainor also had either enough training or enough sensitivity to know when silence and a gentle touch of a hand were so much more calming than scripted words. Finally, a tall man walked over to them. Felly quickly sized him up to be either an ED doctor or ED nurse.

"Good evening, Dr Kovac. My name is Dr Steve Fairbrother, and I have been a part of one of the teams looking after your husband. I am so sorry about this, and I want you to know we are doing everything that we can."

"Have you been in with him."

"No Dr Kovac. But I have been here on the unit all evening. At this point, he is resting as comfortably as he could be under the circumstances."

"At least tell me what happened."

"The report we have been given is that when his Department of Health and Human Services nurse went to see him this afternoon, his symptoms had grown severe."

"Symptoms? When I left home early this morning... maybe 6:30 AM, Geoff told me he was tired and had a bit of a headache. He took some Panadol. I did ring him just before noon, and he told me about the same thing. Do you know when the nurse visited?"

"I can't be certain, but I believe it was early afternoon. He must have taken a turn."

"Can I see him? Speak to him?"

Dr Fairbrother clenched his teeth and took a deep breath between them. "Dr Kovac, I know that you work with *Zaire ebolavirus* over there at the Yunupingu Institute and I have no doubt you have more experience working at Biosafety Level 4 than I ever will. Of course, the hospital setting is different from the laboratory, but the idea is the same. We are not able to allow visitors in high quarantine no matter what the circumstances. We probably follow all the same rules you do."

Tears were streaming down Felly's face. "Yes, I know all that. Is there any way I can at least speak with him? Is there any provision for remote communication?"

Fairbrother rubbed his chin. "You know, just wait here for a minute. I think maybe we can find a headset or two." He walked off down the corridor.

Helen Trainor reached over and again placed her hand on Felly's arm. "Dr Kovac... I do not for one minute believe that I have any idea what you're going through because I don't. When I read the file on you and Geoffrey before you came to your home tonight, I was very impressed with both your levels of expertise, but even more with both your dedication to helping others. Few people I know would ever volunteer to leave the comfort of good old Melbourne and tromp into the wilds of Thailand tracking down one of the deadliest diseases that humans have ever encountered. The whole world would be so much poorer without people like you and your husband. Rest assured that at the very least, he is in one of the best places he possibly could be in the whole world to give him a chance at beating this."

"Thank you, Helen."

Felly slumped over onto Trainor's shoulder and had a good cry. Four or five minutes later Fairbrother returned with a wireless headset in one hand. "Dr Kovac. We have worked out a way to let you communicate with your husband." He held the headset up. "If you just follow me."

Felly stood. "Thank you, Helen. Thank you so much." She followed Fairbrother down the hallway and into a nursing station.

"Right in here, Dr Kovac." He pulled a chair out, and she sat down. She looked at the two pairs of monitors in front of her. Each set had a bottom monitor with vital sign readouts of two patients while the top monitor in each pair had a CCTV picture of the patient. Again her eyes teared up seeing Geoff on the right set of monitors. "Let's put these on you." Fairbrother handed her the headset, and she pulled it over her hair, the one earphone on her right ear and the microphone now in front of her mouth. "See if that works."

She adjusted it a bit and looked up at Geoff's picture on the monitor. "Can you hear me, Geoff?"

Geoff tried to raise his head, but it was not coming off the pillow. He did manage to look towards the monitor which – like her monitor – must have had the camera in its frame. She heard him reply in a very soft and weak voice. "Yes..."

Fairbrother stepped back. "I'll leave you alone, Dr Kovac. Be mindful that your husband needs rest. Maybe try to cut it off in three or four minutes."

"Thank you, Doc." She turned back toward the monitor. "Geoff. What happened?"

"It just got bad... really fast... I was... was obviously having trouble breathing. "I was still okay when I spoke to you on the phone, but after that, I just started to ache and... and bleed..." He tried to reach for his face but couldn't get his hand there.

"Oh, Geoff, I love you."

"Love you... honey..."

"Did anything happen? Did anything out of the ordinary happen?"

He sighed and again gasped for air. After a weak cough, he again whispered into the headset. "Jogging... yesterday when jogging in the park... girl spilled... spilled coffee all over me..."

"Geoff... Geoff..." She saw that his eyes closed, and he again gasped for air.

One eye half opened, and he gasped again. "She... she did... did it... The girl... she did..." Geoff lost consciousness

Felly stood, kissed her hand and touched it to Geoff's image on the monitor. She started to cry uncontrollably.

PART TWO

"You can drive out Nature with a pitchfork, but she keeps on coming back..."

— Horace Epistles, 65-8 BC

17

Sunday, 21 April; Sharma residence, Fremantle, Western Australia

Sacha unlocked the front door and pushed it open. "Go ahead in, honey, I have your bag."

Asha had her flight bag over her shoulder as she entered the foyer. Seemingly out of nowhere, a well-fed beagle came running across the jarrah wood floor and leapt onto her jeans. "Seymour!" She slid her bag from her shoulder. "It's good to see you too, boy." With one hand petting the beagle, she used the other to drop her flight bag onto the console table. Home! She realised that the hall table with the stone slab top had been there since she was a child.

He pulled the door closed and threw the bolt, turned and opened his arms wide. Asha leaned into him, and the two of them embraced each other tightly for a full minute. Sacha looked at the big mirror hanging over the table and smiled at the reflection of father and daughter hugging each other with Seymour trying his hardest to squeeze in the middle. It was natural for any dad to miss his daughter living on the other side of the world and away from home for long periods. He reckoned it was even worse the past decade or so with Emily no longer by his side.

"Let me get you something... a tea, a coffee, juice, water..."

"Daddy, Daddy... I just want to sit and look at you. You're looking perfectly healthy, Dad." She grabbed his hand and headed for the kitchen.

"I feel good, Asha."

"I love seeing that big smile of yours, Daddy."

"I'm smiling because I haven't heard you call me Daddy for fifteen years!" He laughed. "I feel pretty good, Asha. I have an occasional sore back and a gimpy leg now and again, but all up, I'm doing okay for an old bloke going to be 73 this August." He dropped her suitcase at the end of the hall and turned into the kitchen. He reached up into a cabinet and pulled out two glasses.

"You must be dead tired." She took a seat at the big, wooden table.

"Me! Hell, you just flew 18,000 kilometres or whatever it is from Chicago to Perth. YOU must be tired, young lady."

"Young! I wish! I'm not that young anymore, Dad."

He pointed to his chest and used his best 'Tarzan' voice. "Me 72..." He pointed towards Asha. "You 34... You, young..." He laughed. "It's all relative, you know, dear lady."

"You forgot him." She sat far enough out from the table that Seymour had his paws on the wooden chair and his head between her knees. "Old Seymour must be pushing 10 now, yes?"

"He sure is. He's a good boy, too... a good OLD boy." The sound of 'good boy' had the beagle's tail start to wag at full speed, though he kept his snout propped onto Asha's lap. Sacha laughed. "Seymour always thought of himself as a lap dog, but at nearly 17 kilos on his last trip to the vet's, he just can't quite manage to curl up in a lap."

"It's so good to be home... to see you, Dad."

He pulled a jug of cold water from the refrigerator and sat at the table, filling a glass for each of them. "I love you, Asha."

She put her hand on his knee. "And I love you, Dad. It's just fantastic to be off the plane, here with my dad in Freo and petting my favourite dog." She took a gulp of water that drained half the glass. "That long-distance plane was nice, but no matter what they try to tell you about better air in the cabin, air travel still dries me out."

"You're right, of course. No one has worked that out yet."

"So what time is your Earth Day lecture Monday?" She glanced at her watch. "Jeez, Monday is tomorrow now."

"It is dear... it's the wee hours Sunday morning now. I know it's nice to take that LAX-Perth flight to avoid connection snafus, but it still wacks you out with jet lag and your whole sense of time perception. Anyway, my lecture is at 10:00 AM, so not too early. We will have 600 people there they tell me."

"Make that 601. How fortunate they are to hear one of the world's most distinguished environmental scientists." Her bright smile lit up the room.

"I don't know about 'distinguished', but I can claim that I'm passionate about it all."

"I know that, Dad. They are so lucky to have you giving the talk this year."

"Now then, do you think you can get a little sleep?"

"Yes. I'm going to jump in the shower and wash half the world away from me and then see if I can crash. I did catch sleep here and there on the flight, but I just want to stretch out..."

"...and feel clean sheets! I'm exactly the same after a long flight. You'll be happy to hear that I put fresh sheets on your bed, honey."

* * *

Asha yawned. Looking at her watch, she figured she'd had at least six hours of uninterrupted sleep. She washed her face, brushed her teeth and then headed down the stairs. She rounded the bottom of the stairs and walked into the kitchen wearing a robe and slippers. "This robe smells like it has just been washed, Dad."

"No surprise there, Asha. When you told me you were coming Friday, I figured I'd see what was left in your closet that you might wear, and that terrycloth robe was one of the things I reckoned you'd use. I went through half of your drawers up there and washed socks and tees and jumpers just in case... They've all been just sitting there collecting must for 10 or 11 months since you were here last."

"Dad, you're the best." She put her arms around his neck and kissed him.

"How about some brekkie?"

"I'm happy with toast, fruit and tea, Dad... if you have any fruit?" She sat at the table. "I should be getting some brekkie for you."

"No, no... not after that long flight. And yes, it's April, and the early autumn apples are out." He picked up a small, wicker basket tucked between the microwave and the coffee and tea canisters and placed it along with the half-dozen fresh apples it held in front of her.

"Thanks, Dad." She grabbed an apple. "Hey, Pink Lady... my favourite!"

"They're definitely fresh... new season."

"Oh boy... what's this?" She grasped the wine bottle sitting on the kitchen table, picked it up and began to read. "Penfolds Grange Hermitage 1983... damn, Dad, I know what Grange is. It's probably the most expensive wine in the world!" She rolled the bottle around and kept reading the back label.

"Let's not exaggerate, honey. You're right, it is an expensive drop, but far from most expensive in the world! I think you'd have to argue with some of the French cognac producers for that honour."

"Well okay, it's still Grange, and I know it doesn't come cheaply."

"True enough. That is a very special bottle you have there. Your mum bought six of those bottles in a case in 1988 to celebrate our fifth wedding anniversary. By the way, they'd have been a damned sight cheaper then – I think they cost a hundred dollars a bottle then – but it seemed like quite an investment at that point in our lives. Anyway, we drank the first one that year, and it tasted absolutely great to us. Funny thing though, so many of our friends thought we were as mad as a couple of cut snakes."

"Mad? Why?"

"They say – whoever 'they' is – that you're supposed to let Grange age longer. I'll be the first to admit that I am not an oenophile, but I think I've heard that Granges might be at their best after aging for 10, 15, 20 years. Anyway, experts be damned... We drank the second bottle in October of 1989. Lest your memory doesn't go back that far, Asha, that second bottle was in celebration of one Asha Marie Sharma coming into our world."

"Oh, Daddy..."

"We had the third bottle on our tenth anniversary in 1993 and the fourth on our silver anniversary in 2008. The idea was to have another on our fiftieth anniversary, but Emily won't be able to make that one." His head dipped as a momentary touch of sadness crossed his face.

Asha stood and gave her father a tight hug. "I miss mum, and I know you do, too."

"It's all a part of life, honey. The old adage that time heals old wounds does apply to a point. Emily has been gone for what... getting close to fifteen years now." He pushed her back enough to see her face, leaned forward and gave her a kiss. "Tonight, we're going to drink the fifth bottle and – god willing – on 31 October 2033, you and I will drink the last one on what would have been our golden anniversary."

Asha wiped a tear from her eye. "I'm going to cook you a homemade dinner tonight, Dad."

"My dear Asha... I know you've been away from Australia for a while, but I do hope you still remember what I'm saying when I tell you that 'you've got kangaroos loose in the top paddock'?"

Asha tried not to smile but was totally unsuccessful and started to laugh from her stomach to her head. She finally pulled herself together. "It sounds to me that you have plans, Dad."

"I do have plans, honey. I'm going to show my little girl off to the good people of Fremantle tonight. I have reservations at the Sunset Fish Shack for 7:00 PM if you're free."

"If I'm free... DAD!"

"I already had plans to have dinner with my mate Clive, so I'm hoping you don't mind if I can show you off to him, too."

"Not at all. I like Clive, Dad. It'll be fun to see him as well as you. Besides that, GNN is paying for this trip, and I am supposed to be working. Maybe I can pick Clive's medical mind a bit."

"I'm positive he won't mind at all."

18

Sunday, 21 April; Dr Liz O'Rourke's residence,
Melbourne, Victoria

"I can never thank you enough for this, Lizzy. You didn't need to agree to take me into your home."

"Come on, Fell-O! How long have we worked together... have we been friends? Besides that, I think the Victorian Department of Health and Human Services can stick their quarantine rules where the sun doesn't shine!" Liz reassured her colleague and friend.

"I mostly agree with you, but I thought the world of that Helen Trainor woman who works for them... she was very good to me."

"Thank god there is some good in all this. So, what did they tell you, anyway? What's the scoop?"

"Quarantine... the latest Victoria DHHS rules pretty much echo the Commonwealth rules." Felly threw her hands up as if to show she had no control over it all. "That means that the quarantined person – me in this case – is under observation for three weeks from the last chance of infection. No one seems to have yet determined if that time interval is to be measured from when I last was exposed to any threat in Thailand or from my potential exposure at home yesterday morning. I will have professional observations twice a day or more if needed and, assuming no symptoms involving fever, discharge of bodily fluids, or diarrhoea, we're okay. In that case, family and household co-residents – you in this case – are all clear."

"What does the visiting nurse do twice a day?"

"I know I will soon find out firsthand, but I believe she or he will ask me questions, check my temperature and blood pressure and otherwise see if I show any changes in my overall physical condition."

"I know the public health folks are just doing their job. As you and I both know, EVD is damned difficult to diagnose if and when a person is first infected simply because the early symptoms are so universal and look like nearly anything else. I mean fever, headache, flu-like indicators... Doh! That all sounds just like salmonellosis or malaria or typhoid? We could go on forever with this list!"

Liz again comforted her mate. "I'm just not worried, Felly. I have no doubt you'll be just fine."

"Oh...They did add the caveat that we are not permitted to have sexual relations with each other under ANY circumstances." The on-going tension seemed to find its way to the surface, and Felly responded to it by bursting into hysterical laughter.

"Well, I hope you don't find me THAT repulsive!" Liz's hurt expression quickly turned into full laughter as she tried to break the seriousness of the situation. The two of them sat on the sofa for the better part of a minute laughing at each other.

"Damn!" Felly's laughter suddenly was replaced with a gloomy expression. "I'm so worried about Geoff, Lizzy. I just don't have a good feeling about this. Hell, you and I know the numbers. Statistically, anyone who contracts EVD faces a mortality rate of over 50%, but at least we are way better here than in any third world country. Australia has had so few cases that statistics really don't apply, but hopefully, we are ahead of the curve here. Globally, when volunteer healthcare workers have been infected and returned to the States and Europe, survival rates have been close to 80% to 85%. I guess my biggest problem is that I fear exactly what it is that we're dealing with."

Liz's eyes widened. "You mean the synthetic virology research the team has been doing?"

"Yes."

"But Felly, I am confident that at least our research efforts are contained by our extreme biosafety level 4 measures. Besides that, if anything horrendous were to happen, it'd sure as hell happen to one of us first, not to Geoff, don't you think?"

Felly's face again went dour. "That's what you would think, but..." She started to cry. "Remember... it was ME who thought it would be a good idea for him to come along to Thailand. Hell, if it isn't bad enough that Geoff is involved in this whole Ebola thing because of me, now it could wind up being ME who actually kills him." She tucked up on the sofa and cried.

"Well, wait a minute... you're mixing two things here. At first, you're talking about Geoff being infected in Thailand, and that would at least make sense since he was working in some horrendous conditions with EVD patients. Then you mentioned the synthetic strains we have been working with here in Melbourne. Well, how could a Melbourne strain have infected him if both of you were up there?"

"Of course, you're right, but I just feel lousy, Lizzy."

"Come on, girl." Liz shimmied on the sofa closer to her friend until she was sitting with her hip pressed into Felly's side. She wiped tears from Felly's face. "Nobody is going to die..."

"Don't, Lizzy. I'm sorry for the tears, but you can't touch my fluids."

"To hell with the fluids, Fell-O! You and I know damned well that you aren't infected..." She placed the back of her hand on Felly's forehead checking for a temperature. "You certainly don't show any symptoms. We're going to work this out, mate. I promise you, Geoff is going to be just fine."

19

Sunday, 21 April; Sundowner Fish Shack, Fremantle, Western Australia

"Even though I grew up here, it's almost as though I forget just how beautiful it really is."

"That's why I never left." Sacha looked over the top of his glasses at his beautiful daughter.

"Jobs, Dad... jobs..."

"No, no... I didn't mean that you shouldn't have gone. I'm happy you are in Chicago. What an opportunity GNN has presented you. Hell, how many women do you know in their mid-30s who have several years of experience as a presenter on global television and now have editorial responsibility for environmental stories that could impact political decisions for countries across the Earth. In the end, I spend my entire career studying ecological systems and disasters and have few decision-makers willing to even listen to our dire warnings. Ho, hum… along comes my beautiful daughter, you spend a decade working your way up the GNN journalism ladder, and now you have an impact on decision-makers way beyond my wildest dreams."

"Well, thanks for the confidence, Dad, but we will see about just how far that impact might go."

"We will also see when the hell Clive gets here. I dropped a 41-year-old bottle of Grange off here this afternoon! I'm dying to pop the bottle to share with my girl, and he's probably still looking for a clean pair of undies! That damned Clive!"

"Did I hear my name mentioned in vain?"

"Clive, you old bastard!" Sacha stood and pumped his friend's hand.

"Thanks for inviting me, cobber."

"I trust you remember my daughter, Asha."

"Remember? Hell, how could I forget her!" Clive laughed. "I see her on TV at least once a week." He leaned down and gave her a kiss first on one cheek and then the other. "Besides that, about every fifth word out of your father's mouth happens to be 'Asha'."

"Hi, Clive. It's so nice to see you again."

"It's so nice to see you too, Asha. Thank goodness you survived that killer flight."

"Ah, it wasn't all that bad."

Clive took a step towards one of the two chairs left vacant, but a waiter beat him to it. "Let me get that for you, sir." He pulled the chair and adjusted it as Clive sat down.

"I have a special bottle of wine that I dropped off this afternoon." Sacha handed the waiter a note. "I was hoping you could set this up for us?"

"The waiter looked at the note and smiled. "Very good, sir. I'll be back in a minute."

"So, what do you think of that sunset, Asha?" Clive sat back in his chair and turned towards the big picture window next to their table-for-four.

"It's shaping up to be spectacular." Her seat looked straight out the window. The orange globe was still twenty-minutes above the horizon and situated just right to have Rottnest Island's shadow dance across the sea towards Freo. "There are just enough of those feathery clouds that I reckon will make the sky glow fire red in a few minutes."

"You are trying to say cirrocumulus clouds, right dear?"

"Dad... you and your science! Of course, I was saying cirrocumulus clouds!" Her smile sparkled.

The waiter returned with a tray holding a crystal decanter, the open Grange bottle, the cork and three large wine glasses. He set the tray down and handed the cork to Sacha.

"Oh boy... Take a whiff of that! I think we have a ripper here." As he passed the cork to Asha for a sniff, Sacha looked to the waiter and nodded his head. "Please." Asha had a sniff of the cork and passed it along to Clive.

"Would the gentleman like to have a taste?"

"Please."

The waiter poured a small portion of wine into Sacha's glass.

Sacha gently swirled the wine in the glass, took in a sizable sniff and finally had a sip. He smiled broadly. "That is marvellous."

"Very good, sir." The waiter poured some Grange into the other two glasses and then topped up Sacha's glass. "Enjoy."

"Let me propose a toast to the two women in my life who have made me who I am. To my beautiful Asha, I am so happy you are here tonight... and to my beloved Emily, may she rest in peace." He raised his goblet. All three touched their glasses, and the crystal made a distinct ringing sound. They all sipped.

Asha was the first to speak. "It is SO nice being here with you, Dad. Thank you for being you."

Clive's eyes looked back and forth between them, and a big smile crossed his face. "You are both beautiful and both my friends. Frankly, any wine would surely take a back seat to the privilege of being with you both tonight."

"All right, all right... this must be a conspiracy! Neither of you bastards is going to mention the Grange, so I guess I have to be the one to say it... This is the BEST wine I've ever had in my life."

Asha held her glass toward the window and let the setting sunlight pass through. "Maybe that's because it's aged, Dad. You told me that Grange is best after 10 or 20 years. Wow... this one has had 41 years of ageing."

Clive quietly laughed. "I think it's the best wine that old codger has ever had because of the company. Now when I say, 'the company', I obviously don't mean me. I mean you, Asha. Do you know, Ash, you are the pride of this man's whole life? If I had a dollar for every time he mentions you, I'd be wealthy enough to drink Grange every night. This is the best wine ever because YOU are here to drink it with him tonight."

"Aw... thanks, Clive." She raised her glass again and again, all three toasted. She continued to swirl the wine in her glass, almost afraid to break the warm mood she was feeling. The sun just touched the horizon, and the sky didn't disappoint, a red and orange explosion of colour stretched as far as they could see across the Indian Ocean.

"So, work has brought you down to Australia this time, Ash?"

"Yes... I'm working on a story about mutations... mutations of bacteria, mutations about viruses... pretty much we're working on a story about mutations of any microbes that can hurt us humans."

"Oh boy... Anything in particular at this point?"

"Well yeah. I was in Philadelphia last week chatting with an epidemiologist there concerning some microbes that seem to be coming back to life as the melting permafrost accelerates. The America press is stirring fears and claiming they could cause these zombie diseases that have been in frozen form for tens of thousands of years."

"Zombie diseases they're calling them, huh? Leave it to the damned Yanks! And what are you finding out about these zombie diseases?"

"Well, it seems there could be some truth to it. There have been problems with one, in particular, *Bacillus anthracis*. Several dozen people have died up in Alaska, and a similar number have passed away in Siberia and in Scandinavia." Asha arched her eyes at the thought. "I guess the biggest issue is whether this is the same *Bacillus anthracis* we know of, or it is a different variety."

"And that's where the mutations may come in?"

"Exactly."

"Well, you know, mutations happen all the time. Probably the best example we can think of – and the one I point to in my med school lectures here at Notre Dame – is common influenza. We prepare flu vaccines every year, and sometimes we are more successful at outguessing the mutation gods, and sometimes we are less successful. Microbiology is a wonderful teaching tool for evolution because generations can be observed in a relatively short time because their lifespans are running at highly accelerated rates compared to us humans."

"Good point, Clive." Sacha took another sip of his wine. "I know so many of our med and vet students take genetic units where they do lab work with fruit flies for a semester or two. I think fruit flies lay eggs, they hatch into larvae, they moult a few times, metamorphose into adults and are ready to reproduce in a week or ten days. Besides the sheer science of it all, the historical dimension of Gregor Mendel basically establishing the foundations of modern genetics using fruit flies a hundred and fifty years ago is also instructive."

Clive smiled. "You're exactly correct on the use of fruit flies, mate, but as a point of order, Mendel worked with peas, and it was an American – Thomas Hunt Morgan, I believe – who did the first genetic work breeding *Drosophila melanogaster.*"

Sorry... you can tell I don't work in a medical school." Sacha laughed. "Anyway, what wonderful creatures your *Drosophila* are for teaching genetics. I haven't given a great deal of thought to bacteria or viruses, but I guess they would be even faster, right?"

"Exactly, mate. Bacteria and – in a different way, viruses – can go through their own cycles in an hour, a half-hour, maybe 15 minutes at the correct temperatures... You probably wouldn't have the same teaching tool in the university labs because the inherited traits are not so visible as fruit flies, but the speed of reproduction is almost beyond our ability to comprehend."

Sasha ran one finger over his cheek in thought. "Damn..., you've got me thinking here, Clive. Naturally, you're right. Interesting..."

Asha picked up the conversation as she looked towards Clive. "Dad mentioned that you have a friend in Melbourne who is a biochemist, microbiologist, epidemiologist..."

Clive sipped his wine. "Yes, for sure. One of my old mates from medical school, Geoff Kovac. Well actually, it isn't exactly Geoff that Sacha was referring to, it's Geoff's wife, Felicia... Felly. She pretty much looks after the Yunupingu Institute of Medical Research... right in the CBD of Melbourne. I don't know if she's officially the director or not, but I'm fairly certain she's the lead researcher. Anyway, the two of them just spent several months in Southeast Asia, Thailand mostly. I believe their key interest is *Zaire ebolavirus*. I just chatted with Geoff Thursday or Friday... poor bugger is quarantined at home."

"Quarantined! Oh my god!" A worried look flashed across Asha's face.

"No, no... it's no drama as far as I can tell. The Victoria Department of Health and Human Services was evidently acting on orders from the Premier's office. You know, it's an election year, and the pollies gotta be seen to be protecting the public! Anyway, Geoff has shown zero symptoms and has gone nearly three weeks since he last set foot in a level 4 biosecurity facility, so he should be back on board his day job this week."

"Did he mention the kind of things his wife is researching?" It was obvious that this could become a part of the story on which Asha was working.

"Actually, yes he did. I think their team is looking into mutations now that you mention it." Clive arched his eyes. "This could be just what you're looking at, Ash. In the race to develop effective vaccines, it sounds as though they have been manipulating DNA over there?"

"Manipulating as in synthetic viruses? Oh boy... just what we need." Sacha had been fairly quiet until now.

The waiter came and placed an open menu in front of each of them. "I'll be back for your order when you are ready."

Clive never heard the waiter. "That might not be fair, Sacha. Humans have every right to protect themselves against viruses. Some of the new synthetic virology research has proved a wonder to developing more effective vaccines with fewer nasty side effects."

"I'm not arguing effectiveness, Clive, I'm arguing throwing a spanner in Mother Nature's ecological systems."

Asha turned her gaze from the sunset back to the table. "You know, one of my GNN colleagues just sent me a message overnight that there is some fear that EVD might have shown up in Singapore this week."

"Singapore?"

"That's what he told me. If it's working its way through Southeast Asia even into the most urban, most western of countries, can any country be safe anymore?"

"Well, we better hope that Australia stays far away from all of that." Clive finally noticed that the waiter had returned.

"Singapore? Hell, that's as close to Perth as Sydney is." Sacha looked up at the waiter...

"Are you happy to order now?"

* * *

The waiter cleared the rest of the plates. "Are we ready for dessert?"

Sacha looked at both his fellow diners' eyes. "We will definitely have dessert, but could you give us ten or fifteen minutes to let this all settle. In the meantime, could you please bring us appropriate glasses for this?' He handed him a smaller bottle.

The waiter took a quick glance at the bottle. "Right away, sir." He scampered off.

Clive sat back. "How long have we known each other?"

"Damn Clive, undergraduate days I imagine... over fifty years now."

"Right. And you know, I can't help but think that you have spent your entire career in ecology and the environmental sciences, and my entire career has been in medicine, and yet we both look at our subjects through such similar sets of lenses."

Sacha leaned back in his chair and thought about it. "I can see that you could draw some similarity between the Earth as a body and an individual's body."

"Just consider that for a moment... the parallels between a healthy planet Earth and a healthy human being. Frankly, I always go on at length with my first-year medical students in drawing just that comparison. Mother Earth is so like a human body... just a gigantic body. I say Mother Earth, though you use the term *Gaia* often enough, Sacha?"

"Both are appropriate." Sacha was keen to see where his mate was heading with this.

"Just ponder for a minute the human body in terms of it having its own ecological systems. Interestingly enough, this might just be a good metaphor for the project you currently are working on, Ash. Consider that each human shares our bodies with upwards of 60 or 70 trillion microbes... trillions, not billions! I repeat once more, that's 60 or 70 TRILLION microbes, all alive and mostly well, living quite peacefully and in nearly perfect harmony with us. I am not making that up... we are home to THAT BIG of a community! In a sense, we are each like our own, little Mother Earth. For that matter, just like Mother Earth, we don't even know exactly WHO we live with, let alone how these relationships actually work."

"I see what you mean – all quite impersonal with neither the person nor the microbes actually knowing the others are even there." Sacha had obviously taken his mate's words to heart.

"Yes, we are all totally unconscious of the reality that the human body is a microcosm of organisms. Likewise, for day-to-day matters, we are all pretty much oblivious to the fact that we are all a part of Mother Earth and that she is actually the only home we have." Asha affirmed her father's comment. "And if I follow you correctly, once in a while that 'human body ecosystem', as it were, may go out of kilter. Then, when the balance is tipped too far, that's when we need your medical expertise, Clive."

The waiter interrupted the conversation as he returned carrying a tray holding three port wine-sized glasses and the small half-bottle Sacha had given him. It was open, and the cork sat on the tray. He poured three glasses and placed one in front of each of them. "Enjoy."

"What is this, Dad?" Asha sniffed the liquor. "That smells marvellous."

Sasha lifted the bottle and read. "Talijancich Julian James Reserve Muscat 1961... I believe that I was about ten years old when the sun shined down on the Swan Valley grapes up in the hills behind Perth and locked that energy into this wine." He raised his glass. "*Salute.*"

All three sipped the sweet, fortified wine.

"Oh, Dad. This stuff is like drinking heaven." She turned her eyes towards the ceiling and licked her lips.

"I know I'm not supposed to say this Sacha, but I believe this might have outdone the Grange." Clive blessed himself in an act of contrition.

Asha dabbed her lips with her serviette. "Dad, you're making me a bit nervous here. First, the 1983 Grange... now the 1961 Muscat... I know that you told me this morning that you are not an oenophile. If that's the case, I'm starting to be fearful that my own flesh and blood has become an alcoholic!" She laughed and had another sip of the dessert wine.

"Don't you worry, honey. Consider the fact that I have saved both these bottles for more than four decades. Now honestly, if I really do have an uncontrollable urge to drink ethanol, it sure is a very, very, very slow urge."

Clive smiled but was keen to get back to their conversation. He set his glass down. "You made a good point there, ma'am. To follow up on your body-systems-out-of-kilter comment, Asha, that is exactly what I'm saying. It's important for young medical students to understand that there are systems intertwined with the workings of the human body that are way too complex for us to understand, even from a medical doctor's point of view. Sometimes all the education in the world doesn't give us enough information to save the patient. At that point, the body – the individual – will either turn on its own defence systems and save itself or else cease to exist... it will die."

"Spot on, mate. And I always argue that Earth is exactly that way too, only much, much, much more complex. You mention 60 or 70 trillion microbes or players in the human ecosystem example. Damn, in the case of Earth or *Gaia*, there would be... I don't remember what comes next... Quadrillion? Quintillion? In the case of a planetwide ecosystem, there are players and systems beyond comprehension.

"Maybe trying to tie this whole conversation together, when Asha's anthrax or Ebola microbes infect a human body, the first reaction that we note – the first symptom if you like – is that the body raises its temperature to throw off the infection. In light of my ecological research over the past 40-some years, I've grown convinced that Mother Earth might be infected too and similarly, her first reaction also seems to be raising her temperature." Sacha hesitated and ran his fingers through the sparse tufts of hair on his head. "You know, I believe that *Gaia* has a fever."

20

Sunday, 21 April; The Royal Melbourne Hospital, Quarantine Unit, Melbourne, Victoria

Nurse Cassie Schneider looked up from the console at the nursing station to see Dr Fairbrother come in the door. "Hi, Doc. We only have the one patient tonight, yes? Dr Kovacs?"

"One patient is enough, Cassie. He's in pretty serious shape."

"Yes, I know, Doc."

Fairbrother looked at the big clock on the wall. "Damn... after 11 PM already. Like they say, time flies when you're having fun."

"Tell me about it. It's Sunday night, and I've worked the whole weekend." A scowl crossed her face. "Is Kovac a medical doctor?"

"Yep. He's one of the mainstays in the Emergency Department across town at Royal Yarra. I know you had your report from Courtney before she went home and I have no doubt read through Dr Kovac's chart, but basically, he came down with the Ebola Virus Disease symptoms very, very quickly. Contracting the disease is not totally out of the blue since he had worked with EVD patients in several tent EDs in Thailand for the past three months. The troubling piece of information though, is that his wife is a leading researcher over at the Yunupingu Institute and she probably knows more about *Zaire ebolavirus* than nearly anyone else on Earth. From the conversations she has had with our staff here, something isn't sitting right with her. Now right away you'd think 'it's her husband', but it's more than that. Whatever it might be, it sounds like it is beyond the fact that this is her husband."

"What's the treatment plan... I mean above and beyond just what is written here?"

"Pretty much that's it. I mean, it's not like we see many EVD patients."

"I've never seen one."

Fairbrother nodded his head. "I've seen a few cases when I spent a month working in Africa and generally, we wouldn't find much cause for optimism. Anyway, at this point, Dr Kovac's body has responded to the infection with a typical cytokine storm..." Fairbrother looked at her to see if she was following him. "I don't know how familiar you'd be with this because as you've pointed out, our caseload of EVD here is exactly one – Geoff Kovac. Anyway, the cytokine storm results in an overproduction of his immune cells to such a degree there are cytokines, antibodies, white blood cells everywhere to the point that they start to actually attack his own body. It's quite classic EVD from what I've read, though as I say, thank god we just don't see this happening in Melbourne. For that matter, it's great that Royal Melbourne has these two beds that – in their highest biosecurity configuration – allow for full biosecurity level 4.

"Anyway, Kovac's blood vessel cell walls have now become weakened, permeable and are leaking blood and plasma. This is happening throughout his body, and he is starting to leak fluids through eyes, nose, ears, mouth, sweat... That's why you can NEVER go in there without full biosafety bevel 4 PPE gear on."

She nodded her head in the affirmative.

"Yes, I know... you KNOW all that! You just can't take the precautions lightly, Cassie. Now what we are seeing is his blood pressure dropping and his systems becoming more and more dehydrated." Fairbrother pointed to the trace on the monitor above Nurse Schneider. "At this point, his body is releasing nitric oxide, which results in even lower blood pressure. We've got to be careful because he is now very close to going into septic shock."

"So, the plan is to keep pumping IV fluids and electrolytes?"

"Exactly. The bag hanging there should go several hours yet, pretty much through the night."

"That's good."

"Well good is a relative term, but he is as comfortable as we can make him right now. I do think that we've reached the point that we need to use a vasopressor medication also. That will help to constrict blood vessels and – fingers crossed – increase his blood pressure. I'll write up an order, will probably include norepinephrine in that and you can suit up and replace his drip."

"Replace that one?" She tilted her head towards the CCTV monitor above the vitals screen.

He hesitated and thought about it. "No, I wouldn't do that. He's pretty calm right now. As long as he stays that way, we will swap bags when that one is done. Courtney just suited up an hour ago just before the end of her shift and did what she could in there. You can check the numbers on the monitor, but I think that will be several hours yet, closer to when you knock off in the morning."

"So, I needn't suit up right now."

"No, not as long as he seems to be resting... Look, since it'll be near the end of your shift and following all the biosecurity level 4 procedures are time-consuming, I'll put in for some OT for you if you're okay with that?" He looked for her approval.

Cassie's smile telegraphed her approval. "Damn... yeah... That's all good, Dr Fairbrother. I have Monday off anyway and could use the extra cash next pay. As far as whatever meds you order, Penny Li is one of the nurses on duty next door in ICU, and she can do a med check with me."

"Excellent..." Fairbrother took a step into the hallway outside the nurses' station, scratched his chin and turned back inside. "Look, Cassie. We're not giving Kovac any controlled substances in this drip, so I'm not overly worried about the med checks. It's Sunday night, and the place is practically empty. I'll write the order to the pharmacists and see if someone down there can bring it up. You can double-check each other from here before you take the bag in, but I'm happy to have the pharmacy prepare it. The bigger deal right now is to take care that the cannula is well flushed."

"I'll do that, Steve."

* * *

"Hi, Cassie."

Cassie was almost startled as she turned towards the door and saw Gemma Ridley from pharmacology standing alongside a cart. "Damn girl, you caught me texting." She pressed the send button and dropped her mobile into her bag.

Ridley smiled. "Sunday night at work... yippy, right?"

"Sunday night... hell, it's Monday morning now."

Ridley glanced at the clock. "It's nearly 5 AM. I'm out of here at 7."

"Off to bed?"

"Not right away. I have a brekkie date."

"Better you than me, girl... I've agreed to do a bit of OT this morning, but it's bedtime for me once I'm out of here. At least we only have this one patient tonight, but he's in a bad way."

"Yeah, I got the order from Dr Fairbrother. What is it... EVD?"

"Yeah, nasty stuff that."

Ridley's head dropped. "Damn... it sure is. The poor bugger probably would be better if he just let go."

Cassie let out a sigh.

"Well look, Dr Fairbrother ordered another IV drip with electrolytes. That's the same as what's in there. He added norepinephrine at 1 mcg/kg/min, and that's already in the bag. I'm pretty sure your pumps in the quarantine accept the mcg/kg/min reading, but if not, give a holler. Your nurse's app here will convert the numbers if you need it. Do you want me to wait?"

"No, I'm good. You checked all the numbers, right?"

"Yep... I have you covered. I wrote all the numbers on the bag, too."

"Good. We've been running drips since Dr Kovac was admitted, so I'm sure it won't be a problem. Thanks, Gemma. Enjoy your brekkie date."

"I will..." Ridley smiled and turned to go.

"Cool." Cassie covered her yawn. "You'll probably be gone when I suit up and hang this bag, but if you are here, I'll give you a ring and let you know how he responds."

21

Monday, 22 April; Townsville District
Police Headquarters, Queensland

Inspector Rumford was getting an early start today. He set his coffee on his desk, fired up his computer and watched as it checked for overnight mail. At once he noticed an email from the research folks at ASIO. He took a sip of coffee and opened the attached file. As he started scrolling through, it was immediately apparent that this was the latest update on the three students involved with Professor Pratt.

He maximised the window and started reading. Damn... this was the third update he had seen on these kids, and each of them seemed so squeaky clean he reckoned he could send their names off to the Pope for canonisation. He guessed it all made sense. Becky Whitehall was *Dux* of her high school, and that was of a fairly large class – 286 year-12s. She was also Head Girl. She completed her undergraduate degree with honours. Vasquez wasn't far behind. She was also *Dux* of her school but had a little bit lower Australian Tertiary Admission Rank. Finally, John Rivkin was all-everything at his school, finished in the top five grade-point average at his high school and scored over a 99 in his ATAR. Like the other two, he graduated with honours, but from a Victorian uni. He was also an accomplished athlete, captained his Aussie Rules football club and even played the trumpet. Damn... these kids were really cream-of-the-crop material.

Tap, tap... There was a light knock on his open door. "Leon... I hope I'm not bothering you." Agent Navarro leaned into his office.

"Damn, I wasn't expecting you so early. I shudder to think what you've found out, Clint." He gestured for him to have a seat. "D'ya mind if I call Hasler?"

"No, please do. You'll save me from having to go through this more than once."

Rumford grabbed his handset and pressed a couple of buttons. "Yep. Clint Navarro... right now. Yeah, okay." He set the phone back in its cradle. "She'll be right here."

"Did you review the additional background info the office sent over?"

"Actually, that's just what I was doing now... reviewing that. Damn, these three kids are picture-book perfect, goody-two-shoes, halos over their heads – you think of any virtuous terms that you can, and all three of them fulfil the description."

"I haven't had the chance to go through them yet, but that's no surprise. From what I understand, Pratt attracts some great students from all over Queensland..."

"...as well as around the country." Rumford finished Navarro's sentence just as his partner came into the office.

"Hi, Clint." Inspector Hasler seated herself before anyone had the chance to say anything.

"Hi, Katie... Good morning. I wanted to get you both together. I would have called ahead, but frankly, I was just getting a jump on the day, and since I live on this side of town, I thought I'd just give you a try. I've got a lot on this arvo, so better now than later."

"So, I assume you have an update from your forensics team." Rumford was keen to hear anything new.

"I do. Professor Wentworth was spot on with the explosives call... the lab has confirmed all that. We now have zero doubt on the polyurethane and the reinforced phenolic PCB they collected, too. That bloody well confirms the burner phone theory beyond doubt. And on top of all that, the new piece of news I have for you is that we have matched all the pieces here to other events."

"Matched? Other events?" Katie leaned forward.

"What are you talking about, mate?" Rumford tapped his pen on his desk.

"We've seen this MO before... about five months ago. Do you remember hearing about an explosion in the middle of the night last November in Gladstone? You know the MP down there, um... Gleason?"

"I don't know him personally, but I've heard of him. Labor? Greenie?"

"Hardly... that's a pretty conservative district... Division of Flynn, I think. Anyway, I'm pretty sure he's with the Bush Party."

"The Bush Party... Gotcha." Katie made a note of this new bit of news.

"So why would anyone want to blow up a pollie's office, especially considering he was with the Bush Party. Those folks are pretty conservative themselves, no?" The inspector looked right at Navarro.

"The voters there mostly are. That doesn't mean all the pollies follow along blind-like."

Hasler was trying to work out where Clint was going with this. "Blind-like? Depends on what the issue is, I guess."

"Oh, sorry... we think the mining industry here... the Wynwood Mine, we think..."

"Mining?" A quizzical expression crossed Rumford's face as he thought about what he was hearing. "But I reckon a Bush Party MP would be supportive of just about any mining development. Besides that, the proposed Wynwood mining leases are in the Capricornia Federal District, not Flynn, yes?"

"True enough, but I think Gleason might have been having doubts about that Wynwood Mine deal no matter. Don't forget... some of the pastoralists aren't exactly crash hot on miners coming in, tearing up the land and disrupting their livestock." Navarro ran his fingers through his hair. "But in this case, I think maybe someone was trying to persuade him to vote yes when it came up for environmental clearance."

"I'm confused here." Katie turned from her boss to the ASIO agent. "I confess to not know where the Commonwealth government ends and the Queensland government starts as far as giving the final go-ahead for a mine site, but let's get back to the evidence first. What connection are you guys drawing between the *Reef Explorer* and the Gladstone bombs?"

Navarro smiled. "You're looking at this exactly right, Katie. We know... KNOW... that both bombs used the same type of cheap, throwaway phone. The boys traced it to the Diànhuà Company..."

"Diànhuà? Never heard of them."

"Nah, you wouldn't have heard of them, Leon. They're a Chinese company, are fairly new in Australia and sell a line of super-cheap, prepaid models for like under 50 bucks. Anyway, the samples match up – both bombs used the exact same model phone from the bits we have left at both crime scenes.

The problem is, you can buy these damned units practically anywhere in Australia now including online mail order."

"How about the explosive traces?" Rumford was also taking notes.

"Well, there we made a real find. To start with, the actual bombs were a bit different. Obviously, the *Reef Explorer* was petrol and diesel set off by the blasting cap. The Gladstone bomb had the same type of blasting cap ignite an ammonium nitrate and fuel oil mix, and it looks like a homemade device. Where we really lucked out is that... we are damned certain that both used the same kind blasting cap. The traces matched exactly, but the Gladstone bomb left a bit more behind. The boys pinpointed that blasting cap to the exact kind used."

Rumford broke into a smile. "Bingo... we got them!"

"Not so fast, Leon. We did identify the cap and traced it to the Orica people who manufacture it."

"And?"

"And... about every freaking mining company in Australia use this particular cap somewhere in their mine site. Regrettably, that narrows it down to about everybody!"

22

Monday, 22 April; The Royal Melbourne Hospital, Quarantine Unit, Victoria

Cassie didn't mind. She had already lost the weekend to work, so agreeing to stay on another three hours was no tragedy. Considering the penalty rates that she'd be earning, she could put that extra cash away for the UK trip she was planning for this coming August. She'd been awake all night, so another few hours wouldn't make that much difference.

"Can you check my back, Penny? Is that sealed up airtight?"

Nurse Penny Li had come over from ICU to help her suit up. "I can hear you, but I don't know how well you hear me."

"Nah, it's cool, Penny. The suit covers everything, but it isn't that heavy. Once I'm in the patient's room, I'll need the headset, though." She stood and adjusted the headgear. "Are you sure there's nothing open back there?"

"Nah, you're right."

"And the IV bag?"

"I took it from the locker. Did you say Gemma brought it up earlier?"

"Yeah... Gemma Ridley."

"Yes, I saw her signature on there. We see her in ICU all the time."

"Cool. She's a dear. Fairbrother put the order in, and Gemma saved me the hassle of mixing in the norepinephrine."

Penny held the bag up. "Yeah, cool... It's all written here... the electrolytes, the norepinephrine. I can also see that she followed all the protocols, and the bag is double packed and labelled. You'll have to pull the chord, remove the outer bag and put that one into the disposal container in there. All that gets incinerated then, I guess. Damn, I'm glad we seldom have to do level 4 biosecurity patients."

"Tell me about it! No choice though... that's the procedure here." As Cassie raised her gloved hand, she was reminded that she was in the biosecurity suit. "I guess I'm ready. This suit isn't so bulky, but it is confining. It's a good thing I'm not claustrophobic."

"Be happy that you're confined, I reckon... I'll see you into the airlock and monitor the air pressure both there and in the patient's room. Am I coming through the headphone?"

"Yep, the headset is working. And me?"

"Yep, loud and clear." Penny followed her to the airlock. "Let's hope the norepinephrine helps get Dr Kovac's blood pressure back up."

23

Monday, 22 April; Earth Day at Murdoch University, Perth, Western Australia

"Good morning. My name is Tom Greenough. I am both a *Nyungar* elder and a member of the staff here at Murdoch. I want to welcome you and to acknowledge that Murdoch University is situated on the lands of the *Whadjuk Nyungar* people. I pay respect to their enduring and dynamic cultures and the leadership of *Nyungar* elders both past and present. The *boodjar* or country on which Murdoch University is located has, for thousands of years, been a place of learning. We at Murdoch University are proud to continue this long tradition and, especially today, to join in the global celebration of International Earth Day."

Professor Greenough turned and quickly walked off the stage as Sacha walked to the podium. He unconsciously tapped his lapel microphone and looked over the 600-odd people in the lecture theatre. The large screen behind him lit up with a slide showing the planet Earth floating in space and the words "Welcome to Murdoch University and International Earth Day 2024. Dr Sacha Sharma, Emeritus Professor."

"Thanks, Tom... Professor Greenough is not only my colleague and friend but more importantly, a *Nyungar* elder who we are so fortunate to have here on staff at Murdoch. This being International Earth Day, I can't help but add the words of another colleague from the University of Canberra, Dennis Foley. I want to quote him here.

"The land is the mother, and we are of the land; we do not own the land; rather, the land owns us. The land is our food, our culture, our spirit and our identity." The quote was projected behind him over an image of a native Western Australia forest with a mix of jarrah and marri trees.

"Professor Foley's quote is an insightful way to begin this Earth Day 2024 talk by reminding us all that we are not the first – or the last – peoples to occupy this land we call Australia or this planet we call the Earth. It also reminds us that even though many of us who practise western ways may have a unique view on our relationship with Mother Earth, it certainly is not the only view or even the best view. Professor Foley tells us that 'we do not own the land rather the land owns us...' In the truest sense, that reflection is probably much closer to reality than the much of our western philosophy has professed.

"We can go all the way back to the Bible, where Genesis 1 proclaims time and again the 'goodness of everything the creator made before he created humans'... though any praise of nature itself seemed to fall by the wayside.

"Both Greek philosopher Aristotle and Roman philosopher Lucretius may have appreciated wild nature for her beauty, but again echoed the thinking of their time that nature existed to be conquered by mankind. Much later Saint Thomas Aquinas argued that only rational creatures – humanity that is – could know and love that creator and therefore fulfil the true purpose of his creation. Descartes argued the soulless nature of any life aside from humans, and John Locke believed that nature had little or no value until the labour of humans gave it value. In case you're counting, that's several thousand years of learned thought proclaiming humankind's superiority over nature." A series of colourful slides projected on the big screen behind Sacha showing the likeness of each scholar he mentioned.

"In the United States, the early history is filled with two centuries or more of a western movement that called on spirited Americans to 'tame the wild frontier' by any means necessary. Of course, part of that movement meant 'taming the indigenous people' already living on the land. In the early part of the 1800s, the so-called 'Trail of Tears' saw more than one hundred thousand Native Americans marched westward away from their native country in the southeast of America. Exact numbers could never be known, but probably several tens-of-thousands of those indigenous Americans died in the relocation.

"But please my fellow Australians, don't feel too smug about our own past until you consider the checkered history of European settlement. A permanent colony was established in Sydney when the First Fleet of British ships landed there in January of 1788. The then Governor representing the Crown, Arthur Phillip, claimed sovereignty over all Captain Cook's recently discovered New South Wales and instituted the concept of *terra nullius* which basically claimed that no people at all lived here. In the British case... our case... the Aboriginal people were more likely to be shot and killed rather than moved away from their homelands.

"Through this rather one-sided history of man-conquering-the-environment, there have been critical voices expressing a more harmonious perspective that offer us hope. Henry David Thoreau's *Walden* and Rachel Carson's *Silent Spring* are great examples of recognising that *Homo sapiens* might just occupy a different rung in Mother Nature's ladder." Images showing the covers of each of these literary works appeared on the screen. "Likewise, Australian works including Paul Gilding's *The Great Disruption* and Clive Hamilton's *Defiant Earth* have expressed the belief that we are only one of the uncountable species occupying Planet Earth and that our respect of the intricacies of nature is paramount. And of course, one notable bright light during the last fifty years of the environmental movement is represented by the celebration we honour today. I wish to pay tribute to farsighted minds who first proclaimed an annual day on which we can pause to recognise Mother Earth. Today is the 54th anniversary of that first Earth Day in 1970, and there are now more than 190 countries so honouring *Gaia*.

"When I thought about this address, I considered the many, many speakers over the past half-century who have taken on this task to call the attention of their fellow travellers on this spaceship Earth. Many of these speakers traditionally have pointed to the fact that *Homo sapiens* have had such an immense impact on the planet. Many have used this day to point to statistics confirming this impact. Numbers... numbers that often seem to make it all too easy. But being an academic, I would be remiss without employing any statistics so I will give you a flavour of numbers with a 60-second blur of facts and figures..."

"Consider, 24 of the hottest 25 years ever measured – EVER MEASURED – are in the 21st century. That, of course, includes the hottest ever measured just last year, 2023. The most recent carbon dioxide readings from Mauna Loa in Hawaii are now over 420 parts per million this morning, 150% higher than 75 years ago and the highest level in a million years or more. The Paris Agreement that 195 countries signed less than ten years ago targeted holding temperature increases to 1.5°C. We have just about surpassed that global target last year and have close to zero chance of meeting that goal in 2030. The ice caps are melting, the glaciers are disappearing, the Arctic permafrost is less and less permanent, and the sea levels are rising. And making these numbers even worse is that fact that nearly all of them are accelerating. ACCELERATING! Many have argued that our scientific models are faulty. They are correct – our models ARE faulty – nearly every prediction our models have made UNDERSTATE the scope of our planetwide problem. I can sum up the reams of data supporting all of this by saying that we no longer need to speak of climate change, rather assert that climate CHANGED... and I emphasise the past tense."

"But I promised that I was not here to talk to you about numbers." Sacha put both hands over his head with his fingers extended in an 'I-give-up gesture'. "I'm here to talk to you about Mother Earth... about *Gaia*, for today is Earth Day... *Gaia's Day*. Now the name and the concept of *Gaia* has been around for thousands of years for she was the primal Greek

Mother Earth, the ancestral goddess of all life. A more scientific concept we call the *Gaia* Principle has been around for over fifty years at this point... actually pretty much established about the same time as the Earth Day celebration we commemorate today. We have English chemist James Lovelock and American microbiologist Lynn Margulis to thank for the initial formulation of the *Gaia* Hypothesis.

"I have been trying to understand more and more about *Gaia* over my fifty-year career, so I am not silly enough to pretend to be able to explain *Gaia* in any great detail in a fifty-minute talk. I will say this, however: the *Gaia* Hypothesis has been tested, argued against and ridiculed for half a century, and yet the concept is stronger than ever. It is so strong today that the China National Space Administration, the European Space Agency and America's NASA all agree that any search for life on extraterrestrial planets must look for planets either teeming with life or totally dead. In other words, we no longer think a planet can have 'a little bit' of life. The point? A planet is either alive, or it isn't... no halfway levels of life seem possible.

"Why does this seem to be the case? Simply because based on our total sample of one planet – Planet Earth – we learn that organisms co-evolve with the planet. Obviously, the planet affects organisms in terms of atmosphere, water, temperatures, etc. I hear you thinking out loud, 'organisms change the planet?'. Yes indeed... of course, they do. Consider that plants exhale oxygen and over millions of years totally changed Earth's atmosphere. Microorganisms fix carbon in carbonaceous rock, building kilometre-deep layers of limestone and calcite. Organisms fixed carbon within the Earth... in the soil, in coal, gas, oil, peat...

"And the Earth's geology greatly affects the biosphere. Palaeontologists read the fossil records and agree that five Mass Extinction events have happened to our Earth over the past 500 million years. The causes of these events were both homemade and extraterrestrial. Of the homemade events, the causes range from global cooling and sea-level changes to planetwide disruptions of chemical equilibriums to massive volcanic events. Of the extraterrestrial caused events, triggers include things such as meteor impacts, the variability of our sun, nearby supernova explosions and cosmic ray events. The most recent great dying, the so-called K–T Extinction that occurred some 66 million years ago, was primarily caused by a massive 10 to 15 kilometres in diameter asteroid slamming into the Earth off the Yucatán Peninsula in the Gulf of Mexico. About 75% of all the species on Earth disappeared within a 'short' few thousands of years including what we refer to as the great dinosaurs.

"There is evidence of an even earlier great dying not included in the five mentioned here. That was a VERY long time back, about 2.5 billion years ago just after green, chlorophyll-laden plants evolved. This one is of particular interest since we are talking this morning about organic and inorganic co-evolution. This great dying period has been named the Great Oxygenation Catastrophe, which occurred soon after green, photosynthesising plants evolved on the planet." A grin crossed Sacha's face. "I have to smile since we often hear how good or bad carbon dioxide might be without recognising the fact that chemically, no substance is 'good or bad' in and of itself. The reality is that in too small or too large a quantity, ANY chemical can be either good or bad or at least unharmful to we *Homo sapiens*. I mention this because palaeontologists often refer to this sudden surge of oxygen in Earth's atmosphere as the Great Oxygen Catastrophe or the Oxygen Holocaust. The first time many of my students hear that they scratch their heads and say, how can that be? Oxygen is a good thing... we all die without oxygen... Let's take a look at that from another point of view.

"In the carbon dioxide-rich atmosphere that covered our planet two-and-a-half billion years ago, the green plants found themselves in a photosynthesis nirvana. The things these cyanobacteria needed most – water, CO_2 and sunlight – were all found in excess quantities. Over hundreds...thousands... millions... of years, these green plants exhaled incredibly great volumes of oxygen. Initially, *Gaia* was able to offset this chemically active element through geophysical means... Mother Earth sequestered much of that evil oxygen gas all around the world. We here in Western Australia have for sure been very thankful for that since so much of our economic wealth is a direct result of it." Sacha reached behind the podium and pulled out a large piece of reddish rock. "Of course, I refer to the miles-thick layers of this stuff..." He held the rock over his head. "This is a piece of iron ore which was deposited here and globally those billions of years ago when the nearly unlimited supply of oxygen combined with dissolved iron and the iron oxide rained to the seabeds. Yes, that's right – simple geology and chemistry saw the ionic form of iron ions literally 'fall' out of seawater in the form of what you and I might call rust.

"There is more to the story, though... After 500, 600, 700 million years, even Earth's geology couldn't compensate for so much oxygen, and the atmosphere became toxic and flammable. Remember, at that time there just weren't the multitudes of oxygen-breathing animal species to stabilise this system. Eventually, though, Earth's biosphere helped out when these animals showed up in mass with their ability to breath in the oxygen and balancing that with exhaling carbon dioxide.

"When James Lovelock and Lynn Margulis originally proposed the *Gaia* theory in the early 1970s, many scientists felt abhorrence for the idea that a planet could be alive." Sacha used both hands raised up with his fingers indicating quotation marks around the word alive.

"In the first instance, this was due to Lovelock and Margulis's inability to explain the detail of how it all worked. Naturally, no scientist can explain it all... in the 1970s... in the 2020s... ever... I believe it is fair to argue that fully understanding how nature works is beyond human capabilities.

"The second problem many in the scientific community had was that somehow the *Gaia* Hypothesis was a theory built on mysticism or religion. Again, Lovelock may have inadvertently caused this misunderstanding simply because he chose to name his idea after a Greek goddess, *Gaia*. But let's put this into historical context. Remember, this was a time that the western world was coming out of the 1960s when culturally, the hippy-movement was all about beautiful people consuming large quantities of cannabis, LSD and god-knows-what, the birth control pill led to an era of free sex and the American's Watergate scandal seemed to put an end to community faith in much of anything. This was the 'Age of Aquarius'. This was the *'Lucy in the Sky with Diamonds'* era... The moniker *Gaia* certainly fit the cultural times.

"But Lovelock and Margulis NEVER suggested that Mother Earth was alive in the living, breathing sense that we are. They simply pointed out that Earth displayed many properties that living systems have. The most important parallel is that *Gaia* displays homeostasis. I realise most of you are not science students, so let me simply say that homeostasis is a term often used in biological that refers to self-regulation. You get hungry, your brain tells you to eat. You run in a footy game, your body needs more oxygen, and your body tells your lungs breath faster. It's a hot summer day in Perth, and your body makes you perspire freely so that the evaporating perspiration removes heat from your body. You needn't know ANYTHING about these events, and your miraculous body just does them. There's nothing mystical here, just the laws of physics, chemistry and biology.

"Homeostasis is used in chemistry, too, in relationship to *Le Châtelier's* Principle that refers to equilibria. This one, simple chemical law governs so much biochemistry from our blood supply to neurotransmitters. And chemical principles don't stop there... Think of a pile of firewood and a campfire. At the beginning of the night, you start the fire, and the fuel uses oxygen to produce heat, light, carbon dioxide and water vapour. When the fuel runs out, the fire goes out. If you never studied fire chemistry in your life, the fires will still go out when you use up the fuel.

"In economics, homeostasis applies too. The whole notion of supply and demand keeps things in equilibrium. If it's a bad year and farmers don't harvest many apples, the price has to go up, so people buy fewer apples. In years the apple harvest is plentiful, there are so many apples that the grocers can't sell them unless they lower the price. There's no mystery here... just supply and demand.

"Systems of any kind can stay in balance because of the laws of nature. We can capitalise that and call it the Laws of Nature, but that doesn't change the meaning." The slide projected at the front of the theatre now showed the capitalised words. "They are NOT magical, NOT religious, NOT spiritual... They are merely statements that we humans make based on our collected observations of the regularity, the uniformity we see in the world. In short, the Laws of Nature simply describe the way the world is and the way the world works.

"If there is nothing else you take away from this talk today, I cannot emphasise enough that *Gaia* is NOT mysticism... *Gaia* is NOT spiritual... *Gaia* is NOT religious..." The big screen behind him had a slide up with two-metre-high letters spelling NOT for each comment he made. "This, my friends, is science! This is all based on the Laws of Nature! It is the absolute best science we can relate to you today... and just like Lovelock and Margulis, we don't understand it fully. But just because we don't understand it fully, we still see it happen.

"Doubting any newly discovered science is not new. We humans make a habit of mistrusting new discoveries. Sometime before 1514 Copernicus proposed his heliocentric or sun-centred solar system. A hundred years later, Galileo got in big trouble with the Catholic Church because he supported Copernicus's ideas about a heliocentric, sun-centred solar system. It wasn't until Isaac Newton published his *Principia* 150 years later that the idea became widely accepted. Einstein prosed his Special Theory of Relativity in 1905 and his General Theory of Relativity in 1915, but it took decades for this to be accepted. Charles Darwin presented his theory of evolution or natural selection in 1838, and I'm sure most of you know what a controversial issue that caused... evolution rather than creationism... I say 'caused' in the past tense, but in the most recent polling I can find today – TODAY – some 9 or 10 per cent of Australians, some 20 per cent of Canadians and a whopping 30-something per cent of Americans still believe we are all here through creationism, not evolution.

"So, whether we call her Mother Nature or *Gaia* or just plain old Mother Earth, we all live on this planet together... together with the other animals, with the plants, all the microbes big and small, the mountains and bush, the atmosphere and oceans... We do not need to fully understand the trillions and trillions of working systems, of equilibriums, of shared relationships that allow for *Gaia* to have gone on now continuously for billions of years. It just happens without us fully understanding it. On this Earth Day, we only need to have enough awareness not to disrupt *Gaia* from doing what she does best... keeping our Earth as the best place in the whole universe for us to live and thrive."

24

Monday, 22 April; Centre of Excellence for Coral Reef Studies, James Cook University; Townsville, Queensland

Becky Whitehall and Nikki Vasquez came into the big science block through the front entrance past the two-plus-story-tall, cylindrical aquarium in the middle of the spacious lobby. "Look, Nikki ... It's unusual for Monte to be out in such bright daylight." Becky pointed towards the big moray eel curling out of a clump of coral oblivious to the steady flow of students around the big tank.

"He must be hungry." Nikki smiled.

"Or horny…" Becky's laugh was contagious, and both of them giggled their way up the open stairway and down the hall to Sean's office.

Professor Pratt's two-room office suite had a large meeting table in the middle of the anteroom with a bright window on one wall. The opposite wall had a large, narrow service table on one side with a small refrigerator, coffee maker and water cooler next to it. His office was on the back of the meeting room, the door halfway open. The professor and John Rivkin sat at the meeting table.

"I hope we're not late." Becky and Nikki came in the open door.

"No, you guys are on time. Would you pull the door shut behind you, please?" Sean gestured towards the service table. "Help yourselves to a cuppa…"

"Don't mind if I do. You want tea, Nikki?"

"Please."

"John?" She noted that Sean already had a full mug.

"Thanks, Beck."

Sean stood and took a few steps towards Nikki. He opened his arms and gave her a hug. "Damn, you gave us all a fright last week. I'm glad to see you back to near-normal."

"Yeah, I'm good. I probably spent more time sleeping than usual over the weekend, but I feel fine. My leg's a bit sore yet." She ran her hand down over a bandaged thigh, visible below her shorts.

"Look… I wanted to get us all together this morning just to give you a bit of an update. Inspector Rumford gave me a ring an hour or two ago and filled me in on where the investigation is at."

"Sounds like this is getting serious." She set a mug on the table as Nikki sat and a second in front of John. She walked to the other side of the table and grabbed the third mug from the service table and sat. "So, what did he have to tell you?"

"For starters, all the assumptions about the *Reef Explorer* explosion being a bomb are now confirmed... it was definitely an intentional act. I say bomb, but we actually know the petrol tank set off the diesel fuel. Still, it was set, since they have now confirmed the blasting cap and the burner phone that was rigged as the detonator. The police call it a type of IED or improvised explosive device."

"But we knew all this, yeah?" John tasted his coffee and nodded his thanks towards Beck. "What do we know that is new?"

"You're right John, we did pretty much know this, but it's confirmed now. We know more, though... the blasting cap was one made by Orica, and the burner phone was a Diànhuà."

"Diànhuà? Those things really are throwaways! My mum bought one for my little brother so he could ring her to pick him up. I think she paid like $29.95 for it at the shops, and it could do practically nothing besides making a phone call."

"Damn... you wouldn't want a phone that just made phone calls!" Sean laughed to himself. "Anyway, here's the new revelation... which will explain why I wanted to see you guys this morning. The ASIO people have matched the phone and blasting cap to an identical apparatus used to detonate a homemade bomb at a pollie's office in Gladstone last November."

Nikki's mouth opened, and she ran her finger over her lower teeth. "First of all, ASIO is now involved in all this?"

"They have been, Nikki."

"Oh boy... And now you're saying that someone blew a bomb in a politician's office? Do we know what the hell that was all about?"

"No, not really... there is still an active case going on there. At this point, they haven't proved that the Gladstone bomb and the *Reef Explorer* explosion are absolutely involved with each other. The phones are easy to come by and near impossible to trace, and it seems every mine site in Australia is a source for those particular blasting caps. Still, it seems difficult to believe that it's all just one big coincidence... I get the idea that the police and ASIO are pretty damned sure they are connected, but keep looking for a smoking gun, so to speak."

"So, what did your contact tell you that they are thinking? Do they suspect anyone?"

"No, not in terms of an actual suspect. Yes, in that they reckon it must involve someone or some group who want to push through the Wynwood Mine."

"Wynwood isn't even in Gladstone."

"I know, John... I said the same thing. But it just might be political in that whoever is setting bombs wants to make people think twice against voting against the mine. Again, this is their working hypothesis, but they don't actually KNOW it's Wynwood."

"Yeah, okay... understood... But all this relates to the four of us how?" A grim look accompanied Becky's question.

"I don't know..." The professor shook his head. "That's what I want to ask you guys. We haven't done any work directly related to Wynwood."

"Maybe not directly, but some of the data we collected on the reefs around the Whitsundays might be construed that way. As the silt levels increased, the health of the corals declined. I read that some people were using our data on silt to support their arguments against dredging channels for bulk carriers. Obviously, once they haul that coal out of Wynwood Mine to a port, they will need a long line of deep draught ships to transport that off to customers." Nikki looked at Becky. "Do you remember that woman who was yapping on with us that night at the Spinnaker Club?"

"Now that you mention it, yeah... I sort of remember her."

"What's this? Some woman yapping to you at the Spinnaker Club?" Sean's ears perked up.

"Don't get your hopes up here, Professor. That was months ago, and frankly, I doubt I could even point that woman out even if I tripped over her. It was a Saturday night, and we were... I think it was a Saturday night... let's say we were celebrating just before Christmas. This lady just rocked up to us at the bar and started asking us questions about our research." Wrinkles appeared on Nikki's head where she didn't have wrinkles. It was obvious she was deep in thought.

"Now wait a minute... Let me get this straight. A woman you didn't know walks up to you two out of nowhere and asks about your research?"

Nikki nodded her head yes.

"Are you saying she didn't know you were doctoral students? She didn't know you are environmental science students? She didn't know any of your work could be remotely connected to coal production? Do I hear you correctly?"

Becky took a turn. "Look, Nikki is right. Neither of us could tell you a name or even describe this woman. As for your 'did she know us' question..." Beck's head dropped. "I'm sorry, Sean, but I never gave two thoughts to it. Now that all of this has gone down, I reckon she did know who we were. I think at one point, she might have even mentioned Professor Pratt. Please don't hate us... I KNOW that should have set off our psychic security alarms, but I admit to having one too many drinks and being more in party mode. Hell... it was Christmas break..."

"I don't hate you guys... quite the opposite. Christmas drinks... hell, you're grad students. Of course, you can drink one too many as long as you don't drive. But now when I hear this story, I do worry that someone might take our work to be something it isn't. Hell, what ecologist in their right mind would LIKE to develop more coal. But none of what we have been doing has been aimed at disrupting Wynwood or any other coal project. And how about you, John? Any ideas?"

Rivkin let his head slowly rock from side to side. "Damn, Sean, not really. I wasn't with Nikki and Beck that night and never heard about it until now. Frankly, I've never had anyone question me about my – our – research, other than people you would imagine would do so... at conferences and whatnot..."

"Do you think the same folks who blew the Gladstone pollie's office blew the *Reef Explorer*?"

"Believe it? Hell guys, from what the Inspector tells me, they have as much as confirmed that both explosions are related, but they still need a piece of proof."

25

Monday, 22 April; Murdoch University Bush Court, Perth, Western Australia

"Karl... this is Asha. I got your message." She held her mobile to her ear.

"Thanks for getting back to me, Asha. Where are you?"

"I'm sitting on a bench under a stand of gum trees in the quadrangle on the Murdoch Uni Campus. I just got out of my Dad's Earth Day lecture here."

"Was it good?"

"Good? It was fantastic, but then again, it was my Dad who gave it, so I confess my bias!" She laughed.

"Do you want to Skype?"

"Actually, no – the phone is better here. I'm outside in bright sun, and both the picture and sound will be tough to deal with here. The phone is okay for you, yes?"

"Yeah, sure... the phone is fine."

"Where are you?"

"Well, obviously it's pitch dark here since it's Sunday night. Believe it or not, I'm in a hotel room in Philadelphia. After you left, we got some interesting news out of GNN's Philly Office and by last night, I thought I'd better get my butt back east here to see what I could find."

"Aw damn... sorry Karl, but I turned my phone off last night. I'm sure you got an out-of-service message, and by the time I saw it this morning, we were coming here for the lecture. I apologise... I didn't get to my father's place until like 2 AM on Sunday morning, and yesterday I was a bit jet-lagged. Anyway, I had a dinner date with my father last night and reckoned the phone could survive without me having it on." Asha could almost see him nodding his head in approval through the phone connection.

"Absolutely no problems there, Asha. I just made an executive decision to come back here to sniff out whatever's happening."

"Happening?"

"Well, damn... I mean, since you were here last week, several people have contracted anthrax, and three have died since Friday evening."

"Died?"

"Yeah, like died and are no longer living."

"Enough sarcasm, Karl. I get the picture." Asha flashed on just how many stories Karl and she had worked on together and was reassured in the banter they used in their conversations. "You just surprised me with that news. Hell, multiple deaths in Philly a few days after I was there? That's quick! When I met with Stetzer last Tuesday, there was no mention at all about people at U Penn being exposed to anthrax let alone contracting it."

"Well, I don't think he'd have known it then. That's what's funny. Anthrax is supposed to take only one to five days to show symptoms, but at this point, no one can figure out exactly what the source is." He hesitated for a few seconds. "I guess I'm not strictly honest here in that they all assume they know the source – anthrax in the U Penn laboratory. What they don't know is how it got out. As far as I know, there are three ways you can contract it – ingesting it, through the skin or inhaling it. I doubt anyone has been eating anthrax here in Philly, so that isn't a suspected pathway. That leaves through the skin or inhalation. I didn't meet Stetzer today, but I met a couple of his off-siders."

"And?"

"And no one seems to know anything... more realistically, no one is willing to talk about it. One doc – Gail Lynskey – admits they have a couple of labs working on samples they collected in Alaska, but they aren't too quick to speak about any details. I believe that their work is with the zombie anthrax you mentioned last week before you left for Australia, but that's only speculation on my part."

"Any word on the grapevine on Scandinavia or Siberia? Stetzer told me they all seem to be having the same problems."

"I'll get right on that. From what this Dr Lynskey said to me today, I think I might head off to Atlanta since even though U Penn has these samples, the big work is happening at CDC in Atlanta."

"Please keep me up on what's happening, Karl."

"Will do."

I promise not to turn my phone off again, but unless it's an emergency, let's agree not to call in the middle of the night. With you on the east coast and me in Western Australia, don't forget that we are 12 hours off sequence. I may be heading over east tomorrow, and if I fly to Queensland, that'll make it 14 hours' time difference from Philly and 15 from Chicago."

"We'll touch base either verbally or by text."

"Great."

26

Monday, 22 April; Dr Liz O'Rourke's residence, Melbourne, Victoria

Felly heard the bell but couldn't figure out who'd be at the door in the middle of the day. Lizzy was at work, and any of her friends would know that. Since she and Geoff lived in a single-family house, she didn't know the routine for mail order deliveries and the like. She always thought one of the advantages of living in a unit in a high rise was the security, the confidence in knowing that no one could just walk up to your door. She pressed the intercom on the wall, and the CCTV flickered on. She was surprised to at once recognise Helen Trainor from the Victorian Department of Health and Human Services. "Ms Trainor. Why... what can I do for you?"

"Please, Dr Kovac, do you mind if we have a chat?"

Felly was worried enough without seeing Ms Trainor's face on the CCTV, and now her mind when into overdrive considering all the scenarios that might bring her to Liz's apartment. "No, no, not at all. I'm in unit 1804."

"Yes, yes... I can see that on the intercom here."

"The lifts are right in front of you there through the big door, Ms Trainor."

"I see them. I will be right up." She paused long enough for Felly to press the button that opened the glass door to the foyer where the lifts were located.

Felly slowly walked to the door of the unit and waited. Had Geoff taken a turn for the worse? Had someone else at Yunupingu Institute showed EVD symptoms? Did the Health Department or Royal Melbourne Hospital need her expertise? It was only a minute, or so she spoke over the intercom but seemed like a thousand years. The door chime sounded, and

Felly quickly opened it. She reached her hand out to Ms Trainor. "Hello, Ms Trainor.

"G'day, Dr Kovac."

"Please call me, Felly." She closed the door and turned towards the living room. Let's go have a seat. Can I get you anything, Ms Trainor?"

"No, no... Felly. Look, I'll call you Felly, and you stick with Helen, okay?"

"Sure, Helen." They both sat on the sofa and Felly was busting at the seams to determine why Trainor was there. "Is everything okay? Has Geoff taken a bad turn?"

Trainor's eyes were sad, and she ever so slightly bit her lip. Before she began to speak, Felly could feel tears welling up inside. Helen reached out and took Felly's hand. "I'm so, so very sorry..."

Felly's tears erupted, and she broke down. Her crying grew louder now, and she leaned into Helen. Instinctively, she hugged Felly with both arms and tried to comfort her, but she knew it was an impossible task. The two of them sat there for several minutes, Trainor embracing Felly and letting her grief pour out. Finally, after a good five minutes, Felly pulled back just enough to look in Helen's face. "Is Geoff... Geoff... gone?"

"I'm so, so sorry, Felly."

Again, she burst out in another shower of tears and again, Trainor hugged her. After another few minutes, Felly's uncontrollable crying transformed into quiet sobs. Again, she pulled back, her red eyes filled with grief. "Can you tell me what happened... how it happened?"

This was obviously not a situation Helen was faced with too often in her position with DHHS. "I wasn't there, Felly, but I spoke with the doc on duty. He said Geoff was mostly comfortable through the night and continued receiving IVs with fluids and electrolytes. I believe the fear was he could go into septic shock, so the doctor decided to add added a vasopressor and ordered something... maybe norepinephrine... in the new IV bag sometime after 7 AM this morning. At first, he showed no response at all and continued to rest calmly. As they continued to monitor him, his blood pressure dropped lower and lower. Both the nurse and doctor were in isolation with him for over an hour and worked hard. Regrettably, they were unable to bring him around. His heart just slowed and slowed until it stopped. From what they told me he was no longer conscious, so at the very least, he would have been very peaceful. I realise my words can't possibly ease your pain, but I am so very, very sorry, Felly."

Again, Felly burst into tears with her head against Trainor's shoulder. After several more minutes of sobbing, she sat up, wiped her face and somehow collected herself. "Please give me a minute."

"Of course." Helen watched as Kovac disappeared into the bathroom and closed the door. She could hear the sink running.

In a few minutes Felly returned, her eyes still very red, but her face powdered. "Thank you for being so sympathetic, Helen. This is the hardest thing I have ever faced. But face it, I must. I need to let people know what happened for starters... Our families, Geoff's friends and colleagues, my workmates... We need to work backwards and figure where this *Zaire ebolavirus* came from. You know, these little microbes don't just pop up. I never thought this virus was contracted in Thailand, and I still don't believe that."

Helen Trainor was at least reassured to see Felly's deep grief seem to ease somewhat and watch as Dr Kovac's analytical researcher side of her personality kick in. "I can stay with you if you like, Felly."

"That won't be necessary, Helen." Felly's tone was sincere and filled with gratitude.

"You've done so much already, Helen. I know this must have been very difficult for you, too. I need to get on with it now... on with notifying everyone and charting the course forward."

27

Monday, 22 April; Murdoch University Sir Walter's Faculty Club, Perth, Western Australia

Five of them sat at the table on the far side of the Faculty Club as guests of Professor Della Bakhshi, the Dean of the School of Environmental Science. "Thanks again, Sacha. I really enjoyed your take on it today... very different from the normal doom and gloom environmental talk."

"Well, I wouldn't say you exactly left them laughing in the aisles, Sacha." Brenden broke into a broad grin. Professor Gramm was also on staff and the School and second-in-command to the Dean. "I did like the way you presented a case for environmental cybernetics without ever mentioning the term."

"Cybernetics... control, communications, information processing, yes?" Asha was somewhat familiar with the term. "We did a story on artificial intelligence – AI – last year at one of the big tech companies out in Silicon Valley. They were up to their ears in cybernetics."

Professor Gramm was quick to respond to her. "Totally understood. I think the IT crowd and AI guys are out there on the forefront, but frankly, we ecologists aren't far behind."

The Dean nodded her agreement. "Truth be told, it was... it is... living systems in which we recognised cybernetics in the first place. You are spot-on, Asha. I still teach a unit in cybernetics and can sum it up quite simply by stating the three essentials in any energy and matter relationships by..." Della pressed a finger from one hand against the other. "...one, analysing the collecting data from the environment. Two, you have to run these data through a controller or a brain of some sort. Then three..." She pressed three fingers against her hand. "...the system must somehow command some sort of actuators to respond to the environment.

"I'll give you two examples. In an industrial situation like a manufacturing plant, the engineers use electronic sensors to measure pressures, temperatures, pHs, etc. Then they will set up a sophisticated software program in a high-powered computer to analyse all that. Finally, the system uses a collection of pumps, heaters, coolers, conveyor belts, etc., to act on the system to cause it to deliver the output desired. Now the system is a continuous feedback loop though, so the output will in itself be sensed by the sensors, that data is reviewed by the controller and then once again acted on by the actuators. Our chemical engineering people do this kind of thing in their sleep.

"My second example is a biological one, and I was happy to hear Sacha mention this in his talk this morning. The concept of homeostasis is, frankly, the true essence of cybernetics. In a sense, your body runs similarly to the manufacturing plant, and the circulatory system takes oxygen and fuel in the form of glucose to your cells and removes carbon dioxide and waste. If your glucose levels get too high, there is a chemical signal to your pancreas that causes a release of insulin, which will lower the amount of glucose in the bloodstream. If glucose levels drop too far, the pancreas increases a chemical called glucagon, which causes the liver to release any stored glucose. Of course, there is also a signal your brain sends to your appetite mechanism that says 'eat'! Once again, the system collects data, a controller uses these data to cause an action... and this happens over and over in a continuous feedback loop."

Asha laughed. "You should have been at our dinner last night, Della, because that was the same point Clive made, sans the cybernetics reference and using a body temperature example. Amongst you, Clive and Dad, I'm starting to think you are all in some sort of cybernetics conspiracy."

"That's my daughter! I think you hit the nail right on the head, but the real cybernetics conspiracy is that of *Gaia,* and we are all a part of it whether we are aware of it or not." Sacha smile beamed his pride in Asha.

"Good point, Sacha." Della nodded in agreement with his point.

Sacha's smile never left his face as he still looked right at his daughter. "You mentioned last night's dinner to Della, and you mentioned Clive's example of a feedback loop! Asha, Asha, Asha... You missed the whole point of last night's dinner, my dear. Somehow you failed to mention that your dear old father brought along a 1983 bottle of Grange that we drank."

"Amen to both of you." Clive sat back. "For starters, the Grange was superb. I will definitely let my homeostasis example take a backseat to that." They all enjoyed a chuckle.

* * *

"That was an absolutely fantastic lunch. Thank you so much, Dean Bakhshi." Clive dabbed his mouth with her napkin. "I hope you give my own Dean at Notre Dame some pointers on taking staff to lunch."

"Next time I see him, I will." She tasted her coffee. "Asha... where to from here? Your dad tells me you are on assignment."

"Yes, I am. I've been working with a colleague on an in-depth story looking at what seems to be some variations in the mutation rates of various microbes."

"Microbes?" Now Clive's ears perked up, too.

"Yes. It's just that the colleague with whom I'm working on this project – Karl Grimsley – took notice of how several communicable disease outbreaks have started to occur more regularly the past decade or so. He saw it all graphed in an academic paper out of... I think it was the University of Chicago, and over the past 75 to 100 years, mutation rates have grown exponentially."

"But when you speak of human outbreaks – I assume you are looking at human disease..." Brenden looked towards Asha.

"We are."

"Then the seemingly unusual increase in human outbreaks could result from better news gathering methods, greater communications or even more population in susceptible areas."

"I appreciate what you are saying here, Professor Gramm, but our research unit actually looked into that. Frankly, your school here at Murdoch would be envious of some of those GNN researchers since they are a nerd's dream." She smiled and looked for reassurance that she hadn't offended anyone.

"I know that – several of my undergrads have been employed by our ABC and local newspaper here in Perth. I give a lot of credit to the top-of-the-line journos like you and your GNN mob for doing your homework. A good statistical study can tell us when a change in occurrence isn't simply by chance... just because of spurious factors." Brenden's head rocked back and forth in approval.

"I won't burden you with the whole thing since you don't have the time and we are just scratching the surface right now, but I am convinced it's a story worth reporting. Considering the MDR-TB – that's multi-drug-resistant tuberculosis – that is now found in almost all the countries on Earth, we started looking for other maladies that have changed in severity, range or method of infection. The Zika virus was originally mosquito-borne, but there are indications it has mutated. The Lyme Disease is caused by the *Borrelia* bacterium and results from tick bites, though increasingly there has been evidence that it is finding other vectors, other methods to spread. I know you have all read about the so-called 'zombie microbes' being resurrected in the Arctic areas from melting permafrost that, in some cases, has kept deadly diseases like anthrax in suspended animation for tens of thousands of years. And in the past year or so, we have seen *Zaire ebolavirus* break its African roots and now show up in Bangladesh and into Southeast Asia. There is also some evidence that *Zaire ebolavirus* has undergone some mutations, but it is too early to make a definitive comment on this."

"Well, since my ears were first to perk up at the word microbes, let me be first to ask you just how far you have gotten here, Asha?" Clive was keen to hear more both from his personal point of view as well as his role as a lecturer to the next crop of medical doctors.

"I wish I could tell you more, Clive, but we are just exposing the tip of the iceberg right now. I am very fortunate to work for a group such as GNN because they seem quite happy to fund journos such as Karl and myself to dive into this kind of story headfirst. I seriously doubt we could do this working for most outlets that are happy to grab their 'if-it-bleeds-it-leads' story for the local evening news every day."

"And are you finding that just maybe something is there under the iceberg's tip?"

Asha arched her eyes. "You don't realise how appropriate that question is, Clive. The things they are finding in Alaska, Siberia, Greenland... they are finding bacteria and viruses that have been locked away in suspended animation for 20,000, 30,000, 40,000 years. Frankly, no one knows if some of these microbes were actually pathogens to amoebas, to birds, to mammals or to humans. Some of the thawed-out viruses they have found are behaving quite abnormally... acting in unpredictable ways. To me, the biggest takeaway is that we are only starting to experience this thawing phenomenon since the temperatures just keep rising. Absolutely no one has a clue what strange mini creatures will turn up next year or the year after that or the year after that..."

"So, you really ARE finding the unexpected under the tip of the iceberg?" Della looked over the top of her glasses at Asha.

"Well, yes, I think so. I can't give specifics yet for the simple reason that we are still working hard on it, but I have a gut feeling it's almost as though…" She stopped as she panned the faces looking at here.

"What is it, honey?" Sacha tried to reassure her.

"You are all academics. You all spend a career using the scientific method to tease out the truth… the way things really work. I haven't any science to point to at this point, but I swear that I can somehow feel that these diseases somehow communicate with each other… with nature…" She sat back and awaited the condemnation she knew would be coming from a group of pointy-nosed, ivory-tower academics… but it never came.

"Aha… it's funny you say all this since there are several research studies here in the School of Environmental Science that seek to explore just that aspect of Earth's ecology. How does Mother Nature seem to so easily coordinate global changes?" Dean Bakhshi seemed to be a hundred per cent in agreement with Asha. "I certainly hope your dad has passed along work our researchers are involved with looking at rapid changes with coral polyps, phytoplankton and zooplankton up north along the Ningaloo Reef. Obviously, many of these changes are echoing what others are finding on the Great Barrier Reef over east, the New Caledonia Barrier Reef in the South Pacific and the Saya Del Malha in the Indian Ocean."

"It would be impossible to do any serious ecological study without being aware of this 'Gaia grapevine' as it were." Professor Gramm added.

"For sure. The older I get, the more I understand the power of communications, but maybe not exactly as you may think." Sacha looked at his daughter. "I admit that the microbe communication idea is new to me, but that's only because it's not something I have looked into over my career. I do know that when Clive mentions the micro-universe that the human body is to trillions of microbes makes perfectly good sense to me. It also offers a wonderful metaphor for the Earth behaving in the same way as a system... a much more complex system... but still working as a whole."

"Thanks for that, Sacha. And Asha, you have certainly grabbed my interest. I take my role as a teacher of the next generation of doctors quite seriously, you know. I – all of us in medical research and education – have all taken a keen interest in how microbes seem to stay one step in front of us. We have been very fortunate here in Australia in that we haven't had any big outbreak of multidrug-resistant tuberculosis, of Zika or Lyme Disease. I believe I am correct in saying that, other than Antarctica, Australia is the only continent that has never recorded a fatality from EVD, Ebola." Clive was interrupted by his vibrating mobile that had been sitting on the table in silent mode. "I apologise, but this looks important."

Sacha smiled at his daughter. "I almost thought you were going to get some resistance from a mob of academics. I think having me for a father, you would have had to have heard this idea of communication amongst all of life many times before. Don't you remember when Emily and I would read *The Story of Doctor Dolittle'* to you as a kid that we'd talk about the 'if I could talk to the animals' line?"

"I do. Actually, I remember YOU talked about it and mum sang it!" A broad grin crossed her face.

Clive looked up from what must have been a shocking text message, and he seemed shaken. "Oh my god..."

"Sacha put his hand on Clive's shoulder. "Are you okay, mate?"

"Not really... I seem to have spoken too soon. I don't know of a subtle way to put this, but we can confirm that *Zaire ebolavirus* is now in Australian and one of my old medical school mates who was a patient in The Royal Melbourne Hospital just became its first official Aussie casualty."

28

Monday, 22 April; The Royal Melbourne Hospital, Quarantine Unit, Melbourne, Victoria

"G'day Doctor. I'm Inspector Tony Benson." He extended his hand to Dr Fairbrother. "This is Inspector Sonny Liu of the Victoria Police and Dr Lloyd Gephardt of the Coroner's Office."

"I can't say that I'm exactly glad to meet you under these circumstances, but thanks for coming. I'm Dr Steve Fairbrother, and this is Nurse Jo Ferguson. Look, forgive me, but I feel absolutely terrible that we lost Dr Kovac. Frankly, I was really hoping we were going to turn the corner with him today. Also – and no excuse offered here – I admit to being flat out knackered. I'm damned close to 24 hours into a 24-hour shift, and I do feel exhausted."

"Bloody hell! Twenty-four hours! Hopefully, we can do what we need to do without a hassle here."

"No, no... that's fine. They do allow for two, two-hour breaks." He smiled as his head rocked front to back. "My replacement will be here soon, and I am determined to stay on until you guys get what you need."

"That'd be great. Look, can you give me a little background here? Can you tell me what we can and can't do because of the... well, you know, um..."

"The Ebola. Yeah, sure... Look, we have been very fortunate in that we haven't had but one or two suspected cases of Ebola here ever and they were similar to Dr Kovac... medical people returning from helping Ebola patients overseas. Because of that, a 'normal' quarantine unit like this is not set up for level 4 biosecurity, and I think we've done a pretty good job upgrading this one."

"What did you have to add?" Inspector Liu was both interested and nervous.

"We all wear certified personal protective equipment whenever we enter. It's fairly straight forward. The engineering staff set up a negative pressure room with a portable compressor. Anyone going in there wears the proper PPE – ah, that's personal protective equipment – including a set of coveralls, a full gown, a double set of gloves, surgical headgear, a face shield and boots. At the end of use, any healthcare worker isolates everything but the face shield and boots and then that all gets incinerated. The shield and boots are also isolated and then either sterilised or disposed of. Kovac has only been here a few days, but each day we have at least four PPE kits that need to be disposed of. Look, Ebola is transmitted through bodily fluids, so even though we are not so worried about air transport, we still use a negative air pressure room."

"Negative pressure?" Benson was writing notes.

"Yeah. There's a little bit less air pressure in the patient's room so any air leaking will go in, not out. The air that is being removed from there to maintain the negative pressure passes through a HEPA filter – that's the high-efficiency particulate air filter. These are medical grade, take out particles incredibly small and also treat what passes through with an ultraviolet light designed to kill microbes."

"Sounds like quite an ordeal going in and out of there." Liu nodded towards the room where Kovac's remains were still in the bed.

"It is. It takes maybe 15-20 minutes to disrobe, put on all the PPE, go through the check-off procedure and the enter. You basically have 30 or 45 minutes to work with the patient only because being sealed up like that, the health worker can get quite warm and perspire a lot. Finally, when you come out, you are in a much smaller isolation room, and you go through the procedures in reverse before showering with a sterilising medium. Eventually, you finish up in a conventional shower."

Inspector Benson tilted his head to one side. "Well, damn... I can see why the Sergeant told us to beg you people to help us out, but I'll leave that to Dr Gephardt. Ultimately, it's the Coroner's Office that has the responsibility here."

Fairbrother nodded. "Coroner's Office... interesting. Surely there is no foul play suspected here?"

"No, no... no foul play, Dr Fairbrother." Liu tried to reassure him. "This is just such an unusual death... I don't think we've had one previous death from EVD anywhere in Australia."

"I believe that's correct."

"So, the Coroner's Office – off the record, of course – is just covering our butts here. I would be very happy to have you collect what we need when you suit up again." Gephardt sounded happy that he wasn't personally going to collect what needed to be gathered.

"I fully intend to do that, sir. I'm going to get whatever you need using the proper procedures, organise Dr Kovac's remains to be removed, and then I'm going home to bed, sir. Our hospital staff people can suit up later and do what they do to make it all safe in there again. I'm happy to do this now if you like. I'd rather you were here to be certain I do what you need, collect whatever you think is essential. Whatever remains will be incinerated so we won't get a second chance at this should you need other articles... evidence..."

"Understood. That's fantastic that you are happy for us to stay while you go in again, Doc. I have a tick list here if you don't mind." Gephardt handed him the paper.

Fairbrother looked over the list. "Tissue sample, fluids samples, bedding sample, IV fluid sample, samples from water from bedside glass, nurse's gear..." He looked at the two Inspectors and Gephardt. "I assume that's blood pressure cuff, stethoscope and whatnot? I just want to be sure, because as I said, we will only get one shot at this. Pardon my repetitiveness, but once they do the cleanup, everything remaining will be destroyed."

"I'm sure that's correct. Look, if there is any doubt, take the sample, bag it, label it, properly isolate it, and she'll be right. If we have more than is needed, we'll just dispose of that later. We always would rather err on the side of caution."

Fairbrother nodded. "Understood, Doc."

"Fortunately, Liu and I will be here through it all and monitor you on the CCTV. If there is ever any question, just fire away. By the time you finish this, you'll be ready to become a constable." Gephardt laughed.

29

Monday, 22 April; Dr Liz O'Rourke's residence, Melbourne, Victoria

She sat hunched over with her head pressed onto Liz's shoulder, still sobbing and taking deep gulps of air. "I just... I just can't stop crying, Lizzy."

"You don't have to stop crying, Fell-O." Liz felt so frustrated. She was at a total loss of exactly what she could do to make it better. "You need to cry... Just cry on my shoulder, hon. It's okay."

The two of them remained like that for another fifteen or twenty minutes. Felly's crying slowly became sobbing and then silence. At first, Liz thought she had finally fallen into a well-deserved sleep. She gently stroked her friend's hair, trying to reassure her that she wasn't about to leave her alone.

"It doesn't make any sense, Liz... He should have been getting better."

"They'll figure it out, Fell."

She took another deep breath and slowly exhaled. "This is Melbourne, Lizzy. This is a first world country. You know as well as I do that mortality rates in Africa... in Bangladesh and now Southeast Asia have all been very bad. EVD deaths have ranged as high as 90% but recently has fallen to 50% or 60%. Think about that... that means that as many as half the people who contracted the disease survive. We're getting better as a world in our treatment of EVD. The very few cases of returned healthcare workers to Europe, the Americas or the few cases here had survival rates as high as 90% and 95%. Hell, how is it that Geoff shows a symptom or two, is admitted to the hospital, gets an IV drip for a day or two and dies." She started to cry again.

"Try to get some sleep, Fell." She again brushed her fingers through her friend's hair.

"I never, ever thought that was *Zaire ebolavirus* from Thailand. I never thought Geoff was infected there. I'd have known... He'd have known... The authorities are going to have to look into this, Lizzy."

"They will, hon, they will. That's not our job, Felly. It's okay to grieve now. You need to let it out as much as you possibly can, Fell."

"No, no... you know as well as I do, Lizzy... It IS our job. The Victorian Department of Health, The Royal Melbourne Hospital, the Police Department... I don't doubt they want to help, but they just don't have the proper facilities or expertise to look into it. Hell, no one in the whole southern hemisphere has the proper equipment or qualified personnel to follow up on this the way that we can... the way that the Yunupingu Institute can..."

Liz ran her fingers through Felly's hair and continued to comfort her friend as much as she possibly could. She was prepared to sit on that sofa through the entire evening if that's what it took, but she wasn't about to leave Felly alone right now. "You can't worry about this, Fell."

"I'm afraid they will do something stupid... infect someone else... destroy samples... overlook something..."

"Rest assured, that won't happen. I was going to save this, but I think you need to hear it now. The Victoria Police have been right on top of this. The Coroner is involved now, too."

"The Coroner? Why would the Coroner be involved? Do they suspect something?"

"No Fell-O... that's not how it works. The Coroner's Office has the responsibility to determine the cause of death. That isn't just in the case of nefarious fatalities, but in any situation where COD is not obvious. Coroners look into anything from a suspected communicable disease such as this to lightning strikes, car crashes and industrial accidents.

"In this situation, the Coroner has worked with the hospital healthcare workers, and they have collected every sample imaginable. They might be novices with *Zaire ebolavirus*, but they are not novices with collecting forensic evidence. Fortunately, the medical staff could safely isolate any and every sample needed, and they have done that."

"How do you know that, Lizzy?"

"They gave me a ring while I was running back over here, Felly. They told me what they had collected and then asked if we – the Institute – would work with them to determine whatever was needed to be determined. As far as I know, all that was collected is on its way to Yunupingu Institute right now. They are well aware of the expertise we have as well as our level 4 biosecurity laboratory and all the equipment. Besides that, I assured them that we are only too happy to be of any assistance, any sampling, analysis..." Lizz again patted her friend on the shoulder. Trust me, we'll get to the bottom of this, Fell-O. We'll get to the truth of the matter."

30

Tuesday, 23 April; The Qantas Club Lounge,
Perth International Airport, Western Australia

"Hi, Karl."

"Hey, Asha. You still in Perth?"

"Yes, but not for long. I'm sitting in the Qantas Club at the airport here, having a cuppa and an English muffin... with Vegemite, I might add."

"Oh my god... the dreaded Vegemite!" Karl chuckled.

"Anyway, I'm on my way to Townsville. It's kind of a pain since there isn't a direct flight from here to there and I have to go through Brisbane. It's absolutely lousy connections, and I spend three or four hours in Brisbane... I don't think I get to Townsville until tonight."

"Does Brisbane have a Qantas Club?"

"Oh yeah... at least I can use their internet connections and eat their food." Asha smiled over the phone.

"Who are you tracking there? Is it that professor?"

"Yeah, yeah... Professor Sean Pratt. I actually know him. He was one of Dad's favourite doctoral students years back. I think he can help us both ways, with the overall whole-planet scenario as well as with the microbe issues, at least as far as the Barrier Reef goes. When I spoke with him on the phone, he told me he has one doctoral student in particular who is really keen on microbiology as well as the other small creatures... zooplankton and phytoplankton."

"Good stuff." Karl muffled the phone as he cleared his throat. "Anything more on the Ebola outbreak?"

"Um, yes and no. In the first place, though, don't refer to it as an outbreak. One poor bloke was infected, but it sounds as though he contracted the disease while working in a tent hospital in the jungles of Thailand. What makes it interesting to us is that his wife, a... um..." Asha looked at her notes. "Dr Felicia Kovac... She is the director of the Yunupingu Institute of Medical Research there in Melbourne. I wasn't able to speak with her, but I did chat briefly with Dr Deshi Tang, another of the researchers there. He assured me that they would help us out and contribute whatever was in the public domain."

"That sounds promising. When do you meet?"

"Don't know as yet. Sadly enough, the director I told you about is out of contact right now. I mentioned that it was Dr Felicia Kovac's husband, who died, so she isn't in any shape for meeting with me as yet. For that matter, I think she is in quarantine, though it is a home quarantine. I think Deshi and one other... Dr Liz O'Rourke... they may both be willing to meet later in the week. So much depends on what happens there with the investigation."

"Investigation? There's no question concerning COD, is there?"

"I don't think so. Doesn't the Coroner's Office always look into any deaths that are a bit unusual? That would be the same here in Australia or in the States. Hell, I don't think Australia ever had an Ebola death, so for sure you'd have to say it was unusual."

"True."

"How about you, Karl? I imagine you're back in Chicago, yes?"

"Yep, though I think I'm heading to Atlanta – the CDC there – tomorrow. Then depending on what I find out from them, I'm either flying off to Alaska or Siberia."

"Damn... you sound like you love that cold weather."

"Well, fortunately, it's the end of April, so both Fairbanks or Krasnoyarsk won't be middle-of-winter cold. The

Fairbanks situation is interesting, and I'm curious as all hell what I learn in Atlanta... if they let me know anything."

"Huh? What's that about, Karl?"

"Well the rumours I've heard are that the CDC has a program looking into zombie microbes at UA-Fairbanks, but it isn't labelled as such. I think it comes under the general heading of public health or something like that. Interesting, huh?"

"I'll say. And the Siberian city... Kras-no-skie..."

He chuckled. "Krasnoyarsk, my dear friend."

"Right! You know, I pride myself on my grasp of geography, but I can't for the life of me see Krasnoyarsk in my mental map of the world."

Again, Karl laughed. "I confess it wasn't right up there in my bucket list, either. I did do a bit of background reading on it though, and it's in the middle of nowhere over 2,000 miles east of Moscow. It's also way north, but not quite in the Arctic Circle... only 350 or 400 miles south of the line. Still, from all reports, it's meant to be a very pretty city with – believe it or not – a million people."

"Damn! A million people and I don't even know it exists!"

"Don't feel bad, Asha. I didn't know of it, either. Anyway, they have a notable research centre there at the Krasnoyarsk State Medical University. It seems they have datasets going back a couple of decades on permafrost microbes even before serious thawing really kicked in."

"Oh boy. Just in case you get hungry, I wonder whether or not they have a McDonald's?"

31

Tuesday, 23 April; Townsville District
Police Headquarters, Queensland

"G'day, Leon."

Rumford looked up from his desk and saw Agent Clint Navarro standing in the doorway. "I swear I just hung up the phone."

"Well, I told you I'd be right by."

"Damn... I'm starting to think you ASIO blokes only work one case at a time. You see this folder?" Rumford tapped his hand on a manila binder on his desk. "The Queensland Police Service expects its public servants to work a pile of cases all at once!"

Navarro patted his chest somewhere near his heart. "Can you see my heart feeling bad for you, mate?"

Rumford cracked a smile. "Yeah, okay. That's just about how much sympathy we get from anyone else. Now then, you know, I tried to tell you that I was happy to come to see you this time, mate. That said, I'll be damned if I know where your office is?"

"And you never will." Navarro laughed. "You know us spooks... If I told you where my office was, I'd have to kill you." He laughed and pulled up a chair across the desk from Inspector Rumford. "All kidding aside, I just wanted to get back to you. You know, after you told me about Whitehall and Vasquez's night out on the town at the Spinnaker Club, I got the boys straight on it."

"Good stuff... what did they find out?"

"Give me a chance... give me a chance... I'm going to get to that. Now Pratt's kids... sorry, mate... I guess late-20s doctoral students don't actually qualify as kids... His two students didn't give you a date but did say they were celebrating sometime before Christmas, probably a Saturday. So, we started with weekends... Friday and Saturday 15 and 16, 22 and 23 of last December. Now, this proved to be a stretch since that's a long time to have CCTV footage. Fortunately, that Atlas Security company under contract with the Spinnaker Club downloads and backs up the whole CCTV hard drive every Sunday and stores it just in case there is ever any issue with barroom fights, dodgy sexual harassment claims and whatnot. The Atlas folks proved to be a pretty damned sophisticated bunch. We gave them times, and they gave us footage. So, we ran the data through our facial recognition software and... Bob's your uncle." Navarro snapped his fingers. "We found what we wanted way more easily than I thought we would. Those damned AI algorithms are getting scary if you ask me. I swear you could scan a photo of a particular horse fly here in Townsville into the system and our damned ASIO AI will track that fly down and find him on a horse's ass a couple of hours away in Charters Towers!"

Leon had a snicker over that description of the software. "Good one, Clint. Next time I am searching for a fly gone bad, I'll give you ASIO blokes a call. So, what did you find this time?"

"Well, like I said, we didn't have to look too far. We found them there on Saturday night the 16th of December... We found them both... Nikki Vasquez and Becky Whitehall right there at the Spinnaker Club just like they said. And you know, they can both hold a bit of booze. They're pretty girls if I can say so myself." Navarro unconsciously looked around behind him to make sure he wasn't being overheard. "We watched them from about 8 PM for an hour or two with half the blokes in the bar buying them drinks. Anyway, somewhere around 10 PM – I have the exact time on the report back on my computer – a woman comes up to them just like they said."

"Any audio?"

"Don't press your luck. Atlas Security is good, but they don't record audio... but the AI came through again."

"It identified her?"

"Sure did..."

"And?"

"The woman's name is Sienna Olsen, 35 years old, a Townsville resident... back to high school, anyway. She's a divorcee with no kids. Her husband must have beat her up a few times... maybe ten years ago. He left Australia and went back to the UK – Scotland, I think – and she stayed on here, mostly as a shop clerk, waitress... She's been employed with the Lion Creek Mine people who have some development going on in the Central West region, but their offices are here in Townsville. Actually, one of our agents discreetly inquired about 'employment' with Lion Creek yesterday and learned that Sienna may be the only staff on duty in that office most of the time."

"So, no one's talked to her as yet?"

"Nah."

"Damn, Clint... It sounds to me like you guys hit pay dirt. If this Olsen woman was pumping Vasquez and Whitehall about the environmental work they were involved with and she has connections with some coal mining company, we just might have a done deal here. We need to do a bit of digging, but I reckon as sure as all hell you'll find that Lion Creek folks must have been behind both the Gladstone bombing as well as the *Reef Explorer*."

"Don't know... I can't confirm that, but I do believe we are onto something. This Olsen woman is with the Lion Creek people, and I think Professor Pratt was talking about the Wynwood Mine project maybe being complicit. I guess it's a good bet in this part of Queensland that some mining interest would be involved, but we need to nail down the right one since we're on top two different bombings."

"We also searched everywhere imaginable around Lady Lyman Beach up north thereabout... 110 kilometres, I think. Damn, that's some desolate bush up there. There really aren't very many houses within range of the beach, so there's no CCTV we could find. The nearest is a road house six or eight kilometres south of there, and anyone driving back to Townsville would probably have to go past there. The boys are checking if they have any CCTV footage, but I haven't gotten a report as yet."

"Hell, you wouldn't really know what you were looking for, would you?"

"Nothing obvious… yet. But hey, that's what they pay us for. Sometimes the best info is the 'not-so-obvious' info."

DAN CHURACH

PART THREE

"In nature, there are neither rewards or punishments
— there are only consequences."

— Robert Green Ingersoll

32

Wednesday, 24 April; Centre of Excellence for Coral Reef Studies, James Cook University; Townsville, Queensland

Asha walked into the science block and was immediately impressed with the size of the big room. The central area was brightly lit by a large skylight with a brilliant sun shining down onto a cylindrical aquarium she estimated had to be seven or eight metres high and ten or more metres in diameter. Two curved staircases bracketed either side of the giant tank and schools of colourful reef fish darted between sea turtles and groupers.

She glanced at the GPS app on her mobile and noted the location of Professor Pratt's office. She opted for the stairs and walked up the spiral to the third floor and turned down a long hall. It was easy enough to find the door. She checked the brass plate: Professor Sean Pratt, Environmental Science. She knocked.

"Come on in."

She opened the big, wooden door and entered.

"I'm back here." His voice came from the office on the far side of the meeting room in which she stood.

"Sean?"

"Asha." He immediately stood and came into the large anteroom. "How are you?" He took her hand and shook it, then awkwardly sort of gave her a loose hug.

"I'm great, Sean... so good to see you." She chuckled to herself. He obviously had no idea of what was appropriate and what wasn't. It'd been a long time since she last saw him, but he was still as handsome as she remembered him.

"Here... have a seat." He gestured towards the table. "How about a cuppa?"

"I'll have tea."

He grabbed two mugs. "English Breakfast tea okay?"

"My favourite."

He dropped a tea bag in each cup and held them under the big hot water urn on the service table. "Milk?"

"Please."

He pulled a carton of milk from the little refrigerator, poured some milk in one mug, closed the door and carried the two mugs to the table. "I hope that's enough milk?"

"That's great, Sean."

"Jeez... I'm trying to remember the last time I saw you... In person, of course. I see you every now and again on GNN. And you'd better damn well believe Sacha keeps me informed as to what you're doing."

"I know. Believe me, I feel the same about him."

"I'm glad we get to chat a bit before my crew comes in. My crew..." He sat back in his seat and smiled. "You know, you lived with a father that was so through and through an academic that it probably seems second nature to you. I find myself following in his footsteps. Your father is my 'academic dad' as it were, and in many ways, he's almost a dad in the personal sense, too... probably the dad I never really had. And like your father, I take my doctoral students to heart... To me, they are very much like a family... they ARE my family. The older I get, I find myself actually thinking of them as my 'kids', yet that probably reflects more on my never having had a serious partner."

Asha considered it, but then let that comment go. "He's a great person, Sean... and I know he thinks the world of you."

"The feeling is mutual, believe me."

"I'm sure." Her radiant smile seemed even brighter than usual this morning. "You two must chat fairly regularly."

"For sure. We talk at least once a week and probably two or three times a week is more the norm. Hell, in the past seven or eight days, I swear I must have talked to him nearly every day, which, considering his beloved Asha is visiting, is pretty amazing." Sean smiled and nodded his head at her. "So your dad tells me you're working on a major in-depth story on mutations... on how so many different diseases seem to be changing their stripes simultaneously, so to speak."

"Well, yeah... In the first instance, we were onto a story that nominally caught my colleague's attention involving multidrug-resistant TB. I don't actually know where the term MDR-TB came from, but the World Health Organisation pretty much uses that moniker exclusively anymore. Sadly, we seem to have gone from a world that had all but defeated tuberculosis to being up to our ears fighting it all over again. My colleague Karl – that's Karl Grimsley with whom I am working on this – quickly learned that there is no great mystery here. Actually, tuberculosis is a wonderful example of modern medicine demonstrating how science can alleviate human pain.

"Over thousands of years, untold tens-of-thousands of people would have died from TB. When maybe 125-150 years ago it was finally recognised just how contagious the disease really was, people were at first isolated... put in sanatoriums. By the 1920s, the first vaccines were developed and eventually used throughout the western world, at least. By World War Two, the discovery of streptomycin led to successful treatment of the disease."

"That sounds like a tremendous success story. So, what happened?" Sean knew the answer but enjoyed seeing his mate's daughter for the first time in a decade.

"Somehow, I think you know this, Sean, but basically what happened was sloppiness. Increasingly, modern pharmacology has produced more and more effective antibiotics, but in some cases, treatment must be followed for up to six months. I guess it's human nature, but often people feel better and just stop taking the drugs. Of course, that means some of the bacteria that causes tuberculosis survived because it was preferentially more resistant to the antibiotic. Over time, a new strain of TB bacterium evolved that was resistant to some of modern medicine's best efforts." Asha caught herself. Here she was chatting with an academic who had spent half a career dealing with just this sort of situation, albeit more attuned to marine biology and the ecology of coral reefs. "I'm sorry, Sean. Listen to me going on with someone who already knows all this. I'm here to ask YOU about this."

"Already knows all this... I'm NOT an academic in medical sciences, you know. I do find your story interesting though, but you can't blame multidrug-resistant TB solely on sloppiness. I don't know whether or not we have any numbers, but I'll bet that many times the whole regime of antibiotics wasn't given because of lack of funds, not sloppiness. Many third world countries didn't – or don't – have the funds to follow up treatment for six months. I guess that maybe that's human nature too... having half the world's population poor."

"Now that's a good point, Sean. We come up with first world cures for diseases that affect first world people but don't often fund the cure for third world people. God forbid there are third world diseases like malaria... they don't even get much effort in finding a cure."

He smiled. "Asha, I haven't seen you since... jeez, it has to be eight or nine years ago. I LOVED hearing you tell me what you're working on. Again, I may be a biologist, but it's not like all of us share a depth of medical history. I like your explanation here, and it's a great example of how we humans can mess with Mother Nature. I absolutely agree with you on the ability modern medicine can use to apply science to alleviate human pain, but we can also use science to cause a great deal of human agony, too. Regrettably, my work and my students' work increasingly shows us the latter. We are wreaking havoc on global ecologies, and our magnificent Great Barrier Reef here only emphasises that problem.

"So, don't apologise... I actually want you to go on. I'm curious now since you mentioned the idea that multiple diseases seem to be 'changing their stripes' simultaneously. Can you tell me more about what you mean there?"

Sean's words set Asha at ease, and she definitely felt more comfortable. "Well yeah... besides multidrug-resistant tuberculosis, we're seeing similarities with many other bacterial pathogens causing headaches. Everyone knows about *Staphylococcus aureus*, the so-called Golden Staph infection driving our hospitals crazy of late. We find similarities with other common infections such as gonorrhoea, pneumonia, meningitis, diarrhoea..." Again, she caught herself and hesitated. "There I go again. Please stop me if I am running on too much."

"Please, Asha, I am very interested in what you're telling me."

"Okay... I mentioned diarrhoea... Are you aware of the fact that diarrhoea is one of the leading causes of death of children globally? We have found from WHO statistics that nearly 2,500 kids a day die from diarrhoea... 2,500 A DAY! These are all diseases caused by bacteria. Now once we start including viral diseases, it starts to get particularly scary. You know, the past few years with the return of avian influenza – the 'bird flu' – we have seen a resurgence of the H7N9 virus. When that first showed up in Asia a decade ago, it proved to cause a very lethal form of flu but, fortunately, didn't spread so easily. Now this new variety seems to be both lethal and more easily spread. It got Karl and me thinking that it almost seemed as though these nondescript microorganisms KNEW what they needed to mutate into. Now I know that is not the case, but when I heard Dad and his colleagues go on about cybernetics, about systems and how they seem to respond to data..."

Pratt nodded his head yes. "Asha, you're spot on here. These sorts of things actually DO happen in nature. No one –

especially your father – is saying that there is anything mystical here. It's simply following the laws of nature. You just gave me an excellent example with MTB – *Mycobacterium tuberculosis* bacteria. The first bacteria to die are the ones most susceptible to isoniazid and rifampicin, and the ones that survive are resistant. Now when people don't take the full course of antibiotics, the microbe survivors are statistically more and more resistant. Considering that a generation of bacteria can begin reproducing in hours, mutations are super quick. In this case, humans helped. In most cases, Mother Nature helps by throwing differing environmental conditions at the organisms."

"I know for sure you can tell me a thing or two about TB... that *Mycobacterium tuberculosis* bacteria and isoniazid and rifampicin rolled off your tongue a little bit too easy for you to play dumb to my ramblings. And I'm surprised a marine biologist... er, an environmental scientist... just happens to know of isoniazid and rifampicin." Her expression was almost an 'I gotcha' look.

"Be nice, Asha. You shouldn't be surprised to hear that antibiotics keep showing up in water... mostly lake and river water, but even in coastal waters over the reef. God knows what people wash down their drains and... what agriculture washes away as runoff from cattle feed, pig feed, chicken feed... We humans don't just discharge toxins and trash in the waters, but even pour medicines into our waterways."

"You have convinced me... I wasn't thinking about antibiotics showing up in the world, so to speak." She looked at him and was encouraged by his smile. "I really want to pick your brain on the whole mutation issue, though."

"For starters, remember that I am one of Sacha's biggest disciples. I have been devoted to his *Gaia* inclinations since I first met him fresh out of undergraduate studies. I do not have the smallest modicum of doubt that the whole of Earth is one interconnected system that encompasses like trillions of trillions of smaller systems all operating together." Pratt waved his hand toward a decorative sign hanging on the wall behind Asha. "I believe that bit of John Donne was written 400 years ago, but his 'No man is an island entire of itself' quote stands as a testament to all of us being part of a community. Yes, yes... maybe Hemmingway used that to reflect on war 300 years later, but I read Donne the way a Buddhist would read him, no one... no part of nature... is an island. We are as much a part of Gaia as is the *Mycobacterium tuberculosis* bacteria is... as much as the H7N9 virus is. The only difference between *Homo sapiens* and *Mycobacterium tuberculosis* is that we actually think we know more than old Mother Earth... *Mycobacterium tuberculosis* just is."

33

Wednesday, 24 April; Yunupingu Institute of Medical Research, Melbourne, Victoria

"Are you okay, Fell?" Liz sat in her office chair and had her company phone on speaker.

"Yeah... yeah... Don't worry about me, Lizzy. There's nothing I can do, anyway. I'm stuck here in your unit in a soft quarantine and just hope it stays that way. I've been scared to death the Victorian Department of Health is going to lock me away somewhere."

"Don't be silly, Felly. That's not going to happen."

"Well, I'm still pretty useless to anyone. I guess all I can do is sit here and cry." She sobbed into the phone."

"Fell-O... I have a meeting shortly, and I will try to get out of here early. How about I pick up Chinese on the way home?"

"I don't know if I can eat yet."

"You have to eat, woman!"

There was a hesitation... "You know, Lizzy... I can't even grieve properly yet. Hell, this is so out-of-the-ordinary. I can't even be like a normal widow – whatever normal means – and plan my husband's funeral. I have to wait for the Victorian Department of Health and Human Services to let me know when they will release the body so that that can happen."

"They will soon, Felly."

"Will they? Helen Trainor stopped by this morning and – in the nicest way she could possibly do it – told me they can't approve of even allowing cremation until the Victorian Coroner's Office gives them the go-ahead. This is so far out of my hands... out of our hands..."

"Aw man, Fell... Maybe we can hurry that along over here at Yunupingu. I mentioned the meeting I'm heading to. It's actually with people from the Coroner's Office and the Victoria Police. You know that we have agreed to do whatever analytical work they need to be done. Damn... simply put, we're the only logical group in Victoria capable of doing it safely and competently. I think by the time I get home this afternoon, I'll be able to at least give you a bit of certainty... a bit of light at the end of this tunnel."

"Damn Lizzy, I hope so. Once they clear all of this we can get on with the cremation and then at least plan a funeral service. I have resigned myself to never seeing my Geoff again, but I somehow need to come to terms with the finality of his passing and then at least begin to think about moving on with my life."

"It'll happen, Fell. Trust me when I tell you that if there's anything on this end that I can do, I will."

"Thanks, Lizzy."

"I'll be home after the meeting. Oh... I'm making an executive decision... I'm buying Chinese at Chin's on the way home!"

* * *

"I'm glad we are all here this morning. I want to start by freely admitting that I – well, at least those of us here at Yunupingu Institute – have a personal stake in this too since Felicia Kovac is our colleague and friend. That said, I speak for all of us when I say that we will do our professional best to perform whatever analytical tasks you need."

"Thanks, Dr O'Rourke. I know this must be very difficult, but you are doing a great service for both our institutions and the community at large. This would be such a difficult task without your help." Dr Gephardt spoke for the Victorian Coroner's Office.

Liz nodded. "Let me at least make sure we all know each other. You do know me... This is Dr Deshi Tang. Felly, Deshi and I are the three lead researchers here at the Institute. I thought I'd bring along one of our laboratory technicians, too. This is Wendy Ingman."

"Thanks, Dr O'Rourke. Now if I haven't introduced myself, let me say that I am Dr Lloyd Gephardt from the Coroner's Office. Next to me is Inspector Tony Benson and Inspector Sonny Liu, both of the Victoria Police Department."

There were several cards exchanged across the table. Liz sat back and surveyed the officials seated across from her. "Now exactly what can we do?"

Dr Gephardt tilted his head. "Let me start by saying this is a peculiar case in that we pretty much know what happened, and yet the nature of the cause of death requires us to check every possibility. Even more, because of the presence of *Zaire ebolavirus*, we are required to sterilise – read that destroy – all items at the end of data collection. Of course, that means all biological and non-biological pieces of evidence."

"Dr Gephardt, you say 'evidence' almost as if you suspect foul play. Is that the case?" Deshi gritted his teeth.

"No, no... please don't make any inference from me using the term evidence. It's just that everything we have collected could help us more fully understand what happened here. Now, remember, I say it 'could' help us, but we just don't know."

Liz spoke up. "Okay, so there is nothing suspicious here. What exactly do you want us to analyse? To look for?"

"In the first instance, we would like to analyse tissue samples and confirm that it was the *Zaire ebolavirus* that was the cause of death. Frankly, we did collect everything from clothing to PPE packets that we have transported over here in proper isolation containers, but I honestly believe we can wrap this up fairly quickly just by confirming the *Zaire ebolavirus*."

Again, Liz looked at Dr Gephardt. "That sounds pretty straight forward, Doc. We can have Deshi and Wendy do those analyses if you like, probably this afternoon." She looked at her colleagues, and they both were shaking their heads yes. "I'm happy to have any of your technicians look over our shoulder if need be, but it does get crowded in our biosecurity level 4 laboratory."

"No, no, I don't think that will be necessary, Dr O'Rourke. We are all professionals here. There is nothing any of our lab techs could do to make your job easier or more complete. Besides that, the way a Coroner's Inquest works here in Victoria is that we would call any specialist we like to the hearing and you will be required to testify under oath. It's all fairly straight forward, and in this case, we don't anticipate anything contentious. In a sense, you two..." He looked at Deshi and Wendy. "...are, in reality, providing this work as a community service to the state. Now the Victorian government will reimburse you for all equipment and supplies used and of course, your time."

Liz nodded her head. "That all makes sense."

"What kind of time frame are you talking here?" Deshi scratched his chin using one finger.

"ASAP... Absolutely. You tell us – in what sort of time frame can you complete the work?"

"Oh, we'll be quick. I mean five or ten years ago, this could have taken two, three days or a week or more. We have the latest gear here." Liz looked down at a paper on the table in front of her. "Tissue samples, DNA runs, mass spectrometry, pharmaceutical analysis, chemical traces... I don't promise you a report today, but we should get this together in twenty-four to forty-eight hours. Look, tomorrow is a Commonwealth holiday, so I would assume we can have a preliminary report to you by sometime Friday."

"Wow. That's a damned sight faster than either the police or the Coroner can generally get things done, Dr O'Rourke. As for tomorrow, I know it's ANZAC Day, and most people will have off, but the Police Department never sleeps, you know." He smiled smugly and nodded his head.

"Fair enough. Anyway, as I told you, we are lucky to have the latest equipment. I do admit to wanting this completed post-haste for a very personal reason. Felicia Kovac is my friend, and she is right now stuck in that lousy first stage of grief. The sooner we get this over with, the sooner she can put the shock and denial behind her. It is nearly impossible to move on from that until we can clear Geoff's Kovac's body for cremation."

"I understand, Dr O'Rourke."

"Well, let's get on this." Liz pushed a piece of paper toward Deshi. "These are the bits that Dr Gephardt needs, Deshi. Let's do this ASAP."

"Will do, Liz."

34

Wednesday, 24 April; Townsville District
Police Headquarters, Queensland

"You do have Bluetooth on that bucket of bolts, yes?"

"Hey, hey, Clint... you be nice to my brand-new computer. You ASIO guys obviously don't have the same appropriations routine that we everyday Queensland coppers do, but it took me three years of requisitions to get my old one replaced, and that was..." Leon counted on his one hand and moved to the other. "...six or seven years old. This, mate, is the latest technology." He clicked a button or two.

"My mobile should be visible to you now."

"Under control, mate... I got it." A click or two and Rumford had copied the video file onto his desktop. "You might drag that chair around this side if you want to see this. You're looking at a high definition 38-inch monitor here, Clint. It's a piece of beauty, isn't it?" Rumford ran his fingers over the side of the screen, his smile telegraphing his pride at his new, high definition monitor.

"Yeah, yeah... just play the damned thing, would ya?"

The screen flickered and then came to life with a full-screen image looking over two petrol bowsers. There was a big sign on the left side of the picture, but it was too obtuse to make out the name. "Where's this again?"

"It's the Snake Bend Road House maybe 65 or 70 kilometres north of us along the coastal road. This is their CCTV footage from Monday the 15th. Now the boys have been through this, so we have avoided the many tedious hours of goannas and pink galahs. Here, you'll see in a minute..."

"See? There ain't a freaking thing to see but..." As soon as Rumford started complaining, a white Toyota HiLux ute came into the screen on the left and quickly headed north and off the screen on the right. "That's it?"

"Well, that's not all of it."

Rumford used his mouse to freeze the screen, back up and run it again. After the third run, he froze it and zoomed in on the back of the ute. "Damn. I can't read a plate number."

"Nah, too obtuse. We ran the AI on this and son-of-a-bitch, even that couldn't come up with a number. But zoom in on the bed."

Rumford did. "Big deal... there's a few two by fours, several bags of... looks like mulch and a duffle bag. By the way... does the road keep going north or is it a dead-end near Lady Lyman Beach up there?"

"No, that's pretty much the end of the line. There are a couple of cattle roads off the sides, but no real road."

"Fair enough."

Navarro waved his finger towards the screen. "Right. Now let it go again."

Leon let it run. It was obvious that the ASIO blokes had cut out the junk and included the segments worth seeing. In less than a minute, they both watched the white ute travel from the right side of the image to the left, obviously heading south along the same stretch of road."

"Freeze and zoom again."

He did, and they saw the exact same contents in the back of the ute. "Okay, what am I missing. You see a ute go north and..." Leon was looking for a timestamp.

"About an hour later – forty-eight minutes to be precise – it goes south with the bed looking identical. Remember, this is Monday. Now go forward. The next two instances are on Tuesday, 16 April... that's the day the *Reef Explorer* was blown up."

They watched. Again, the Toyota drove past the road house to the north and again, the back bed looked untouched. "What time is this one?" Rumford zoomed on the bed, and again it was identical to the previous day.

"The ute drove north, passing the Snake Bend Road House at 7:32 AM. Keep in mind, the boat was exploded around 9:44 AM."

"Yeah, okay. This bloke – kind of looks like a bloke – drives up the highway two straight mornings and doesn't change a thing in the ute's open bed."

"Right. Now check this out..." The last vision showed the ute coming back south again. "The time stamp here is 10:01. That road house is maybe 15 or 20 minutes south of Lady Lyman Beach." The Toyota came into view on the right and headed off to the left. It was very noticeable that it was moving at a much faster speed this time than the first three appearances. "Check the bed."

Rumford did. The duffle bag was no longer there. "All right. Put this all together. First of all, we can't see the licence plate. That's a freaking bummer. Second of all, we see the ute go up and down that highway two straight days. What in god's name does that have to do with the *Reef Explorer*? Granted, the second day he was travelling faster, but that in and of itself doesn't matter."

"True, but the duffle bag is gone, too."

"Come on, Clint. We KNOW the *Reef Explorer* blew when a burner phone activated a blasting cap that set off a jerry can of petrol. No one needed a duffle bag with – I guess that was your point – a bomb in it."

"No, no... that wasn't my point at all."

"Well?"

"My point is this. Imagine this bloke goes up the road on Monday and sees the university technical guys bringing the *Reef Explorer* in so it'd be ready for Pratt and his students the next morning. Now I don't know if the suspect here actually set the trigger on Monday or not, but when he was happy, he drives back south. On Tuesday morning, he goes back up there early and maybe sits on the beach a bit. We've got to account for over two hours here. He went north at 7:31 and speeds south at 10:01... What would he have done all that time? The scenario that I'm thinking says he probably grabbed his bag, opened a towel and played beach bunny for a couple of hours. When he went back to his ute, he tossed his bag in the front seat, pulled out the burner phone, made the call that set off the explosion, then high tailed out of there.

"Well, this is all well and good... great circumstantial evidence here, but we don't have the ute's numbers."

"There are two more CCTV bits on there, Leon. Click on them."

Leon did. The first showed a white Toyota Landcruiser heading north on the coastal road. "Read the time stamp... Tuesday at 8:14. Zoom in."

Leon did. "Fair enough – James Cook University seal on the side. Obviously, that's Pratt." He moved the image to the cabin. And sure enough, there's Pratt and the three students. I notice we can't see their plates, either."

"You can't bitch at the road house. They are looking at folks ripping them off for fuel and food. They want to see the cars where they are parked, so the angle is impossible for seeing car plates on the road."

"True enough. But how do you know there weren't more cars... more times the ute passed..."

"A couple of things here. I chatted with the owner of the Snake Bend Road House... nice bloke. He said this time of year they don't get traffic. School is still in, the weather hasn't changed enough down south, and it's slow. He said they did a good business on the long Easter weekend, but that was way early this year... the end of March. Most years the traffic starts to pick up in mid-to-late May and is really good in June, July and August... sometimes into September. It's cold down in Sydney and Brisbane, and you get a lot of folks taking kids up to Innisfail, Cairns and Port Douglas for a bit of a warm getaway during the winter months. This road does dead-end, but folks still use the beach in winter. Basically, he has to make his money four or five months a year and then just lay back."

"Well, what's the last segment. You said there were two more bits, right?"

"I did."

Rumford clicked on it, and the video ran. A little, bright red Nissan Micra came into the screen from the south, slowed and pulled into the road house. A young man climbed out of the driver's side, disappeared out of the picture for a minute and came back into view carrying what looked like a bottle of drink in one hand and a bag of chips in the other. "Damn, this has potential if they saw the ute."

"Zoom in."

Rumford did. "Yeah, okay... that's a big bottle of Pepsi and a bag of chippies. Ah... ah. Wait a minute." He zoomed on the front of the parked car. "Pretty as can be. That plate number is as plain as day."

"It is... and look on the dash."

Leon moved the zoom up. "Hot damn... that looks like he has a dash cam."

"Looks like... That IS a dash cam."

"Hot shit! You've seen the video?"

"Slow down, mate. We just saw this early this morning. The boys are on it. They have contacted the bloke, and he works here in Townsville. They are interviewing him now and downloading the video. If those two go anywhere near Lady Lyman Beach, we definitely will know about it."

35

Wednesday, 24 April; Centre of Excellence for Coral Reef Studies James Cook University, Townsville, Queensland

"I wasn't expecting you to feed me, Sean." Asha followed the group into his office suite.

"Hey, that's the least I could do for you and for my team here."

Nikki sat on the far side of the table and looked towards their guest. "Believe me, Asha, it's not like either Sean or the university treats us too often. You know the old adage that 'there is no such thing as a free lunch' and all..."

The others followed suit, and all pulled up a chair. "Are you all Queenslanders?"

Becky was first to fire back. "I knew I liked Asha the minute I met her. Most folks from WA call us Banana Benders."

Asha laughed. "Indeed... and then call us Sandgropers!" She pointed at herself.

"Nah... we wouldn't call you a Sandgroper... You live in America now so I think that would make you an honorary Seppo now, aren't you?"

Sean quickly interjected... "Peace, peace... we are all proud Aussies here. Becky's from Brissie, Nikki is from Rockhampton and John... actually, John is kind of a foreigner. He's from someplace called Melbourne."

They all laughed.

"So, Asha, you must be tired. That lousy flight through Brissie is a killer. Why in god's name we can't have a direct flight from Townsville to all the major cities is beyond me."

"Nah, I'm okay, though it did take me almost as long to get from Perth to Townsville as it did from Los Angeles to Perth."

"Damn." John shook his head.

"You guys have had a tough few years, haven't you?" Asha looked towards Sean. "Weatherwise, I mean..."

"Yes, actually. In the past five years, we had those awful bush fires just inland, Cyclone Gillian a few years back and then three – count them, THREE – five-hundred-year floods within five years!"

"Coincidence?"

Sean put the silliest expression he could manage across his face. "Coincidence! Hell no. Our Coral Sea end of the Pacific is closing in on two degrees hotter than the hundred-year average. When you start to do the calculations on how much water that is, the heat capacity of water and therefore how much energy we're talking about, it is blatantly obvious that it's no coincidence. We see it every time we dive over the Reef."

"I can vouch for that." John raised his hand.

"We can ALL vouch for that." Nikki agreed.

"I have no doubt you guys are really close to it all, but even city folks should know beyond a doubt that we reached DEFCON 1 several years back. Sitting here on top of the largest reef on Earth has to drive that home."

"It does, though since you are a journo collecting data, I'd like to take issue with your 'largest reef' comment."

Asha spun her head at Becky's comment. "Ah... help me here. We have a larger reef somewhere?"

Becky smiled. "Well, sure... you grew up near that one. The Great Southern Reef is a system of interconnected temperate reefs that stretch from Kalbarri in the west to Brisbane in the east. I mean, if we just want to go by numbers, the Great Barrier Reef here is maybe 2,200 or 2,300 kilometres along Australia's northeast. The Great Southern Reef extends somewhere like 8,000 kilometres from one end to the other so it would triple the size of the Barrier Reef."

Sean interjected. "True enough, but the tourism folks find it much easier to sell a warm and beautiful tropical Cairns in mid-winter than a cold and rainy Melbourne, Adelaide or Esperance."

"Damn... I never knew that. For that matter, I appreciate your tourism take on things too, Sean."

"We aim to educate." The professor arched his eyes at her. "Maybe it's time for a bit of chemistry. Where do you reckon the most life would be found... the tropical reefs like our Great Barrier Reef or the cooler ones like the Great Southern Reef?"

"That's simple... I'd say the tropical. Look at all the fish we see there. I reckon that's a no-brainer." As soon as Asha said it, she knew she had been lured down the garden pathway to scientific illiteracy.

"Now don't get mad at me, Asha, but that's what just about everyone would say. The reality is that the cold water can hold so much more dissolved oxygen allowing life to explode dramatically. That's why colder water is greener... more phytoplankton. And phytoplankton means food, my dear. That's why the Arctic and Antarctic waters are teaming with life. Now you may laugh at that, but that's also why the largest beasts on Earth... blue whales, the right whales, the finbacks and the humpbacks... all feed in cold waters. It's not coincidental that the largest whales are filter feeders and spend the summer months on both the north and south sides of the equator in the cold Arctic and Antarctic waters eating krill, copepods and other small zooplankton. The very base of the ocean food chain explodes in those colder waters."

"Wow. I didn't know all that."

"My point in all this wasn't to tease you, Asha. My point was to have you meet my students and to share some ideas amongst us all. And to draw a line between what the tourism people put out for mass consumption versus what is factual... what is based on science. I am keen on the work you are doing and want to learn more about it. I tried telling you this morning when you mention that some diseases were 'changing their stripes' simultaneously. We see that, too, though on a macro scale compared to your micro scale or... if you will, microbe-scale."

"How do you mean?"

"Who wants to go first?" Pratt looked around the table.

"I have a strong interest in biochemistry, and we've measured some interesting things on the Reef lately. I don't mean to claim this is brand new, but we are getting a better handle on it now... chemically, I mean. There's a funny story here." Becky's enthusiasm was obvious. "You can be floating over a perfectly healthy reef and notice a brown patch where near all the coral has died and algae are draping all over it. Why? Well, the initial irritant could have been a boat anchor breaking some coral or a shallow clump that was more exposed to bleaching. Whatever, once the algae start to explode in growth, the coral polyps excrete a chemical compound that wafts its way through the water where it is sensed by little goby fish. These fish read that signal as a dinner bell and come for a free feed of algae. Consider... the same chemical is a danger signal for the polyps, but a dinner call to the fish. There are many of these kinds of 'reef-wide' methods of communication going on all the time."

"We've found even more far-reaching chemical signals." John joined the conversation. "I won't go through the whole lifecycle of coral polyps spawning, but let's just say it is truly a miracle of life on Earth. All of that said, the result is a tens-of kilometres long milky cloud of coral larvae floating in the ocean. Technically, these larvae can survive in the sea for weeks, yet they are ready to settle, attach themselves and grow into coral polyps within a week of spawning. How do they know when to settle? Again, they read chemical signals. Though much of their movement is at the whims of currents and wave patterns, they somehow 'know' when to attach."

Nikki nodded towards John. "These are good examples of communication, but I'm sitting here looking out the office window at a stand of magnificent *eucalyptus grandis* in the quadrangle. We can start with how this species has evolved to handle the extremes of Australian climate starting with the deep tap root the seedlings send down the first year after the seedlings have germinated. Consider the leaves... unlike temperate deciduous trees that hold their leaves horizontally to capture the maximum amount of sunlight, all the *eucalyptus grandis* leaves hang straight down vertically to minimise the harsh sunlight of Australian summers. And recently, our colleagues at Macquarie University have discovered this species has generational memory... seedlings produced by parent plants that have experienced severe heatwaves are better able to survive extreme heat because they produce more protective proteins than their cooler weather relatives. Again, this is an example of chemical communications, but in this case, from one generation to another."

"Damn... that's all fascinating stuff. How do they all know?" Asha had heard her dad answer this question a thousand times but thought she'd get a different perspective on it.

Sean leaned forward. "They don't. I'm sure your father has gone on at length about these things, but they needn't KNOW anything. Mother Nature just follows scientific principles and causes these things to happen. I'm the first to admit that these little stories don't, *per se*, feed into your question of worldwide communication within *Gaia*, but they do echo the questions we have that are so very similar to what you are asking.

"In the end, probably our whole educational system's approach to cranking out PhDs may be flawed in that it causes such a myopic study to satisfy examiners' expectations. By that, I simply mean that doctoral research historically calls for such a narrow-focused study." Sean put his hands together with tips touching, indicating a sharp point. "When trying to understand *Gaia*, the focus needs to be exactly the opposite... as broad a view as possible." He extended his fingers and stretched his arms apart as far as he could. "Frankly, I'm not sure it is within human understanding to even appreciate the expanse of *Gaia* because she is EVERYTHING.

"At the end of the day, it's not so easy as just finding a chemical or taking larvae samples or recording whale songs... It makes no sense to say this global communication is not happening simply because we are unable to understand the trillions and trillions of interactions that may happen right in front of our eyes and ears, and yet we are incapable of sensing them. It IS happening."

36

Wednesday, 24 April; Dr Liz O'Rourke's residence, Melbourne, Victoria

Liz came in the door and set her cloth bag with several containers of Chinese food on the counter. "I told you I'd be early. Felly... Felly..."

Felly came walking out of the bedroom wearing a robe and slippers. "Hi, Lizzy."

"I'm so sorry I woke you up."

"You didn't." Her eyes were red, and it was obvious she had been crying. "I was just lying there... thinking..."

"Oh, Fell..." She gave her mate a hug.

Felly's head rested on her friend's shoulder as she spoke. "Did the Coroner's Office people come by today."

"Yes, yes... it's all sorted. Deshi and Wendy are acting on behalf of the coroner. The representative from the Coroner... a Dr Lloyd Gephardt... seemed to have everything they needed under control. I don't know all the technicalities, but he and the Police Inspector told us how concerning a Coroner's Inquest, Deshi and Wendy will be considered actors for the community and will be asked to testify under oath. It sounds to me that anytime the police or coroner need specialised people to help determine whatever they need to determine, they cover it all by swearing those people is as expert witnesses. Look, don't quote me on any of this, but I just know that our people are acting on behalf of the State at this point. Oh... and they will reimburse the Institute for our equipment and time, too."

"Fair enough. I still don't know what it all means..."

"What it means is that this will all be behind us in a day or so. With any luck at all, you can then get on with honouring Geoff and somehow go about trying to pick up the pieces."

Felly was still standing there, her head resting on Liz's shoulder. She pulled back and looked at her friend. "I only wish it would be that easy, Lizzy."

"Whatever you must go through, you know I'll be here at your side. You're my mate. We get through the police stuff by tomorrow, I reckon, and then you can get on with whatever you need to do."

"No... that's what I'm trying to tell you, Lizzy. I don't think it's all going to be that easy... with the police, I mean."

"What are you talking about?"

"I can't believe I didn't tell you this already, but I'll try again. Sunday night... the last time I spoke... spoke to Geoff..." She broke down and dropped onto the sofa, big sobs interrupted by deep breaths.

Liz sat next to her. "Take your time, Fell..."

She pulled herself together as well as she could. "That Helen Trainor from the DHHS took me to the hospital. We went into a nurses' station outside of Geoff's... Geoff's room. A doctor came in and helped me get a headset on so I could... could speak with Geoff..." She broke down again, though managed to pull herself together enough to finish her story. "He was mostly too weak but sounded coherent. He told me that he was jogging in the park on Friday, and some girl came out of nowhere and spilled coffee all over him."

"An accident?"

"I don't know, but I don't think so. Geoff seemed to think it was out of the ordinary."

"Did he recognise her? Did he say anything else?"

"I don't know if he recognised her. Understand, Geoff didn't have an honest-to-god conversation with me since he was pretty much out of it. The last thing he said was that she did it... the girl did it..."

"And what does that mean?"

Felly started crying again. "I don't know... I don't know... I don't..." She curled up and continued to sob.

* * *

Liz thought it was an accomplishment just to coax her friend into eating some of the Chinese food she heated up in the microwave. They chatted minimally at dinner and then sat in the lounge area for a short while until Felly finally drifted off to sleep. Liz lifted her friend's legs onto the sofa and tossed a throw over her, doing what she could to encourage the rest.

"Tweet tweet... tweet tweet..." The ringer on Liz's phone was in the daytime mode. Damn, why didn't she think to put it on silent? She grabbed her mobile and noted that Felly's eyes slowly opened. Liz could see whoever was calling was at Yunupingu Institute. "Liz O'Rourke here."

Deshi responded on the other side of the connection. "Liz, are you able to talk?"

"No, we're just here in the lounge room."

"Is Felly right there?"

"Yes."

"Okay look, we have finished the tick list here, save for a couple of tests I will let run again overnight just as a double-check. I need to talk to you, Liz."

174

"Yeah, yeah... you two have worked way too much for one day." She looked at the time. "It's nearly 10 PM... Why don't you and Wendy get out of there, and I'll check in with you in the morning."

"Got ya." Deshi knew Felly was right there. "I'll be in early... probably by 7:30 or 8:00. There's stuff we need to talk about before I contact Dr Gephardt."

"Don't forget that it's a public holiday tomorrow, yes?"

"Yes, I know I told Wendy not to bother since I can fill you in on all of this. I hope you don't mind coming in, Liz."

"Mind? Of course, I will be there... certainly by 8 AM."

37

Thursday, 25 April; Townsville District
Police Headquarters, Queensland

"Amazing... I can't believe you're actually in today."

"Like I have a choice. I don't reckon the crims take a day off, ANZAC Day or not." Rumford sat back in his chair. "Besides, I reckon I'm going home at lunch today. My missus has some plans... I think we are doing something with my in-laws, and I sure as hell wouldn't want to miss that." Leon's eyes rolled up towards the ceiling.

Navarro laughed. "I'll bet!"

"And you?"

"Well, I had my wife and kids to a sunrise service at ANZAC Park, The Strand... Damn, 5 AM is a bit before I'm usually up, but after I dropped them home, I thought I'd check on you."

"Out and about by 5 AM! I'll give you that, mate... you are way more ambitious than I am as far as ANZAC Services go."

"Well, with any luck, I'm planning on knocking off after half a day, too. I couldn't avoid checking in with you. Besides, I've got good some good news for you and some bad news."

"Let's hear them both."

"Let's do the Bluetooth thing again... Is your computer fired up?"

"It is." Rumford used his mouse to open the link to Navarro's mobile. "What am I looking for?"

"It should be the only thing there... It's a video just labelled Nissan."

"Gotcha." He clicked on the file as Navarro came around to the side of the desk. "So, the Micra's dash cam was working... good stuff."

"It gets better." Clint pointed to the screen as it showed the view over the little compact's bonnet as it turned into the unsealed car park. As the Nissan slowly rolled into the clearing, first the university Landcruiser came into view... obviously Pratt's vehicle. As the Micra turned towards the far side of the car park, the white HiLux ute came into full view. "Freeze it."

Leon did. "Spot on." He used his mouse to zoom in. "They got a great view of the plates."

"Yep. We've already followed up on this, and the HiLux is registered to a Lester Wilkicki. We've got his residence south of town on the Bruce Highway, but haven't been able to get to him as yet. The boys have been there, and they're watching. Maybe he took off for a long weekend. We will see him, count on that."

"He'd be our prime suspect now, right? Is there a bulletin out on him?"

"Yes... check your bulletins. We issued a 'Keep-A-Lookout-For' on him a few hours ago but haven't gone public with it. The last thing we want to do is spook him. I reckon that Wilkicki most likely isn't a threat to the public at large."

"Two bombs? Not a threat?"

"Two bombs that were obviously not intended to hurt anyone. Why risk driving him underground or out of the country?"

"Yeah okay... True enough. At least you issued a KLO4 across all police communications. How about the Nissan Micra? You must have chatted with the owner, no?"

"Yeah, yeah... It's registered to a bloke named Brad Langdon. We obviously caught up with him since you're looking at his video. He and his squeeze... a Lynn McCabe... never saw the driver of the HiLux. They didn't even remember seeing anyone on the beach. They parked at the far side of the car park, so 100 or 125 metres north of where the HiLux was parked here. They went on their beach stroll and walked north, so away from where Wilkicki must have been. They did see the boat and must have jumped when it blew, though they were nearly two kilometres away from it by then."

"So, they didn't chat with anyone?"

"No, but they phoned in the explosion. Langdon said they had a bit of a struggle getting a strong enough signal, but as they walked back towards the car park, they did make the call. Obviously, they don't have great mobile coverage up there. They waited until a rescue vehicle got there about 10:15 or so... pretty good time for being in the middle of nowhere. Fortunately, there was a fishing boat not too far from where the *Reef Explorer* went down, and he had Pratt's people on their way back to the dock by then."

Rumford was counting on his fingers. "They were lucky... picked up within 10 or 15 minutes and then they had Vasquez with the ambos within half an hour. Thank goodness that she wasn't bleeding too badly."

38

Thursday, 25 April; Yunupingu Institute of Medical Research, Melbourne, Victoria

"Liz, Liz… You can't believe how glad I am to see you."

"No problems. I'm just so keen on getting to the end of this." She dropped her jumper on the wall hanger. "When did you get in?"

"You don't want to know… probably about 5 AM or so."

"Deshi… you put so many hours in yesterday that I was hoping…" Liz's words were interrupted.

"Good morning, Liz." Wendy came in from the back of the office suite, obviously having been here for a while.

"Wendy! You too! What are you doing here on a holiday morning?" Liz showed her surprise. "You really didn't need to come in today. I'm sure Deshi could have filled me in."

"I couldn't sleep."

Deshi looked at her. "Me neither."

"Aw jeez… what don't I know here?"

Deshi tilted his head. "I really was afraid we made a mistake, but instead of running the sequence three times, we ran it again – three runs simultaneously – and got the same result. Then I checked that we hadn't used contaminated capsules, or the equipment hadn't been autoclaved… Everything keeps saying we followed all regs."

"For crying out loud, Deshi. What did you find already?" Liz's impatience was getting the best of her now.

"Well, better that I show you the printouts. Let's go into the staff room, and I can project them for you."

All three of them sat around the big table. The overhead projector came to life as Deshi sat with his laptop in front of him. "We did what we always do running the polymerase chain reaction technique... the PCR. We had several samples run in parallel... two of the Thailand *Zaire ebolavirus* samples that Felly brought back and two of the samples from the synthetic virology research we've been working on. Finally, we had two samples from Geoff... um, Dr Kovac. One was from his sputum and one from his blood."

"Okay, so far, so good. You ran the PCR, and I assume you recycled it repeatedly through the spectrum of temperature variations, yes?"

"Yes."

"How many cycle repeats?"

"Last night... 35. The overnight run we did 50."

"And..."

"And when Wendy and I did the same with the overnight results, we fed the whole pile of data into the AI program and matched them up... Here's what we got."

He flipped through a series of slides showing hundreds of combinations of A, C, G, T... differing orders, differing sequences... Some were shown in different colours, and the artificial intelligence matched shorter segments against the long chain of the samples. All of this would have been gobbledygook to the untrained eye, but Liz, Deshi and Wendy stared at the screen and winced.

Liz finally broke the silence. "Sample DTG2024-0238 is ours, right?"

"Yes." Wendy knew the number by heart since she ran the original sequencing.

"And the blue sequencing is Geoff's?"

"Yes."

Liz sat back in the chair, rubbed her eyes and then let them drift to the ceiling. She let out a long, slow breath and then inhaled. "I sure as hell don't think there is any mistake here. Geoff's virus was ours... Geoff definitely didn't die from the Thai strain of *Zaire ebolavirus*. This indicates very conclusively that he died from the synthesised virus we created right here at the Institute a couple of months ago."

"But that doesn't make sense, Liz." Deshi was almost angry at himself for the results of his work. "As far as we know, that synthetic virus was deactivated."

Wendy was quick to add her take on it all. "Yeah, as far as we knew..."

"Regrettably, it all has to make sense. Neither Geoff or Felly actually thought he had contracted EVD in Thailand. They were both so certain that the quarantine the Victorian government ordered was all a big furphy. Felly went on with that a dozen times last week. Then all the sudden Geoff came down with symptoms... It's possible to show symptoms within a day or two of exposure, but that's a damned unusual occurrence. Generally, you'd expect several days to a week or more." Liz was thinking out loud now. "We follow every level 4 biosecurity procedure here. I have no doubt that every one of us does that."

"It couldn't be not following procedures." Deshi voice was sure. "Hell, we'd all be showing symptoms if that were the case. For that matter, I don't remember even seeing Geoff here at Yunupingu since they came back last week, do you?"

"Na... and I've been around every day." Wendy stared at the wall as if hoping the answer would somehow just pop up there.

"No... no, I didn't see him here either. He went back to work the first day or two. And Felly is living with me at my place now, and she shows no symptoms at all. *Zaire ebolavirus* doesn't just spontaneously appear. It had to come from somewhere..." She leaned back again and whispered to herself... "Spilled coffee?"

"Pardon me, Liz?"

"No, it was nothing, Deshi. Look, we have to report this to Dr Gephardt tomorrow. You have to give them everything you have and don't sugar coat it. They are going to have you and Wendy testify at the inquest eventually, so be one-hundred per cent honest with them. Remember, both the Coroner's Office and the Victorian Police are competent professionals. They will get to the bottom of this, I have no doubt."

39

Thursday, 25 April; The Strand, Townsville, Queensland

"It's all just beautiful, Sean."

"It is. Like anywhere else in the world, if you stay in one place long enough, it is too easy to forget all the reasons you originally had for settling there. In my case, The Great Barrier Reef was a no-brainer, but there is so much more to Townsville. The weather is mostly great, the scenery spectacular and the lifestyle fitting to my personality. Best of all, it isn't the Big Smoke like Sydney or Melbourne. I'm just never all that comfortable in the big city for more than a two or three-day conference."

"I can understand that. Whether you are an academic or not, it's always nice going to work in shorts and thongs. I've been in Chicago for half a decade now, and in the summertime, we dodge thunderstorms and tornadoes, and in the wintertime, we scrape car windows in negative 20 or 25-degree temperatures. Plus, with three million people or so, I can identify with feeling overwhelmed by wall-to-wall people, too."

"Listen to you... all those years in the States and you have difficulty saying minus 5 to minus 15!" He laughed.

"My using Celsius temperatures were all in deference to you, Professor Pratt!"

"Speaking of which, it must be 27 or 28 already, and it's not quite noon."

"Yes, it's actually warm... the sun feels great for being late in April. I'm impressed with the relaxed feel here on the Strand."

"Well, it's ANZAC Day, and almost everybody has the day off from work. The weather sure is conducive to a day on the waterfront, wouldn't you say?"

"I would."

"Hey, how about a gelato?" He reached out to hold her hand and gave her a gentle tug toward a little al fresco café under a magnificent banyan tree. "These guys have the greatest gelato."

"I love it." Asha wasn't sure if he held her hand as a sign of being nice to his academic mentor or if there was something more happening here. "What a perfect spot."

"What'll it be." They both looked into the refrigerated display at a rainbow of flavours. "I LOVE the banana chocolate swirl."

"Oh... I don't know... maybe that vanilla blueberry crumble sounds good... like it's calling my name."

"Settled... two grandes, right?"

"Oh... I was thinking maybe the piccolo size."

"Piccolo... that's the small one, Ash. I watched you eat lunch and – though I don't know where you put it – you seemed to have fun enjoying the eggs benedict croissant."

Asha was enjoying the banter. "So are you saying you think I'm a big eater... maybe a bit overweight."

Pratt knew he had gotten himself into an awful, no-win situation, and he hoped his boyish grin would help extract him from it. "Of course not! I just reckon you must do a lot of running or rowing or be a regular at the local fitness centre to be in such good shape as you are."

"Thanks, Sean. I'm not as regular as I should be, but I do jog when I can. I tend to travel a lot for GNN and at least pack my runners. Regrettably, I don't always use them. How about you?"

"I guess the same. I try to run... and swim when I can. Fortunately, we dive a couple of days a week."

They grabbed their gelatos, Sean held his mobile out to the scanner over the counter, nodded to the clerk and they took a seat looking out at the sea.

"Is that Magnetic Island?" Asha gestured towards the ocean.

"Yep... most of the locals call her Maggie Island. It's an interesting spot if you ever have the time to see her, but it will take you the better part of a day. I don't get out there regularly, but the ferries run frequently, and it's a bit less than an hour each way."

"Any good beaches or will the crocs eat you?" She giggled.

"Crocs? Hell, you have more worry with stingers – the little jellyfish – most of the time. They do have protected areas, though."

Asha tasted a scoop of gelato. "Yummy... this is so good."

"It's so nice to be able to spend a day with you. I can't believe it's been so long."

Asha took another mouthful of gelato and dapped her lips with her serviette. "It has... You know, when you were Dad's student, and I was still in high school, I used to be so infatuated with you."

Sean could almost feel himself blushing. "Well, I never knew that."

"Certainly, I would never have said it... and Dad knew I would KILL him if he ever mentioned it to you."

"You told Sacha this?"

Asha looked down at her half-eaten gelato. "No, of course not. I have no doubt that he figured it out, though. Dad is a damned perceptive bloke, you know. Try as I might, it was always hard trying to pull one over on him, even back when Mum was alive." It crossed her mind to mention that her dad still teased her about it but thought better of that.

"So where to from here?"

"I'm really into this story, Sean. My off-sider, Karl Grimsley, is on his way to Alaska and the Siberia right now. He's tracking down the so-called zombie organisms they're finding in the melting permafrost. We are wondering if there is any relationship between those and the *Zaire ebolavirus* spread across Southeast Asia and now even touching Singapore. Of course, I don't mean any relationship between the actual microbes, but just with the seemingly accelerated speed of mutations. There just seem to be more mutations happening than there should be, and we have been wondering if there's some sort of unseen communication going on between nature and the microbes."

"Communications between nature and microbes? Interesting thought here..." Sean shifted in his chair. "I don't know how we can actually say there are more mutations. That's a difficult thing to put numbers on. Hell, as we see Earth heating up, we also see changes speeding up. That's just a law of chemistry you learn in high school, I reckon. Heat speeds reaction rates up. Obviously, I spend my life looking at the marine biology end of things... spend so much time floating over and studying the reef. We see changes in the reef all the time, and some of that includes mutations of microbes, mutations of coral polyps.

"You mention communications within nature, we see that sort of thing all the time. Do you know *Acanthaster planci*, the crown-of-thorns starfish?"

"Yes, of course, I've heard of the crown-of-thorns starfish. Growing up in Australia, it'd be difficult not to have heard about them, even living in WA."

"Well next to coral bleaching and cyclones, both accelerated by global warming, the next biggest threat to the Great Barrier Reef is the crown-of-thorns starfish. You'd know that these creatures live on a diet that consists mostly of eating the coral."

Asha nodded her head. "Yes, yes... to the point they could kill the coral, right?"

"Exactly. But what you may not know is the excellent example they offer demonstrating the idea of communication amongst creatures in nature. We've recently had a team of Aussies and Japanese researchers who have sequenced the genome of *Acanthaster planci*. They also analysed these 'plumes' of chemicals the starfish seemed to follow to find mates and mapped these proteins to the starfish genome. Surprise, surprise... they were able to synthesise a starfish 'perfume' – don't take that term literally – that lured love-sick creatures all to one spot from which they could be gathered and disposed of. How's that for communications."

"Bloody hell... That's is just what I'm talking about. I wonder if bacteria and viruses can do that, too?"

"I assume, but I confess to not being at the forefront of viral research."

Asha drank half a glass of water in one swallow. "This is why I have been keen on picking your brain – and your student's brains and Dad's brain, for that matter – about communication in nature. Karl and I are trying to find any link between Mother Nature – *Gaia* – somehow making a concerted effort to damage *Homo sapien*."

"Wow... that's a fairly extreme piece of conjecture."

"Keep in mind, I've listened to Dad for my whole life and often consider his work with how cybernetics functions on a planetwide level to keep things within survivable parameters.

You no doubt know this in greater depth than I do since he was your PhD supervisor. We – Karl and I – just wonder if it is that much of a stretch to think that *Homo sapiens* may be at least as deadly to *Gaia* as the Great K-T Boundary Meteor 66 million years ago?"

Sean leaned back in his seat and pushed the now-melted remains of his gelato around with his wooden spoon. He looked at Asha and arched his eyebrows. "You know, I'd imagine 90% of my colleagues doing environmental research at the level we do in the university system would agree with you... But I also would bet you that 95% of them would be scared to death to say what you are suggesting out loud. I reckon if we did, we'd be on the pathway to dried up funding and no more publications. I needn't tell you that no grants and no papers equal no jobs in an academic setting."

"Surely, you aren't saying that the only reason you do what you do – your research that is – is to win funding and write papers, Sean."

"No, not at all... Give me a break! If anything, we have to temper our actual results and make things seem more optimistic than they really are so as not to scare pollies and business folks to death! I actually believe what you are implying, but that's downright scary to the average citizen. What you are proposing sounds like some wild science fiction thriller written by some science hack. I mean, after a hundred years of 'man-against-nature' scenarios, you seem to be suggesting that it will all end with a 'nature-defeats-man' final battle."

"Or worse yet, a 'man-defeats-nature' if we *Homo sapiens* prove to be the next giant meteor impact that actually causes the Sixth Great Extinction."

40

Friday, 26 April; Dr Liz O'Rourke's residence, Melbourne, Victoria

"Son-of-a-bitch! I had to show my ID at my own freaking front door... TWICE! Downstairs and then again in the hallway."

"There's a cop outside the door?"

"Yes... on a seat. It doesn't look like he'll be leaving any time soon."

Felly got up from the sofa, her robe half open revealing her pyjamas. "I can't even believe this... believe any of this."

"Oh my god, Fell-O." Liz looked below the robe at the electronic monitor tethered around her friend's ankle. "Where in the hell do they think you're going?" She gave her friend a hug. "Oh, Felly... I'm so sorry all this is happening."

Felly had shed so many tears the past few days that she started to think she'd never be able to cry again. "Thanks for being my friend, Lizzy."

Liz exhaled. "Let's sit down."

They did... side by side on the sofa. "What happened, Liz? Why did they put me under house arrest? The Inspector said I was under suspicion of killing Geoff. Killing Geoff..." She sobbed on her friend's shoulder.

"It's stupid, Fell. Deshi and Wendy ran all those tests repeatedly. With yesterday being a holiday, they ran the whole battery of tests for the third time. I saw all the DNA nucleotide sequence printouts and the chromatograms... Sure enough, the samples from Geoff matched up with the synthetic virology research we've been doing. It wasn't the Thai strain of *Zaire ebolavirus* samples you brought back. The good news is that you were exactly correct... Geoff didn't contract the

EVD up there. The bad news is that the EVD he has contracted came from Yunupingu Institute. We know you had nothing to do about it, but we somehow need to prove that."

"We need to PROVE that I am innocent. I'm a scientist, not a lawyer, but I seem to remember somewhere in my schooling that in Australia, the burden of proving someone committed a crime falls on the Crown, yes?"

"Yes, of course. This is a very strange situation though since the Institute seems to have the only expertise capable of doing that in Victoria and possibly in Australia. So far, it seems as though we have found evidence pointing at ourselves!"

"But how about the coffee?"

"The coffee... oh yes, the spilled coffee. You know, I didn't think of that. Since Deshi told me of the results he and Wendy found, I've been so concentrating on what we did wrong... on how the tests could be misleading. I forgot what you told me Geoff said to you."

Felly slowly rolled onto her side and sobbed. Liz sat there with Felly's head now lying across her lap, letting her hands play through her friend's hair. She had to come up with a plan...

"What am I going to do, Lizzy?"

Liz bit her lip. "It's what are WE going to do, Fell-O. You aren't alone in this. This has to do with the whole team. We are ALL in this together."

"Thanks, Lizzy."

"For starters, we need to somehow look into the coffee cup mystery here. I met a couple of coppers yesterday that seemed pretty openminded. They were... damn, what were their names?" She felt through her jumper pocket... "Wait a minute, Fell." Liz stood and walked over to her bag. She quickly found a couple of business cards and returned to the sofa. "Okay, let's see here. They were Inspectors Tony Benson and Sonny Liu, and Sonny is part of their forensic team. How about I give them a call and see if we can have a chat with them. We have to start somewhere, Fell."

Felly never lifted her head but grunted her agreement.

* * *

"Can you think of anything else, Fell?"

"That's all I can think of."

Liz could see that Felly seemed to have actually turned a corner here. Though she was hesitant at bringing the coppers in right away, she could see that Felly almost rose to the occasion. Now maybe facing the challenge of finding out what really happened would be the best way she could celebrate Geoff's life. Possibly her friend had now turned her grief into determination.

"So, let's go over the coffee incident in a bit more detail." Inspector Benson had his notepad out and his pen at the ready. "Can you tell me more about the park... about how long Geoff jogged?'

"The park is nearly between our Medical Science Building where Yunupingu is and Yarra Hospital... I'm pretty sure it's Fraser Park."

"Yes, yes... there's a Fraser Park there, at the end of Lismore Street, yes?"

"Yes. That's the one." Felly moved a piece of hair from her eye. "Now I couldn't tell you exactly how long he was running on Friday..."

The Inspector interrupted. "No, no, Dr Kovac. I understand you don't have exact details from Friday. Can you give me an idea of what his normal routine would be, though?"

"Well, it wouldn't have been a normal routine, since he was not allowed to work then with the quarantine. Normally he'd run in the morning... four or five days a week, anyway. This would have been maybe mid-morning on Friday, and I was at the Institute. Anyway, Geoff always wore trackies or shorts if the day was warm. I'd think he wore track shorts Friday because it was a nice morning from what I remember, anyway."

"I checked the weather. It was 26.7 Friday morning at 11 AM and got to a high of 29.2 around 12:30 PM. Remember, that front came through later in the afternoon, and we had a downpour. The official gauge had 22 mils by 7 PM... down to 16 degrees then, too." Inspector Liu was reading from his own pad.

Felly nodded. "I'm sure he'd have worn shorts and a tee. Anyway, he usually went outside the house, would do his stretches, sometimes hanging onto the back of the car if it was out of the garage. Then he'd jog off. Occasionally I'd go with him on the weekend, and he'd jog over to the park, lap it a few times and then come back the other way down Philpot Street and over Evans back home. He'd mostly go for about 30 minutes. Hey, the bloke was a medical doctor and pretty disciplined about his exercise."

"Who do you see in that park? I mean... what sorts of people?" Benson kept writing as she spoke.

"Just what you'd expect in Melbourne, Inspector." Felly's eyes were mostly dry now, and she spoke very matter-of-factly. "Mums with babies and prams, kids running and climbing, old folks strolling... For sure, it attracted lots of joggers and the occasional the yoga folks."

"Do you think he knew the woman?"

"I'd have no idea, Inspector. He was having great difficulty speaking. He struggled to say something like 'girl spilled coffee... she... did... it...'" Finally, it proved too much for Felly, and she sobbed, dabbing her nose with a tissue.

"Anything else, Dr Kovac?"

"I can't... I can't... Look, it's not that I don't remember. I only spoke with Geoff for a minute or 90 seconds at most. He was nearly incoherent and frankly, it wasn't like we had a normal conversation. What I've told you here is what he told me."

"Hum..." Sonny Liu rubbed his chin. "Fraser Park is a sizable place. Surely the city has CCTV cameras in there. This was late Friday morning, is that correct?"

"Somewhere between mid and late Friday morning, yes."

He looked to his pad. "So that'd be Friday, 19 April sometime before noon. I think that's enough to point us in the right direction, Dr Kovac."

41

Friday, 26 April; Townsville District
Police Headquarters, Queensland

Hasler stuck her head in Rumford's door. "We got him here, Leon. I trust that you got my message, yeah?"

"Sure did, Katie. You picked up Wilkicki, right?"

"Yep, but we also got Sienna Olsen. It turns out she was with him... over there on Mitchell Street right off Strand Park."

"Damn... what a bonus. Where do you have them?"

"They're writing Wilkicki up at the front desk, and then we'll put him in the holding cell. I have Olsen in interrogation room one right now."

"Good. We'll go talk to her. There's nothing to hold her on, so we might just have a chat and turn her loose. Wilkicki is suspected of some heavy shit, so I hope that paperwork reflects the Terrorism Act."

"Yeah, boss... the bombs... We are writing him up for an act – acts – of terrorism."

"Good. We can hold him with no change for a couple of weeks that way, though I assume we'll charge him pretty quickly. So, how'd it go? Was there any resistance?"

"No, no... just the normal cursing and bitching and 'what did I do' stuff. Zane and I cuffed them both and brought them in with no issues."

"Did you find the ute, too?"

"Yeah, that's actually how we found him. The cruiser's camera and the AI software picked up the plate, and it was easy to locate him from there. I'm pretty sure he had no freaking idea we were onto him, so it's not like he was looking out for us."

"Ya got him?" Clint Navarro popped his head in the door.

"Sure do, thanks to Katie here and Constable Zane. They got them over near Strand Park."

"Good stuff. Are you charging Wilkicki under the Terrorism Act?"

"Well, we will. We're holding him under that now but haven't formally charged him yet. I reckon we'll have a talk with him, but not until we talk to his girlfriend."

"Damn... girlfriend? You reckon Wilkicki and Olsen are an item?"

Rumford tilted his head and grunted. "I... I don't know that at this point." He glanced at Hasler.

"They could be, boss. They were having a coffee when we picked them up and seemed to be all lovey-dovey..."

"Hum... This gets more and more interesting... I wasn't expecting to find both of them at the same time. Maybe this whole case is coming together." Rumford grabbed his notebook. "Let's go see what we can find out.

* * *

"G'day Ms Olsen... Ms Sienna Olsen, correct?"

"What's it to you?"

"Come on, Ms Olsen. You are in a heap of trouble here."

"I'm in trouble? How the hell could I be in trouble? I didn't do anything."

Leon pulled a chair out and gestured for his mates to have a seat. "Let me start by saying I'm Inspector Leon Rumford and this is my partner Inspector Katie Hasler... I believe you have already had the pleasure of meeting Katie. Finally, this is another colleague, Clint Navarro, who works with our friends at ASIO."

Her ears perked up when she heard ASIO. "Now wait a minute. ASIO? I didn't do a damned thing wrong here..."

"I don't know if you are familiar with the Terrorism Act, Ms Olsen, but involvement in bombings is terrorism in any Magistrate's Court in Australia. That's serious stuff, ma'am."

"What are you talking about... bombings? I've got a job, sir. I'm not a terrorist."

"Well okay, Ms Olsen... we'll start with that, but I have to caution you that you have a right to silence. You don't have to tell us anything or do anything for that matter, but if you do decide to talk with us, we can use what you say as evidence. Do you understand that?"

She nodded.

"This is being recorded, Ms Olsen, so could you please respond out loud?" Katie spoke in a calming voice.

"Yes, I understand. I didn't do anything wrong, so I don't have anything to hide."

"That's good, Ms Olsen. Now you said you have a job. Can you tell us where you are employed?" Rumford tapped his pen on his notepad.

"I work for Lion Creek Mine as the office administrator."

"And where is that. Ms Olsen?" Leon maintained eye contact with her.

"It's out in the Central West region... outside of Longreach... Barcaldine..."

Katie asked for clarification. "And you work way out there, Ms Olsen?"

"No, no... I work at the home offices here in Townsville, over on Cloncurry Street by the IGA there."

"Aha. So, what sort of work do you do there?"

"Answer the phone, take messages, organise meetings with our management team... Sometimes I greet visitors from down south or overseas." Sienna was becoming a bit fidgety.

Navarro looked at Rumford and widened his eyes, quietly asking if he could ask a question. Leon's nod of approval was nearly imperceptible. "Tell me, Ms Olsen, would one of your jobs include doing a bit of detective work... maybe chasing up some students concerning work they were doing that might impact Lion Creek Mine?"

"What?" Olsen's face was sour, and her voice gruff. "What are you talking about, detective work? No... I told you I was administrative. I don't do any detective work."

"So, you never represent Lion Creek away from the office? Look, I'm not trying to trap you here, Ms Olsen. I'm just asking if you ever do any background research for the company away from the office? You know... for example, maybe track down some people who could help the company get some environmental approvals for mine development?" Clint rubbed his chin.

"No, not really. That's not my job. Mr Green is our liaison person, and he does most of the communication with government people."

"I see, Ms Olsen." Leon slowly opened the manila folder in front of him and pulled out two A4 pages with colour photos printed on each. "Do you know either of these women, Ms Olsen?" He pushed the pictures of Nikki Vasquez and Becky Whitehall in front of her.

Olsen pulled her chair closer and stared down at the photos. She ran her fingers through her hair and slowly shook her head from side to side. "No... I never saw either of these women in my life. I'm sorry, but I can't help you here, Inspector."

Leon looked at her, his eyes locked on hers. "Are you positive?"

"As positive as I can be. I never saw either one of these women, sir. What is this all about, anyway?"

Rumford curled his lip over his bottom teeth and touched his hand to his chin. He kept staring at her while slowly stroking his jawline. "Hum..." He again opened the folder and pulled out another A4 photo. "One more picture here, Ms Olsen... can you explain this one to me? Um... note the date stamp there, Ms Olsen."

She again pulled the photo closer and looked down. There was a surprisingly clear photo that had been blown up and cropped from the Spinnaker Club CCTV. The date stamp at the bottom of it read 'Saturday 16-12-24 22:08'. They were three smiling women in the photo, all sitting together at the bar. It appeared that someone had just told a joke because their smiles were such that they appeared to be laughing together. All three had half-filled drinks in front of them.

"Now you tell me you never saw these two women in your life, Ms Olsen." Rumford again turned the first two photos towards her. "And yet here we see you with both of them in a very social situation. It's difficult to believe the three of you weren't getting along very well on..." He tilted his head to read. "...Saturday night the 16th of December at just after 10 PM. I think you'll find that this photo was taken at the Spinnaker Club here in Townsville. Can you explain that, Ms Olsen?"

She kept her eyes down, looking towards the table. "Can I have a lawyer?"

42

Friday, 26 April; Qantas Club, Brisbane, Queensland

"So, you're flying from Townsville to Melbourne... why are you in Brisbane? My mental map of Australia isn't that good, but don't you kind of fly right over Brisbane to get to Melbourne?"

"Don't ask, Karl. Just blame it on the realities of a country with 26 or 27 million people versus America with 340 or 345 million people. Anyway, a couple of hours layover here at least allows me to use the Qantas internet connection to Skype with you."

"True enough."

"So, how was your trip?"

"I'm still trying to work that out. I got here last night, but it's only..." She could tell his eyes moved from the laptop's camera to the clock. "...about 4:45 AM here in Fairbanks. Actually, I'm giving you a hard time with your connection from Townsville to Melbourne... don't even ask me about Atlanta to Fairbanks. It seems no one ever plans on connecting flights being late into Seattle..."

"Oh boy. Well, you're there."

"Yeah, that I am... I'm meant to meet with an academic at the University of Alaska Fairbanks this morning. Evidently, this..." He looked at his notes. "Professor Thomas Zandercon... is a medical guy with a strong background in biochemistry. I think he pretty much leans on the Atlanta CDC folks for expertise, but he is their representative up here and clears biological samples, organises site visits and whatnot. I don't expect too much from him, but I wanted to touch base before I go to Siberia."

"Burrr... That just sounds cold."

"No, not really. I checked the web when I got in the room here last night and the high and low in Krasnoyarsk yesterday was 56 and 28... Fahrenheit, of course. So, what's that to you Celsius folks... 13 or 14 and minus 2 or so. Hell, that's probably warmer than Chicago was yesterday. I spoke to Lisa back at the office, and she said they had snow flurries this morning."

"Damn! At least the weather has been pretty good here, though I'll hold that report until I see what Melbourne is like." She sipped her coffee. "So, what did you learn in Atlanta?"

"It's not even so much that I learned a great deal, but at least I did make contacts. I learned about this Zandercon guy I'm seeing up here in Alaska later today. I think the person at the CDC who can really help us is this Dr Thompson... Gerry Thompson. When you consider that everyone at the CDC is basically responsible for the national health security of all of America, that is a pretty broad task. This Thompson guy seems to look after the area that is specifically of interest to us, namely potential threats... new or changing diseases that could cause pandemic-like outbreaks. I know, I know... that's fairly nebulous, but his name kept coming up regarding anthrax and Ebola."

"Sounds like you learned a lot from him."

"Um... not yet. I said I learned a lot about useful contacts but haven't been able to dig into the nitty-gritty as yet. It seems that Thompson is off in Europe somewhere this week. He's meant to be back next week, so I will either communicate with him at a distance or – better yet – get back to Atlanta. All that will depend on how Siberia goes... and what you learn down there."

"We'll have to see on that. Townsville was good, but I admit I learned way more about the Great Barrier Reef than virology. Now that I'm heading to Melbourne, I think that I'm hot on the trail. The folks I'm chasing at the Yunupingu Institute of Medical Research there could really prove of great value to us, but some weird things are happening there right now."

"Like what?"

"Like the lead researcher's husband just became the first EVD death in Australia ever. Even more than that, I guess I sort of have a personal connection."

"Personal... how's that?"

"My dad's best mate – Clive Moseley – went to medical school with the bloke who died from EVD in Melbourne. Actually, I just chatted with Dad before I rang you and he told me Clive is heading for Melbourne right now, too. No doubt we'll see each other there. We coordinated enough that Clive and I will be in the same hotel."

"Wow, Ash... sorry to hear about your dad's mate."

"Thanks, Karl. Actually, in light of the tragic situation, I reckon I am fortunate to be able to talk to some of the other researchers at least. They are the top people working in this area in all of the southern hemisphere. I believe they are doing some work with synthetic viruses here, which initially seemed strange to me, but they do this in the hope of developing new vaccines."

"Synthetic viruses, you say?"

"Yes."

Karl leaned back a bit from his laptop's camera and scratched his head. Asha could see his hotel bed behind him with the rumbled sheets offering testimony to his interrupted sleep. She could also see that he was deep in thought during his moment of hesitation. "Man... I met a really weird kind of guy yesterday... hell, I've lost track of days."

"It's Friday evening here, so it must be early Friday morning there."

"I got you, Ash. I guess that makes it two days ago already. Anyway, I met this really strange character in Atlanta. I sat next to him while waiting after I first got there, then he came up to me a few hours later at this little café they have there for the public."

"Hold on a second... Why do you say he was weird, and what has this got to do with synthetic viruses in Melbourne?"

"To start with, he seemed more like a salesperson than a medical type. I wouldn't have even connected the dots here, but once you mentioned synthetic viruses, you got me thinking. This fellow... Milt Warner and that was mister not doctor..." Asha could see Karl holding a business card. "It says here he is a consultant with the NBS, the National Biodefense Strategy, whatever that is. Anyway, he mentioned he had been to Australia recently, but we never got into it. You might see if anyone in Melbourne heard of this guy."

"But Mr Warner seems to have stuck in your mind."

"Well yeah, he did. He went on a bit about how this synthetic virus stuff – I think he said synthetic biology – could possibly be used in the wrong way. He also mentioned that he thought the Pentagon would be keeping an eye on people working with these things to make sure there weren't terrorist links to them."

"Synthetic viruses... terrorists..." Asha pulled a pen from her bag. "Give me his details again."

43

Saturday, 27 April; Fitzroy Police Station,
Melbourne, Australia

Inspector Tony Benson heard the knock at his office door.
"Come on in."

Sonny Liu poked his head in the door. "You got a minute,
Inspector?"

"Yeah, sure... what do you got?"

"I ran down some CCTV video from Fraser Park last
Friday... 19 April."

"Great... let's see what you got there." He looked at Sonny.
"Is it on the network drive?"

"No... I never got that far, but I cut out the lengthy times
with nothing in them. Check this." He held his hand out with
a thumb drive.

"Yeah, fine." Benson took the drive and plugged it into his
computer. "I assume it's the file named 'Fraser Park 19-04',
yes?"

"Yep." Liu came around to the side of Benson's desk so he
could see the big screen.

"Okay, what do we have here?"

The file opened and started playing. Both men remained
quiet as a 45-ish-year-old man came jogging in one end of the
park. The camera was fixed, so as the man jogged closer and
closer, he eventually ran out of view. "Clearly that is Geoff
Kovac looking perfectly healthy at 11:12 AM last Friday
morning. Keep watching... I pasted in footage from a second
camera next." The second camera winked in and pretty much
picked up where the first left off, but it was clearly a greater
distance away. Kovac was jogging towards the camera now

and grew larger as he came closer. Suddenly, a heavily clothed body stepped out of a clump of bushes and walked at a quick pace towards the path. In an instant, the covered body seemingly feigned a stagger and let the coffee cup spill onto Kovac's face and body. The figure quickly spun around with the cup still in hand and now ran back into the bushes. Kovac stopped, wiped himself with his hand and then tee-shirt and looked towards the bushes. He was obviously saying something, but there was no sound, and his mouth was not in clear view. The video again blinked, and a third camera picked up Kovac as he turned and resumed his jog until he exited the park on the far side of where he had originally entered.

"Sonny... Sonny... Hold it here." Benson stood from his seat. "If you don't mind, would you sit here and take over. I think you're way more adept at this than I am. Let's go through this a bit slower this time."

"Will do, Tony." He sat and took hold of the mouse. "We'll replay, but I'll slow it down a bit." The first camera again showed Kovac entering the park at a fairly brisk jogging speed. Liu froze the image and zoomed in. "He's still pretty far away here, but the blow-up still shows some detail. It's obvious who we are looking at, and there is no doubt that's Geoff Kovac. Note the time stamp is 11:10. As soon as I forward it, and he runs another 15 or 20 metres, the clock ticks over to 11:11."

"Take it back again and freeze it. Do we see the suspect anywhere here?"

Liu stopped the video. They both squinted and ran through it twice, but other than some mums with prams, several little kids and an older couple walking a dog, no one else was around. "Here's where we flip to the second camera." Again, Kovac was farther away, but jogging towards camera two. Sonny ran the video very slowly, and both studied the area. Other than a few other people in this view, there was nothing of note. "Maybe I'll stop it here, and we can zoom on that stand of grevilleas. We know the perpetrator is in there somewhere..." He zoomed in almost enough to look at individual leaves."

"Back out again and take it frame by frame. As soon as we see the perp, freeze it again, and we'll zoom and study, zoom and study. We might need some stills printed up here."

Liu followed the Inspector's lead and slowly moved forward until the first glimpse of the suspect appeared in the grevilleas. "Go back until we don't see them and then zoom. Can we go frame by frame enlarged like that then?"

"Can do, Inspector." And he did. In the very first frame, the perp became visible and showed an arm and a leg before pushing through the bushes. Frame by frame, they watched until the entire body was visible. They probably spent ten minutes watching that key 20 or 30 seconds of video over and over, the bit showing the perp literally throwing the coffee onto Geoff's face. They continued the super slow motion, frame by frame analysis. "You want me to rerun it?"

"Well, sure, but wait a minute. Let's compare notes." The Inspector's words couldn't be taken literally, because he now grabbed his notebook sitting on his desk and opened it to begin to write. "What did we just see? I'm curious for us to compare each other's perspective on this."

"Well, first of all, I reckon we'll never ID the perpetrator from these cameras. Let me go back..." He manipulated the mouse and backed up until the suspect was standing upright several metres after coming out of the bushes. "Look here. I'd say the suspect isn't very tall. If you compare them to that rubbish bin, I'd say the maximum height the perp could possibly be is maybe 150 or 152 centimetres. Now I say that knowing that the standard Melbourne rubbish bin – the green one there – is exactly 100 centimetres up to the top of the container and the lid adds a few more centimetres of height. Again, look at the proportion of the body and the runners this person is wearing... they are really small. Besides the fact that they look small proportionally, look at the design." Liu zoomed in to the maximum, and one of the runners completely filled the screen. "Look at the style of shoe and pay particular attention to the laces. That really looks like a women's style running shoe. First of all, it is pinkish... Second of all, the laces are very thin and contrasting, darker pink. I'd bet you a freaking doughnut that's a woman."

"Damn, Sonny... good observation there. I didn't pick up on the size or shoes. By the way, how'd you know that the bin was exactly 100 centimetres high?"

Liu grinned. He took both of his hands and pointed at his chest with extended fingers and tapped himself. "I'm forensics, mate... I've had to measure them, and they are exactly 100 centimetres high. When a city the size of Melbourne buys several million bins, they just don't vary in dimensions."

Benson laughed. "Good job, Sonny."

"How about you, Inspector? What's your takeaway here?"

"Well, what strikes me is how well covered this person is. Can you go back to the head-to-toe zoom level again?" Liu did. "I was struck by the fact that even on a day when the temperature was pretty warm..."

Liu interrupted as he flipped his notebook back a few pages. "I checked earlier this week, and the Bureau of Meteorology has 26.7 Friday morning at 11 AM."

"You impress me once again, Liu." Benson cocked his head and smiled. "So even on a mid-to-upper 20s, sunny day, our perp is 100 per cent wrapped up. Zoom and then pan foot to head."

Liu did just that.

"You see, there is no view of skin at all on the ankles. As you sweep up the side, it looks like sweatpants, but they almost seem full enough that the wearer may have something underneath. Same with the long sleeve sweatshirt. And here's what hit me over the head the first time you zoomed. Focus in on the hands." The entire screen as from one fingertip to the cuff. "You notice right here?" Tony pointed to where the cuff came over the woollen glove.

"Damn, good eyes, mate."

"Yeah. You can see there a flash of plastic or rubber here."

Sonny still sat in front of the screen and leaned forward. "That's not rubber, Inspector. That's either latex, polyvinyl chloride or neoprene. And if we look at the other hand... "He panned over and kept the zoom at maximum. "...I thought I noticed a second glove... Yeah, look right here." He touched the computer screen with his index finger. "Can you see a second flap here, just a very little bit of it."

"God damn, Liu, you're starting to scare me. I think the IT boys slipped an AI chip in that freaking brain of yours."

Liu smiled and sat back.

"Well anyway, you can zoom back and continue up the torso... You can't see a damned thing around the neck or head, either..."

"But you can see the outline of glasses. I think if we have the IT boys enhance this, I imagine they're lab glasses because they look big and push the ski mask out more than regular eyeglasses would. Whoever this is wasn't just hiding their body from cameras... they were hiding it from whatever was in that coffee cup."

"Well, we can't even catch a clue as to who this is from this video. Do you have any ideas of where to from here?"

"Tony, Tony, Tony... This is the Big Smoke you're talking about... Melbourne. Hell, what are we up to... maybe 4.6 or 4.7 million people? I swear that CCTV cameras are freaking EVERYWHERE! I reckon that whoever this was, they didn't want to walk too far in that getup on a beautifully warm autumn day. That means they'd have had to suit up somewhere close by. Now that could have been in a car or a restaurant."

"Or maybe a workplace?"

"Maybe." Liu had minimised the video and was working the Inspector's web browser. "Look at this map of the city. I'll zoom here on Fraser Park. I reckon the perp either has a car or a private area somewhere... like a private office or toilet somewhere over here along Lismore Street or Wayland Avenue. I wouldn't be surprised if we can get some footage from... Aw hell, look... There's a hotel, a library, another public building – don't know what that is – a Macca's over here..." Liu looked up at Tony. "Give me a day. Want to bet we'll see who the stranger is behind that garb?"

44

Saturday, 27 April; Yunupingu Institute of Medical Research, Melbourne, Victoria

"I feel terrible that you're in here on a Saturday morning."

"Really, Ms Sharma, it's not at all like we wouldn't be here anyway. If you only knew how flat out we've been here the past week or ten days." Deshi extended his hand towards the staff room table. "Please have a seat."

"Thanks. And please, call me Asha."

He smiled. "Same here... I mean, call me Deshi." Liz had been on the phone in her office and now walked into the staff room. "Good morning, Liz. Let me introduce Asha Sharma from GNN. I believe you communicated earlier this week. Asha, this is Dr Liz O'Rourke, one of our researchers here at Yunupingu Institute."

"Nice to meet you, Asha." She leaned over and shook her hand. "Let's stick to Liz, please. Do you care for a coffee or tea?"

"Tea would be great."

"That sounds like an Aussie accent to me, Asha."

"It is. I am West Australian, born and raised, though I've been in the States the past several years with GNN."

"Western Australia... Our lead researcher, Dr Felicia Kovac, married a Western Australian... Geoff Kovac. Sadly, it was Geoff who passed away from Ebola Virus Disease this week. It's hit us all pretty hard."

A gloomy expression washed over Asha's face. "I am so sorry for you all. Please understand that my purpose of coming here as a journo had nothing to do with Dr Kovac, Geoff Kovac, that is... but I certainly was aware of all this. By the strangest of coincidences, my dad's best mate went to medical school with Dr Kovac."

Liz nodded. "By the strangest of coincidences, your father's friend is Dr Clive Moseley, and he's at my apartment right now with Felly Kovac."

"Oh my god... I knew he was coming over since my dad told me that yesterday, but I didn't realise he was already here."

"Yes, he flew in last evening and came by. He has accommodation just a block or so away from my building. He is very helpful and supportive of Felly."

Though Asha knew that Clive and Dr Kovac had been friends for a lifetime, it still seemed incredible that this kind of cosmic coincidence just happens. "I began to say that my intention here was never about Felicia or her husband or Clive Moseley for that matter. It's simply dumbfounding to find myself in the midst of all this."

"It all does stretch the imagination, that's for sure." Liz lifted her mug.

"If you don't mind, could you tell me how you got to this point? I think Clive mentioned that both Felicia and Geoff were working with Ebola victims in Southeast Asia?"

Liz sat back in her seat and began... "From what you wrote to us this past week, I know you are working on an in-depth story about viruses and other contagious diseases. I'm sure you already know that the Yunupingu Institute is the foremost research facility in the southern hemisphere working on – in particular – *Zaire ebolavirus*. Late last year Felly was notified that her grant to do site research up in Thailand had been funded. Geoff knew a few people and was able to tag on as an Emergency Department doctor at several of the tent-hospitals now set up to handle the overflow of Ebola patients. In January, they departed from Melbourne..."

* * *

"I feel self-conscious in taking so much of your time, Liz... Deshi..."

"Please don't feel that way, Asha. First of all, we had to eat lunch, too. Second of all, we are happy to contribute to your story. Regrettably, there is so little real science involved in the public's understanding of contagious disease... especially EVD. If we can help educate the public, that is a good thing. If we can help educate the global community, which is exactly the audience that GNN has, that is an excellent thing."

"I – we, Karl and I – will certainly try to do just that."

"But for me personally, there's a third reason..." Liz looked at Deshi as if to say, 'I'm not dobbing you in'. "I have some skin in this game, too. Fell-O is one of my best mates. In the first instance, I feel terrible for the grief she is going through. In the second instance, this trumped-up charge of her having anything to do with her husband's death is absolutely ridiculous."

"Of course, it is. It sounds to me as though you know what happened, but that because of circumstance, you feel the burden of proof has fallen on your team here." Asha still had several chips left on her plate, picked one out and put it into her mouth.

"For sure, but I don't think it is all because of circumstances. I am more convinced than ever that someone else has – how shall I say this – maybe greased the skids a bit. At first, I thought there was a perfectly reasonable explanation to all this based on accidental exposure, a malfunction of Geoff's personal protective equipment or something like that. But now I think someone has organised this and tried pointing a finger at Fell."

Ash nodded in agreement. "Of course, you mean the person spilling the coffee?"

"Exactly. I just hope the police can make some headway on that and, frankly, the quicker they do that, the better."

45

Saturday, 27 April; Townsville District
Police Headquarters, Queensland

"G'day, Mr Wilkicki. My name is Inspector Rumford... Leon Rumford."

"Right." Lester stared down at the table.

"So, Mr Wilkicki, we sure were fortunate when Inspector Hasler and Constable Zane were on a routine patrol yesterday, and the AI in their police cruiser matches your ute's plates to a KLO4 order in the Queensland-wide communication system. I reckon that was a nice piece of luck. But that was only the start of our luck yesterday, Mr Wilkicki. Imagine our surprise when they locate you in that little café off Strand Park then we find you having morning tea with Sienna Olsen. I say surprise because no one had any idea the two of you knew each other. We had two totally different Keep-A-Lookout-For orders, one for you and one for Ms Olsen. Now, what are the chances we'd find both of you together? What kind of odds would Queensland Sportsbet give you on that, Mr Wilkicki?"

"Look... you know you've got nothing to hold me for, and you need to either charge me or let me go. I've been here twenty-four hours, and you coppers can't hold me any longer without arresting me."

"Come on, Mr Wilkicki. I can't believe the constable writing you up yesterday didn't mention the fact that we suspect you in a bombing... in two bombings, actually. That's terrorism, sir. We can hold you up to 14 days without charging you under the Terrorism Act. For that matter, let's see how you answer some of these questions, and we might just charge you today."

"You can't do this."

"Oh, but we can do this, sir. You met me yesterday... I'm Inspector Hasler. Let me take care of the formalities here, Mr Wilkicki." She lifted a small card from the table and read. "I am informing you that you do not have to say or do anything, but anything you say or do may be used in a court of law. You may also communicate with a legal practitioner should you so desire. Finally, we are recording this interview, sir. Do you understand this, Mr Wilkicki?"

"Yeah, yeah... Look, I don't need a lawyer. I didn't do a damned thing."

"Thanks, Inspector Hasler. Tell me, Mr Wilkicki, are you employed?"

"Yeah."

"And where do you work, sir?"

"I'm a... I'm a farmhand..."

"A farmhand? And where do you practise this trade, Mr Wilkicki?"

"I'm sort of a contractor... I pick up jobs where they need me."

"So where would you be working right now, sir?"

"Let's just say I'm between jobs."

"Hum..." Rumford flipped a page in his notebook. "So as a farmhand do you dig post holes and stretch wire... maybe drive a tractor sometimes... help round up some cattle?"

"Could do... depends on the job."

"That's your white Toyota HiLux we have locked up out there..." Leon looked at his notes. "...plate number 395 DLP?"

"Yeah, I guess so."

"You guess so?"

"That's my ute."

Hasler sat forward. "Just so you know, Mr Wilkicki, we did have a search warrant issued and we have executed that looking through your ute. Now we came across some lipstick, a makeup kit and some... well, some girl things in the glove box. Would I be safe in assuming that they belong to Ms Olsen?"

Lester grabbed his chin with his hand and rubbed it several times as if in thought. "Maybe."

"That's fine... I can check with her on that."

"Yes, yes... that would have been Sienna's stuff."

Hasler nodded and turned towards Rumford. "I reckon you might want to ask him, Leon."

Leon played along. "Yeah, let's give it a try even though he doesn't seem to want to be too helpful here. Mr Wilkicki... in your farm hand duties, would you have much need for blasting caps? Now I admit I've never been a farmhand, but I didn't reckon you'd use a lot of explosives in that line of work. Can you explain why you had a partial box of Tang R38 blasting caps? You wouldn't use those herding cattle now, would you?"

Wilkicki let the sarcasm go. "They weren't mine."

Katie Hasler ran a hand through her hair. "But wait a minute, sir... they were inside your toolbox, and that was locked. Besides that, our forensic team found your prints all over both the toolbox and the blasting cap box."

"Maybe you can rephrase that, Mr Wilkicki. Maybe you DID find a need for blasting caps on the farm?" Rumford nodded his head. "You must have needed the caps, Wilkicki."

"I forgot... I did a job for the mining company, but it's a few months back, and I never took the caps out of the tool locker."

The mining company, Mr Wilkicki? You wouldn't be talking about the Lion Creek Mine, would you?"

"Yeah... yeah, that's the company."

"Funny thing, sir..." Katie flipped through her notebook. "When I talked to the administrator of the head office of Lion Creek Mine here in Townsville, there didn't seem to be any record of you working there."

"Interesting, Inspector Hasler." Rumford nodded his head. "Who did you talk to over there?"

"The Administrative Assistant at Lion Creek Mine, a Ms Sienna Olsen." Both inspectors turned their gaze to Lester.

46

Saturday, 27 April; Dr Liz O'Rourke's residence, Melbourne, Victoria

"Poor Lizzy... you will get so tired of eating take away food, you'll tell them to cart me off to the prison farm."

"Damn, Fell-O – there's no way that's happening. Besides, that was a pretty good pizza."

"I agree with that. It might not be quite up to Fremantle standards, but I admit that you Melburnians can whip up a decent Italian pie." Clive loved the thought of a Western

Australian putting a dig into Victorians even considering the circumstances. He smiled to himself... it was the Australian way.

"Thanks for having me here tonight." Asha felt that she was the intruder. "I mean, you guys are doing me a favour just to be willing to talk to me about my GNN project. All of a sudden, I'm in the middle of your Saturday night."

"Don't underrate yourself, Asha. Let's not forget my little friend here." Felly patted her hand against her electronic ankle bracelet. "It's not like Lizzy and I were going to be doing the town tonight. Besides that, Clive is here, and you are his friend. I don't think I've seen you for what... a year or two, Clive? Is that about right?"

"Yes, that's about it, Felly... maybe a year and a half. I saw you both at that medical conference in Darwin... maybe August or so the year before last." Clive smiled. "Remember that damned crocodile in the enclosure!"

"Oh my god!" Felly started to laugh and then seemed to catch herself.

"It's okay, Fell." Liz patted her hand. "To be perfectly honest, I wish we'd just get your mind off this whole freaking week for a little bit. I wish you liked footy or something – we could watch the Saturday night game."

"I like viruses..."

At first, a look of shock crossed Liz's face and then it transitioned to a smile. "I'm not sure that liking viruses more than footy reflects on you, my dear, or on footy!"

They all laughed.

"You know, that's my damned Fell-O! I swear you would work on your annual leave if they let you." Liz continued. "For that matter, I should ask Asha just exactly what she's working on. Maybe that would get your mind onto something a bit distracting."

"Aw jeez... I don't know. I don't think you want to talk about mutating diseases."

Clive scratched his head. "Well, from what I heard about your project at dinner on Monday night, I found it all quite interesting."

"Okay, I'll bite... What are you working on, Asha?" Felly's interest seemed genuine.

"Well, my colleague Karl Grimsley and I are looking at mutations of microbes. He's in Alaska now and heading for Krasnoyarsk State Medical University in Siberia and is basically trying to find if any of the so-called zombie microbes coming back to life from the melting permafrost are mutating in strange ways?"

"Strange ways?" Felly's interest was piqued.

"Well, is it possible that microbes somehow communicate what works and what doesn't? I'm not being silly and I sure as heck don't mean anything mystical or magic here. Look, I'm considering input from a variety of inputs: my environmental science academic father, Professor Sean Pratt with whom I was just visiting up along the Great Barrier Reef in Townsville and a Dr Lawrence Stetzer, Director of Epidemiology at the University of Pennsylvania in the States. All this definitely has me wondering."

"And don't forget old Clive Moseley here who went on at great length the other night about the human body as a miniature universe for trillions and trillions of microbes."

"Your example is excellent, Clive, but I will argue against the 'old' part forever!" Asha leaned over and squeezed her friend's hand.

"Communications, right? I read that in your note, and it had me interested from the start..." Felly lifted her glass and took a swallow of juice. "You know if you trace the history back, and you probably should do that in your doco, yes? I assume that you and Karl will produce a GNN documentary from all this, right?"

"That's definitely the plan, Felly."

"Well, I'd suggest you set it up just stating something obvious that nearly all of the general public simply ignores through ignorance, apathy or – most likely – both! Let's just consider... the eighteenth century and into the nineteenth century saw an explosion of chemistry from atomic structure to the quantum model of the atom. I dread mentioning names like Dalton, Avogadro, Mendeleev, Curie, Rutherford, and Bohr for fear of all the others that I overlook. The explosion of chemical knowledge had an impact on everything from energy to materials science to agriculture and diet. The early twentieth century produced the physics revolution. From the foundations of Galileo and Newton sprang the likes of Faraday, Maxwell, again Curie, Thomson and Einstein. Some argue that physics may be the most fundamental of all sciences, but in practical terms, the everyday results of all this included everything from transistors to spaceflight to supercomputers. By the middle of the twentieth century, we experienced the marvel of seemingly unlimited information technology, data handling and the nearly unlimited communication that spun out of the miracle of the internet.

"And that all set the stage for the biological revolution from the latter half of the twentieth century and into our twenty-first century right up to today. Every one of these developments is all intricately intertwined, and arguments of one or the other being 'key' are as silly as the seventeenth-century angelologists arguing about how many angels could dance on the head of a pin. You and Karl are the journos writing the doco script, but I'll simply give you my two cents here. Consider the 'Human Genome Project' proposed in the 1980s, started in 1990 and declared complete in 2003. Nominally, the cost of this was around three billion 1991 USA dollars and was a project many argued was impossible. We're talking about sequencing or figuring out the order of some three billion base pairs of DNA making up the whole set of chromosomes in a human being. You don't need to know biology or biochemistry or genetics... Just consider three BILLION of anything. That's three thousand million of something. Imagine writing three thousand million words, all in the correct order.

"Fast forward 20 years or so and we can sequence that and more... in a couple of hours using the computers that we have at Yunupingu Institute... And the cost? Probably forty or fifty US dollars if we can get one of our doctoral students to run the samples!" Felly smiled.

Liz's mood lifted, seeing her grieving friend finally able to be distracted even for a little bit. "Maybe the bacteriophage would be a good example of how even a virus might communicate, as it were."

"Good point, Lizzy. A bacteriophage..." Felly hesitated to see if Asha was at all familiar with the term and quickly saw that she wasn't. "... has been known for over a hundred years and the name basically means 'bacteria eater'. These viruses work like any virus. By that I mean, they enter a cell, take over its genetic machinery and reprogram it to make more bacteriophage material, then destroy the cell until it releases all the new bacteriophages in neighbouring cells.

"In this active phase, the whole lifecycle can be repeated and repeated until all the neighbouring cells have died. If that's all that happens, the bacteriophages will die since they cannot survive without fresh cells to infect. Viruses are no different from any other life. To be successful, they must survive. Viruses can only live by using the machinery of a living cell by hijacking that cell's life processes. If the active form of any virus kills all the healthy cells around it, the virus itself must die." For the first time in a while, Liz actually smiled. "Enter a phenomenon that absolutely mesmerises a nerdy virologist like myself."

"Me too..." Liz put her hand above her head.

"This phenomenon developed way back in the early days of any virus's evolution, and it represents a fascinating method of communication called 'quorum sensing'. This quorum sensing is nothing more than a chemical excretion given off by viruses, and when the percentage of them dying gets beyond a certain point, some viruses can be triggered into a latent phase rather than the active phase. In this state, the virus can be passed onto another cell, but doesn't activate and therefore doesn't destroy the cell. It's almost as if the viruses can hibernate like a bear to get it through the winter without starving. Please don't take my simile too literally, but you get the idea. Actually, we would probably avoid confusion better by not even using the term 'communication' since it almost implies some sort of human understanding. Think of these microorganisms interfacing or giving feedback to one another... it is not a conscious thing, rather an expression of the laws of nature."

"Oh boy... does that sound like Dad." Asha looked towards Clive.

"Indeed, that sounds like Sacha." Clive had sat quietly through all this until now. "That was an absolutely fascinating description, Felly. You certainly know more than I do in this area, but research is looking to use this idea, correct?"

"Absolutely it is, Clive. If we can learn how to send the same signal to a virus to go into the latent phase, possibly we can keep it in that state indefinitely. If that is the case, we may be able to simply turn off a virus, so to speak. I confess to oversimplifying this way too much, but it does speak to Asha's curiosity of how even viruses can interface or give each other feedback... or yes, communicate if you like. It also speaks to our work trying to find the specific segments of DNA that might allow us to do this, and to that end, we are employing the use of synthetic virus sectors."

Asha's face perked up. "I've heard this idea recently... actually, my colleague Karl did. He mentioned this to me on Skype last night. For that matter, he bumped into a strange fellow while on assignment at the CDC in Atlanta early this week."

"A strange fellow?" Now she had piqued Liz's curiosity.

"Yes." Asha rooted around in her bag and found her small, travelling notebook and flipped a few pages. "His name was...

um... Mr Milt Warner... He told Karl that he worked for the Pentagon in the Biological Defense Program."

47

Sunday, 28 April; Fitzroy Police Station, Melbourne, Victoria

"Bloody hell, Liu... don't you ever take a day off?"

"Not when I'm in the middle of something big, I don't."

"Well, fair enough, Liu... Hey, I get it – maybe you just want TOIL?"

"TOIL."

"Come on, Liu... it's Australia. TOIL means Time-Off-In-Lieu... Get it, Liu? Lieu?"

Liu's eyes shot to the ceilings like rockets! "Holy bat shit! I don't even believe you said that, Inspector. You're telling me it's Australia? Hell, I was born in Sydney!"

"Fair enough." Tony Benson's smirk quickly disappeared. "I'm just trying to inject some humour into a Sunday morning at work..."

Sonny hid his smile, shook his head and walked in the door, his fast-food coffee cup in his hand.

"Well, you're here at 7 AM on a Sunday, so you must have thought it worthwhile. I'm just being my cheery self. What do you have there?" Benson looked at the thumb drive in Liu's hand.

"I did check on the CCTV cameras on Lismore Street or Wayland Avenue, and they might just help us crack the case." He leaned over Benson's shoulder, grabbed the mouse and clicked on the folder icon.

"You get any closer, and you'll have to kiss me! Would you just sit here already? I thought we went through this yesterday... You are way better at manipulating the video than I am."

Sonny sat at Tony's desk and within seconds opened the first video. It showed a view looking back towards Fraser Park from Lismore Street. "Note the time stamp here... Friday at 11:09." The video ran for 20 seconds or so with everyday street traffic and a few pedestrians. Suddenly they could see a fully cloaked body with the ski mask, balaclava and sweatsuit who walks at a very quick pace across the street and disappears into the park.

Benson shook his head. "Damn it, Sonny. How do you find all these cameras?"

"Tony, that's not even a challenge anymore. I think the official CCTV cameras now listed on Melbourne City Council papers are nearing 10,000... that's 10,000 official eyes all over the city. Pretty much if there is a streetlight or traffic light, there are CCTV cameras. Now in addition to that, there is at least an equal number of businesses with their own CCTV, though those cameras may be pointed differently. On top of all that, I don't think anyone has an idea of the number of residential... home CCTV systems. This has grown exponentially. Ten or twelve years ago, the city had 26 official cameras and bragged to the public about that."

"I'm amazed at the quality."

"Hell, the official ones installed in the past few years are all Ultra High Definition, so you can blow them up enough to make positive IDs."

"Okay, so we see where the perp enters the park."

"Let me just speed up a bit..." Sonny manipulated the mouse again. The timestamp clicked by 11:10... 11:11... and just on the blink over to 11:12 the dark figure is jogging out of the same Fraser Park bushes. "There's our suspect." The person backtracks the same way only jogging this time. There was no longer a coffee cup in their hand.

"Aw, man... we lost them."

"Inspector..." Sonny made his favourite gesture of putting both hands in front of him and turning them towards his chest as if to say, 'this is me your talking to'. "We didn't lose a thing. This is a camera over on Wayland Avenue looking back up Lismore Street. She's still jogging."

"She... you said she... We don't know that yet, right?"

Liu smiled. "You don't know that yet." He switched to a third camera that showed the suspect entering a McDonald's on Wayland Avenue.

"You mentioned Mackers yesterday. Did you suspect this at that point?"

"Well, the coffee cup stayed hidden enough that we couldn't see the lettering, but the colour made me think it was Mackers. You know, I buy one of these every morning." He lifted his cup and took a sip of his McDonald's coffee. "But now it gets really good. Here, look..."

The camera view was now inside of McDonald's and showed the counter and the hallway to the public toilets. The suspect hurries into the picture on the left and goes into the hall, disappearing from view. "Look here." Sonny pointed his finger towards two people sitting in a booth who appeared to look, tilt their heads questioningly, then resume chatting. "I reckon they were wondering why someone was dressed like that. By the way, check the time stamp here... 11:15. Let me speed it up for a couple of minutes."

"Any problem getting the Mackers' footage?"

"Nah... they're good with the police. Once I saw that she went into the building, I knew we'd get her. I made one phone call, and the magistrate issued a search warrant so we can use it all... all legal footage." The video fast forwarded at 6x, still slow enough to see people placing orders and walking in and out of the scene, but fast enough to offer a bit of humour.

"Okay, now check this..." A 30-ish-year-old woman comes from the ladies' toilet into the hallway and walking towards the restaurant proper. She is carrying a large shopping bag with the top folded over. As she walks into the main area, she cuts across the front of the service counter and out of sight on the far side. "I had the AI check height after we viewed the video yesterday, and it measured our suspect at 154 centimetres, which is just a tad under five foot one on the old scale."

"You were way off... what did you say? Maybe 152 centimetres..." Benson laughed.

"Well, if you look at this photo..." He went back to the best head-on view and zoomed in. "...this woman is about that height. Also, before you ask, we watched that door until 12:30 PM and no one even close to that size came out, so I'm sure this is our suspect."

"Did you follow her from here?"

"Not yet, but we didn't have to. Thank you to our Victorian Police AI software..." He clicked, and the screen flicked to a photo of the woman with basic details listed beside the image. Gemma Ridley, 154 centimetres, 51 kilograms, DOB: 14 January 1997, 12082 Sandford Avenue, Unit 1604, Carnegie, Victoria.

"So, have you had the chance to run any more info on her at this point?"

"Tony, I am happy to tell you that I am my own biggest supporter. I am happy to be here so early on a Sunday morning. I'm also happy to tell you that I – Sonny Liu – gave up my Saturday night movie because I sat at my home computer going through these videos and putting together the snips you see here. All of that said... the only other thing I can tell you is that she is a pharmacist and works at The Royal Melbourne Hospital."

"Damn... Thanks to you. Sonny, this whole thing has come together just like that." Benson snapped his fingers.

"Let's give a little credit to thousands of CCTV cameras and the police AI software – top-notch stuff."

"Look, this is what we're going to do. "It's ah..." He looked at his watch. "... it's nearly 8 AM. We know who the perp is, but we need to work out why. I'm happy to arrest her today if that works out, but let's gather a bit more information first. How about you and I go back over to The Royal Melbourne. I don't know if we'll find the same staff working that was there last Monday, but it doesn't really matter. Let's go see what we can find out.

* * *

"Yes, of course, I remember you. That was last Monday, right? That was the day that the doctor died here... EVD..."

"Yes, that's right, Nurse Schneider."

"Please, Cassie is fine, Inspector."

"Another Sunday, Cassie?" Benson tried his best to frown.

"No... it's all good. Last week I worked overnight Sunday and overtime Monday morning. This week I'm day shift and go home at 3 PM. Even better, we don't have anyone in any kind of quarantine this week, let alone biosecurity level 4. That takes so much effort suiting up and worrying about maybe an accident."

"I see what you mean." Now Sonny took a turn. "Do you mind if we ask you a few questions."

"No, not at all."

"Were you responsible for giving Dr Kovac any pharmaceuticals last week?"

"Of course. I was the ICU nurse on duty and happened to be the biosecurity 4 person. As you can see here today, we don't often have a quarantined bed, though these two can both be quickly set up for that. Biosecurity level 4 is a real pain, and few of the nurses ever volunteer to do it. You have to do special professional development workshops to qualify, but you get a pay bonus to do so. It's very rare that we ever need BSL3 let alone BSL4, but I always volunteer. I like the extra pay, plus you really ever only have one patient when it is required. Since you always have to suit up, most of the night you just sit here looking at monitors. Frankly, the most difficult part of ICU quarantine is staying awake on the night shift."

"Is there any way we could look up Dr Kovac's treatment chart? For that matter..." Benson had his notebook open. "...is Dr Fairbrother here this week?"

"There's more than a chance for both. Dr Fairbrother is on a six-day rotation of 24-on-24-off schedule, so since he was off Friday and Saturday, he's back this morning... just started, like me. As far as patient charts, that's all saved electronically now, though you'll have to ask Dr Fairbrother about that since I don't know what legalities are involved."

"Did I hear my name being used in vain?"

"Good morning, Dr Fairbrother. I don't know if you remember us. I'm Inspector Tony Benson, and this is Inspector Sonny Liu. We met you last Sunday."

"Yes sir, I do remember... both of you."

"We are just chasing a few things up here. Cassie tells us she was responsible for giving Dr Kovac his meds last week, regrettably, on the morning he passed away. I wonder, could you tell us what meds he would have been given? If we need a Magistrate's Court..."

Sonny politely interjected. "No need, Inspector Benson. We got all that along with Dr Lloyd Gephardt of the Coroner's Office last week. The Coroner's inquiry covers all of that."

"Spot on, Sonny."

Fairbrother was quick to respond. "Look, it's all recorded on the system, but frankly, I don't need to look. Dr Kovac's case was so unusual for us that I remember it all in detail. I won't burden you with that unless you need it, but basically, Kovac's body responded to the Ebola virus with an overproduction of his immune cells to such a degree that it started to attack his own body including breaking down tissues like blood vessels. That causes two things in particular, namely dehydration and septic shock. The dehydration calls for fluid resuscitation, which is best done using a combination of oral fluids as well as an IV drip of 0.9% sodium chloride solution. At first, we attempted to maintain oral fluid intake, but that became increasingly difficult with time, so we upped the IV drip.

"Overnight last Sunday night, Kovac's vitals became increasingly unstable, and his blood pressure was approaching dangerous levels. By morning, I decided to use an additional pharmaceutical to increase his blood pressure, namely a medication called a vasopressor. I ordered that. Generally, we can just put that right in the drip, especially in a biosecurity level 4 setting since it's not possible to have a nurse or doctor checking in every few minutes or so. So that's what I ordered."

Both Benson and Liu were busily writing. Sonny was the first to speak up. "Sorry, Doc... what was the vasopressor you ordered?"

"Sure... I ordered norepinephrine at 1 mcg/kg/min. I sent that order down to the pharmacy. You are welcome to check that on the system here, but it is a pretty standard order."

"And did the pharmacy mix that into the bag, or did you do that, Cassie?"

"Normally I would do that myself... not even by myself, but I would have another nurse check me. It was the middle of the night though, and Dr Fairbrother reckoned we weren't using a controlled substance, so he was happy not to do the double-check."

Benson looked at Fairbrother. "Is that unusual, Doc?"

"No, not really, and that's exactly what I told Cassie. She's one of our most experienced nurses here in the unit." He smiled at her as he nodded his head. "I mean, considering the situation, neither sodium chloride solution nor norepinephrine is really the kind of medication that is easily abused, plus the fact that Dr Kovac was isolated in a difficult to get to level 4 quarantine, I think it's a stretch to refer to that call as unusual. Remember, Inspector... we just don't have to face Ebola cases here in Melbourne, thank god!"

"Fair enough, Doc." Benson looked at Schneider. "So, do you remember who brought the medication up from the pharmacy, Cassie? I know it's a big hospital and you might not know..."

Cassie interrupted him with a smile. "Sure, I remember exactly who it was because I know her personally. She brought the meds up on a tray, and I told her I was happy to add the norepinephrine, but she said 'no need'... she had already done that for me. She read the label where she had written what was in it according to proper procedures, and I thanked her."

"And what was her name, Cassie?"

"It was Gemma, Gemma Ridley, one of our pharmacists."

48

Sunday, 28 April; Victoria Police squad car, Melbourne, Victoria

"I'm so sorry to bother you at this time on a Sunday morning, Dr O'Rourke."

"It's no bother, Inspector Benson, though I wasn't expecting to hear from you this morning.

"I have a request for you, Doc. Your group over there at the Yunupingu Institute has contributed a great service to the Victoria people over the past week. Because of the level 4 biosecurity requirements of looking at any of the evidence we collected from Dr Kovac and his belongings, you people have been able to conduct all the analytical work our forensics teams have required. Now you are fully aware that we have more potential evidence we collected in high-level storage at the Institute."

"Of course... That is all locked away with a police seal on it in our level 4 laboratory facility. Now if you need something out of there, I can get it, but it would still not be able to be analysed without the level 4 precautions, Inspector."

"Of course, I am fully aware of that. That's why I am calling. I think we've had a break in the case."

"A break?"

"Yes... a big break, Doc, though I am not at liberty to reveal all the details to you right now. I'm not asking you to take a sample of evidence out of the level 4 lab. Rather, I'm asking if you can run an analysis for us."

"An analysis? Jeez, I can, but it depends on what you need to be analysed."

"Well... listen, I'm in a squad car right now with Inspector Liu... you met Sonny Liu, too, I believe."

"Yes, yes..."

"We're on speaker here, so I'll let Sonny tell you what we need. He's the forensics bloke here."

"Hi, Doc... Sonny Liu here. The bit of evidence that Tony... that we need to be analysed is the IV bag that was hanging next to Dr Kovac's bed."

"The electrolyte solution?"

"Yes, yes... it seems there may be another medication in there. Basically, we're looking for a routine analysis that could determine the level of saline and norepinephrine in the bag."

"Well, that's not something I've done for a few years, but I could run that analysis. From memory, I think we'd just do a high-performance liquid-chromatographic and maybe use the mass spectrometer if needed."

"Are these devices you would have access to?"

"Inspector Liu, there's not much we don't have access to at Yunupingu Institute."

"That's fantastic."

"When do you need this?"

Benson sounded almost apologetic. "Any chance you could do that this morning?" His voice trailed off.

"This morning? Damn...Frankly, the equipment is the least of my worries. I will see if I can get one of our techies or a doctoral student to help out. I hate to admit this, but I don't so much run this equipment over the past several years, just read results. If I can't find anyone, I will still do the analysis, but having some young hands on board would help. You say this is critical."

"I can't begin to tell you. This might be just the break we needed to get that damned ankle bracelet off Felly's leg."

PART FOUR

"Although Nature needs thousands or millions of years to create a new species, man needs only a few dozen years to destroy one."

—Victor Scheffer, Biologist, 1906 to 2011

49
Sunday, 28 April; Seaview Bar and Grill, Townsville, Queensland

Katie Hasler sat across the street at a Mackers keeping an eye on Sienna Olsen. The suspect sat with an unknown man under a sun umbrella outside the Seaview Bar and Grill. Katie was conscious of the fact that she never worked undercover simply because three-quarters of the people in Townsville knew her. She reassured herself that in a sense, she was just enjoying a Sunday morning in a tourist area, wearing a colourful blouse and a pair of shorts. She enjoyed working with Constable Jon Zane and even put up with the way he always teased her. So here she was, sipping a coffee and sitting in the al fresco area getting paid at penalty rates for the extra work. "That woman just loves The Strand, I reckon!"

"Yeah, I'm sure she does. We got her honey in the lockup, and she's back here in a flash with another bloke. Talk about being a two-timer..." Zane wore jeans and almost looked the part of an Asian tourist. In his case, he'd transferred up from Brisbane and hadn't been in Townsville long enough for many people to know him.

"Nah... you're wrong on that, Zane."

"Wrong?"

"She isn't sweet on that bloke."

"How can ya tell?"

"Just look at her. The body language isn't right. Her face is too serious. She's not joking... not smiling. Her arms are even folded across her chest right now. For that matter, neither is he... comfortable, I mean. I reckon it's business."

"Business... Sunday morning... Hey, maybe he's a lawyer."

"I doubt it. The guy looks too sleazy."

"Wait a minute... I said that maybe he was a lawyer. Now how in the hell can a lawyer possibly look too sleazy?" Zane looked at her and smiled. "You are either full of shit or else you're psychic. Frankly, I'm hoping you're psychic."

"I'm too recognisable... Could you go over there and answer your phone and very nonchalantly snap a half dozen photos. That mobile of yours has a zoom, yes?"

"Yep, good enough for the AI to read it, I'm sure."

"Well, don't look so obvious, okay?"

"Obvious? I was a spook in a former life, you know!" Zane pulled his phone from his waist, looked at the screen and then across at Katie. "Sorry, honey, I've gotta take this one."

Hasler smiled a pretty smile and spoke in a soft tone heard only by Zane. "Honey, you bastard! I'll get you for this." She then blew him an air kiss that looked for all the world as though they were an item."

Zane stayed on their side of the Strand but got to a spot where he had an unobstructed of Olsen and the bloke with whom she was speaking. He kept pretending to speak on his mobile and – after a minute or so – smiled, said a goodbye that was easily lip-read and pretended to end the call. He then held his phone closer to his eye and placed his free hand over the top as if shielding the screen from the sun, the way he would when reading a text message. He held that pose for 20 or 30 seconds and was able to snap off a half dozen photos. Satisfied he had what he needed, he again swiped at his phone and put it back on his waist. Zane slowly walked back towards where Katie was and sat down once again. "Now then, what were you saying, honey?" He smiled.

Hasler still grinned ear to ear. "Keep that up, and I'll spray paint in your locker, you horse's ass!" She blew him another kiss.

"I'm sure I got what we wanted." He thumbed through the photos. "Let's go back to the office and check this guy out."

* * *

"I'd swear you guys didn't even put in for overtime the way you're both dressed today." Leon Rumford sat way back in his chair.

"Overtime. Hell, we should be getting double time for working as undercover agents." Zane feigned a serious look.

"Double time? They should pay me quadruple time for working with a bastard like you, Zane!" Hasler sneered but left no doubt that she was teasing him.

"Hah! Undercover agents! You guys are both watching too many cops and robbers' movies. At least you sound like you work well together." Rumford tried to egg them on.

"That's what you say but check this out. I just ran those photos through the Queensland Blue Net software, and we got an immediate hit. I think this will surprise you." Zane passed the paper over to Leon.

Rumford held the page in one hand and pulled on his chin with the other. He read for the better part of a minute. "Damn... I didn't see this coming. If you'd have asked me ten minutes ago, I'd have said Olsen was meeting with some mining types. But this is even better... Malcolm Michaels... Senator Malcolm Michaels."

"I sure didn't recognise him, but I confess to not following politics even a little bit." Hasler almost sounded proud of herself.

"I didn't recognise him either, Leon." Zane was more apologetic for his ignorance.

"Well, neither one of you needs to feel embarrassed for the simple reason that just about no one knows the bloke. I think he grew up bush... maybe near Mount Isa somewhere. Anyway, he is part of that batshit-crazy NFP group – the Nation First Party – and wound up winning a Senate seat with like 30 or 40 votes in the special election."

"I've already confessed to not understanding much about politics, but how'd he do that? Even as a state senator, that's not many votes." Katie was shaking her head.

"Good one, Hasler. It's bloody hell obvious that you don't follow politics. Queensland doesn't have a senate, just the lower house. Michaels is a Commonwealth Senator."

"Damn... that makes it worse? Please explain?" Zane was shaking his head now.

"I don't pretend to know either, but with the Commonwealth, the pollies are more interested in killing off each other rather than governing. We seem to have an election every year or two. Now they have these high tech, AI-guided 'preference whisperers' who can figure ways to get people elected on a wing, a prayer and less than a hundred first preference votes."

"God bless democracy." Hasler gave him a thumbs up.

"Well, I do know those NFP people are mostly raving lunatics. They are anti-climate change, anti-immigrant, anti-taxes, anti-vaccination, anti-academics... damn if I know exactly what they are actually for."

"Unless we're reading this all wrong and Michaels isn't involved with any bombings, I don't know what all this means." Zane looked to Rumford. "Where do you reckon we'd go with this now, Leon?"

"I guess for starters, we go talk with Professor Pratt. Maybe the good Professor knows something about this Michaels bloke."

50

Sunday, 28 April; Yunupingu Institute of Medical Research, Melbourne, Victoria

"Inspector Benson... This is Liz O'Rourke. I just got out of the shower, and we've completed the analysis you wanted. Look, I think it's best if you can come over here."

"You're at the Institute, yes?"

"Yes, and I'll be here. One of the PhD students came in to run some of these tests... He's been a great help... Jai Yang. I don't believe you've met him. Anyway, he's happy to hang around too. If Sonny's with you, bring him along."

"Yep... Sonny is here, and I'll make sure he comes along for the ride."

* * *

Liz's phone buzzed, and she answered. "Dr O'Rourke."

"Liz, it's Tony. The damned door is all locked up."

"Sorry, Tony... I forgot it's a Sunday. I'll be right down."

"I got it, Liz." Jai did a slow jog out the door and was back in a minute or to.

Benson and Liu came in the door. "Well, we met Jai... Thanks for getting us off the street, mate."

"No worries."

"I can't tell you how much I appreciate this, Liz... and you, too, Jai. Make sure she pays you double time for this morning, mate."

"Will do... you'd better believe it." He laughed.

"Grab a seat, would you?" They all sat at the staff table.

"Believe me, Liz... as soon as I am free to do so, I'll tell you the whole story, and this will all make sense to you, I hope!"

"You know what I told you when I met you a few days ago... I just want to get this over with." Liz rocked her head back and forth. I can't help but think I said 'since I met you the other day'... It seems as though this has been going on for years!"

"I'm with you... So, what did you find, Liz?"

"I should let Jai tell you. Go ahead, mate."

Jai was happy to present the findings. "Well, when Liz told me what you were chasing... the IV drip with the electrolytes and some norepinephrine... We suited up and went into the lab and opened the box. There's no need to worry about anyone tampering there since it is the highest biosecurity level you can have... that's a 4. Anyway, what was written on the IV bag was 0.9% sodium and electrolytes along with norepinephrine at 1 mcg/kg/min... Right away I thought something wasn't right since the IV with sodium and norepinephrine in solution should have been nice and clear. Well, the bag had an orange-brown cast to it. Whatever was in there was light-sensitive.

"I don't know how long that hung in the hospital, but it's been pretty much in the dark closet there for a few days. Whatever was there must have started decomposing right away."

Benson felt his leg tapping ever so slightly, the tell-tale sign of his impatience. He looked at Sonny and almost broke into a smile. Inspector Liu was obviously in his element, dead set intent on the explanation Jai was giving.

"Well look, to keep this short and to the point, we tried running some high-performance liquid chromatography, but that result was unsatisfactory. We were getting no sign of norepinephrine. Sometimes that can show up with traces of epinephrine, but that wasn't showing either. You know that both are both similar neurotransmitters, but the norcpincphrine works more on vessel walls and epinephrine on cardiac muscles..." Jai could see Inspector Benson was getting a bit fidgety.

"Here's the upshot. I'm going to hold all the science – but it is cool stuff when you have the time..." Jai smiled. "Our best technique with his sample was the ESIMS, that is the electrospray ionisation mass spectrometry. I'll give Sonny these printouts here, and I can get them to you electronically if you like, but the point is, there was no norepinephrine in that bag... zero. Instead, it contained sodium nitroprusside and Furosemide, which is a Lasix."

Benson's patience had reached its limit. "Look, um... this is really impressive work, Jai. I can't tell you how much I appreciate you're coming in here on a Sunday morning. At the end of the day, though, what have we learned?" He looked at Liz.

"Well, I don't pretend to be a medical doctor, but I do understand some basic pharmacology here. Dr Fairbrother was trying to hydrate – that is to replace and build up water – in Dr Kovac. He also was trying to raise Kovac's blood pressure since it was getting dangerously low. What Jai's analysis found – and I do give Jai all the credit – is that instead of the medications Fairbrother ordered to do that, the bag contained sodium nitroprusside and Furosemide. In everyday language, the Furosemide was acting to make him lose fluids, not gain them. The Furosemide also results in lowering blood pressure, not raising it. Additionally, the sodium nitroprusside was acting to lower blood pressure, not raise it. The medications in that bag were aimed at making Dr Kovac get sicker, not healthier."

"And this happens when he is teetering on the edge."

"Yes, that's exactly the case."

"Do you think it possible this could happen by mistake?"

Liz looked at the table. "I don't pretend to know how hospitals work, but that seems highly unlikely to me."

"You do realise that you are suggesting someone intentionally tried to harm Dr Kovac?"

"I do."

"And you, Jai?"

"I reiterate what Liz said, and I'm no medical doctor, either. Still, it just seems impossible to make that mistake."

51

Sunday, 28 April; Professor Pratt's residence, Bushland Beach, Queensland

Sean turned the gas stove-top burner down and grabbed his phone. "G'day."

"Professor Pratt?"

"This is he speaking."

Professor, this is Inspector Leon Rumford, Queensland Police Service here in Townsville. I'm so sorry to bother you on a Sunday morning. I was hoping I'd get a hold of you before you were out of range."

"No, no... it's fine. I'm still at home in the kitchen here just frying up a couple of eggs. "He turned the burner off. "I was wondering what had become of your investigation."

"Well, obviously you knew we had enough evidence to convince us the *Reef Explorer* explosion was not an accident. We have now charged a fellow with the act, but we are struggling to discover what exactly his motive was. Would it be possible for me to stop by and ask you a few questions?

We're just trying to see if anyone had it in for you or one of your students."

"I'm going to be here until noon at least."

"That's plenty of time. Look, I'll head over there now, so should be there in ten minutes or so. Thanks, Professor."

* * *

Sean no sooner finished his fried eggs on toast than the doorbell rang. "I'm coming." He could see the Inspector through the screen door. "Good morning, Inspector. Come in." He opened the door and ushered Rumford into his living room.

"Again, Professor, I'm so sorry to bother you this morning."

"And again, no problem. If I can be of any help that'd be great. I look forward to clearing this whole thing up. You say you have arrested someone?"

"Well, yes, we have charged someone, but there are big holes. If you don't mind, I want to run some faces... names by you and see if any of them ring a bell." He opened a folder and pulled out an A4 colour-printed photo and laid it on the coffee table. "Do you recognise this woman? Have you ever seen her before?" He laid Sienna Olsen's picture in front of Pratt.

Pratt picked it up and stared at it for half a minute. "I can't ever remember seeing this woman, Inspector. Is this who you have charged with setting the explosive device?"

"No, no... that's ah... no, she isn't the suspect at this point. She works for a company called Lion Creek Mining. Do you know about this company?"

"Know of them? Well, of course, I've heard of them. Probably most people in Townsville have heard the name. They want to develop that coal project in the Central West region out by Longreach and Barcaldine, yes? Being a professor at James Cook, especially in environmental sciences, I get invited to probably a dozen community meetings a year. Several are sponsored by the Townsville City Council, but there are others at other local councils. Inevitably questions come up from concerned citizens asking about the effects of this kind of project on the local environment. Of course, with something like Lion Creek, the local environment doesn't only include the Central East communities around the proposed mine site, but also the rail line to the coast and all the issues concerning loading and shipping tens of millions of tonnes of coal from coastal ports here along the Barrier Reef."

"I assume that coming from your environmental perspective, you wouldn't have a lot of friends in the mining industry."

"Funny you say that. You do realise I'm sure that the mining industry is not one, monolithic point-of-view that always supports anything mining. I do have a few mates who work in mining, but believe it or not, most of the time they agree with me. People in the mining hierarchy can be just as environmentally minded as anyone else. My life is dedicated to saving our Great Barrier Reef, but I don't reckon we need to give up a first world, high technology lifestyle to do that. It's just that sometimes we need to put Mother Nature first."

"Good on you, Professor. It sounds like you and I are on the same page. All of that said, however, someone probably doesn't like what you are saying at some of these meetings. So, this woman..." He again pointed at Olsen's photo. "...and Lion Creek Mining doesn't specifically ring any alarm bells in your head."

Leon pulled out another picture and laid it on the table. "How about this fellow, Professor? Any recognition of this face?"

Sean looked at the photo of Lester Wilkicki lying before him, picked it up and took his time trying to remember him. "Nah... I'm sorry, Inspector, but again, I can't say I remember this fellow at all. Is he with Lion Creek, too? Is this your suspect?"

"Look again, Professor… it's too early to say that. We just are looking into several possibilities here. For that matter, we aren't even sure if he is involved with the Lion Creek people." He fished around in his folder and pulled out a photo of Malcolm Michaels and placed it on the coffee table. "How about this bloke?"

Pratt looked at the photo, and before he could even pick it up, his head started rocking back and forth. "Yep… Senator Malcolm Michaels. This bloke is batshit crazy!"

The Inspector quickly covered his mouth with his hand and ran it back and forth as if in deep thought. He very consciously tried to cover his smile, realising full well that he had referred to Michaels using the exact same nasty reference in his conversation with Hasler and Zane.

"He's one of those NFP people – that Nation First Party! I'm trying my best to help you and do not mean to be getting political here, but these people – this Michaels guy in particular – are against everything dealing with the environment or social justice."

"Again, sir, we certainly have much more in common than not, but I need to know why you recognise Michaels and whether or not you have had any interactions with him."

Pratt shook his head from side to side. "Yes, we've interacted. He's probably been at four or five of those community meetings I referred to, and he is always one of the first in line at the microphone. I believe he's faded a bit since being elected, but last year he really hassled me several times."

"How did he hassle you?"

"Damn… I believe every time he began a question to me, instead of calling me Sean or Professor, he'd address me as 'you greenie communist'. It's pretty weird since many of the 'pro-mining' folks go on with economic statistics, the number of jobs that will be created, the amount of money that will pour into both Queensland and Commonwealth budgets and the like. Michaels never goes anywhere near that sort of argument. He gets quite personal, shouts about how NASA statistics prove climate change is a hoax, how communist academics like me are profiting to the tune of millions of dollars in research funds." Pratt took a breath. "He also uses a lot of foul language, and it doesn't even seem to faze him a bit. It amazes me because I think he really, really believes that nonsense. We academics are just rolling in cash because of the big climate hoax. I wish he'd realise for one minute how it takes days or weeks to apply for a grant which most likely you will not win and when you do, it's for ten grand or twenty grand... in short, spend two or three hundred hours to win a grant that will just barely cover a couple of grad student stipends for a year. Oh yeah, we are all rolling in cash, that's for sure." Sean realised he was speaking fast and getting upset.

"Understood, Professor. I believe we may have found someone who might not hold you in the highest esteem."

"That's putting it mildly, Inspector."

52

Sunday, 28 April; Victoria Police squad car, Melbourne, Victoria

Inspectors Benson and Liu pulled away from the Medical Science Building and took a slow lap around the block. "What do you reckon, Tony."

"Obviously Ridley is suspect number one, but we're missing something here. What the hell motive would she have to just up and kill a doctor...Actually, she up and kills him twice."

"Sonny kept his hand on the wheel and glanced over at Benson. "Twice?"

"Not twice, but I mean, first of all, she risks her own life with the Ebola-laced coffee. Then if that wasn't enough, she goes and risks her job, her reputation and her entire career by swapping over medications. Why? It seems it was all aimed at helping Kovac lose his battle with his EVD infection, his dehydration, his septic shock... Hell, it doesn't make sense."

"There is no obvious money motive... There's no obvious career motive, like a promotion or anything..." Liu turned another corner. "I guess the obvious motive we just don't see right now might be a love interest. Maybe Ridley's tied up with some bloke who had reason to harm Kovac."

"I don't know. I guess my head tells me that we should to go find this woman and arrest her. From everything we know right now, this sounds very much like a murder one case cut and dried, and we shouldn't mess around with it." He shook his head and let out a sigh. "But my gut tells me otherwise, Sonny... My gut says we need to find out more here before we tip her off."

"Exactly, Tony... once she gets wind that we were nosing around Royal Melbourne, I fear that would spook her."

"Agreed one hundred per cent... Look, I want to go back to the hospital to see what we can learn. We won't spook her right now because we know she's off this weekend. But we'd better play our cards right here. How about you set course for the hospital, and I'll phone in a silent stakeout on her residence." He pulled another copy of the printout from his file. "Inspector Tony Benson here. We need a silent stakeout on a Gemma Ridley, 12082 Sandford Avenue, Unit 1604 in Carnegie. You can find the details and photos under case VK90761-24."

* * *

"You're back so soon, Inspector?"

Benson glanced at his watch. "Well, a lot has happened in the past few hours, Dr Fairbrother." He pulled his notebook out and flipped through some pages. "Now you told us that you ordered an IV drip of 0.9% sodium plus norepinephrine at 1 mcg/kg/min, is that correct?"

"Yes, that is correct."

"We had that IV bag analysed, Doc, and we found that the medicines in there didn't exactly follow your order."

"It didn't?"

"No, Doc. As a matter of fact, they may have had an opposite effect than what you wanted."

"What was in there?"

"Our laboratory analysis showed the bag contained sodium nitroprusside and Furosemide. What do you reckon that would that have done to Dr Kovac?"

"My god... we wanted to increase fluids in his bloodstream and increase his blood pressure and these two medications would have the exact opposite effect!"

"Yes, that's the advice we had had before we came back to see you. Tell me, Dr Fairbrother, is there any way these medications could be switched by accident? I mean, are these used often enough that the pharmacists and even the nurses would know the difference."

"Well let's be clear... anyone looking at the IV bag would have no idea what was in it other than by reading the label. As for pharmacy... they surely would know the difference and couldn't possibly mistake sodium nitroprusside and Furosemide for norepinephrine."

"One more question, Doc. Do you know Gemma Ridley?" Benson read her name from his notes. "I believe that's who Nurse Cassie Schneider said brought the medications up to the unit here."

"I certainly know who she is... she's been around several years now, I reckon. She seems like a perfectly pleasant and competent young woman, but I'd be the first to admit that I don't know her other than to say hi to and I never directly worked with her. As an ED and ICU doc, I pretty much only interact remotely with the pharmacy folks... I put in orders, and they bring it up for the nurses to administer. Maybe you could ask Cassie that. I notice she just came back from break." Fairbrother gestured toward the nurses' station next door.

"Thanks so much for that. We'll check in with Cassie now."

When they were out of earshot, Sonny spoke softly to Tony. "That was a big bust. I mean, he confirmed our fears, but didn't seem to know a thing about Ridley."

"Well, let's see what the nurse can tell us." Benson rounded the doorframe and entered this little room. Schneider was looking at one of the monitors and using her mouse to tick a few boxes.

"Hi, Cassie." Liu smiled.

"Hello, Inspectors. I didn't expect to see you two back so soon."

"We just needed to follow up on a few things with Dr Fairbrother. Frankly, we're trying to wrap this whole sad story up now and just have a couple of loose ends. Would you mind if we asked you a question or two?"

"No, please. I'll answer whatever I can."

Benson again looked at his notebook. "When we spoke with you this morning, you said that a pharmacist named Gemma Ridley..." He started to read. "...'brought the meds up on a tray, and I told her I was happy to add the norepinephrine... she said she had already done that for me. She read the label and had written what was in it according to proper procedures'... Does that sound accurate."

"Spot on, Inspector. That is exactly how I remember it."

"And you never saw the packet label for the norepinephrine?"

"Well no, Gemma saved me having to do that and added it downstairs in the pharmacy. She knew what it was, though since she read it to me. Besides that, when I suited up and took it in to hang on Dr Kovac's IV line, I again checked the label. He's the only patient we had in there, thank god, and I distinctly remember the 'norepinephrine at 1 mcg/kg/min' handwritten on the label with an indelible sharpie pen. I remember the rate because I had to set it. It also was a fairly standard order for a patient who was dehydrated and in danger of septic shock."

"Excellent, Nurse Schneider." Sonny noticed her eyes crinkled, and he sensed she didn't like the 'nurse' title. "You prefer Cassie, yes?"

"Please."

"Me too... Sonny. One more question, Cassie. How well do you know Ms Ridley? Do you know her other than strictly professionally?"

Cassie smiled. "I've known her for three... four years now, though mostly at the hospital. That said, we've shared lunches and breaks many times over the years. A couple of times I've seen her away from work... just in a club or what have you."

"Pardon me for asking, Cassie, but did you ever meet a boyfriend... meet a mate of hers or partner?"

"I certainly didn't meet a boyfriend because Gemma's gay. It was never a secret, and I think just about everyone knew that. As far as I know, she does have a serious mate, but I never met her."

"Thanks so much for your time and honesty, Cassie."

"Is Gemma in trouble?"

Benson tucked his notepad away. "No, no... this is all just routine, Ms Schneider."

* * *

They both slid into the squad car and slammed the opposite doors behind them. "It's all very interesting."

"Yeah... I mean it's not like we've met the woman, but I wasn't anticipating that one. That fact that she's gay has no bearing on the case, though if a love story is a motive, it will certainly change where we search. Look, how about I call O'Rourke and Kovac and see if we can have another chat. I'm sure they – especially Kovac – will be thrilled when I tell them we are coming by to remove the electronic ankle bracelet. I'll also check in with the constables on the silent watch over there to see if they've had any contact."

53

Sunday, 28 April; Dr Liz O'Rourke's residence, Melbourne, Victoria

"Please come in Inspectors Benson and Liu."

"G'day Dr O'Rourke... Dr Kovac... We just wanted to update you on how the case is going and tell you that you are no longer a suspect, Dr Kovac."

"Thank god. I was afraid you were going to tell me you have changed your mind about this lousy electronic ankle strap, Inspector."

"No, no... nothing like that... For that matter, why don't you have a seat and I'll start with that."

Felly didn't give him a chance to change his mind, and she nearly raced over to the big sofa and sat. Benson stooped in front of her in a funny scene that almost looked like he was about to propose or at least to sell her a pair of shoes. He reached into a small over-the-arm bag he had set on the floor, produced a small electronic key, then slid it into a depression on the side of the bracelet. The electronics in the strap caused a beep-beep sound, and the back of the bracelet flapped open. Benson pulled it off and dropped it into his bag. "I'll bet that feels better already, Dr Kovac." He looked at his mobile and tapped away for thirty seconds then put his mobile back in his pocket. "Sorry for that – I had to make sure the folks monitoring knew it was me who took it off and deactivated it."

"Thank you so much. After rescuing me from that, the least you can do is to call me Felicia... Felly..."

"I'll do that, Felicia." Benson stood, grabbed his bag and then took an easy chair across from the sofa.

Liz looked at Benson. "So, from what you have said on the phone and confirming that by removing Felly's ankle strap, I guess it's fair to assume you have wrapped the case up at this point, Inspector Benson."

"Well, we can't exactly get ahead of ourselves here, but we are confident that Felicia had nothing to do with her husband's death. We did locate CCTV coverage that confirmed Geoff's conversation with you concerning someone spilling coffee while he jogged through Fraser Park. We have also corroborated that story through other evidence and have no doubt now as to the identity of the suspect."

"And that suspect is..." As the last word left Felly's mouth, her jaw had dropped, almost in the middle of her last word.

Liu leaned forward, but Benson was first to answer. "I apologise, Felicia. I promise that in the fullness of time, all of this will become known to you, and I will make sure you hear it from us before it shows up in the press. Right now though, we're still collecting evidence and solidifying our case. I only wish it were all as easy as it seems in the movies..." Benson smiled. "Just rest assured that we have this under control now."

Liu nodded and looked towards his partner. "And Inspector... Mr Kovac..."

"Thanks for that, Sonny. I apologise again. I wanted to also tell you that since you are no longer a suspect, the ankle bracelet is off and we have all the evidence we need from the hospital secured, we are now able to release Geoff's remains. I know that it is a daunting task facing you, Felicia, but you may now organise whatever it is you choose with his remains. I'm sure the Health and Community Service people will work with you on this, but I believe you will be encouraged to opt for cremation. I cannot even imagine the grief you feel, but I honestly hope you can at least find some solace, some closure now."

Felly grabbed a tissue from her pocket and dabbed her eyes. "Thank you, Inspector. At least now we may be able to begin that process... the healing. It's all been so up in the air, so surrealistic..."

Benson leaned over enough to pick up his bag again. He quickly produced a folder which he placed on his lap. "Would you mind looking at a photo for us, Felicia?" He handed the A4 photo to her.

Felly took the photo and held it angled towards the window to catch the full light. "I... I don't recognise her. I can't remember ever seeing her. Is this the suspect... the person who threw the coffee?"

"Please, Felicia, I'm not at liberty to confirm or deny that."

Liz interrupted. "May I see the photo?"

"Sure." Benson took the page from Felly and handed it to Liz.

As she reached for it, Liz's eyes still rested on her friend, realising how difficult this was for her. She took the photo and looked at it. Her eyes went wide. "I've seen this woman... recently..."

"Pardon me." Sonny was as surprised as everyone to hear such a quick reaction. "You think you've seen this woman before."

"I've either seen her or her twin."

Benson didn't give Liz time to finish. "Where, Dr O'Rourke? Where have you seen her?"

"Downstairs in the café... the Medical Science Building where Yunupingu is located has a public café downstairs, and I generally grab a coffee there once or twice a day. One of our doctoral students... Jai..."

"Jai who we met with you this morning?" Liu was on the edge of his seat, too.

"Yeah, exactly. I've noticed him sitting with a few women in the café... I even mentioned Mallory to you, Felly."

"Mallory Fowler..." The tone in Felly's voice left no doubt that Mallory was not a friend of Kovac's.

"Yes..." Liz swept her gaze from her friend back towards the two inspectors. "Mallory Fowler is a laboratory technician for the Microscopy Centre located in our building. All the research programs housed in there have access to their services. She comes up to Yunupingu to pick up samples, and I know Jai has used their services in his doctoral research. We all know Mallory because she used to work with us when she was a PhD student, but..." Liz quieted and looked to Felly.

Both inspectors also looked to Felly, and she responded in a terse voice. "I was co-supervisor for Mallory... she was working on her doctorate with both my colleague at U Melbourne and me. She and I may have had some personality clashes, but I believe I gave her every benefit of the doubt. Anyway, there were some issues of plagiarism and some... well, some other unethical behaviour. My colleague at the university – Dr Rachel Milner – and I fully concurred on the decision that we had to let her go. Frankly, it wasn't pleasant, and I thought she had disappeared. Liz told me she had reappeared around Yunupingu while Geoff and I were in

Thailand." Felly looked at Liz. "You thought maybe she and Jai were an item, no?"

"I'm not saying I knew that, but they did have tea and lunches together often enough, so it was an easy supposition on my part."

"But Dr O'Rourke, you just said you recognised this woman." Liu pointed to the photo still in her hand. Somehow I'm not following where Mallory comes into this..."

Liz brushed her hair back. "Let me start by saying I don't know Mallory well and never did, but I certainly recognise her. I also have no idea who this woman is, but I swear it is her whom I sometimes see having tea with Mallory and Jai. Also, when I mentioned to Liz that Jai and Mallory may be an item, I want to reiterate that I have no basis for saying that other than seeing them exchanging samples or having tea together."

Felly slid over on the sofa a bit closer to Liz and patted her knee. "It's okay, Lizzy. I'm not upset with you..."

Inspector Benson finished writing in his notebook and looked up. "Felicia, you stated that Mallory Fowler may have plagiarised written work and also committed some other unethical behaviour. Can you tell us what that 'other unethical behaviour' entailed?"

Felly's eyes looked more at the carpeting than the Inspector. "I don't exactly know how to say this professionally... I mean, trying to be politically correct... Mallory Fowler was hitting on my colleague, Rachel Milner... in a sexual sort of way..."

54

Sunday, 28 April; The Regency Arms Hotel,
Melbourne, Victoria

"Yes, I arrived safe and sound. You may be surprised to hear that the weather is absolutely beautiful. It's 26 degrees – that's in Celsius, Ash – and it's sunny... well, it was sunny. It's nearly 8:30 PM now, so..." Karl looked out of the window. "...it's nearly dark. Actually, the sun must have just set. Damn, that reminds me how close to the Arctic Circle we are here. Anyway, I'm happy you finally Skype me when it isn't smack in the middle of the night!" Karl laughed.

"Don't be blaming time zones on me, Karl." Now it was Asha's turn to smile. "I'm here in my hotel room in Melbourne and getting ready to go to dinner with my Dad's best mate, Clive. He's the medical school lecturer I mentioned to you. We've had a crazy weekend here."

"Well, I can match you since I had a crazy time in Alaska and a hell of a trip over here... I needed to catch three flights! Anchorage to Krasnoyarsk sounds about as bad as Townsville to Melbourne...

"Hardly..." Asha rolled her eyes. "So, what did you find out at the University?"

"I met with that University of Alaska at Fairbanks fellow, Professor Thomas Zandercon. He wasn't all that helpful, to be honest. Yes, he nominally is contracted as a consultant to the CDC, but he pretty much sounds like a medical school academic. He also was minimally involved with the anthrax outbreak last August and into September, but I think the CDC had several folks come up from Atlanta for that."

"Sorry, Karl... it sounds like a wasted trip."

"Well, it wasn't totally a waste. I learned more about this Milt Warner."

"Aw... yeah, I was going to ask you about him. He was down here in Melbourne a week or two ago, too."

"I did have a good chat with Zandercon more about the whole idea of biological warfare. Now I didn't research this as yet since I'm on the road here, but I think most of the world pulled away from biological warfare back in President Nixon's day in the early 70s. There was a Biological Weapons Convention signed back then, and almost all countries did sign including America, Russia and eventually, Australia... eventual China signed, too, but ten years later or so."

"Do we believe that nobody has a biological warfare program now?"

"That's a difficult one, and maybe you and I should tee that up for our next project after this one. There are so many freaking loopholes here. For starters, the agreed ban is on the offensive, but not the defensive programs. There has not been a uniform interpretation of what is biological, and questions arise with whether or not some toxic substances fall into this category."

"Doesn't the Geneva Protocol cover the ban of poisonous gas in warfare?"

"Again, I haven't researched this yet, but I'm pretty sure that is the case, though it's not as if poisonous gas hasn't been used in warfare recently. Well, bite my tongue, I should say other than the Syria situation..."

"So where does this Milt Warner and the Pentagon fit in?"

"He claims the Pentagon's interest is one-hundred per cent defensive. I think that's where his interest in the synthetic viruses comes in. It seems the latest approach to developing people-friendly vaccines increasingly employs a synthetic virus." She could see him look at his notebook. "Professor Zandercon went on trying to explain how this approach to synthetic viruses was revolutionising the world by using large-scale, genetically altered organisms. He was throwing terms around like CRISPR gene editing and extending that to whole-genome synthesis... By the time he started in with creating 'ultra-safe' cell lines, I was getting pretty damned nervous."

"Ultra-safe cell lines, huh! Obviously, we both need to dig deeper into this stuff since it's not just everyday genetics we're getting at here. I'm hoping I can learn more about this on my end, Karl."

"I do too because much of what Zandercon was saying went right over my head." Karl threw his one hand up and swished it over his head.

* * *

"Hi, Clive... I hope you weren't waiting too long."

"No, not at all, Asha. I just came down from my room a few minutes ago. Boy, this is way more crowded than I would have thought for a Sunday evening."

"Well, we are in the 'Big Smoke' don't forget. Melbourne is always pretty damned busy."

I thought the 'Big Smoke' referred to Sydney, no?"

"I reckon the 'Big Smoke' refers to any big city..."

Clive smiled. "I guess so... So, you sounded happy to dine right here, right?"

"For sure. I'm still dealing with bits and pieces of jet lag and travel, plus the restaurant actually looked pretty good. You have to admit, the view out that window of the Yarra River and the city skyline is spectacular." Asha gestured towards the big plate glass window.

"I thought Chicago would have spoiled you for skylines." Clive looked at the hostess. "Dr Clive Moseley, you have a table for two... Any chance we could have a window seat?" The hostess nodded with a smile, grabbed a couple of menus and led them towards the set of big windows.

"You're right that Chicago has a beautiful skyline, but you have travelled enough to know that every city has its own, distinctive skyline. Maybe some are more memorable than others, but they all have a certain uniqueness that sticks in your memory."

"You're right, of course."

The waitress pulled a seat out for Asha and then Clive. "Could I get you some drinks?"

"Absolutely."

She handed Clive a drinks menu and walked off.

"What can I get you, Asha? I think I'll just have a Victoria Bitters... you know the old saying... 'when in Rome'..."

"Good one, Clive. I reckon a Victoria Bitters is a downright creative drink when in Victoria!" She giggled. "I'm happy with a Chardonnay. I can't be certain they have heard of Western Australia on this side of Aussie, but maybe I could at least ask for a Stella Bella Chardonnay from our beautiful Margaret River."

"Excellent choice, Ash. Surely they will have that."

The waiter returned, took the drink orders and left them with two menus. In short order, they had their drinks in front of them, and their dinner orders were taken. Asha sipped her wine. "You know, the North Americans keep importing more and more Australian wines, but they seem to have trouble finding where Western Australia is on the map."

Clive laughed. "That's our benefit, I reckon. Seriously though, so many WA wineries produce a wonderful drop, but often only bottle a couple of thousand cases a year. That being the situation, it's even difficult for customers over this side of the country to get wine from some of the smaller WA wineries let alone customers on the other side of the planet."

"That makes sense. I do miss this one, though. It doesn't exist anywhere I've been in the States..." She took a breadstick from the container and snapped a piece from it. "Clive... I had a long chat with Karl, my GNN colleague, before dinner. He's way up in Krasnoyarsk, Siberia, right now working on our project. Anyway, he was sharing with me some work he learned about at the University of Alaska – Fairbanks dealing with synthetic viruses. Do you know anything about that?"

Clive nodded yes when the waiter asked if he'd like another VB. "Do I know anything about it... well please remember, I lecture in medical school, not in a biochem research facility. That said, the entire world of medicine has been abuzz with 'synthetic biology' for the past few decades. Basically, it's my understanding that synthetic biology allows us to better understand how a cell, a bacterium, a virus is constructed and that allows us to better figure out how to get them to do what we want. By better understanding how they are constructed, I literally mean examining them atom by atom... Surely Felly and Liz can do a much better job explaining this than I can, but there have been some wonderful results from all of this work including tremendous progress in how vaccines are developed and manufactured and the quality and effectiveness of these new preparations.

"I can best explain from my non-expert level of understanding with an example I have used with my second-year med students. Back 10 or 11 years ago, there was a nasty outbreak of an H7N9 flu strain. Interestingly enough, the genomic sequence of this strain had been charted and reported online by a Chinese researcher and just sat there for the whole world to see if they so desired. I would assume to nobody's surprise, a pharmaceutical company downloaded the viral gene sequence, synthesised artificial genes and inserted those into a viral backbone. In less than one week – ONE WEEK – this pharmaceutical company did what usually would have taken six or seven months of laboratory work. In that case, they pretty much followed the standard methods of producing the vaccine, but in a so much quicker timeframe."

"And the vaccine worked?"

"Yes, of course, it did. They went through the American FDA approved procedures, but increasingly, the pharmaceutical companies are pressing to go from synthesis to production. If they include some sophisticated AI in the process, it is probable that within the next few years, they will go from the appearance of a new strain of flu or another viral disease to a full production vaccine within a week or two."

"Damn..." Asha finished her wine, and the waiter quickly topped it up. "But all this is risky, no?"

"Risky? Obviously, there is always some risk involved. In the truest sense of all, though, not doing these things may be riskier. I think you are aware of the Spanish flu pandemic in 1918. The name is a misnomer since it didn't originate in Spain, but since Spain was neutral in World War One, most of the reports on the extent of the pandemic came from there. Estimates are that over 500 million people were infected and that is out of a global population of only one-and-a-half billion people. We reckon 50,000,000 people died from that outbreak. It finally got to Australia in 1919, and around two million people caught it here and somewhere around 15,000 or so died, and that was out of our total population of about five million people. Think about that... over three per cent of the entire population of Earth died in a year or two from one disease outbreak. Just suppose that synthetic biology would have allowed an immediate response to that outbreak and stopped it in its tracks..." Clive picked up his beer and took a gulp.

"I knew of the big flu pandemic, but never really considered the numbers. Jeez... If we have eight billion people on Earth today, that kind of pandemic will kill so many people..."

"If you do the maths and use the 1918 to 1919 percentages, over a quarter of a billion would die from that kind of pandemic today... Now that, Asha, is a serious risk. And we're only talking about modern medicine here. The whole exploding field of synthetic biology is impacting manufacturing with the likes of 'growing' plastics and other chemical products to making synthetic fuel by designing bugs that can 'fix' atmospheric carbon dioxide into biofuels."

"But shouldn't we fear using this for bioterrorism?"

"We certainly should be conscious of that and keep our military and policing divisions alert to maintain an eternally vigilant eye on these things, but at the end of the day, the biggest bioterrorist of all might just be Mother Nature..." Clive leaned back in his chair just as dinner arrived.

55

Monday, 29 April; Townsville District Police Headquarters, Queensland

Leon Rumford carried two mugs of coffee through his office door and set one in front of Inspector Kate Hasler and put the other on his side of the desk. He took a seat. "Let's see if the bastard calls at 7 AM like he said he would." He glanced down at his watch and was reminded that he spent big bucks buying this fancy one. It was always connected to his mobile and the internet assuring it displayed the exact time. He counted 57 seconds... 58 seconds... 59 seconds... The phone rang. He pressed the speaker feature to answer the phone. "Inspector Rumford here."

"Morning, Leon... it's Clint."

"You old bastard... you're late."

"Bullshit!" Navarro was also obsessive enough to know he called right on time.

Rumford smiled at Hasler and grabbed his mug. "Yeah, all right... you were only one second slow. Look, I have Inspector Hasler sitting here with me. We're hoping you're going to fill us in on what your boys found out yesterday."

"Yeah... I got a report last night and then chatted with my mate Felix down there."

"ASIO agent, right?"

"If you want good information, where else would you go?"

Kate Hasler was quietly laughing through it all, but Leon could see she was getting a bit impatient. "Okay, enough already... what can you tell us?"

"Good morning to you, too, Inspector Hasler. Look, Felix finally tracked that Bush Party MP down – Mr Patrick Gleason – but I think he was chasing him all afternoon. He eventually did catch up with him at his Gladstone office after dinner, and they had a chat."

"Did Gleason ever have any issues with Michaels? I mean obviously, he knows him since they are both in Parliament now. I know Gleason is in the Lower House and Michaels in the Senate, but they must come across each other." Hasler leaned forward in her seat now.

"No doubt, but from what Gleason told Felix, I'm sure he avoids Michaels like the plague."

Leon picked up his pen. "Why do you say that?"

"Well, before Michaels stood for a Senate seat in the last election, he evidently chased around several Queensland pollies, both at the state level and the federal."

"Chased?"

"Well yeah, sort of. He would show up at community meetings and not only within the Federal Division of Flynn."

"Where have we heard this before?" Rumford mumbled.

Kate spoke up. "Let me guess... Michaels attacked him on being a lefty, being an environmental crazy, being against mining..."

"You got it. I guess that sort of surprised me, though since most Bush MPs aren't generally viewed as lefties and greenies." Clint added. "They do push the agricultural side of things though, and many times that can clash with the mining interests, but they're damned conservative otherwise. Why do you say you heard this before?"

"Because we heard nearly the same story from Professor Pratt the other day." Leon answered while looking at his notes. "I asked him the questions that Felix must have asked Gleason, and Pratt gave me just about the same responses... same characters, same script, just different times and places."

"Oh yeah?"

"Yeah... Michaels called him out in front of a couple of hundred people in community meetings up this way, so obviously, he didn't restrict himself to one district. He parroted all the same nonsense that anyone associated with the Nation First Party, though Michaels wasn't an elected official at that point." Rumford grabbed his mug.

"Now listen to this... Gleason checked his diary and went back like 19 or 20 months... well before the last election. He made a note of three community meetings, in particular, one in Gladstone, one in Biloela and one in Tannum Sands. He claims that Michaels literally went off at him in each meeting and shouted, cursed and called him all sorts of names... evidently, Michaels isn't afraid to use foul language. It's both funny and sad that it seemed to work in favour of both of them."

"How do you mean, Clint?" Kate scratched her head.

"Well, Gleason reckons his supporters got pissed off at Michaels and rallied around the MP. But there is also some indication that a small group of NFP advocates who attended these meetings cheered Michaels on and absolutely approved of him seemingly taking on a sitting pollie."

"Can you pin any connection to the Gladstone bombing?"

Navarro let out a deep breath. "Here's the thing... Though Michaels harassed Gleason for several months, these three incidents were a year and a half ago in September. Recall the election was in November. Well, the Gladstone bomb at Gleason's office was in early October only a few days after the third community meeting run-in, the one at Tannum Sands, right there near Gladstone."

"So, is that it, Clint?"

"Um... one more thing. Michaels has Lester Wilkicki's and Sienna Olsen's contact details both on his mobile phone and his office system."

Rumford hesitated and made a funny face as he and looked towards Hasler questioningly. "Now how in the hell do you know that?"

Though they couldn't see Navarro, they could almost 'hear' him smile over the phone line. "Felix told me that if I told you that, we'd have to kill you both."

56

Monday, 29 April; Victoria Police squad car,
Melbourne, Victoria

"This looks like the place, and I think we're in luck... There's a parking spot right there." Sonny pulled over a few doors away in the front of the little coffee shop on Laverne Street. They both slid out of the squad car and entered the café. Liu immediately spotted Jai Yang and gestured in his direction. "There he is, Tony."

"Good morning, Inspectors. I didn't expect to be starting out the day with you two."

"Well, thanks for agreeing to meet. Dr O'Rourke gave us your number, and we were fortunate in getting a hold of you before you got to work.

"I'm not a big brekkie person, but I do stop in here most mornings for a coffee and a look at one of their complimentary copies of *The Age*. I admit that I never buy one but enjoy reading it."

"You sound like a doctoral student, Jai." Benson laughed. "Thanks so much again for your analytical lab work with Dr O'Rourke yesterday... That was really a big help to us."

"It was a big help to me... Liz signed my pay form, and I got penalty rates since it was Sunday. I'll be able to afford two coffees next week!" He smiled.

"We won't keep you long." Tony fished his hand into his folder. "We're just wondering if you know this woman." He placed the photo of Gemma Ridley in front of him.

"Jai immediately nodded his head yes. "Of course, I do... that's Gemma Ridley."

Sonny took a turn. "And you know her how?"

"She's my good friend's mate. My friend, Mallory Fowler, works in the Microscopy Centre at the Medical Science Building where I am based. She used to work for Yunupingu Institute, but that predates me. Sometimes she stops by the Medical Science Building and has lunch with us at the café there."

"Fair enough. Look Jai, can you tell me what sort of relationship you have with Mallory? Are you two like... like a couple?"

Jai had a hearty laughed at Benson's suggestion. "Oh, god no. Look, Mallory and I are friends, that's all. In my doctoral research work, I regularly have samples I need to take in for imaging in the Microscopy Centre in our building. Mallory works there, and that's how we became friends. I quite like her, actually... but no, we aren't like... like that. I don't think she'd mind me saying this since it is public knowledge, but Mallory is lesbian. For that matter, she and Gemma are the item. They are way serious and increasingly even talk of marriage now. Anyway, that's how I know Gemma."

Benson looked over at Sonny and then to Yang. "One more question, Jai. You say that Mallory worked at Yunupingu before you got there. I assume that's before you started your doctoral studies."

"Yeah, yeah... the Yunupingu job more or less came out of my doctoral program since the major aim of my research is in virology, especially the *Filoviridae* family of viruses, and Yunupingu is focused on parts of that."

"Are you aware of any personal issues, conflicts that maybe either Mallory or Gemma have with Dr Kovac?"

Jai paused an instant and scratched his neck. "Nah... no, I can't say it's ever come up. I..." He scratched his head this time. "You know, one time I remember Felly and Liz came into the café and just picked up a cup of coffee. I said something like 'hi', but Mallory and Gemma kind of looked away and kind of bit their tongues. I think maybe Mallory mumbled something to Gemma, but that was about it. Frankly, I never asked her about it, and it never came up again. You probably ought to ask Liz or Felly about that."

Both Inspectors stood up. "Thanks, Jai, thanks for that."

* * *

"Let's get over to the University... Medical Sciences building." Benson looked at the clock on the squad car's radio unit. "Dr Milner will be expecting us right about now. I'm going to check in with the boys on the stakeout. I'm amazed that no one has shown up at Ridley's Carnegie residence for 24 hours now. They haven't gotten a track on Fowler since when they checked her listed address yesterday, it seems she hasn't been living there for months, and no one seemed to know where she had moved. I think we might find that she moved in with Ridley."

"I bet you're right on that, Tony."

* * *

Dr Rachel Milner's office was easy enough to find, and the door was open when they got there. "Hello... Dr Milner?"

"G'day. Rachel Milner here." She stood and extended her hand to them both.

"I'm Inspector Tony Benson, and this is my associate Inspector Sonny Liu."

"My pleasure. Please close that door behind you." She walked around from behind her desk and ushered the inspectors to a small coffee table with four comfortable chairs arranged around it. "Have a seat."

"Thanks so much for agreeing to meet with us on such short notice, Professor."

"No worries... after I chatted with Felly last night, I was only too happy to help in some way."

"Excellent. I wasn't sure if you had spoken with her. I assume she filled you in on where we are with the investigation."

"She did. Look, Felly is about as close to me as can be. I often tell her she's the sister I never had. Frankly, we were personal friends before we even worked professionally together. Happily for us, even our husbands get along..." She looked towards the floor. "...got along... just fine."

Sonny looked at Tony and arched his eyes. "Please know that Tony and I are both so sorry for your loss, too, Dr Milner."

"It has been difficult, but obviously nothing at all like what Felly is going through. Thank god you have found the guilty party."

"Please, Professor... we do have a suspect, but we haven't made an arrest, and we are a long way off from a conviction."

Benson thought he might accelerate his interview to ease some of Milner's conjecture. In almost one motion, he lifted his bag, dug into his folder and produced a photograph of Gemma Ridley. "Do you know this woman, Professor?"

Milner took the photo and stared at it for fifteen seconds or so. "I may have seen her somewhere, but I certainly don't know her. I honestly wouldn't swear that I have even seen her, Inspector."

"And this woman." He pushed a photo of Mallory towards her.

"Well, of course... that's Mallory Fowler."

"Dr Kovac tells us that you and she used to be co-supervisors for Mallory when she was a PhD student, yes?"

"Yes, we were."

"Tell me, Professor, what kind of student was Ms Fowler?"

Milner let out a deep breath. "Look, she was very bright, but she wasn't a good student. I've been in academia for twenty years now and time and again I see the same thing... Doctoral-level work has more to do with interest, personal motivation and dedication than with sheer brainpower. Fowler is a very smart woman, Inspector, but she lacked... how can I say it... the personal skills."

"Dr Kovac told us she washed out of her doctoral studies because of plagiarism and other ethical failures. Could you please comment on that?"

Rachel shifted in her seat. "I... I guess so... Look, the plagiarism was straight forward. It is so simple nowadays to check that with the latest software incorporating AI baselines. Throughout the first 5 or 6 months of her second year in the program, Mallory submitted several papers that were blatantly plagiarised. When Felly confronted her with that, she simply denied it even though Felly had the printed copies of papers from which she literally cut and pasted whole pages."

Sonny spoke up. "That sounds pretty black and white to me, Professor. I guess that in and of itself would be enough to end a student's doctoral hopes."

Milner nodded yes.

"As far as the 'other ethical failures'... Liu continued. "...can you tell us about that?"

"It's quite sad, really." Rachel's head turned down as she talked. "Look, you have to understand that I am not at all comfortable talking about this, but if it is going to help Fell... and Geoff..." Milner took a deep breath and slowly exhaled. "This is obviously confidential, police business, right?"

"Of course, this is all confidential police business, Professor." Benson shifted.

"There was never any secret here, and Mallory was fairly open with her fondness for women... Both Fell and I knew that Mallory was gay, which I can assure you, was perfectly acceptable to both of us. It was just one of those things that never came up, and we would never talk about since it was nobody's business but her own. We probably went the first 6 or 8 months of the two years she was studying with us, and it was just like that... no mention of it at all. Now understand, I don't mean the lack of conversation that had anything to do with her being lesbian, and that would have been the same if she had been straight. For god's sake, Fell and I were – are – best of friends and we never have conversations about our sexual lives. That's what I mean... sexuality just never came up... never SHOULD have come up..."

Both inspectors nodded their heads and continued taking notes.

"Somewhere near the end of her first year, Mallory started saying little things... like that's a nice dress... I like your earrings..."

"She's saying these things to you, Professor?" Sonny's eyes were arched high.

"Yes, yes... to me. Frankly, those sorts of little things aren't that unusual amongst the 'girls' as it were, though a little bit unusual considering the supervisor-student professional relationship. I'm guessing somewhere in December something strange happened. We had the staff Christmas party over at the Institute, and I assume Mallory had a few too many drinks. She started getting rather touchy-feely, and I felt uncomfortable about it. Somewhere near the end of the evening, I was getting ready to leave, and she came over and hugged me very close. Of course, I tried to pull back without making a big scene, but before I could do that, she gave me a kiss... but it was a very strange kiss... an open mouth kiss and VERY inappropriate.

"That bothered me over the whole several week holiday period, but I thought maybe it was just the alcohol and that it would all go away. In retrospect, I fear I erred in not coming down firmly right then and there. When we all got back on board in mid-January, it drifted to the background for a few weeks. My birthday is in February, and the day before it, Mallory came to this office in the afternoon and closed the office door and threw the deadbolt. She had a wrapped pressie in her hands and asked me to sit right here and open the present. I was nervous, to say the least, but not knowing how to deal with this, I pulled at the paper while she sat in that chair and nudged herself a bit closer to me. I opened the package, and there was a very revealing lacey lingerie set."

Milner stopped and took a deep breath and then let out a sigh. "I apologise... this is difficult for me."

"Take your time, Professor." Benson knew she was having trouble telling the story and was happy to give her all the time she needed.

She let out another sigh and continued her story. "When I looked at this lingerie set, I must have swallowed my tongue! Oh my god! I'm glad I don't have a photo of what my face must have looked like right then. I was literally shocked and said nothing at first. Mallory said I should try it on, and that she wanted to give me a very special birthday present. I probably swallowed my tongue a dozen times before I could find my voice and asked her to leave. She was very hurt and said that she loved me. Inspectors, please believe me when I tell you that I have never felt so unprepared and totally speechless before that moment or since. I just didn't know what to say. She leaned over and tried to kiss me again, and I let loose. I tried hard to remain professional, but I had great difficulty. I told her how inappropriate this was... that I was married... that I was heterosexual... She told me not to lecture her and that she wasn't a little girl."

"I'm sorry to put you through this, Professor." Benson was amazed at hearing her story. "And I imagine that was the end of that."

"No, it wasn't. We went through similar inappropriate moments at least four or five... maybe six, seven or more times over the next couple of months. Each time I would say no, she'd have a hissy fit and get increasingly upset. I didn't know who to tell this to. I did hold on to this alone for several weeks, but it was eating me up. I didn't even mention this to George – George is my husband. Finally, I spilled my guts to Felly, crying hysterically and expressing guilt even though I could find no reason for feeling that way. I was so upset that I couldn't see this coming... that I couldn't have prevented it. Thank god for Fell... She was so strong... so supportive... I don't know how I'd have gotten through this without Fell.

"We discussed it all at length, and Felly agreed to take on way more responsibility... at that point, I refused to see Mallory alone. I didn't see Mallory much after that, but I heard about her often from Fell. Fowler must have been more and more of a pain in the butt to Felly to a point where I think she – Mallory that is – blamed her for screening me out. That went on for another 4 or 5 months of that second year until Fell and I both agreed she needed to drop out of the program. Felly spoke to her about it several times, but Mallory continued to take it out on Felly. She used to say things to Felly such as blaming her, saying that it was Felly who kept her away from me. She was persistent... always claiming that it was all her fault – Felly's fault – that I resisted her advances. One day towards the end of that second year, Mallory was in the level 4 biosecurity lab and came out late in the afternoon when just she and Felly were still here. She 'accidentally' forgot to dispose of a glove or cover and left it near where Felly had her bag on a desk. Fortunately, Felly noticed, but she hit the roof when she realised Mallory had not only broken protocol but seemingly did so on purpose. I believe that was the last time Mallory was ever in the Yunupingu Institute, save for in her new role as an employee of the Microscopy Centre over there."

"Did you or Dr Kovac report this to the University... to the authorities?"

Milner's head dropped. "No, I didn't... We didn't... Fell and I talked long and hard about it. I was not keen on ruining this woman's career and just wanted her to go away. Felly probably had a good case considering the glove incident, but she too just wanted her to go away. Actually, when you consider the news headlines and student-teacher relationships, too often if a child accuses a teacher of unethical behaviours, many times the burden of proof seems to fall onto the professional. I realise we weren't in that school-level; teacher-student relationship, but in some ways, this could be construed to be even worse. I couldn't even imagine what a female graduate student supervisor accusing a female PhD student of making unwanted advances would look like to the community." She tipped her head. "Fell was nervous about how that would look, too. "In the end, we decided that it would just go away, and fortunately, that seemed to work. Neither one of us saw her for a long, long time. I only heard of Mallory reappearing since Felly came back from Southeast Asia. She told me she saw her at their office, evidently collecting samples for the Microscopy Centre or going to tea with one of the current doctoral students there."

Sonny noticed that Milner was actually shaking. "I'm so sorry we put you through this, Professor. We needed to know this, and you have helped both Felly and Geoff Kovac telling us all this. I – we – can definitely see why this is so very difficult to share with us."

"I'm sorry I am so emotional now. I have pushed this out of my mind for a long time now and don't at all like revisiting it. I thought this was all behind us. I'm so sorry that Felly has gone through this. I pray that Mallory Fowler is in no way involved here, but if precedent is any predictor, I very much fear that she could be."

57

Tuesday, 30 April; Townsville District
Police Headquarters, Queensland

"Good morning, Senator." Rumford led the way into the interrogation room with Navarro and Hasler close behind. All three sat across the steel table from Michaels.

"Your heads are going to roll for this. You can't bring a Parliamentarian in like this. You can't keep a sitting Senator in the lockup overnight. I'll have your head, um... um..."

"Oh, sorry Senator... I should introduce us. These are my colleagues, Inspector Kate Hasler and ASIO Agent Clint Navarro. And my name is Inspector Leon Rumford, and my serial number is QLD953-076 if you should need that. I'm sure my colleagues will be happy to supply you with their ID number, too if you so wish."

"You have no right to detain me, scum."

"My, my, Senator... I think my mother taught me to be a bit more civil with people I just met... maybe when I was just five or six years of age. Did your mum teach you that, Inspector Hasler, Agent Navarro?"

"She sure did, Inspector."

"And my mum taught me to be extra nice to police officers." Navarro was quite conscious that he had to focus on tampering his short fuse.

"I want to see my lawyer. Jake Hollister... he's my attorney... I want to..."

Rumford slammed his hand on the table, and the steel sheeting retorted with a loud bang. "I've already spoken with Attorney Hollister, Senator Michaels. And you are wrong, sir... We needn't let you see him right now, and frankly, we have no intention of doing so. You, sir, are in very big trouble."

"But I'm a Senator..."

"And I, sir, am a cop. Last I heard, you parliamentarians make laws and us coppers enforce them. At the end of the day, we all need to educate ourselves in exactly what the law is. You, sir, should have spent more time learning what you can and can't do legally. You, sir, are being held under terms of the Terrorism Act... You, sir, can be held without charge for 14 days..."

"You can't fucking hold me, copper. You're nothing more than fucking communist jackboots! You will never work again, believe you me!" Michaels was shouting now. "I'm going to have your fucking badge... your fucking career..."

"And you should learn to use a bit nicer language. Maybe you should listen for a minute, Mr Michaels. I'm going to say Mr because I think your days as a Senator are numbered. You are in one hell of a lot of trouble. Terrorism... you could get life in prison. Terrorism... the minute you are convicted of any felony... but especially terrorism... that Senator title will be removed, retroactive to right now, sir."

"I've got rights!"

"Rights... Thanks for reminding me, Mr Michaels... Before we go on, let me get over the formalities here, sir. We have kept the magistrate up half the night because of you, but she did issue a Commonwealth search warrant for your home, office and belongings. Kate, do you mind?"

"No, Inspector, I don't." She looked at her card. "I am informing you that you do not have to say or do anything, but anything you say or do may be used in a court of law. You may also communicate with a legal practitioner should you so desire. Finally, we are recording this interview, sir. Do you understand this, Mr Michaels?"

Michaels did not respond.

"I believe you should respond, Mr Michaels. It's one thing to have the coppers on your case, but you now even have ASIO chasing you... and regrettably, I tend to have a nastier temper than these two..." Clint's voice was calmer and quieter than it should have been.

"Look, man, I didn't do fucking nothing!"

Navarro leaned forward until he was centimetres from Michaels' face. This time he raised his voice to just short of yelling. "Be respectful of Inspector Hasler. She asked you a question, Michaels. Do you understand her words? Was it clear to you what your rights are and that you are being recorded... and being recorded, I might add, means this can all be played back in a court of law?"

Both the volume of Navarro's voice and the reminder that other people might hear this seemed to settle Michaels enough that he mumbled an answer. "Yes, I understand."

"Very good." Rumford opened his folder and produced a manila envelope from which he pulled several A4 sheets that he laid on the table. He took extra care in making sure the official seals were visible. "You, sir, will shortly be formally charged and placed under arrest for the bombings of MP Gleason's Gladstone office and Professor Pratt's team while diving off the *Reef Explorer*. Attorney Hollister has a copy of these papers now. I repeat that under the Terrorism Act, we have every right to question you here this morning and will do so until we get to the bottom of this."

"This is all bullshit... When did these bombings occur?"

"Well sir, the first one was just before midnight on Thursday, 12 October last year about a month before the election. You should remember that one since we know you attended several community meetings at Gladstone, Biloela and Tannum Sands. Actually, the Tannum Sands one was two nights earlier on a Tuesday night the 10th of October. The second bombing was near Townsville up off the coast from Lady Lyman Beach. That one was just two weeks ago on Tuesday, 16 April... in the morning..."

"I have alibis."

"Alibis?" Hasler's gaze remained glued on his eyes.

"If you're trying to frame me, you'd better be a hell of a lot more on the ball than this, suckers. Parliament was sitting two weeks ago, and I was in Canberra, 1,500 kilometres away. No doubt you can see that on the digital recordings they have. I don't even need my calendar to check October because I remember that Tuesday night in Tannum Sands, but I drove up to Townsville the next day doing campaign appearances. Thursday night I was in Townsville, more than 800 kilometres away. Once again, you can check me since I was interviewed by Sky News, so there'd be a digital record of that, too..." Michaels sat back in his seat with a smug expression on his face.

Navarro grabbed his chin and rubbed it several times. "You place a lot of faith in having digital alibis, don't you, Michaels?"

"The video never lies, ya creep."

Clint let his mouth hang open for several seconds until he fished in his pocket, pulled out his mobile and set it on the steel table. "You know. I thought I'd toy with you a bit, Michaels, but a piece of shit like you really isn't worth wasting time on. You somehow forget that when you link the word 'terrorism' with the 'Australian Security Intelligence Organisation', you might just have outfoxed yourself in terms of digital records." His fingers worked the mobile's screen until he looked up from the desktop. At first, there was a beep, and Clint turned the volume up full. Suddenly voices could be heard that obviously were from a recorded phone call.

"Hello, Malcolm?"

"Yes."

"Sienna here. Lester called... things went well."

"The office?"

"Yes... a really big bang. He said it must have woken up half of Gladstone."

"Were there any people in there?"

"Nah., he thought the place was clear. The throwaway phone bit worked a charm, and the bomb went off just as planned."

"Okay, Sienna, let's leave it at that for right now. I'll get back to you tomorrow."

The phone followed with a computerised voice. "Timestamp Tuesday, 10 October, 11:37 PM Australia Eastern Daylight-Saving Time."

"Jeez... that sounded just like your voice, Malcolm. And we know that was Olsen because she's already dobbed you in, mate."

Michaels looked startled. "You fucking..."

"SHUT UP, MICHAELS!" Navarro's voice nearly shook the walls of the investigation room. I've got one more for you to listen to, you bastard!" He again fiddled with the screen on his mobile, and again, the phone could be heard ringing.

"Michaels, here."

"It's Sienna, Malcolm. I just heard from Lester, and everything went according to plan. The explosion was on target and Pratt's university boat went down."

A laugh could be heard. "Excellent. Hopefully, he was out of any camera range."

"I'm sure he checked."

"I've made the arrangements, so you'll see your European holiday refund in your bank account by tomorrow."

"Good on ya." She chuckled. "We might just think about planning another holiday... maybe Bali."

Again, the computerised voice was heard. "Timestamp Tuesday, 16 April, 9:44 AM Australian Standard Time."

"You can't do that! That recording is horseshit, and you know it. You don't have my permission to use that, and I'm a Senator."

"Rumford ran his fingers through his hair. "For some reason, Mr Michaels, you don't seem to be able to let it register in your brain that you are under arrest on a terrorism charge. You don't really have any ground to stand on to say we can't use that data."

"But the government can't just record a conversation and then use it against you without permission."

Kate Hasler smiled. "You just don't get it, Mr Michaels. Those recordings were not from your phone, sir. They were from Sienna Olsen's phone, she recorded them, and she gave us permission to use them."

"Well, that bitch! She's a rat! She cut a deal with you..."

58

Tuesday, 30 April; Fitzroy Police Station, Melbourne, Victoria

Tony Benson and Sonny Liu sat in the meeting room across the hall from Benson's office. Benson stood at the whiteboard with a marker in his hand. "I just want to go through it all here to see where we stand. In the past 24 hours, I have felt as though we have this case all wrapped up, and yet we don't even have an arrest at this point. We need to push hard now, Sonny."

"I know what you mean. Look at what you have up there now. Obviously, Felicia Kovac is off the board. For that matter, others we talked to have been valuable, but are pretty much out of play. Dr O'Rourke was never suspected of anything. Dr Deshi Tang... Dr Rachel Milner... Jai Yang..." Every time Sonny mentioned a name, Tony put a red tick by their name. "...that lab tech, ah Wendy Ingman."

"And other than Ridley, the hospital folks are all out of it at this point." Benson checked off Fairbrother and the other staff to whom they had talked. "I know you must have arrived at the same place that I have... I think that Mallory Fowler was the motivating force behind it all and never did get over her Rachel Milner fantasy. I can't say if she pretended to fall in love with Gemma Ridley to activate her plan or if she actually fell in love with Ridley first and then devised the plan. It probably doesn't matter since the end result is the same."

"Would she have known that Geoff Kovac – or Felly Kovac, had it worked out that way – would have wound up in Ridley's hospital?" Sonny turned his seat to the side and stretched his legs out in front of himself.

"No problem there, mate... Any cases in Melbourne involving Ebola are so rare, so nearly non-existent, that there is only one facility in the city that could hope to handle it. I'm of course referring to level 4 biosecurity facilities..."

"Good point, Tony. But damn... if Fowler planned this thing that far out... far enough to feign falling in love... you're suggesting she isn't only psychotic, but most likely psychopathic. That means this was most certainly not a crime of passion, at least not on Fowler's part. She'd be a stone-cold killer, calculating every step of the way and acting everything out as premeditated as she could possibly be."

"Well said... I think that's most likely exactly the case." Benson drew a red circle around Fowler's name. "So that leaves us with Ridley. She is so obviously the actor here, and I don't think there can be any doubt that she infected Geoff Kovac in the first case using the coffee in the park and helped hurry his death along in the second case by switching the medications in the IV bag. But what's the motive? Is it one-hundred per cent love... her love for Fowler?"

Benson unconsciously picked at a tooth with his fingernail and Sonny nervously tapped his foot on the floor. The two inspectors remained like that for nearly a minute, contemplating the final part of the puzzle...

Sonny was the first to speak. "You know, Tony... I guess we won't be able to figure that final piece of the mystery until we bring them in and interrogate them separately. My gut instinct tells me that Fowler is truly the psychopath and that Ridley is quite simply a demented sweetheart willing to even commit murder to preserve her lover's affection."

"If that's the case, Sonny, we'd better go bring them in... now, before Fowler gets some more crazy ideas..."

59

Tuesday, 30 April; Dr Liz O'Rourke's residence, Melbourne, Victoria

Felly gave Rachel a big, tight hug before she could even close the door. "I am so, so sorry you had to go through all that yesterday, Rachel."

"Come on, Fell... That wasn't your fault. Frankly, we could have gone through this several years ago, but horrifyingly enough, I might have gone through it all without you. I'll never know why that glove she left wasn't contaminated."

Rachel followed her friend to the living room. "Hi, Liz. Damn, this whole thing has no doubt been amazingly difficult for you, too."

"It has, Rachel. After more than a week, we can at least see some light at the end of the tunnel... For starters, Felly getting that damned electronic ankle bracelet off was a huge deal. Now having Geoff's body released... we can finally get some closure."

"Thank god. When I called last night, I was still upset from my interview with the two inspectors, but when I thought about what you were going through, I somehow just wanted to get over here and give you a hug."

"Thanks, Rachel. I hope Inspector Benson and Inspector Liu were kind to you."

"They were." Rachel threw a lock of hair over her shoulder. "You probably know that I still haven't really told that story to anyone other than George, and even that took me a long time to do... it is still so very difficult." She looked to Liz as if to say, please keep this confidential.

"I did tell you that Geoff's funeral is Thursday, yes?" Felly reckoned she was almost out of tears now.

"You did." Rachel pouted. "It's probably best to organise it so quickly."

"When you think that Geoff's been gone… died last Monday morning… it isn't that fast. He has so many friends near and far that, considering the situation, I thought it best to have a small burial service Thursday and then a larger memorial service in a month or so where we can celebrate his life." Felly tried to force a smile. "I hope by then all the police stuff will be over with."

Liz leaned forward. "It will be, Fell-O. With any luck at all, we'll get you settled back at home." She suddenly realised the Health Department issues with that. "Oh boy… I wonder what hoops the Victorian Department of Health and Human Services will have you jump through to get back in your own home."

Felly answered. "With any luck, I think it's just ticking boxes now. Health and Community Services released the house yesterday, too. Of course, the problem with the house is that it needs special cleaning and since that was a level 4 biosecurity issue, that is a special decontamination process. For all I know, I probably have to buy all new furniture. I've organised for the decontaminating to be done now and hopefully, it will be cleared by the weekend. We'll see."

"But in a way, that makes no sense. If the Department of Health and Community Services and the Victorian Police Department have both determined that the strain of Ebola that infected Geoff was from Yunupingu Institute, then Geoff couldn't have been able to infect your house with it…" Rachel was almost thinking out loud.

"Well, not technically. He took his jog that Friday morning and when he returned home, he would have still had some of the spilled liquid on him. It's debatable whether anything would have survived, but we don't actually know that. I guess it's better to do the cleaning than not." Felly nodded her head, resigned to the fact that she really had no choice in the matter.

"Have you heard any update on Mallory?" Rachel almost feared to ask.

"I know they are looking. Evidently, she hasn't been home since the weekend, though according to Inspector Benson, even the police aren't exactly sure where home is. She may have been living with the other woman... Ridley... Gemma Ridley." Felly breathed deeply. "I just want them to find her... them... and for this to be over."

"Soon, Fell-O, soon." Lizzy leaned over and tapped her friend on the knee.

60

Tuesday, 30 April; Fitzroy Police Station,
Melbourne, Victoria

Benson looked up from his desk computer as Sonny Liu walked into his office. "What time do you have?"

Sonny looked at his mobile and then back at Benson. "It's nearly 10:30 PM, Tony. You know, my wife has just about forgotten what I look like."

"That's probably an advantage considering she's been looking at your sour puss for what... ten years now." Benson smiled.

"Eleven years, you old bastard! One of these days, my wife and I are going to take a holiday someplace far away from here where I'll be certain that you can't call me back in to work after dinner."

Benson ignored him and turned over a page in his notebook. "Look, let me bring you up to date with the latest I heard from Fisher and the boys on that detail over there watching Ridley's unit. It's kind of crazy considering that have now been watching for 55 or 60 hours, and no one has turned up anywhere around there. At this point they have established that Fowler left her Hawthorn place a few months ago, so the assumption is that she moved into Ridley's Carnegie flat, but that is still not confirmed. The trouble is that in the past two days, nobody that they have talked to and showed Mallory Fowler's photo to has any recollection of her, though many know Gemma Ridley. That's kind of funny, no? Maybe they have been living secretly."

"And yet Professor Milner, Jai Tang and Felly all told us Fowler is openly a lesbian." Sonny's face disclosed his confusion.

"And we have no reason to doubt that. Maybe Fowler didn't make herself visible because she didn't want anyone to recognise her later." Benson's eyes arched high. "Look, just before you got here, Fisher might have gotten a break. He told me they did track down Ridley's mum somewhere over there... Footscray or Essendon – he never gave an address... She did see Gemma Saturday night and didn't have much to say about the conversation. But he did find out that mum gave her daughter car keys as well as keys to her beach house in Apollo Bay down there on the Great Ocean Road."

"Apollo Bay... that's two or three hours down south past Geelong."

"Yep. Fortunately, Fisher already has the local coppers chasing the beach house tip and looking to see if they are still there."

"They have the details on the car, too?" Benson checked. "It's a Holden Spark... Vic plates FGM-276..."

Sonny stared at his partner and noted him flipping through his note. "Tony, if you don't mind me asking, how come you use a notebook. I mean now days just about everyone in the department uses a tablet computer or a mobile to take notes. I've worked with you for several years now, and you always have that damned notebook... What's with the old paper and pencil, mate?"

Benson looked at him with the most serious expression he could manage. "I'm glad you asked that, Liu... Maybe there's hope for you as a copper yet. Did you ever hear of Sherman Lockhart?"

"Um... I can't say that I have, Tony."

"Well you know, I'm a decade or so older than you and have been here for... hell, going on 25 years now. When I first came into the department, Sargent Sherman Lockhart sort of took me under his wing. He was a hell of a detective. I'm surprised you never heard of him."

"Lockhart?" Sonny shook his head.

"He was so good at tracking down the bad guys that he earned a nickname. Sherman Lockhart got shortened into Sherlock, so everyone called him Sargent Sherlock, but usually just Sherlock. Old Sherlock was a legend to all Melbourne coppers... a real legend."

"Damn, I did hear of him. I think he fell off the perch the first year I was around here, but I never knew his real name, just Sherlock. Didn't he just up and die from a heart attack or something?"

"Yep... that was Sherlock. Anyway, I learned the notebook from him. The first tablets were coming in before he passed, but he always argued that a paper notebook never needs charging, never gets fried by lightning and can't be hacked. He also taught me a little trick when interrogating perps who may not be coming clean with you."

"A trick? What's that?"

Benson made sure he held his notepad in his hand. "One of the best devices for focusing a suspect and making him or her think you know more than you do is to keep looking down at your notebook. If you do it right, you can almost convince the suspect that you KNOW what the answer is and are just checking to see that they give you the true response."

Liu was almost impressed. "All right... so now I know. Can't you do that with a tablet?"

"An electronic tablet... you're dreaming, Liu."

"Well, let's hope they track these two women down, and I can watch you do your notebook routine a bit closer this time..."

"I'd advise you to take a lesson from an old pro, Liu, and maybe..." Benson's words were cut short by his desk phone. He grabbed for it. "Benson... Yeah... Where?" Benson looked at Liu and nodded his head. He pointed to the handset with his free finger and arched his eyebrows. "How many bodies? Any ID? We're on our way..." He slammed the receiver back into its cradle and popped out of his seat. "They got 'em."

"Both girls? What were you saying about bodies?"

Benson grabbed his bag. "That was Fisher. His boys found the little Holden run off the road pretty much in the middle of nowhere... someplace just off the Princes Highway where there's a turnoff towards Moriac. It seems the car had run off the road and must have been wrapped around a tree or something. Hell, there's nothing down there. I know the road... two-lane, sheep paddocks and trees..."

"What about bodies. Tony?"

"There is one dead body at the scene and no sign of anyone else. At this point, they haven't IDed the body."

* * *

It was nearing midnight by the time Benson and Liu saw the police and rescue lights on Hendy Main Road, only a hundred metres or so off Princes Highway. They pulled off the dual carriage highway and onto the to the two-lane side road. There were a few cars backed up on the two-lane road, but at this hour of the night, the country traffic was sparse. Benson radioed in a check to the station as Liu slid out the driver's side. Benson was only seconds behind.

"G'day Inspector. I'm Constable Lewis... based in Geelong. What a nasty crash here. I was first on the scene, and when I found her, I checked for a pulse on her neck and couldn't feel one. The ambos came screaming in a few minutes after me. They worked on her for a bit, tried damned hard to resuscitate her, but they never got a pulse. They had a hell of a time trying to get the body out of the car, so they waited until the wrecker got here. They finally pulled the smashed-up car out of the ditch and away from the tree and the rescue people were able to get her body out of the front seat."

"The report said one body?"

"Yes, that's it, Inspector. We have found some ID now... a Gemma Ridley from up in Carnegie... near you guys up there in the big city."

"Ridley, huh? Yeah, we were looking for her. The word we got was that she was at a family beach shack in Apollo Bay. Funny thing though... there were two of them... we were looking for two women."

Constable Lewis shook his head. "We have no sign of anyone else... no bag, no wallet, purse... there is no sign of another person that I could find."

Liu spoke up just as the rescue team was moving the stretcher with the covered body towards the back of the rescue vehicle. "Any idea on the COD yet?"

"Cause? Well no, nothing official, but I've been here since about twenty minutes or so after the call came in. Hell, she hit a tree, the airbags went off, and I guess the impact must have been too much. I assume she whacked her head on the dash and windscreen. There's a smashed window there, so looks like some serious concussive forces. I hate to sound so routine, but you do one of these late-night crashes, and you've done them all. You get kids half pissed, and they run off the road. I reckon that's what happened here."

"Hum. Mind if I check with the rescue team?"

"No, go ahead. I'm sure the ambos won't mind."

By the time Liu got over to the ambulance, the rescue people had already pushed the covered body into the back of the wagon. "Do you mind if I take a look at the body?"

The ambo looked at his name badge. "No, go ahead, Inspector Liu. She isn't' a pretty sight."

Liu climbed into the back and sat on the side bench next to the gurney. He pulled the cover back. It was obviously Ridley. He was surprised that her face was in pretty good shape. There was a bang on the forehead, but considering it was a lethal accident, she didn't look that bad. He pulled the cover down to her waist and notice a pool of blood on her side towards the back of her ribs. He leaned over and pulled the gooseneck lamp down closer."

"What are you checking there, Sonny?" Benson stood at the back of the wagon now, looking in at his partner.

"I'm not sure, Tony." Liu grabbed a pair of disposable medical gloves from a box on the rack behind the bench. He quickly pulled them on and ran his hand along Ridley's side. "Damn." He pulled the blanket down farther and loosened her blouse. As soon as he could see her skin, it was obvious she had been impaled. He rolled her just enough to get a better look.

"Come on, mate. You aren't doing a full autopsy in there."

"Sorry, Tony. Look, Ridley has definitely been impaled. That's not unusual in a car accident, but this almost looks like it was a spear or rod, but there's nothing obvious here. We'll take a look at the car. Anyway, I think it went in from an angle below her hip and penetrated the – I'm counting four or five here – it's difficult to tell in such tight quarters. Anyway, if I had to guess, I'd say the rod entered low and slid in upward through the fourth and fifth ribs into the heart muscle. There's a hell of a lot of blood here. I know the ambos tried resuscitating her, but that was never going to happen."

Liu shimmed his way back the bench seat and jumped out of the ambulance. He looked at one of the rescue blokes. "Did you ever get a response?"

"No... she had no pulse when we got here, and my mate and I both worked... maybe ten or fifteen minutes... we even hit her with the paddles a few times...Nothing was happening. Besides, she had lost a lot of blood and was in a very difficult spot to get to her until the wrecker moved the car away from the tree."

"Thanks, mate." He looked at Benson. "Let's check the ditch over there."

Constable Lewis was sitting with his bum on his squad car seat and his legs outside, feet on the ground. "Told you it wasn't a pretty sight."

"You were spot on there, Constable. Hey, did you get some photographs before the car was pulled up?"

"Yeah... here – take a look." He handed Benson and Liu his phone with the first photo open. They thumbed through, both taking turns looking. Zooming in and out and then going to the next photo."

"Do you mind giving those to me, Constable Lewis?" Benson pulled his mobile out and tapped the Bluetooth icon. Within a few seconds, he had all the photos on his mobile. "Thanks."

"Over here, Tony." Liu could see Benson had finished getting the photos. "Look at this." Sonny held a big torch and pointed it into the car. "There's a hell of a lot of blood on that seat, but not much on the windscreen. Also, look at those." He pulled one of the deflated airbags back and pointed to three different points-of-impact on the glass screen. You'd reckon that if the glass were hit from outside – from impact with the tree – these impacts would push in. You can see all three impacts push out. Also, if Ridley's head hit the screen, there'd be one big impact pushing out. We don't see that here."

"Let's check the ditch." Benson had his torch pointing down now and the both took short steps down the gravel and dirt incline into a ditch maybe a metre-and-a-half deep. "Son-of-a-bitch!" Tony bent down and looked at a rock. "I think there's blood on this."

Just as his hand extended towards the rock, Sonny shouted. "Hey, Tony... careful with that. If it's evidence, you don't want to contaminate it. Take some photos, and I'll grab more gloves." He ran back up to the ambulance and grabbed another pair of gloves, borrowed a clean towel and returned to the ditch. "Let me get it." Liu stooped and picked up the rock. "Shine that here."

"See what I mean?"

"Damn right I do. That is blood... fresh blood..." Liu lifted the rock and carefully place it on the towel. He wrapped it up and then stood. "Heavy enough... maybe three or four kilos."

"So, Constable Lewis... Who called this in?" Benson stood with Lewis while Liu kept looking around.

"It was a bloke driving an IGA truck doing overnight deliveries, I guess. Fortunately, I was only about a kilometre down Princes Highway here..." He gestured towards the west. "...and got here literally within a minute of his call. The trucker told me he was making his last drop of the night in Colac before heading back to the city."

"Did you see him?"

"Yes. I pulled in right behind his rig, and he was just climbing out of his cab. I'm telling you, he must have noticed the car off the road somehow... it isn't all that visible. Anyway, he pulled over and called it in. Dispatch immediately noted where I was and patched it through to me. I quickly checked the car and driver and pretty much accessed it as a DOA and told him he could leave. I do have his details, though. Let me forward them to you."

"Thanks, Constable. Hey, what're the chances that IGA truck driver has a road dash camera on his truck?"

"I'd say pretty good. Nowadays I think more and more of the insurance companies all but require that on commercial vehicles... just to cover their own asses."

"Tony, look at this."

Benson looked over and saw his partner holding what appeared to be a metre-long metal rod of some sort. As he walked closer to where Sonny was standing, it was obviously covered with blood. "What do you reckon, Sonny?"

"I reckon she just might have been knocked out with that rock, killed with this rod first and then the car was run into the tree. Let's get this evidence into the forensics guys ASAP."

61

Wednesday, 1 May; The Regency Arms Hotel, Melbourne, Victoria

"Happy May Day, Karl."

"Well, it's way early here for that..." Karl looked at the clock on his laptop. "Damn, only 4 AM and I haven't seen a spec of daylight yet, though I think it does come up early. We've got to stop meeting like this, Asha."

"We will stop soon... when we are both back in Chicago."

"You mentioned May Day... I don't know if you realise just what a big deal May Day is in Siberia... I guess all of Russia. I doubt I'll make much progress with interviews today since just about everything is closed."

"Damn, I never thought of that. Some of those Eastern European countries, many being old Soviet Block countries, take May Day very seriously. At least I know I've heard that many times, anyway."

"I'm sure you are correct on that. They have a big parade here today from the posters plastered all over the lobby here. You'd be surprised... the city of Krasnoyarsk is way more modern than I anticipated and straddles the Yenisei River. It's over a million people, and the buildings are modern, and the place is pretty clean. Frankly, I was expecting something much more third-worldly for some reason." Karl sat at the small desk in the room and a bit of the night sky could be seen in the half-opened drape behind him.

"Were you able to meet anyone yesterday?"

"I did. I visited the Krasnoyarsk State Medical University yesterday, and they were all quite hospitable. I had the VIP's tour of the place... all very medical school-oriented and it's obvious their main thrust is cranking out doctors. They do conduct a bit of research and – obviously, that's why I am here – they have taken the lead in the 'zombie microbes' investigation, at least as far as the Russians are concerned. They do a fair amount of collaborative work with European Union scholars, too."

"Interesting... how's the English? Did you have any trouble communicating?"

"Yes and no. People in the street, the shops, the restaurants... seem to know enough English to at least point you in the right direction, especially the younger folks. Here at the hotel, most do not speak English, but there is always at least one English speaking clerk on the front desk and the couple of *concierges* I've spoken to have been excellent. No, all-in-all, language hasn't been a problem."

"That's all good... so what have you found out so far?"

"Frankly, I learned a hell of a lot more here than in Alaska. I fear to say that the Russians seem to be taking this whole thing – zombie bugs – much more seriously than my fellow countrymen in the States. Anyway, after my tour around the medical campus and school here, I spent several hours with two scientists, Dr Jelena Popov and Dr Boris Stepanov. They were a wealth of information and have very much collaborated with the *Karolinska Institutet* in Sweden. I've got reams of notes and photos and videos that we will eventually go through together, but basically, they have done much work that they are happy for us to use collecting and analysing samples, site visits including questionnaire data and surveys and good biomedical testing numbers we will have our folks sort through back in Chicago. I have been so very impressed with how open they have been."

"So, have they been able to identify this new – or ancient – form of anthrax that is increasingly causing problems in northern populations the past year or so? Can they do anything in terms of prevention or treatment?"

"I've got to give you another yes and no here. They have arrived at the same place the Americans and Canadians have as far as the new strain of anthrax, though they are no more certain than the Americans are as to whether it is a new mutation or a ten-thousand-year-old *Bacillus anthracis* that's been in a cryogenically induced state of suspended animation since cavemen were around. That said, they have made some important breakthroughs on a more useable and reliable vaccine.

"The current vaccine has fairly good results for people who may be exposed to *Bacillus anthracis* and is targeted for people from 18 to 65 years of age. One of the hang-ups with it is that it takes time to build immunisation by taking an initial intramuscular injection and then a second at one month and a third at six months. Then you basically are to get booster shots at six and twelve months and then once a year afterwards. This is all well and good for people who risk exposure in their line of work, but it doesn't help much with the general population. It also offers about 90% effective results.

"I know you have learned that the worst infection of anthrax comes from inhalation, and that is much more serious than cutaneous infections. Inhalation exposure generally requires a combination of antibiotics such as ciprofloxacin and that would normally be delivered intravenously.

"Now I doubt that I have told you a great deal more than you already know. The two positives though are that first of all, Popov and Stepanov have confirmed all this, and second of all, they are making great headway here along with their Swedish colleagues towards developing a vaccine that is both more effective and easier to administer. There probably would be little value in telling you more here on Skype. I will say this though... I undoubtedly have enough material and – just as importantly for our documentary – enough video to flesh out at least one or two segments of an episode, especially sprinkling in some of the less insightful Fairbanks stuff."

Asha nodded her head in the affirmative. "Sounds like I'd better be adding to your work here, Karl. I do have a lot I've pulled together so far but have a way to go as yet. This criminal investigation has sort of waylaid me a bit, and I am keen to pin down some more specifics with the whole *Zaire ebolavirus* flareup both in Southeast Asia and down here."

"Have there been more cases in Australia?"

"No, thank goodness. Frankly, it seems that the one case... one death... increasingly looks like a homicide, though that in and of itself could prove to be useful material for us."

"Damn... murder by *Zaire ebolavirus*? Well, you keep digging since I am feeling more and more positive that the anthrax side of our work may prove to be discovered, identified and possibly defeated, at least temporarily."

"Keep that 'temporarily' tag in mind... I increasingly think that we may have hit the limit in our centuries-long fight with Mother Nature. I'm not so certain mankind is 'winning' this battle anymore."

"In the end, isn't that exactly where we started this whole story... exploring the increasing body of evidence that somehow, nature has almost turned a concerted effort on ridding itself of the *Homo sapien* menace?"

"Oh god, Karl... it sounds so ominous when you put it in those words."

"Honestly, Asha, I think you were the original source of those words was said to you by one Professor Sacha Sharma."

* * *

Asha wanted to make one more Skype call to Townsville before she met Clive for brekkie. In the last call she had with her father, he indicated that he invited Sean over to Freo both to work on a few things they were collaborating on and to see Asha before she headed back to the States. She had done about as much as she could here in Australia and was determined to at least spend the weekend with her dad before heading back to Chicago and thought it'd be nice to see Sean again, too.

"Asha. Good to see you. You're up pretty early?" Sean was still at his home.

"Early? It's nearly 8 AM here. I'm meeting Clive for a coffee and then trying to wrap up a few things here.

"When's Dr Kovac's funeral?"

"That's tomorrow... 10 AM Thursday, Melbourne time."

"Poor guy. Any word on the suspect? Have they found them yet?"

"To tell you the truth, Sean, it isn't as though anyone would call to tell me that, but as of last night, I believe they were still chasing someone. Hopefully, we will hear more today. I just know that Felly – Kovac's wife – will at least be able to begin that long process of healing."

"For sure."

"What have you heard on your bombing case up there in Townsville?"

Pratt yanked on one ear. "I think they've IDed several suspects now, but I don't have anything official yet. It could be a very controversial result though since the lead Inspector was asking me a lot of questions about one of our Commonwealth Parliamentarians."

"Wow, a sitting pollie?"

"Let me wait on that one, Asha."

"Understood. I did talk with my dad last night, and he said he was organising some work you two were doing and hoped you'd come over to WA for the weekend. Have you spoken to him yet?"

"Yep and yep... He invited me, and I booked flights last night." Sean laughed. "We do have a bit of work, but I think Sacha has designs on you and me. Anyway, I'll fly over on Friday but need to get back here Monday morning." He almost blushed.

Asha tried to ignore his comment on Sacha's attempt at playing Cupid. "Damn... I know what Perth-Townsville flights are like!"

"Best of luck with the funeral tomorrow." He shook his head at the camera when he realised what he just said. "You know what I mean... I know it's not like you've known these people forever the way Clive has, but it still is emotional. Give Clive my condolences."

"Will do, Sean." Now it was Asha's turn to feel a blush surge into her face. "I'm glad you'll be in Perth over the weekend, Sean."

"Me too." He smiled into the camera. "See you, Asha."

62

Wednesday, 1 May; Townsville District
Police Headquarters, Queensland

Clint Navarro tapped his phone and slid his volume control down. "Now I'm sorry we had to make you listen to them again, Ms Olsen, but you can see what our problem is here. We have these phone calls that somehow connect your boyfriend, Leister Wilkicki, to Senator Malcolm Michaels and two bombings. In every case, you seem to be the middle person, Ms Olsen.

"Now Inspector Haslet has informed you of your rights. I just want to reiterate that you can have representation here if you so desire, Ms Olsen. I also want to advise you that Mr Wilkicki has already admitted his involvement with both of these crimes and that we are still in discussions with the Senator.

Navarro tilted his head and looked at her with his sternest expression. "You know, Ms Olsen, I think it is pretty obvious from what you just listened to that those recordings don't leave much to the imagination. You used the words 'bomb' and 'explosion', Ms Olsen. Our forensic boys have already corroborated your voice patterns and the timestamps and your GPS traces, ma'am. I will happily get your attorney in here right now, but he will not change these facts. You are in some very serious trouble, Ms Olsen. Now I'm just an ASIO agent, but I've been chasing criminals my whole life, and I don't see you fitting into that whole criminal mould. I don't see you being a terrorist, Ms Olsen. I really think you are better than that." He ran his fingers through his hair. "Do you want to explain the rest of this to her, Inspector Rumford?"

"Sure thing... Thanks, Clint. I admit I feel the same way Navarro does. I just don't see you being the motivating force behind all of this. It seems to me that Michaels had a beef with what seems to be the entire world. Wilkicki was looking for a get-rich scheme. Ms Olsen... I reckon you just wanted to please... wanted to help your boyfriend out.

Leon pulled a paper from his folder and placed it on the table in front of him. "You can contest all of this since that is your right, but I need to inform you that..." He looked at a paper on the desk in front of him. "...Section 7 of the Criminal Code Act 1899 in Queensland states that it is an offence to aid, abet, counsel and/or procure another person to commit a crime." He looked up at her. "That is what we refer to as being an accessory to a crime, Ms Olsen. This falls under the Queensland State Criminal Code, but frankly, Ms Olsen, the Commonwealth Code may have much harsher penalties. Because explosives were used, government property – the *Reef Explorer* – was destroyed and a Commonwealth Parliamentarian's office was targeted, these crimes fall under the Australian Anti-Terrorism Act of 2005. I don't think that Queensland will ever get a chance to prosecute you, ma'am... I think you're looking at the Commonwealth taking this to the fullest... making an example of all three of you. Do you understand all of this, Ms Olsen?"

She let out a deep sigh. "But I never wanted to hurt a soul."

Rumford's head rocked side to side. "I'm sorry, Ms Olsen. But that's just not the way the law works. The Commonwealth will put all intentions aside and cut straight to the chase... they will try you as an accessory to attempted murder under the terrorism code... Do you understand that, Ms Olsen?"

She raised her hand and wiped away a tear. "I do, sir."

Rumford was encouraged. He detected that she felt defeated, and he reckoned now was the time to push her cooperation. "Under Commonwealth Terrorism Laws, attempted murder carries the same penalties as murder. That also applies to when we charge you as an accessory to murder. That said, you could be looking at 25 years in prison, Ms Olsen. 25 years is a long time. I see from your records here..." He looked down at his notebook lying on the tabletop. "I see that you are 34 years old now. Let's see… if the Crown throws its full weight at you, you'd almost be 60 years old when you were released, Ms Olsen."

Sienna's face was red, and her tears started to flow freely now. "I'm… I'm not a terrorist, Inspector… I was only trying to help Lester. He thought we could earn some easy money, and he promised that no one would get hurt. He… we NEVER wanted to hurt anyone." Hasler walked over beside her and gave her several tissues. She also grabbed the jug of water and filled Olsen's glass.

"I believe that, Ms Olsen. But you may want to somehow indicate that to the Crown. I've already spoken to the Commonwealth Director of Public Prosecutions' Office and have been told that they are agreeable to making a deal with you, Ms Olsen."

"What do you mean, a deal?" She dabbed her face with a tissue.

"I am not in a position to make promises, Ms Olsen, but if you agree to turn prosecution witness for the Crown, I have been assured you would get a substantial reduction in sentencing. For that matter, if you help Commonwealth Director of Public Prosecutions bring down Senator Michaels, it may be possible to receive a lesser charge and possibly avoid any jail time at all… Prosecutors don't like it when a citizen commits a crime against a member of the community. Prosecutors don't like it when politicians comment crimes against members of the community even more."

63
Wednesday, 1 May; Fitzroy Police Station, Melbourne, Victoria

Benson dropped his desk phone in the cradle and stood. He walked across the hall, poured himself another cup of coffee and returned to his office. He sat in his chair and closed his eyes, rubbing them hard with his fingers. Damn... he'd had all of six-hours sleep last night... actually, this morning. But it sounded as though they cracked the case wide open. Now they just needed a little luck.

"Tony." Liu poked his head in Benson's office door.

"Bloody hell, mate... look at you! I confess to sitting here half-asleep and thinking about how tired I feel. But damn, mate... I reckon you look worse than me."

"Thanks... At least I got five or six hours. My wife is about ready to disown me. At least I got a report from the forensic boys..."

"Already! Doesn't anyone around here sleep?"

"Already! The bastards took..." He looked at his watch. "...eight or nine hours... What's that about? I told them it was a rush job!" He smiled. "But they did get a hell of a lot here. They didn't have time to go through the car with a fine-toothed comb yet since the wrecker only brought it into central about an hour ago, but at least they dusted for prints Fowler's are all over it. One of my mates did confirm that the impact on the window came from outside, not in, just like we thought. They still need to match things up, though."

"How about the rock... the metal rod?"

"Good news there. The blood type on both the rock and rod are Ridley's so her body was definitely in contact with the rock and she was impaled by the rod. Of course, we have no prints on the rock since the surface was too rough. The prints on the rod are a definite match for Mallory – we have sample prints for her from both the Microscopy Centre and from Yunupingu. Some of Mallory's blood could be on the rod, too, but we need to find her to confirm her blood type."

"What was the rod, anyway? I thought maybe it was steel rebar..."

"No, no... too light. It wound up being aluminium... like a rod pulled out of a pool fence or something... very light."

"Cause of death?" Benson was scratching notes into his notebook.

"They need toxicology yet, but indications are that Ridley was bashed in the head with a blunt object... probably knocked her out. The scratch marks look like that rock could have done the job. The investigating team at the autopsy didn't think that that was the COD though, rather the single entry of that rod is what killed her... It separated ribs four and five and then punctured Ridley's heart. She'd have died within seconds from the trauma." Liu sat back in his seat.

"Well wait a minute here... Fowler is not that big of a woman. Would she have had the strength to run that rod through Ridley's chest?"

"I think so. The tip of the rod had a point, again, like a pool fence picket. She must have had her adrenalin pumping too since one of those bashes with the rock was pretty serious. Look, we need to ask her how she did it, but at this point, there's no doubt it was her. Fowler's prints are all over the car, too." Sonny yanked on his ear.

"Look, here's how I reckon it happened and, save for a few details, I bet we are smack on the money." Liu stretched his neck and ran his hand through his hair. "Fowler and Ridley went to the Apollo Bay beach house and got a bit lovey-dovey for a day or so, but then started getting nervous about the coppers coming after them. Maybe Ridley even spoke with her mum at some point, but Mallory would have pulled the plug and said they were getting out of there. Maybe they got in an argument, or maybe it was just cold psychopathic murder, but somewhere right near where we found the car, Fowler pulled off the road. I reckon she got out and found a rock... or maybe even had it in the back seat since Apollo Bay. Anyway, she bashed Ridley in the head and knocked her out cold. Then she hit the windscreen and made a few cracks there that we see coming from outside to inside. With Ridley out cold, she puts her behind the wheel and impales her or else impales her and then slides her behind the wheel."

Benson followed Liu's whole scenario but finally interrupts him. "Wait a minute... I'm still thinking about that smallish woman driving the proverbial stake in Ridley's heart. Do you reckon she did it with Ridley behind the wheel or outside on the ground?"

"My guess is outside and then manoeuvre her behind the wheel, but I can't be certain. The forensic folks need to finish going through the car and over the photos, and they'll fill in the blanks here. But whether Fowler impaled Ridley before or after she moved her, it doesn't change the outcome. At that point, she starts the car, props the accelerator – maybe even using that aluminium bar – and then puts it in gear and lets it smash it into the tree and ditch and watches the airbags inflate. She was only a couple of hundred metres from Princes Highway, so she tidies up her handiwork, cleans herself up a bit, walks over to the highway and hitches a ride."

"You might be right, Sonny." Tony was nodding his head. "The picture you paint here seems to fit all that we know so far. Now we just need to find Fowler and let her supply some of the detail."

"Well, I have some good news on maybe tracking her down... I hope..." Tony set his coffee mug down. "We got results from the dash cam on that IGA truck. Remember, he was travelling west on Princes Highway from Geelong before he noticed the crash scene off the side there near on that two-lane road. Anyway, our boys reviewed his dash cam video. He only passed six cars on the other side of Princes Highway between the crash scene and Waurn Ponds. Fortunately for us, the IGA truck had a good system... eight megapixels..." Benson clicked his mouse and turned the monitor so Liu could see it."

"Damn, that is a pretty good camera considering it was pitch black, save for the car lights."

"Yeah, but look. Photo one... photo two..." Tony clicked through the cropped image of the six cars the IGA truck had gone past. "Notice that only one car had two people in the front seat."

"Can you zoom on that one."

"Sure... look..."

"You know, it's too damned dark to get any kind of resolution, but it sure as hell looks like a bloke driving and a woman in the passenger's seat... just because of the hair. You can read the plate number, though. I think we need to give that bloke a call."

"Cool your jets, Liu. I don't spend half my day sleeping like you. I'm way ahead of you. I've called him. It's a veterinarian named Kirby Brown, and he was travelling up the M1 – the Princes Highway – to Werribee. Dr Brown told me he saw a woman waving alongside the highway and he thought at that hour, she'd need some help. He picked her up and her description matched Mallory's. She told him her car broke down, and she wanted to get her roommate to drive back down to fix the car."

"So, where'd he take her?"

"She was happy to get out at a 24-hour Caltex station there in Werribee. He said the last he saw her, she was on her mobile. He offered to take her somewhere if she wanted, but she said she was fine now." Benson looked at his notes. "I also checked with the Caltex station there, and we didn't talk to the overnight bloke yet, but there was nothing in the logbook about anyone unusual coming in at that time."

"Damn!" Liu slapped his hand on the desk.

"What's that about, Sonny?

"I'll bet you and I sped right past Dr Brown and Fowler on our way to the crash scene last night... this morning..."

"You're probably right. Look, we have a nationwide KLO4 on Fowler now and hopefully, she'll turn up sooner rather than later. We also have Tullamarine Airport covered as we do the train and bus stations. AI is on the prowl through CCTV also. She'll be recognised, I'll guarantee that."

64

Wednesday, 1 May; Dr Liz O'Rourke's residence, Melbourne, Victoria

"Everything is set now, so there's nothing else to do before tomorrow's service." Felly seemed to have cried as much as she could for the past eight or nine days and was almost anxious to go through the formality of tomorrow's funeral.

"I almost feel guilty being here tonight, Felly." Asha had accepted the invitation from Clive at breakfast this morning. "I just feel as though I am intruding since I never knew Geoff."

"Nonsense!" Felly was definitive. "Clive was one of Geoff's best mates, and they knew each other for forty years. Don't forget, Clive needs to get through this all, too. Clive has reminded us time and again of his relationship with your father... and with you..."

"Thanks, Felly." He grabbed her hand, leaned over and gave her a kiss on the cheek. He looked at Asha. "I wanted you here, Ash."

"We all wanted you here with us, Asha." Liz stood at the counter between the kitchen and the dining area. "And I could think of nothing better for dinner tonight than Fell-O's favourite, Prima Pizza. You have to grab your own plate, though."

* * *

"Well, that is encouraging news that your colleague Karl has learned in Siberia, of all places." Clive still munched on a piece of crust.

"Not really..." Liz crinkled up her face questioningly. "We have done a great deal of work with Russian researchers and have found them very thorough and competent. I can't at all speak for some of the crazy behaviours of their governments over my lifetime, but some of the science out of there has been top-notch and excellent."

"Fair enough... I didn't mean to be disparaging of the Russian scientists, rather that Siberia seems so far out of the mainstream of travel. I swear I've been around the world, but never to Siberia."

"Understood. Frankly, I've never been there, either. Have you two ever been there?" Liz looked at both Asha and Felly, and they both shook their heads no. "I'm old enough to still remember that the Russia we know grew out of the old Soviet Union and that conjures up all sorts of nasty images of the Iron Curtain, the arms race and biological warfare... I like to think it's not like that anymore."

"Agreed, Lizzy... though I must admit, I had a similar feeling when we met that American bloke, Milt Warner, a few weeks ago. I was feeling guilty that he might have been looking for nasty ways to use our research for evil ends." Felly's face showed her concern.

"Maybe I can give you a few words of encouragement, at least." Asha's reassuring smile was calming. "I did tell you that Karl came across Warner, too... in Atlanta at the CDC there.

He didn't think the bloke was all that threatening and was simply fishing for anything that others were doing that could cause concern for the Americans."

"I hope your colleague is right." Felly still looked concerned.

Asha's curiosity got the best of her. "I guess I just don't know enough to be fearful or dismissive... do you really think Warner or, for that matter, any of the Americans or the Russians or the Chinese, could take this whole idea of synthetic biology and somehow use it in warfare?"

Felly was first to speak. "Biological warfare... that issue has been around forever, and the idea of it never seems to go away. Being a so-called expert in the field of virology, I have absolutely no doubt we have the knowledge and the technology to build incredibly lethal infectious diseases. But it always comes back to the same problem, namely, how do you infect your enemy without infecting your friends? I know the science fiction movies always seem to have the antidote developed simultaneously with the pathogen, but in reality, that doesn't really happen. I'm not saying some haven't tried... or are trying... but there is nothing I have ever come across, in theory or in practice, that indicates it is even possible to employ those kinds of nasty microbes in any kind of controlled way."

"Agreed one-hundred per cent, Fell-O." Liz lifted her glass of red. "It is just so risky that I certainly hope nobody would ever try."

Clive joined the dreadful discussion. "Should we fear some small terrorist organisation? My understanding is that increasingly, engineering new DNA has become almost a backyard, in-the-garage sort of activity. I've read of several community biology laboratories that are open to anyone with the desire to learn biological engineering. I know there's a chain of half a dozen People-Labs in the States that offer the equipment and even expert help to anyone willing to do some basic education and contribute to the rent, so to speak. I believe they are only operating a biosecurity level 1 lab now, but who knows."

"Karl and I did come across People-Labs but haven't actually visited any at this point. But it can't be that easy, can it?"

"Don't kid yourself, Asha. Do you remember the other night I told you the story about the H7N9 influenza?" Clive reminded her of their conversation. "Those folks simply looked up the genomic sequence of the specific strain that Chinese researchers posted on the internet and in less than a week, produced a viable vaccine."

Asha slowly nodded her head, but her squinting eyes telegraphed her concern. "But you'd think that with this technology getting easier and easier, crazy lone wolves would be trying their hand at making nasty bugs in record numbers."

"Our security has thought of this too. In a sense, there is this balance between being free and open, and yet somehow not letting awful things happen. I know – at least I have read about – this whole concept of People-Labs and there are a couple of start-ups here in Australia now, too. Actually, one of our former doctoral students is running one of those sorts of labs in Sydney." Liz looked at Felly. "You remember Sophia, Fell-O, don't you?"

Felly nodded her head. "Yeah... sure... she's a bright woman."

"Anyway, I had a chat with her about this once, and first of all, the key ingredient in these facilities seems to be the openness of it all. It would be difficult to carry out anything nefarious without everyone knowing about it. Secondly, as Clive mentioned, they are all operating at biosecurity level 1 now, so the really lethal stuff just wouldn't enter into it."

"Then, why do it?"

"Simple, Asha... attempts at entrepreneurial breakthroughs. There are many examples in agriculture from viticulture within our wine industry to animal husbandry." Liz had obviously done a bit of research on the trend. "I read about a pet shop in Singapore now where you can buy glow-in-the-dark tropical fish and puppies with striped coats like zebras."

"Damn... but it can't be that easy, can it?" Asha was amazed at what she was hearing.

Clive joined in. "Remember, we're messing with DNA here so you can design viruses, bacteria or – as Liz just pointed out – mammals the likes of puppies. We've had some Western Australian-specific examples involved in the resource sector with designer 'bugs' that could help purify gold employing specialised microbes eating sulphur to bacteria that can help clean up petroleum spills by being able to eat the oil."

"I confess to really oversimplifying here but consider that designer DNA is increasingly in vogue. DNA is basically made using pieces called nucleotides, and all nucleotides are made from just three parts: a phosphate group, a sugar group and a nitrogen base. You want to talk about simple? Surprise, surprise... there are only four nitrogen bases, namely adenine which we abbreviate with the letter A, thymine abbreviated T, guanine with a G and cytosine with a C. Now you can put thousands... millions... billions of these together, but you can also just tweak parts of the chain.

"By that, I mean that I can use an existing genome and only look at one part, let's say the part that determines hair colour. Maybe that codes as ATCGTC for blonde hair and ATCGCC for brown hair and the other tens of millions or a billion of base pairs are just used from the existing genome. The standard equipment – even at People-Labs – is pretty easy to use to do that. In the end, that's how you wind up with zebra-coated puppies."

"Wow." Asha was intent. "You're saying that you take an entire house – so to speak – and just alter a little plumbing under the bathroom sink and wind up with a new house that does something the old house couldn't do?"

"Well, something like that. Maybe compare a long piece of software code with tens of thousands of lines in it. If the right hacker knows what ten or twelve lines to manipulate, you wind up with software that can do something very different, like send money from your bank account to the hacker's!" Liz seemed to like her own example.

"I admit that I am stunned at how easy this sounds because I fear what could result from all this." Asha took another gulp of her wine. "I knew this was happening, but I guess I didn't realise it was so widespread or so easy."

65

Thursday, 2 May; Centre of Excellence for Coral Reef Studies, James Cook University, Townsville, Queensland

"Thanks for coming in this morning even though it is pretty early to be getting you deadheads out of bed. I wanted you to all be here when the Inspector comes over to fill us in on the latest update to the investigation. From what he told me yesterday afternoon, I believe they are pretty confident that they have wrapped it up." Professor Pratt smiled at the head of the meeting table in his office.

"Come on, Sean... We'd have been bummed out if you DIDN'T call us in." Nikki Vasquez ran her hand over her leg, a bandage still covering where she had been injured.

"Too true, Nik..." Becky voiced her agreement while John nodded his own.

"By the way... I'll be over in WA over the weekend, but if you need me, just text or – if you really need to – call."

There was a knocking door. "I'll get it." John Rivkin got up and opened the big, wooden door. "G'day, inspectors."

"G'day." Rumford led the team in. "Hello, Professor. I'm glad you were able to call the whole group together since you all have skin in this game."

"Welcome Inspectors Rumford and Hasler and agent Navarro. Please, grab a seat."

"How are you feeling, Nikki?" Hasler smiled at her.

"I'm doing just fine, Inspector. Thanks for asking. The docs say I'll have nothing lasting from it all, save for a nasty scar. It already has healed enough that I don't feel any pain when I walk. I should be ready to dive again when we go out the end of next week. I just thank my lucky stars that the explosion didn't happen a minute earlier."

"Well, I'm here to tell you I have good news and... better news!" Romford's grin went ear-to-ear. "Having been a copper for twenty-something years now, it doesn't always work out that things fall into line so well. We have made three arrests now, and that should all hit the headlines maybe in time for the evening news, but for sure in tomorrow's papers. I just wanted you to know before that happens because, once this news hits, it's going to be BIG..."

"I knew about the bloke and his girlfriend, but I think things may have gone beyond that, yes?"

"Yes, Professor. Thanks to your help and Agent Navarro here, we got to the bottom of it all. You won't be surprised to hear about the Senator, but I imagine it will be big news across the country."

Becky Whitehall ears perked up. "Come on, Inspector, don't be teasing us like that."

"Let me think where we left you the other week, maybe ten days... Becky, John and Nikki knew about the blasting caps and burner phones, right?"

All three students nodded.

"Well, here's the thing. We pretty much first pinpointed Sienna Olsen and then her boyfriend, Lester Wilkicki, because of you two." He looked at Whitehall and Nicki Vasquez. "You were a fantastic help."

"No way... we had no idea what date that lady started talking to us, let alone who she was." Nikki was surprised.

"Nah, it doesn't work that way anymore. I don't know if you realise there are tens of thousands of public CCTV cameras all over Australia now and an unknown number of commercial and private ones. Add to that the artificial intelligence software we can feed that data to, and it's damned difficult to hide from all of them. We found that woman – Sienna Olsen – almost right away. She works for a mining company, Lion Creek Mine. Using CCTV from a road house near Lady Lyman Beach up north and the dash camera from a couple of locals, we also got to Mr Wilkicki and connected the two of them right away. That's where Clint Navarro comes in... his people were able to isolate mobile conversations and the rest, as they say, is history."

Navarro leaned forward. "I am aware of the fact that the Professor knew about the Gladstone bomb, but I'm not sure you three did... There was a bombing that preceded the *Reef Explorer* incident down in Gladstone last October. Considering these were bombs and both impacted government property – the *Reef Explorer* and a Commonwealth MP's office in Gladstone – we were at once operating under the Australian Anti-Terrorism Act and that gave us way more leeway."

Pratt scratched his head. "So, everyone has been charged at this point?"

"Actually, that's why I started saying we have good news and then better news. The good news is that both Olsen and Wilkicki copped pleas. Olsen pleaded to accessory after the fact, and the Crown agreed to give her a slap on the hands, maybe serve 3 to 6 months in jail and then be paroled."

"After the fact?" Pratt was aware of her knowledge about the explosion when Lester phoned her.

"The Crown was happy to make that concession since 'after the fact' had a lesser penalty associated with it. Now Lester Wilkicki pleaded to attempted murder, and that's a pretty serious charge. When they sentence him, instead of the recommended 25 years, he will maybe get half of that and would probably be eligible for parole in maybe 7 or 8 years."

"Wow, that seems pretty light for that sort of crime." It was obvious Becky had stayed way clear of any run-ins with the law in her life. "Why was the Crown so lax in their punishment."

Inspector Hasler took a turn. "Ha, that's simple. They both turned evidence against Senator Malcolm Michaels."

"Michaels, the nut case?" John Rivkin's eyes lit up. "Remember that crazy bloke that gave you all the hassles at the community meeting, Sean?"

"Do I ever."

"Well, the point is that Michaels has been very uncooperative and, especially since he initiated both explosions, he will face the full force of the law. I reckon he'll get the full 25-year sentence and, obviously, lose his Senate seat and all the perks that go with that."

"Damn... shows what I know. I've been telling Nikki I was certain it was the mining company the whole time." Whitehall shook her head.

66

Thursday, 2 May; Blue Gum Funeral Home,
Melbourne, Victory

Felly had planned a small service for Geoff today and a larger one in a month or so after the pain of the past two weeks had time to lessen. She was surprised by the 150 people who had come to the Blue Gum Funeral Home for the memorial service this morning. The weather was cooperative with partly cloudy skies and temperatures in the mid-20s.

Since neither Geoff nor she had any family left in Australia, she was particularly heartened by Lizzy and Clive standing by her side. They helped her greet a long queue of friends offering condolences after the service. She knew that Geoff would have been honoured seeing all his work colleagues from Yarra Hospital, all the Yunupingu staff and other community friends and neighbours they had known over the years paying their respects and offering Felly condolences.

Inspectors Benson and Liu stood at the back, waiting to be at the back of the queue so they too, could pay their respects to Felly. "Some name for a funeral parlour room right... the 'Condolence Lounge'. Almost makes you think they should have a bar in here."

"Behave yourself, Tony."

"Never fear." He didn't wear a tie often but had one on now. He unconsciously grabbed at the knot and adjusted it. "Good thing I didn't forget to put my mobile on silent... I got a message from JJ toward the end of the service... they got her."

"Fowler?"

"No, Santa Clause's mother!" Tony had a look of disgust on his face.

"Be nice, Benson. This is a solemn occasion..."

"They picked her up at Tullamarine... Just before a domestic flight to somewhere. He said he'll fill us in when we get back."

"Good stuff."

"Good stuff? I say, finally!" Benson looked at the queue and noticed that the last two or three people were chatting with Felly and Liz. "Let's go pay our respects and get back to the station. I want to hear the whole story and then have a chat with Fowler."

67

Thursday, 2 May; Fitzroy Police Station, Melbourne, Australia

"I'll let Burros know we're here, and he can come to give us the whole story." Liu headed down the hall as Benson opened his office door.

He dropped his bag in the corner, undid his already open tie and pulled it through his collar. He let out a deep sigh and sat behind his desk. A quick look at his screen showed a couple of dozen emails had come in while they were at the funeral home including several from Burros. No point in looking at them, since he'd be here in a minute. Any others could wait. He closed his eyes and dropped his head onto his palms, his elbows on the desk. He'd been through a thousand cases in the past dozen years, but this one was an extraordinarily strange one. Murders are never a pleasant thing, but in this case, people were trying their damnedest to contribute to the community... to help people through the emergency department in Geoff Kovac's case and through their research in Felly, Liz and Rachel's cases. Long hours, threatening working conditions, dirty hands... it's not like an ED doc, or academic researchers were ever going to be rich... Man, he needed about a week's worth of sleep. Benson started to doze off and suddenly...

"You meditating, Benson?" Inspector JJ Burros' booming voice shook him from his micro-nap, and his head snapped up like a leaping lizard.

"Nah, nah, nah... I'm just resting my eyes here. It's been a long week."

"Fair enough." Burros sat in one chair, and Liu plopped himself in another.

"So, what's the story? I know you got her, but can you fill us in?"

"Sure can. Look, after that veterinarian dropped her off in Werribee, Fowler tried begging another ride into the Melbourne CBD to hop a train. She must have quickly figured the CCTVs were tracking her. Once morning came and the retailers opened, she bought some makeup, a wig, whatever could throw the AI off her. Don't kid yourself, Fowler is a smart woman. She knew how to design a disguise to confuse the AI, but only for a while."

"Hell, we knew she was a smart bird."

"Well, it must have worked. We – actually, the software – spotted her near Flinders Street Station around 10 AM yesterday, but then she just disappeared from radar. She really had us stumped there for a bit. We had the AI cranking away as hard as we could taking the feed from a thousand cameras. One of the boys tried backtracking in an attempt to work out what kind of wig she bought and how she tried changing her appearance. It was all for naught though, since, in the end, she made a big mistake at 4:52 this morning." The smile on Burros' face announced his satisfaction.

"And that was?"

"She bought a plane ticket using her credit card."

Liu jumped in. "Damn... she must have been getting desperate."

"Well, she was. She knew we were watching and thought the only chance she had was getting out of town." JJ flapped his arms like he was flying. "She must have thought that an international flight wasn't going to work or maybe she didn't have her passport... whatever, she booked a flight to Broome."

"And you picked her up?"

"Well, not right away. We still didn't ID her on any CCTV. The boys just staked out the gate where the Broome plane was departing from and lo and behold, a half-hour before boarding – around 7:30 AM or so – she comes rocking up with curly, blonde hair, blackish eyes, bright red lipstick... well, whatever she did, it was confusing enough to the AI. For that matter, when you see the CCTV footage, your own eyes won't recognise her."

Benson squirmed his shoulders, trying to work out a kink or two. "So, you brought her in?"

"Did do. We sent the message to you but knew you were at the funeral service. Hell, she ain't going nowhere now. She's in interrogation room two."

"Spot on, JJ. We'll let's go have a chat and then we'll book her."

* * *

"G'day, Ms Fowler. I'm Inspector Tony Benson, and these are my colleagues, Inspector Sonny Liu and Inspector JJ Burros. I've been looking forward to meeting you for over a week now."

"Glad to meet you, Inspector. Now can you let me go... I need to get off to work."

Liu was confused by the calmness of her voice. "Do you realise you're in big trouble here, Ms Fowler?"

"Trouble?"

"You do realise that Ms Ridley is deceased, don't you?" Tony's eyes grew tense.

"So what?"

"Did you have anything to do with that, Ms Fowler?"

"Me? No, why would I do that?"

"Well, you were in her mum's car with her, down near Apollo Bay Monday afternoon or so."

"That wasn't me... it couldn't have been."

Tony was confused now. "Why's that, Ms Fowler?"

"I was with my friend."

"Your friend?"

"Yes... I was with Rachel... Rachel Milner."

Liu looked at Benson, and his eyes went wide. "Wait a minute, Ms Fowler. We know you were with Ridley... Gemma Ridley... she was your lover, right?"

"No, no... Rachel is my lover. Rachel has always been my lover... Rachel and I are going to get married."

"Do you realise that we have your fingerprints... your blood... we KNOW you were with Gemma Ridley Monday night... that's the night she died, Ms Fowler."

"I'd remember that if it happened, and I don't remember that. Rachel and I made love Monday night... we make love every night..."

Benson stood, a blank expression on his face. "Thank you so much, Ms Fowler." He looked towards JJ. "Um, JJ, could you please make sure Ms Fowler gets to a very safe place." He gestured down the hall towards the lockup. "Could you please make sure they keep an eye on her there." He nodded his head.

"MH Intervention Team?"

"Exactly... can you stay with her until they are here?"

"Will do, Tony." JJ walked over beside Fowler. She already was wearing handcuffs. "Let's go somewhere more comfortable, Ms Fowler."

* * *

"Damn, she obviously went off the deep end."

Sonny cocked his head. "Hell, she could be going in and out of this all the time. Mental health issues aren't my area of expertise, but I don't think she's faking it."

"No, I don't either, Sonny. Hell, for all we know, Gemma Ridley was involved in the same fantasy world, somehow. At least JJ will await the Mental Health Intervention Team, and they can take her for assessment. We've done all we can do..."

PART FIVE

"Nature is trying very hard to make us succeed, but nature does not depend on us. We are not the only experiment."

— R. Buckminster Fuller

68

Saturday, 4 May; Sundowner Fish Shack,
Fremantle, Western Australia

"So, you two worked all day I trust?" Clive sipped his Shiraz and looked across the table at Sacha and Sean.

"We did. We've been trying to connect the dots using a meta-analysis of dozens of coral bleaching studies around the globe to see what details may be common to the lot of them. Sean and I have been working on this one for a year or two now."

"I see." Clive's fun-loving grin was etched on his face. "Thank goodness he was able to get here this weekend, just before Asha heads back to the States. What a coincidence."

Pratt let the coincidence comment slip right over his head. "Yes, I'm happy to be able to see Ash before she leaves." He dipped his head to her and raised his glass.

Asha wasn't sure if the blush she perceived on Sean's face was actually there or she imagined it.

"Well, I'm glad I'm here tonight and that Dad is here as well as you Clive..." She nodded. "... and you, Sean..." Her smile beamed as she raised her glass.

"You know, if we keep toasting like this, none of us will be able to roll down the stairs after dinner. Imagine the stories we could tell of the night the four of us spent sleeping it off out cold on the floor at the Sundowner Fish Shack in Freo..." They all joined Sacha in a hearty laugh.

Asha's laugh turned more serious as she was again captured by the view of the setting sun dropping like a fiery ball into the

Indian Ocean behind Rottnest Island 20-something kilometres to the west. "It's so beautiful... times like this, I actually feel pangs of a little bit of homesickness."

"You can always remedy that by spending a week back here with your old dad."

"Come on, Dad, you're not that old. You're still cranking out papers..."

"I wouldn't exactly say I'm cranking them out anymore..." He gently placed his hand on Asha's and gave her a little squeeze. "So tell us, honey... how'd your fact-finding mission go? Were you able to gather any useful information for your GNN doco?"

"Mostly, it went very well. I never expected to come down here and magically uncover all the answers to Earth's mysteries..."

"That's a good thing because you'd have run into the three of us and many millions more with our intellectual shovels, all trying to dig out some answers!" Sean's smile seemed to linger on Asha a little longer than it should have.

"I did find a lot, though. I've been trying to explore the idea of nature somehow coordinating the ecosystem's response to destabilising forces. In the time I've been here, I've picked all three of your brains to that end, along with your students, Sean, and your good friends in Melbourne, Clive... Karl and I still think there is so much seemingly happening all at once."

"That could be sheer numbers, Ash." Clive had a more thoughtful look now. "In a world with nearly 8 billion people, the impacts of the mutations you and your colleague are chasing may have outcomes that seem greatly amplified simply because so many people are affected by them."

"That's a point worth taking Clive, and I do confess to being indoctrinated... err, educated, about human impact on nature by my Dad..."

Sacha feigned shock. "There'll be none of that disrespectful tone, my dear... you were enlightened by your dad."

"Okay, okay... enlightened ...educated." Now it was Asha's turn to squeeze her father's hand. "Look, it's just that the metaphor you and Clive used the last time we dined here a couple of weeks ago really stays with me and I just can't get out of my mind." She looked towards Sean since he wasn't aware of the example. "That was a comparison of a single human body with *Gaia*. Our resident medical expert, Clive, used the model of the 'human ecosystem' to illustrate self-preservation. Consider the first thing the body does in defence of an exploding population of microbes – invaders – is to raise the temperature, to respond with a fever. If we carry the comparison of a human ecosystem to a planetwide ecosystem, the first thing Mother Nature does to an exploding population of invaders – like *Homo sapiens* – is to raise the temperature... she gets a fever."

Clive knew full well he agreed with her but thought it time to play devil's advocate. "But wait a minute, Asha... isn't it *Homo sapiens* that are digging the sequestered carbon, burning it willy-nilly, exploding the carbon dioxide levels for the past two thousand years."

"Two thousand years? I consider myself a fossilised carbon dioxide radical, but two thousand years seems a bit of an exaggeration, no? The steam engine is only a few hundred years old." Asha had a doubtful look on her face.

"No, you have to go back way before the steam engine. Archaeologists have pretty solid evidence that the Roman migrants were burning coal in England a few hundred years after Christ, close to two thousand years ago. That said, consider the fact that more than half of all the fossilised carbon dioxide poured into the Earth's atmosphere by humans has been dumped there in the 21st century... just the last quarter of a century. HALF! Surely, we can't blame Mother Nature for rising temperatures, but must place the blame squarely on the shoulders of *Homo sapiens*."

"Now wait a minute. Clive." Sean bristled and sat up straight now. Obviously, Clive had accomplished his mission and spurred on the debate. "We might just consider that human DNA has a previously unknown short circuit fuse built right into it."

"A short circuit fuse?" Clive squinted his eyes as though he was somehow trying to see Sean's example.

"Yes, I see where you're going with this... I'm talking about the prospect of a fuse that old Mother Earth and the laws of science have included in our design. If that is the case, this fuse may allow for self-destruction of the species if we humans start causing so much damage as to kill off nature itself or – in Sacha's way of saying it – killing *Gaia*."

Sacha smiled on the inside but kept his critical expression on display. He knew that Asha and Sean were on the same wavelength as he was and that Clive too agreed, but his mate had done an excellent job of precipitating the discussion. Being the oldest person at the table, he also knew too well that the most tiresome of all conversations were those in which everyone agreed. "So, I hear you saying that if humans evolved within nature's systems, then the 'self-destruct' feature within our DNA is as much a part of *Gaia* as is the fact that birds evolved wings or turtles evolved shells... Mother Earth's laws of science even assured that life survived the Oxygen Catastrophe so many billion years ago. Maybe that self-destruct piece of our DNA is our inability to place cooperation above reproduction, of our blind adherence to the 'survival of the species' instinct to over-populate the planet to such a degree that it causes our own extinction."

"Wow, what a paradoxical headline to be written when the very last *Homo sapien* stops breathing – 'Human 'Survival of the Species' Instinct Leads to Our Own Extinction'." Clive swirled his wine. "But I can see where you are coming from there, Sasha... Sean... We humans can go to great lengths to cooperate and function on incredibly altruistic levels, but in the end, we tend to follow the 'pass our genes on at all cost' imperative. So similarly to a peacock showing his feathers to attract a suitable peahen, maybe humans dumping a trillion tonnes of carbon dioxide into the atmosphere is just our way of trying to attract suitable mates capable of bearing offspring."

"And that means what?" Asha was a bit confused.

"That means that all of our accomplishments, all of our technology, all of our engineering and art, all of our civilisation... all of it... was simply for the sole purpose of allowing us to pass our genetics on to another generation... a larger generation."

"Wow." Asha leaned back. All four of them sat there for a minute digesting what they had just collectively heard from each other.

Finally, Sean broke the silence. "Then if what you say is the case, Clive, we have truly buried that human concept of 'man above nature' forever. I certainly never have agreed with that notion anyway, but considering that nature is king... or queen..." He looked to Asha. "...anyone or anything that seemingly rises above the totality of *Gaia* will be quickly redesigned or eliminated."

Clive felt a pang of guilt at pushing the conversation too far in this direction and thought he would try to lift the gloominess more towards hopefulness. "Let's not carry the power of nature too far here... we do find some encouraging signs, you know. After the funeral on Thursday, Felly and Liz received some excellent news. The early results from the *Takuathung* vaccine trials have been more than encouraging. The effectiveness is into the upper 90s as a percentage, way better than anything accomplished to date. Even more, the effectiveness seems to remain at those levels across several different strains of *Zaire ebolavirus*.'"

"That is encouraging. You know, I'm a marine biologist and, though I've had my share of biological studies, I confess to not knowing much about modern medicine. I understand the basics of developing vaccines, but I don't have any idea how you would go about testing something like a serum to ward off Ebola. You're the medical doctor, Clive... how do they do this?"

"I can give you the basics, but you'd have to speak with the Yunupingu Institute people to get the full-on explanation. Felly and Liz told me this much, though. They started with the genomic blueprint of a proven safe vaccine used against an existing virus and then modify that to contain a surface glycoprotein found in the *Zaire ebolavirus*." He looked at Asha. "This is one-hundred per cent involved in the use of the synthetic biology that you and I talked about a few times last week, Ash. It is an absolutely wonderful example of how positive outcomes can result from these new techniques."

"You say how successful it seems to be... how do they test that with something as deadly as the Ebola virus?" Sacha ran his fingers through his hair.

"Good question, mate. The old, conventional scheme of giving a thousand kids an injection and follow up on how many avoid a disease just doesn't apply here since it would be downright unethical to do that... suppose they all get Ebola and die! Initially, they may employ animal studies, usually rhesus monkeys, until they reach a point of 100% effectiveness. Eventually, they follow what is called 'ring vaccination protocol' by identifying a new case or cases of EVD and then vaccinating all the closest people to those infected as soon as they can. This is the same protocol that was used at the end of the smallpox eradication programs employed in the last century. I believe that was the original drawing card for Felly and Geoff spending their three months in Thailand. That designation, the *Takuathung* trials, takes its name from the *Takua Thung* District some 65 or 70 kilometres north of Phuket. Felly spent most her time in Phuket and Geoff worked both at the *Takuathung* Hospital and at some tent emergency facilities in the outlying areas around there. In short, this is excellent news."

"I guess while we have taken a more optimistic turn, I should report that my colleague Karl has just been in Siberia visiting the Krasnoyarsk State Medical University there. They too have made excellent inroads to the development of a new vaccine showing easier and more effective results against the latest 'zombie microbes' that prove to be 10,000-year-old *Bacillus anthracis* crawling out of the melting permafrost... so to speak... At least we do have reasons to be optimistic." Asha's smile lit up the table. "I'm still a bit nervous about the synthetic biology though."

"In a decade or two when our synthetic bugs eat oil spills, our beef, lamb and chicken are all factory-grown from our synthetically produced DNA, and you fly back to Chicago in an airliner burning recycled carbon dioxide produced by synthetically engineered CO_2-fixing bacteria, you will see the benefit. Then you can finally recompose Dr Strangelove's famous words of sixty-something years ago and tell us all 'How I Learned to Stop Worrying and Love the Synthetic Microbes'."

"Good one, Clive." Sacha smiled at Asha. "And Asha, it's understandable to have a healthy fear of synthetic anything... Still, we do need to take our 'wins' where we can. The positive outcomes fighting anthrax or Ebola are noteworthy, and that's just as it all should be, honey... Though I have just spent a lifetime trying to scratch the surface in trying to understand *Gaia* and have learned to both love and fear her power, never doubt for a minute that old Sacha Sharma is always on the side of *Homo sapien.*

"In the end, I am no different than you or Clive or Sean... In terms of our genetics, we all come into this world as what our DNA dictates, and we will leave it at the end of life the same way. We'd be foolish not to cheer on accomplishments such as vaccines and antibiotics. But we should never get too big of a head... never feel so much in control... Mother Nature is always there. We need to avoid at all costs falling into the 'one step forward, two steps back' syndrome."

69

Sunday, 20 October 2024;
Institute for Immunology and Infectious Diseases,
Murdoch University, Western Australia

"Why are you in the office at this hour of the morning, Sandra? Bloody hell, woman, it's Sunday!" Blaire Peterson raised his mug and sipped his tea.

"Yeah, I know. I had a message after midnight, and frankly, I rolled around for an hour or two and never could get back to sleep. Finally, I gave up the idea of sleep." Sandra threw her long hair back over her shoulder.

"Damn... what was that message?"

"It was from Bream... Dave Bream. He spent the last three days driving through the communities up there in the Kimberley, chatting with the locals and collecting his samples... Kalumburu, Warmun, Halls Creek, Fitzroy Crossing..." Sandra shook her head. "Look, the kids are starting to die in numbers now. We've had feedback from the Royal Flying Doctors, and they are running out of ideas. They just haven't been able to treat this strain."

"Are we certain it's the Murray Valley encephalitis virus bug?"

"Sure as sure can be, it's MVEV. That's what Dave was collecting up there even though he hasn't got it into the lab as yet. It was the same way in August... in September... I mean, there are enough community nurses to cover where limited resources don't allow the RFD to be, but having medical folks there now seems to be a losing battle."

"But hell, MVEV is mozzie-borne, no? I mean, if you don't get bitten by a mozzie, you can't contract the virus, right?"

Sandra tilted her head. "Don't know, Blair... That sure as hell WAS the method of transmission for the past hundred-plus years, but I don't have to tell you, it isn't even the wet season up there yet, and the mozzies haven't even begun to hit their peak. Something else is happening."

"Dave said that?"

"Well if you remember, Dave's been saying that for a year. We've seen it in the lab. Once we thought we had MVEV covered, but then something happened. There are... were..." Sandra's eyes scrunched up. "...two things we knew about this disease, namely, it was rarely lethal, and it could not be contracted from person to person, only through mosquito bites."

"Well then, what in the hell happened? Now it's become lethal and is spreading person-to-person... Why is it all the sudden presenting in such different ways?"

Sandra squinted her eyes and flashed a big frown. "Can a mosquito-borne disease somehow combine with a respiratory virus-like an influenza strain? Look, this stuff is beyond me, Blaire, but I'm just saying... and I think maybe Dave is just saying... the same thing..."

"Well the only way we will even explain this is through some kind of mutation, I reckon, and we hopefully get a leg up on that with the research we are doing right here in Perth... It looks like Mother Nature has thrown us another curveball... Let's hope it's not a pandemic catastrophe just waiting to happen."

ABOUT THE AUTHOR

Dan Churach was born in Pottstown, Pennsylvania. He earned his Bachelor's degrees at Benedictine University in Illinois and the University of Hawaii at Hilo, his Masters at the University of Rhode Island and PhD at Curtin University in Perth.

Dan and his wife Karn are explorers, from Philadelphia to Hawaii in America, from Broome to Perth in Australia, they embrace transitions from urban to rural and back again, always with gusto. In his novels, Dan leads the reader on a voyage where critical thinking explores current scientific questions that shape the physical environment his characters inhabit. *FEVER* is his third published novel dealing with interpersonal relationships and the impact of science and technology on ordinary people.

A career university lecturer and a high school teacher, Dan believes that a good educator must be a good storyteller. His constructivist approach to education recognises that all new knowledge is built upon the learner's existing experience and that storytelling enhances this process. With a formal background in science and academic research, Dan assures the reader that his fictional writing is strongly based on a foundation of scientific reality.

Dan and Karn live with pups Bomber and Rocky in Leeming, Western Australia, but always keeping a keen eye out for what is around the next corner.

PROOF!, *Back to Paradise* and *DREAMS* are all available from Amazon.com.

Check Dan's website at www.churach.com.

FEVER

Made in the USA
Middletown, DE
07 June 2020